Child

PAULA ROE
TESSA RADLEY
CAT SCHIELD

**MILLS &
BOON**

First Published in Great Britain 2017
By Mills & Boon, an imprint of HarperCollins*Publishers*
1 London Bridge Street, London, SE1 9GF

EXPECTING HIS CHILD © 2017 Harlequin Books S. A.

The Pregnancy Plot, *Staking His Claim* and *A Tricky Proposition* were first published in Great Britain by Harlequin (UK) Limited.

The Pregnancy Plot © 2013 Paula Roe
Staking His Claim © 2012 Tessa Radley
A Tricky Proposition © 2013 Catherine Schield

ISBN: 978-0-263-92979-9

05-0917

Our policy is to use papers that are natural, renewable and recyclable products and made from wood grown in sustainable forests.The logging and manufacturing processes conform to the legal environmental regulations of the country of origin.

Printed and bound in Spain
by CPI, Barcelona

THE PREGNANCY PLOT

BY
PAULA ROE

Despite wanting to be a vet, a choreographer, a card shark, a hairdresser and an interior designer (although not simultaneously!), British-born, Aussie-bred **Paula Roe** ended up as a personal assistant, an office manager, a software trainer and an aerobics instructor for thirteen interesting years.

Paula lives in western New South Wales, Australia, with her family, two opinionated cats and a garden full of dependent native birds. She still retains a deep love of filing systems, stationery and travelling, even though the latter doesn't happen nearly as often as she'd like. She loves to hear from her readers—you can visit her at her website: www.paularoe.com.

As always, my girls, The Coven, without whom I'd be a blubbering mess of plot confusion on the floor. But especially to Shannon for that late-night brainstorming, Deb for the sane wisdom of finishing the book, and Margie for her brilliant expertise about fertility treatment and medical procedures.

And a deep, heartfelt thank-you to the man who inadvertently saved me from my book slump: British singer, writer and actor Mat Baynton. Without the wonderful distraction of your show, *Horrible Histories*, and the beautiful, inspirational music that is Dog Ears, this book would have turned out most different and definitely lacking. You're a lovely obsession. Thank you more than you'll know.

One

"That bridesmaid keeps checking you out. Do you know her?"

"Who?" Matthew Cooper turned from the huge skyline window, transferring his attention from the stunning seventy-eighth-floor view of Queensland's Surfers Paradise to his sister, Paige. Her familiar teasing grin remained firmly in place as he gave a cursory glance at the impressively decked-out bridal party. The group of six was slowly making the rounds as a glorious sunset illuminated the aptly named Sunlight Room, Q-Deck's premier reception area.

"The redhead," Paige answered.

He shrugged, snagged a glass of champagne from the passing waiter's tray, then went back to the commanding view. "I don't know anyone here. The happy couple are your clients."

Paige frowned. "And you're depressing me. It's a wedding, Matt. A celebration of love. Loosen up a little. Have a bit of fun." She scanned the crowd again. "Go and chat up a bridesmaid."

He raised one eyebrow, jammed a hand into his pants pocket and took a slow sip from his glass. "The redhead?"

"She is *definitely* interested."

Matt murmured something noncommittal.

Paige sighed. "You are one sad guy. Here you are, thirty-six, prime of your life, attractive, single, excruciatingly rich—"

"Responsible. Successful—"

"And still work-obsessed," she concluded as she watched

him check his phone for the third time in half an hour. "I thought you left Saint Cat's to get away from that."

He frowned. "Running GEM is totally different."

"Hmm…" Paige's brown eyes blinked as she popped an appetizer in her mouth, then held up her palms, indicating scales. "On the one hand, heart surgery. On the other, running an international global rescue company." She tipped one hand down, the other up. "Saving lives for the family business—parents overjoyed. Training emergency medical response teams in developing countries—parents pissed off."

"I'm still saving lives, Paige. And I don't need you on my case, too."

"Seeing nasty, lying ex-wife every few weeks." One of Paige's palms dropped. "Skiving off to exotic locations and even more exotic women." Her other hand shot up as she smiled. "Yet you're still not happy."

"I'm—"

"You're not." She touched his arm. "I may live in London but I still know you."

Before he could answer, the bridal party shifted, a solid mass of movement and noise flowing in a singular wave.

It was Friday night in the middle of an unseasonably warm August, and instead of finalizing project details before he flew out to Perth on Monday, he was in a room full of strangers, celebrating the union of two people so obviously in love it was kind of nauseating.

A vague, irrational anger swept over him. The last wedding he'd attended had been his own—and look how that had turned out.

People parted to reveal the newlyweds, Emily and Zac Prescott, sharing a grinning kiss. As the guests cheered, Matthew's jaw tightened, uncomfortable emotions welling in his throat. Why the hell had he agreed to be Paige's plus-one?

"Your ring looks good," he said to Paige, who'd fallen silent.

"As if you can tell from this distance." Still, she visibly

preened as they both studied the intricate, handmade Paige Cooper diamond band on Emily's ring finger. "Look," she added, sharply elbowing him in the arm. "There's the red-head."

The woman in question was partially hidden by Emily's dress. Her head was turned, body angled away so he could only make out the sweep of neck and bare shoulders, the fiery red hair bundled up in a sleek knot at her nape.

Then she moved and a spear of golden sunlight sharpened her profile.

He gasped as everything went out of focus.

"You know her?" Paige asked sharply.

"No. Excuse me for a moment." Ignoring Paige's frown, he shoved his glass into her hand and moved purposely forward.

She was five feet away, lagging behind the rest of the wedding party and talking to a smooth-looking guy. He paused, head spinning as the past flooded in to seize his senses. Angelina Jayne Reynolds—AJ. *Angel,* he'd whispered in her ear, deep in the throes of passion as she'd writhed beneath him. The nickname suited her. From her pale ethereal skin, long elegant limbs and ice-blue eyes, to the deep auburn shock of hair that tumbled down her back in flaming waves, she was a mixture of heaven and hell all rolled into one. A woman who'd set his blood boiling with her joyous laugh and come-hither grin. A woman who'd driven him crazy for six whole months, burned up his sheets, then walked out of his life without a word. It had taken him close to a year to forget that.

But you didn't really forget, did you?

He knew the moment she sensed him staring. Her back straightened and then her shoulders as she scanned the crowd with a faint frown. His gaze remained fixated on her nape, that spot where her gathered hair revealed vulnerable skin. He remembered kissing that spot, making her first giggle in delight, then sigh in rapturous pleasure....

Finally, she turned and the reality of all those missing years slammed into him, making the air whoosh from his lungs.

AJ had been gorgeous at twenty-three. But now she was… breathtaking. Life and experience had sharpened her features, accentuating her jaw and chin. Creamy skin and high cheekbones emphasized those blue cat's eyes, the corners slanting up in a permanent air of mischief.

Then there was her mouth…a luscious swell of warmth and seduction painted a glossy shade of magenta that conjured up all sorts of dirty images.

Finally, her gaze met his. It registered brief feminine appreciation, skipped away then snapped back to him in wide-eyed shock.

He couldn't help but smile.

Somehow, the distance between them disintegrated and he was suddenly standing right in front of her.

"AJ Reynolds. You look…" He paused, only half aware of the noise and movement pulsing around them. "Good."

"Matthew Cooper." Her voice came out rushed, slightly breathy, stirring something he'd buried long ago. "It's been a long time."

"Nearly ten years."

"Really?"

"Yes."

She threaded her fingers in front of her, the perfect picture of demureness. He frowned, his eyes skimming over her elegant ice-blue dress, the small butterfly necklace at her throat, the tiny diamond stud earrings. Something was off.

"You're not used to seeing me dressed like this."

Visions of tangled sweaty limbs and hot breathless kisses caused a zing of desire to shoot through him. She must've sensed it because she quickly added, "I mean…the gown."

With an inward curse, he got himself under control. "It is kind of…"

"Fancy?"

"Elegant."

Her mouth twisted as she glanced fleetingly across the

room. "I know you don't know my sister. So how do you know Zac?"

The bride was her sister? "Through Paige Cooper."

Her eyes widened. "The ring designer?"

"Yes."

"Your wife is very talented." She smiled politely.

"Sister."

"Ah." She glanced at the bridal party, her expression unreadable. "I didn't know you had a sister."

"There were lots of things we didn't talk about."

She simply nodded and smiled at a passing guest, her fingers still threaded in front of her.

Had she ever been this restrained? He remembered AJ as a colorful, passionate talker, using expression and movement to engage. But now it felt almost painfully polite.

Not surprising, considering how they'd parted.

He shoved his hands deep in his pockets.

"Well…" She shot a glance past his shoulder and when he followed it, he spotted Zac and Emily being seated at the bridal table. Off to the side, Paige was deep in conversation with a blinged-out teenager. "It was nice seeing you, Matthew."

"Wait," he said, curling his fingers around her arm. She stilled, her eyes snapping up to his, and he quickly released her. "Can I buy you a drink?"

She gave a slight laugh. "We have an open bar."

"Later." He held her gaze pointedly.

"No, I don't think so," she said, her smile slowly fading.

"A dance, then."

"Why?"

Her directness startled him for one second before he remembered that it was just one of her many appealing traits. "Because I'd like to."

What the hell was he doing? The rational part of his brain was telling him to just let her go. But the unsatisfied, something's-missing part that had survived his marriage's collapse and last week's agonizing new client contract negotiations egged him on.

AJ wasn't a part of his reality. She was a bright memory from his past—an idealistic, purposeful past full of ambition for the future. She was the beach, short shorts, laughter and sensual lovemaking. His present was vastly different. It was endless meetings and lonely foreign countries, the occasional life-threatening situation, a deceitful ex-wife and nosy parents who just couldn't let the past go. He couldn't let her leave. Not yet.

"A dance," he repeated, fixing her with a firm look.

She studied him in silence. Odd. Wasn't this the woman who gave new meaning to *impulsive?* Yet now she seemed downright cautious.

"Matthew, I'm being as polite as possible, given we're at my sister's wedding. But let me make this clear—I do not want to drink or dance with you. Now if you'll excuse me…"

She smiled, then turned on her heel and headed over to the bridal table, leaving him speechless and frowning in her wake.

He glared at her gently swaying backside and the swish of ice-blue skirts billowing around her ankles.

Huh. Guess she's still pissed off with you, then.

Two

Two long hours crawled by, one hundred and twenty agonizing minutes in which AJ wished more than once she still drank alcohol. A champagne buzz would definitely help get her past this irritating awareness of her ex.

His hair is longer, she reflected as she ate dessert. The shaggy style lent a romantic air to his bold features: the wide Roman nose, the dark eyebrows framing dreamy chocolate-brown eyes, the firm jaw shaded with stubble and the dimpled chin. Oh, he was still lean and angular, with elegant hands and expressive eyes that reminded her of chivalrous knights and romantic poets from days gone by, but in those ten years he'd broadened and matured. It suited him.

Not only was he gorgeous and hyper-smart, he was also a doctor. An actual heart surgeon, for heaven's sake, every girl's McDreamy with a deep, soothing English accent that made her shiver. Yet no TV character could hold a candle to the reality that was Matthew Cooper.

Maybe it was the memory of their mutual past. A past based purely on sex—they hadn't been together long enough to crash and burn under the weight of inevitable relationship complications. Instead, Matthew had brutally cut her off at the knees.

Amazingly, she made it through her toast and then the official bridal party dance without a hitch. Her partner dutifully waltzed her around the dance floor as Zac and her sister glided by, smiling and whispering in that enviously intimate way of all newlyweds.

Eventually the DJ cranked up the music, the lights dimmed and everyone flocked to the dance floor. After refusing to dance with a chisel-jawed blond, she made her way to the bar and ordered a virgin cocktail.

"Having a good time, gorgeous?"The bartender grinned.

"Sure." She smiled halfheartedly.

He placed the drink in front of her, but when she reached for it his hand lingered, his gaze intent. "Hey, what do you say to—"

Suddenly Matthew was there, easing onto the stool next to her, his polite smile aimed directly at the bartender. It was almost funny the way the other man yanked his hand away and quickly asked, "What can I get you, sir?" But when the bartender went to fix a coffee and Matt turned to face her, amusement was the last thing on her mind.

After the year she'd had, she was so not up to facing the man who'd dumped her nearly ten years ago.

AJ stared into her drink, watching the bubbles rise to the surface as she stirred it with the straw. She'd been good enough to have hot holiday sex with but not good enough to introduce to his parents or take out on an official date. To advertise as girlfriend material.

Ah, but it *had* been amazing sex.

The memories made her cheeks flush. With a small sigh she shoved the straw between her lips and took a sip, ignoring his gaze.

The bartender placed the coffee on the bar—espresso, no sugar—and her eyes were drawn to Matt's long fingers curling around the cup. His scrutiny was beginning to unnerve her. Sure, he'd always been intense, examining things from every possible angle. It was part of what made him such a brilliant surgeon. But this…this…singular attention, as if he couldn't quite believe what he was seeing, was something different.

"Stop staring. I haven't changed *that* much," she finally said, irritated.

"You have." He lifted the cup to his lips and took a chug, then carefully replaced the cup on the saucer.

"How?"

One eyebrow went up. "Fishing for compliments, AJ?"

"No."

His expression changed. "Yeah, I remember that about you. You look…" He paused, and an inexplicable rush of anticipation stilled AJ's breath. "Thirty-two suits you," he finally said. "Very much."

Oh. Perversely disappointed, she took another sip of her drink and smiled politely. "Thank you."

"So how've you been?"

If you don't count my surgery, my screaming biological clock and the fertility clinic appointment tomorrow? "Fine." She eased off her chair and smiled once more, only this time it felt as if her face was about to crack. "Well. It was nice seeing you. Again. I—" When he muttered something under his breath, she frowned. "Sorry?"

"I said, crap. What the hell's gotten into you, AJ? It wasn't 'nice' seeing me again and you know it. So stop faking."

AJ took a step back and crossed her arms, trying to rein in her irritation. "You know what? I'm not doing this with you. Not here, not now." And she abruptly turned and stalked off.

Her heels barely made a sound on the stucco dance floor, the thumping music drowning out everything except the anger in her head. She managed to dodge a handful of dancers, then a tipsy guest, before making it through an archway at the far end of the room. With a vicious yank she pulled a door open and stepped inside the luxurious foyer that led to the restrooms.

Pausing at one of the full-length mirrors, she stared at her reflection, then cupped her cheeks, heat flaring beneath her palms.

Matthew Cooper was an arrogant ass. He was a trust-fund kid with upper-crust parents and a British ancestry dating back to the Battle of Hastings. An insanely intelligent silver-

spooner who never knew what it was like to truly struggle…
for a life, for control, for his next meal. He was the most self-
centered, overbearing—

No. This wasn't about him. Her life had been one insane
rollercoaster ride since April: in the space of a week she'd
gone from her normal checkup to being prepped for surgery
to remove ovarian cysts. Determined to keep Emily's happy
prewedding bubble intact, she'd told no one, but her luck had
run out when she'd run into Zac at the hospital, where he'd
been donating some huge sum to the children's ward and she'd
been coming out of post-op. She'd sworn him to secrecy, but
then the rat had insisted on paying for everything, including
a week's recuperation at a private health facility.

*It's highly unlikely you'll be able to bear a child, Miss
Reynolds.*

Oh, her surgeon had his sympathetic bedside manner down
pat, and a few years ago she would've brushed off his concern
with barely a backward thought. The mere idea of *her*—Miss
Single Girl, Life of the Party—having kids was laughable,
right? Her fractured childhood notwithstanding, she loved the
fact she could pick up stumps and move across the state on a
whim, answering to no one, depending on no one and needing no one. Sure, there were those weird little pangs when
she saw Emily and Zac together and she briefly yearned for
something more. And it seemed like all her friends were dropping off her radar one by one, suddenly engrossed in getting
married, falling in love or having babies.

Not AJ Reynolds. She didn't need anyone.

Except now, the most basic choice of womanhood had been
ripped from her and the sudden, inexplicable loss gaped like
a jagged wound.

She'd started to question all the turns she'd taken to get to
this point, every minute choice she'd made. That unfamiliar
self-scrutiny had freaked her out, but finally, after a week of
agonizing, she'd woken up one morning and known exactly
what she wanted.

The heavy sucking sound of the door opening, followed by a sudden brief burst of music and laughter, broke through her thoughts. She narrowed her eyes at Matthew's reflection in the mirror, refusing to turn around even when the silence lengthened and her skin itched with expectation.

"The men's room is next door," she said helpfully.

He ignored her comment. "You're still angry with me."

She whirled, ready to do battle, but took a calming breath at the last moment.

"Being angry means I still care." She tipped her chin up, giving him her best down-the-nose glare, even though he was a good six inches taller. "And I don't."

"Right."

His superiority grated. "Oh, get over yourself, Matt! It's been ten years. I've moved on. Grown up. I'm living my life. You…" She waved a hand, taking in his perfectly suited frame. "You're probably married to some socialite, chief of something by now and pleasing the pants off your parents—"

"Actually, I'm divorced and run an international medical response team."

"—and honestly, I don't think—" AJ paused then blinked. "What?"

"I run GEM. It's a global emergency medical—"

"Wait, wait, wait. You *quit* Saint Catherine's?"

He nodded. "Just over four years ago."

AJ was stunned. "Holy crap. But you lived and breathed that place. It was your entire existence and you… Wow. What did your parents say?"

"Considerably more than 'wow.'" The cloud in those hooded velvet eyes spoke volumes, belying the casual quirk of his lips.

"Wow," she said again. He remained silent as she stared at him.

He'd been married. It was old news, but her heart still smarted. He'd loved someone enough to propose. He'd taken someone else to bed and been loved in return.

Was it wrong to hate someone she didn't know?

AJ focused on his beautiful mouth. She knew the second his thoughts solidified: his brown eyes darkened, nostrils flaring as he slowly dragged in a breath. "Angel…"

She swallowed. "Don't call me that."

She heard a loud click and jumped as the room was suddenly plunged into pitch darkness.

The light timer had run its course. With a soft curse, AJ stuck out her hands and took a step forward.

"AJ?"

"I'm walking to the wall." She took another step, then another…until she found something solid. And warm. Definitely *not* the wall.

She sprung back with a dismayed groan and would've lost her footing if not for Matt's quick response. He grabbed her arms, steadying her. "I've got you."

"I'm fine."

"Yes, you are." The blackness was absolute but she could still hear the smile in his voice.

Her breath hitched as his hands seared her skin. "You can let go now."

"Okay."

But he didn't. Instead, he cupped her elbows and suddenly every one of her senses went on high alert.

His long sensual fingers were warm on her skin and his subtle scent beckoned. When she felt him shift, a wave of body heat swathed her, drawing her into a seductive web.

Damn it. Her heart pounded in familiar anticipation. She heard him draw in a breath, then slowly exhale. That gentle puff of air was way too close to her cheek.

"Matthew. Turn the light on."

"I will."

"Now."

"You *are* still angry."

"That doesn't concern you." She struggled in his grasp so that when he released her, she crashed into his chest and her lips collided with his.

She gasped and pulled back, a second too late. That fleeting moment of delight had done its job.

The door suddenly swung open, and the light automatically switched back on. They both blinked and turned to see Paige standing in the doorway.

Everyone froze in a strange tableau of embarrassment, followed by an immediate gathering of dignity as AJ and Matt both sprang apart.

"Oh, hey," Paige said, way too casually. "I've been looking for you everywhere, Matt. The newlyweds are leaving. You want to go?"

"In a minute." But he stayed where he was, studying AJ so thoroughly that she ended up smoothing down her perfectly straight skirts with nervous fingers.

AJ didn't miss the way Paige's speculative gaze swept over them or the small grin on her lips. *Oh, great.* "I should be going, too."

"We could share a cab if you want," Paige said.

"Oh, I still have the bridal car...."

"Really?" As Paige's face lit up, AJ groaned inwardly. *Damn.*

"You could share with me, if you like," she said reluctantly. *Say no, say no, say no.*

"That'd be great! Wouldn't that be great, Matt?"

His gaze darted from AJ to his sister, and a small frown suddenly furrowed his brow. Then he stuck his hands in his pockets and shrugged. "Wonderful."

At the last minute, Paige conveniently realized she'd forgotten her purse. With an "I'll just grab a cab—don't worry!" she slammed the door on their surprised expressions and the Bentley pulled away from the curb.

The silent drive was awkward. AJ kept her legs crossed, her body angled toward the door, her gaze firmly out the window, but it still didn't stop her from casting furtive glances at Matt's reflection in the glass.

There was something about *this* man, this one particular person with whom she'd shared her body so freely and willingly. Out of all the other guys, she'd actually liked this one. He had ample cause to be a complete jerk—money, breeding, genius-level IQ, brilliant career, lush looks. But he wasn't.

At least, not until *that* night. And to be fair, she'd read far more into their fling than she should've. A mistake she'd avoided making for years afterward. Until Jesse.

She shook her head, refusing to think about her last stupid mistake. Instead, her thoughts wandered back to Matt. Who knew what had shaped him in those ten years? Something obviously huge, considering he'd thrown away a career he'd sacrificed everything for since high school.

Matthew finally broke the silence. "So what are you doing now?"

Crashing and burning. Feeling way too attracted to you. Wanting to touch— "Going to my hotel."

"I meant for work," he replied patiently.

She sighed and slowly turned to him. This was her punishment for bad judgment—death by small talk. "I have a stall at the Gold Coast markets."

"Selling what?"

"Drawings."

"You draw?"

"And paint. I even do a pretty good caricature, which is my best seller."

"I didn't know you were an artist. I mean," he amended, "I saw you sketching once, but…"

"We just shared a bed, Matt, not our deepest thoughts about life and love." She shrugged. "We had fun for a few months."

She remained surprisingly calm under his scrutiny, even though her insides jumped as his fingers softly drummed on the door.

You're not twenty-three anymore. You can hold a man's gaze without backing down like a blushing virgin.

"We had fun," he repeated slowly.

The heat of irritation crept up her neck. "Well, *I* did."

His eyes darkened, mouth tilting into a knowing grin. "I know. I was there, remember?"

Unfortunately she'd been doing nothing but remembering ever since she'd clapped eyes on him. And if she were the old AJ, the one who'd lived and loved with careless abandon, she wouldn't hesitate to follow through. Judging by the sensuous curl of his mouth and the way his gaze devoured her, he was thinking the same thing.

She took in his lopsided smile and the tiny dimple it made, the way his eyes roamed leisurely over her face and hair before coming to rest on her mouth. The way those eyes then darkened with a predatory gleam.

Growing up, she'd quickly learned how to read peoples' expressions, predict a mood then act accordingly. This skill had been a good foil for her smart mouth, which had provoked the bulk of her mother's slaps. That little girl desperate for a mother's love was long, long gone.

The message she saw in Matt's eyes was plain as day. He wanted her. And judging by that smile, he was reading her need as easily as the Sunday sports section.

It seemed he was about to say something more but instead glanced out the window. AJ followed his gaze, to the blazing lights of the Phoenician. Her time was up.

"This is my stop," she said unnecessarily, her smile tight. "Well, goodbye. Have a safe trip back to Sydney."

"Thanks."

She eased from the car and, to her surprise, he followed.

"I'm perfectly capable of seeing myself to my room," she said tartly.

He lifted his hand, her thin handbag strap dangling from one finger. "You know, that hairstyle really doesn't suit you."

She grasped her bag strap. "I'm supposed to be a demure bridesmaid."

He refused to relinquish the bag. "Demure?"

She watched his gaze go past her shoulder to the people coming and going from the hotel. "Give me my bag."

With a small tug, he drew her closer. "I'm staying at the Palazzo Versace. Have lunch with me tomorrow."

Her heart leaped for one second before she ruthlessly shot down that eager spark. "No."

"You have something else planned?"

"Yes."

"You can tell me more about your paintings."

Oh, you are smooth, Matthew Cooper. From his languid, willpower-melting smile to the way his head tilted, she knew *he knew* she was attracted. She'd made some colossal mistakes in her past, but denying her body's desires was not one of them.

How long had it been?

Too long. A familiar sliver of excitement prickled just before she sighed and tugged at her bag again. In response, he tightened his grip and tugged back.

"Damn it, Matt, give me my—"

He took her hand and threaded his fingers through hers. The gentle slide of warm flesh, the firm conviction as he curled his hand around hers had her blood leaping to life.

Matthew had beautiful hands, with smooth sun-darkened skin and lean fingers. Perfect surgeon's hands, miracle instruments of power and talent, whether he was performing intricate lifesaving surgery or bringing her to a panting climax.

Her breath gurgled in her throat.

He began to stroke her knuckles with his thumb. That shockingly personal intimacy did her in, scattering all rational thought.

Then he firmly drew her forward and, in the middle of the hotel entrance in front of a dozen milling guests, placed a kiss square on her mouth.

Alarm made her pulse skyrocket, yet familiar desire dissolved any objections. His mouth was as warm and skillful as she remembered. Her whole body took barely a second to recover, to remember, then it was off and running, eager for more as her eyes fluttered closed and she kissed him back.

She didn't care that his lips curved into a knowing, way-too-confident smile beneath hers. All she could think of was that mouth, tasting of coffee and something forbidden, urging hers wider, devouring her; then his tongue as he gently eased her open and dove inside.

Damn him. He knew how to turn a woman on.

A group of hotel guests abruptly surrounded them, cheering and whistling, edging past with alcohol-infused enthusiasm and bringing with them movement and noise and sudden clarity.

She pulled back and Matthew reached out to steady her, his breath warm across her cheek. When their hips bumped, then their shoulders, a frisson of delight shivered up her spine.

AJ barely noticed the brief, cheerful apologies as the crowd moved on. All she noticed were Matthew's warm palms cupping her elbows, his soapy-fresh scent and his breath as it feathered across her bare shoulder.

"Want to change your mind about me seeing you to your room?" he murmured in her ear, his deep accented baritone making her nerves dance.

"No."

He grinned. "So lunch tomorrow?"

"Contrary to popular belief, the world doesn't revolve around you, Matthew Cooper." She dug in her bag for her phone and checked the time. "I have things to do tomorrow."

"Dinner, then."

She sighed. Sharing food with him, making small talk, was the last thing on her wish list, especially after her appointment tomorrow.

He reached out and took her phone. She scowled. "What are you—?"

He flicked it on and dialed. "Here's my number." He paused and his phone trilled from somewhere inside his jacket. Then he returned hers. "Lunch tomorrow."

With a confident grin, he turned and strode back to the car. She glared at his broad back. *Of all the arrogant…*

The Bentley finally drove off. With a sigh, she turned on her heel and walked into the hotel foyer. This wasn't a problem. She'd just call tomorrow and cancel. There'd be nothing he could do about it, after all.

Yet it didn't stop the niggling feeling that she was throwing away the chance to have Matthew back in her bed again.

Irritated, she punched the elevator button. Sure, she'd lusted. She'd wanted. She'd desired. But she'd never completely offered him her heart and he'd never demanded it. She'd been young and reckless, reveling in life, and he'd been the perfect fling. Yet despite her oh-so-mature outlook on the whole affair, he'd still managed to bruise her.

Matthew Cooper was part of her past, not her future. If she was an expert at anything, it was moving on and letting the past stay buried.

Three

AJ perched on the edge of her chair in the discreet Brisbane fertility clinic, hands clasped firmly in her lap.

She'd managed to get a grasp on her emotions, wrapping them with prudent caution. Yet she couldn't stop the edginess that rose up, catching her breath and making her heart kick.

Forget about Matthew Cooper and just get on with your original plan.

Dr. Sanjay flicked open the file on his desk. "How are you today, Miss Reynolds?"

"Fine. Nervous."

He looked up from the file and peered over his glasses with a smile. "So, this is your second consult. Dr. McGregor did your full checkup and discussed the realities of getting pregnant with you?"

"Yes."

He kept reading. "It says here you had surgery three months ago for ovarian cysts."

"Yes, my surgeon did say my chances of conception were low. Thirty percent."

"You have quite a bit of scarring—"

"But thirty percent is better than nothing, right?"

He sighed, then gave a reluctant nod. "It doesn't mean it's impossible—just difficult. But it will be time consuming, and fertilization may not happen the first, second or even the fifth time. And it can be draining, physically, mentally and financially." He glanced back down at the file. "You've already chosen a donor from our files, I see."

She nodded.

"Okay." Sanjay flipped open the file, then frowned. "One moment." He reached for the phone and made a call. When he hung up, he slowly removed his glasses, closed the folder and fixed her with a silent, considering gaze.

Uh-oh. She nervously twisted the handles of her handbag. "What's wrong?"

"Miss Reynolds, I'm sorry but we cannot proceed at this time."

Her mouth gaped. "Why not?"

"I've been advised your donor is no longer available." He gave her a sympathetic smile.

"What?"

"Your donor cancelled his appointment," Sanjay said calmly. "This means—"

AJ stared blankly at the manila folder as the doctor's explanation faded into the background. No. *No!* This could *not* be happening.

"Miss Reynolds?" the doctor repeated gently. "Did you hear me? How do you want to proceed?"

"What do you mean?"

He paused, silently studying her as if trying to assess her mental state. "You'll need to make another donor choice and then we can go from there. You'll need to make another appointment with reception."

He slid a business card across his desk, almost as if he'd been waiting for the cue, but all she could do was stare at him. "But…but…I don't… It took me three months to get this one! Can't I just—"

"I am sorry about the long wait time but we are fully booked. And I am legally bound to follow procedure." He straightened the files on his desk, then fixed her with a polite smile. "You need time to make a decision and once you have, we can discuss everything at our next appointment. Now, can I help you with anything else?"

AJ shook her head and took the card, her fingers surprisingly steady.

When she finally strode outside, the bright morning sun seared away the vague clinical aroma and the doctor's sympathetic but hands-tied expression. Slipping on her sunglasses, she crossed the road to the parking lot and dug out her phone.

She found her car—a third-hand, beat-up red Hyundai Getz—and slipped into the driver's seat.

Just what was she going to do now?

She stared at the cracked steering wheel, her mind a total blank. Another three months. Could she wait that long? She'd done her research—she knew anxiety and worry played a huge factor in getting pregnant. And there was no guarantee the first time would work anyway. She'd been on a dozen different blogs and forums where women openly shared their stories—the injections, the schedules, prime ovulation times, family pressure, aching optimism and the deep, dark lows of constant negative tests. She'd read about women making the agonizing choice of stopping fertility treatments after years of stress, only to fall pregnant months later when the pressure was off. Her head had spun with overload.

She could spend years chasing this dream. And where would she get the money? She'd never had a loan in her life and there was no way she'd stoop to sponging off Emily. Big sisters looked out for the little ones; they didn't demand handouts.

Her mind was a whirling mass of chaos, thoughts flying everywhere, so it took a few seconds to realize her phone was ringing. Confused, she finally grabbed it and stared at the screen.

Her sharp laugh shattered the still air. It was Matthew. Great.

"Yes?"

"Just checking you'll be here for lunch."

His deep voice, combined with that polished accent, sent her thoughts into further turmoil. She glanced at her watch. Ten o'clock. It felt like she'd been in there for hours. "Probably not. I'm in Brisbane."

There was a pause. "Later, then. The Versace does an exceptional high tea."

She opened her mouth to refuse, but a sudden insidious thought struck her speechless.

Oh. My. God.

She shook her head. *No.*

But wait! What if...? No, you can't.

Sure, you can.

She took a deep breath, then another.

"AJ?"

"I'm thinking," she replied, dragging a hand through her hair.

"Don't take too long," he murmured. "Time's ticking away."

Never a truer word was spoken. Her forbidden idea slowly took shape. Matthew Cooper had the power to grant her most desperate wish. He was the perfect male specimen. The perfect candidate. The key to her plan.

Matt could give me a baby.

Yes! No! Indecision warred inside before she finally overrode her doubts and chose a side.

"I'll be there at one," she said and turned the key in the ignition.

Matt hadn't actually expected her to say yes. Now, as he waited in the Palazzo Versace's opulent coffee lounge, he wondered if this was such a good idea.

His entire life was a study in cool-headed decision-making. He made plans, logical moves, well-informed choices. Choices that had furthered his career, challenged his intellect and increased his standing in the medical community. And when he'd reached his personal crisis point, that cool head had led him to a new calling.

Yet he'd impulsively asked AJ out. In the space of an evening, she'd managed to rub off on him.

Hell, he never could control himself around her.

He shook his head and glanced over at the reception area for the fifth time in as many minutes. Circular couches with plump sun-yellow cushions were scattered throughout the foyer and the sleek, intricately tiled marble entrance bore the familiar Versace logo. Some said this five-star Gold Coast hotel blurred the line between lavish and garish, but he loved it. It was private, the staff was discreet and service was topnotch. He never stayed anywhere else when he was in Surfers.

He glanced up again, and when he spotted a familiar figure walking through the huge glass doors, her low strappy heels clicking sharply on the tiled floor, his thoughts fled like predawn shadows at sunrise.

He'd recognize that distinctive red hair anywhere, even if it was tied back in a controlled ponytail. He also noticed how her brow was furrowed in concentration.

AJ had a habit of frowning when she didn't agree with what was being said, those tiny disapproving lines momentarily creasing her forehead before she opened her mouth and began challenging, questioning.

She may look like a Renaissance painting, but her brain was firmly twenty-first century.

He ran his eyes over her, taking in the beacon of hair, the soft lemon cardigan over a modestly cut cream sundress, the silver sandals on her feet. She looked…demure. Again. A word he'd never consider for a woman who'd worn screaming-orange and electric-blue with impunity, who'd rocked short denim shirts and sexy off-the-shoulder tops, who laughed and loved equally with impulsive, joyous abandon.

Burning curiosity sparked in him as he strode across the foyer.

When she finally noticed his approach, a smile replaced her frown. It was all-encompassing, defining those high cheekbones and creasing her clear blue eyes. It felt as if he was the only guy in the world and she was smiling just for him. And yeah, it also jammed the words in his throat as if he were a boy with his first crush.

Irritating and arousing—that was AJ to a T.

So he did the only thing he could—smiled in return, took her arm and placed a kiss on her cheek. She stilled in surprise, and he immediately pulled back, decorum warring with craving.

"How…?" She swallowed then went on breathily, "How are you?"

Suddenly needing to do more than kiss your cheek.

"Hungry. Are you?" he asked thickly.

"Not particularly."

As soon as the words were out of her mouth, AJ sensed the danger. It was like fire crackling to life, flaring up to bathe her in delicious heat. His eyes were dark, full of forbidden promise, and suddenly AJ recalled another time, another place, where they'd forgone food and instead feasted on each other until dawn crept into the sky.

She dropped her gaze.

His palm cupped her elbow in a soft caress. "I've arranged for us to eat outside. Come."

She let him lead her past the huge windows with a view of a massive, Greco-Roman-style pool and fountains sparkling in the afternoon sun, then out the doors. A bead of sweat formed in the small of her back, and she slipped her sunglasses on. The water looked so inviting.

"Have you been here before?" he asked, his hand a warm brand on her as they wove their way through the pristine cabanas ringing the pool.

"Once, for dinner." Zac and Emily had treated her, and she'd spent the whole time stroking the chair and lusting after the dinner plates.

They stopped in front of a cabana, where a female server greeted them. "Good afternoon, Dr. Cooper. Your afternoon tea is ready. Would you like me to serve you now?"

"No, that's fine. Thank you." When he smiled, AJ swore she saw a blush rise in the girl's cheeks before she nodded and left them.

Their private air-conditioned cabana looked like a sheikh's tent. She glanced around, noting the cotton-draped walls and roof and the table on the far side that held coffee and tea jugs warming on heating plates. A love seat against another wall was scattered with a dozen cushions displaying the distinctive Versace pattern. Two recliners flanked a low table that held an elegant three-tiered display of sweet and savory treats that made AJ's mouth water.

Matt nodded to the chairs. "Take a seat."

She hesitated, then toed off her shoes before settling into the lounge with a sigh. After her crazy morning this was a welcome respite, despite Matt's surreal presence amid the luxurious five-star hotel aura.

He took a seat across from her at the low table. She focused on the spread before them.

"Is that smoked salmon? And cream cheese?"

"Your favorite, right?"

She sighed. "You always knew how to make me smile, Matthew Cooper."

His mouth grazed her bottom lip before he reached for her coffee cup and began to fill it. "I'm planning on doing much more than that."

Oh, wow. She didn't care that her answering grin was full of girlish giddiness, nor that anticipation made her hand tremble as she took her cup.

"Really." She took a sip, eyeing him over the rim.

"You told me you hated playing games, remember?" He met her firm look with one of his own. "I'm just being honest."

Yes, he was. She looked away, unable to hold his gaze any longer. *Here's your chance. Ask him now.* She replaced her cup and reached for a tiny smoked salmon sandwich. "So how long were you married?"

He paused, a sliver of bread roll halfway to his mouth. "Does it matter? It's over."

"It doesn't." She shrugged. "I'm just curious."

"Her name was Katrina," he finally said, then popped the food into his mouth and slowly chewed. "We were married for three years. You?"

"Oh, no. Not me." A memory flashed by, but she swallowed the bitter ashes with a neutral expression as she selected another morsel from the platter. "And you left Saint Cat's." She nibbled on the finger sandwich. Chicken and pesto—delicious.

"To start my own company."

But why? The question hovered on her tongue but she swallowed it back. Did she really need to know?

She took a sip of coffee, studiously avoiding his gaze as she finished the chicken and pesto, then picked a mini chocolate croissant. She bit into it and gave a small murmur as the buttery pastry crumbled in her mouth.

"Good?"

"Oh, yeah."

"I thought you'd like it."

"Oh, you did?" She licked her bottom lip, picking up a stray crumb. And just as she expected, Matt's gaze honed right on in, watching her as she slowly licked one finger, then her thumb.

Her breath staggered on the intake. There was nothing to stop her from leaning over the table and suggesting she was hungry for something more than food. Hell, this cabana was just as good as a private room—they could get naked right here, right now, and no one would suspect a thing.

Yet something made her hesitate. This was Matt. The guy she'd shared a bed with for six whole months. The guy she'd been prepared to let down all her defensive walls for, only to be dumped that same night. The guy who'd been her benchmark, who'd made her vow never to be that vulnerable again.

"Matt…" she began, then paused when he abruptly stood. He was staring down at her with such intensity that the rest of her words gurgled in her throat. She knew that look. It still made her legs weak even after all these years.

"Come with me."

When he rounded the table and held out his hand, she was lost.

His fingers wrapped firmly around hers, slowly drawing her to her feet, to him. Her heart hammered as she stared into those dark eyes, that crazy feeling of anticipation simultaneously scaring and exciting her.

Kiss me.

As if she'd spoken aloud his eyes dipped, then his head, and everything fell out of focus. She felt her eyes close, the familiar arousal bubbling up in her belly. Yet when he was barely a breath away, when her senses were full of his delicious scent, her breath ragged and her belly tight, he stopped.

She'd been leaning in, practically begging for him to kiss her. With a small sound of frustration, she opened her eyes and saw him grinning.

Then he turned and pulled her with him.

They left the cabana in silence, her shoes forgotten as they moved swiftly past the pool. AJ barely had time to register the scorching hot tiles beneath her feet before they were inside the cool foyer, Matt leading her to the long bank of elevators. He pressed the button and then looped his arm around her waist, pressing his warm body into her back.

His solid heat made her mind reel. It had been too long since she'd been this intimate with a man. She'd missed having a pair of strong arms hold her, a hot hard body intimately pressed against hers.

When the elevator pinged open, they rushed inside. He swiped his card, then turned to face her when the doors slid smoothly shut.

And she was staring right back at him.

He was tall, well over six feet, and although she was hardly short, her shoulder barely reached his bicep. She caught a glimpse of her reflection in the elevator mirrors—

conservative hairstyle, demure dress. Hardly the outfit for a seductress, yet he'd—

He swooped in and kissed her.

It was a hot, determined kiss designed to awaken and arouse, a kiss she recalled stirring her from sleep and into full-blown desire in seconds flat. It was just as good—no, even better than—last night. Her fingers curled around his biceps and the tension in those muscles matched the scorching pressure of his mouth. He took fierce control, forcing her mouth open, and with a squeak of surprise she let him in. Everything throbbed—her skin, her pulse, her groin. His arousal pressed between them, a hard reality against the thin barrier of their clothes.

"Angel," he breathed. AJ groaned as memories engulfed her. It was the one word he'd always whispered when he brought her to climax again and again.

She barely registered the elevator had come to a stop. Matt suddenly pulled back, spinning her to face the front with a wicked gleam just before the doors slid open.

An elderly woman got on and AJ murmured a polite greeting, her face warm and her blood pounding. Matt was standing behind her, his hands stuck casually in his pant pockets, studying the glowing numbers as they continued their ascent. Yet his thigh nestled firmly against her bottom, heat searing through her thin dress.

She stared at the slowly changing floor numbers until her nerves felt so tight they began to scream.

What on earth do you think you're doing?

She never dwelled on the past or rehashed it. Moving on was what she did, what she'd always done. She'd come to terms with it all, had matured, grown.

So why was she still thinking about it?

She'd been twenty-three. They'd both gone into their affair with a mutual understanding it was only temporary. Of course his career had come first. Saint Catherine's up-and-coming neurosurgeon didn't belong with an addict's daughter and runaway thief.

When their fellow passenger got off on the tenth floor, AJ took an unsteady breath. *I am me. AJ Reynolds. I am not the broken product of those awful people. I have a sister who loves me. I have friends. I am smart. I love animals. I don't cheat or lie. I'm a good person.*

So would a good person manipulate and seduce to get what she wanted?

Matt gently urged her forward, breaking into her thoughts. She glanced up to see they'd reached the top floor just before the doors quietly opened onto the long plush hallway.

Sweat popped out in the small of her back. She could feel the tickle as it slowly slid down, down, until her dress eventually absorbed it.

"AJ?"

She squeezed her eyes shut as his hand cupped her hip, the familiar firmness creating alternate bursts of doubt and desire in her belly.

You can do this.

The corridor was way too long, its walls adorned with exclusive hand-drawn Versace designs in gilt frames. Then finally they were at his door, a huge, dark wooden thing emblazoned with a fresco of classic Greek gods and a gold number three. He opened it with his card and she caught her first glimpse of the amazing decor inside the cavernous penthouse suite along with a sliver of blue sky from the huge patio windows. As she hesitated at the threshold, he gently pulled her against him. Her bottom connected with his groin and his lips went to her nape.

She gasped. With one hand braced on the door frame, he looped the other low across her belly.

"I want you in my bed, Angel," he murmured in her ear, his hot breath and rough stubble sending tiny waves of longing over her skin. "I want to have you beneath me, above me, around me."

He shifted, the truth of his arousal solid against her butt.

Sinful memories flooded in to hijack her senses. In his pool, slick and hot in the moonlight. On the beach at sunrise, a scratchy blanket against her bare back. And late one night in the kitchen, naked and laughing when they'd realized they'd left the blinds open so anyone walking past could catch an eyeful.

Yet she couldn't ignore the overwhelming resonance of the final few months.

You can't do it, not like this.

Her eyes flew open and she jerked forward, breaking the warm contact of his lips on her neck before quickly turning to face him. She saw confusion in his eyes.

Her fingers dug into the wood door frame, holding her up and keeping her steady while everything inside groaned in abject disappointment.

"I'm sorry, Matt. I…I can't."

"What?" He frowned as his hand slowly slid from the frame. "I thought—"

"I'm sorry," she repeated lamely.

No! No, no, no. Her hands tightened on the door, breath caught in sudden hesitancy. He was right there in front of her, her memories a pale comparison to the reality of his warm body, skilled lips and practiced hands.

No. This wasn't right.

It took all her willpower to steel herself against those seductive eyes and take a firm step past him, into the hall. "I can't do this. I'm… Goodbye, Matthew."

Then she turned on her heel and practically sprinted to the elevators.

Four

It was Thursday, surgery roster day. It was always odd walking the halls of Saint Catherine's as a visitor and not rushing on his way to surgery, post-op or a meeting. Matt had passed reception and greeted the nurses, their unspoken questions creating a tiny frisson of discomfort as they returned his smile and nodded. The corridors held that familiar polarizing smell—people either loathed the mix of antiseptic, antibiotics and clean linen or found it comforting. For him it was about adrenaline, the scent of new scrubs, the weird soapy smell in the washroom. The jitters that always hit him a second after he gowned up. Then the rush of complete and utter calm as he scrubbed, studied his notes and prepared to cut.

He automatically glanced at the door numbers, then turned his focus down the hall. Katrina's office was at the end and, as always, he had to go past the Blue Room to get there.

He picked up the pace, studiously ignoring the innocuous door with its private sign. He'd always hated that room: a room where bad news got officially delivered, where parents learned their child's illness was terminal, where brothers, sisters, husbands and wives broke down and cried. The other surgeons called it "the grief room" in private.

A room he associated with so many names—Kyle McClain. Denise Baxter. Eli Hughes. Valerie Bowman. And the rest. He remembered them all.

Head cloudy with memories, he barely heard his name

being called until he spotted a middle-aged couple heading down a corridor on his left.

"Dr. Cooper?" the woman said again, and he paused as they approached. "I thought it was you. It's Megan Ross," she added with a smile. "This is Jeremy. I don't know if you remember us—"

"Of course," he said, shaking Jeremy Ross's hand. "I operated on your son, Scott." Matt paused, then asked cautiously, "Is he okay?"

"He's perfect." Scott's father waved away his concern with a reassuring smile. "We're just visiting a friend."

He nodded, relieved. "Good. Scott would be what—fourteen now? Oh, okay—" He paused as Megan Ross enveloped him in a huge hug.

"I'm sorry," she apologized, face flushed as she let him go. "But it's the least we can do for the man who saved Scotty's life."

He smiled. "That was my job, Mrs. Ross."

"Oh, no, you did more than that. You walked us through the procedure, answered all our questions and reassured us we were doing the right thing." Her voice wavered and she gulped in a breath, giving her husband a shaky smile when he reached out to rub her back. "You gave up your time, sitting with us, talking about silly, inconsequential things and keeping us occupied while we waited for Scotty to come out of post-op. We were here for a month and you were there for us every time. Not many doctors would do that."

Matt's heart squeezed for one moment, remembering the little boy with the brain tumor, one of his very last cases at Saint Cat's. "You are quite welcome."

"We've just come back from Greece, went to all those places you told us about that night," Jeremy Ross added. "Scotty loved it." He stuck his hand in his pocket and withdrew a small drawstring bag. "We got you something."

He put up a hand, alarmed. "Oh, you didn't have to—"

"Don't you go refusing it," Mrs. Ross chided. "Scott picked it out especially for you."

Could he feel any more awkward? Yet as the parents beamed at him with gratitude, the feeling fragmented. He took the velvet bag Mr. Ross held out and tipped the contents onto his palm.

"It's Saint Luke," Mrs. Ross said. "Patron Saint of Physicians. We got it on Naxos. They make them from the crumbling stones of the Gateway to the Gods."

"It's beautiful," he said, turning the cool stone figurine over in his fingers. Intricate carvings detailed the ancient saint's intricately folded robe and beard. He had a beatific expression on his lined face and he held a thick book in his hand.

A wave of emotion hit the back of Matt's throat. "Tell Scotty it's perfect."

"We will. You know he wants to be a doctor when he grows up?"

He nodded. "He'll make a good one."

After another hug and handshake, they left. And Matt was left standing there in the cool corridor, completely undone.

He remembered everything so clearly, every moment he'd spent in their company, deflecting their grief and uncertainty with hard facts, then with uncomplicated amusing stories of his sister's travels. They were good people, easy to talk to and relax around. Eventually conversation had turned to his own hopes, his plans to travel and see the world—plans that were merely a pipe dream considering his insane workload and commitment to the hospital. And the Rosses had regaled him with their ten-year-old's antics, his love of science and classic *Doctor Who* episodes, his obsession with all things ancient.

Had it really been four years ago? The desire had been planted then, only months before his brother Jack's death, before his life had taken a one-eighty and he'd turned his back on his parents' demands, his career and his marriage.

Matt dragged a hand through his hair and stared down the long corridor. He'd finally seen the world, been to places he'd desperately wanted to go. He'd spent a whole year doing nothing except experiencing life. These days, GEM ensured his travel bug was sufficiently fed: he handpicked his assignments and delegated the rest to his capable staff.

He'd achieved all his goals. Well, except one. One deep desire that burned in the back of his mind, one so powerful that it had contributed to his marriage's downfall, turned Katrina so bitter and angry that she'd demanded way more in the divorce than she was legally entitled to. Wracked with guilt, he'd given it to her.

I don't want kids. She'd made that clear from the very start. And he'd agreed. He'd witnessed the devastation of losing a child, seen the agony and pain every day. You couldn't escape it in a place like this. Plus, where would they find the time to devote to parenthood? Their entire lives revolved around equally demanding careers.

Then Jack had died and life as he knew it came crashing to a halt.

No, Katrina had said calmly when he'd broached the subject. *I told you. We agreed.*

I know, he'd replied, unable to meet her accusing eyes. *But I've changed my mind.*

She'd sighed. *Look, we should take a break. I'll get Kylie to book us a holiday.... We could spend a few days in Bali—*

I don't want a holiday, he'd shot back. *I want you to consider us having a baby.*

Oh, the look he'd gotten from that! And when she'd slowly crossed her arms in that I'm-tired-of-this-topic way of hers, he knew before she opened her mouth that his marriage was over.

That will never, ever happen, Matthew.

His phone beeped, breaking into his thoughts. He glanced at it. He was five minutes late. Katrina hated tardiness.

With a sigh, he approached the conference room door and knocked, then walked straight on in.

Five

"I'm sorry...do you have another meeting, Matthew?"

Matt glanced up from his watch to meet Katrina's cool gaze before leaning back in his seat and crossing his ankles beneath the conference table. "No."

Suddenly Matt and his ex-wife were the sole focus of attention in the room as the department heads' soft chatter came to a halt. Matthew remained impassive in the silence. Sure, for most of the staff his history with Katrina was a nonissue, but there were a few who gleefully anticipated a domestic incident every time they assembled to discuss his company's staffing needs, which Saint Cat's played a large part in fulfilling.

They obviously didn't know her. Or him. Their divorce had been polite, dispassionate and completely professional—just like their marriage.

He cocked one eyebrow up, inviting her to press the issue. She blinked a slow and icy dismissal before continuing with the agenda.

He furtively eyed his watch again. Half past one. Jeez, he hated these meetings. Every year admin rehashed the same concerns about working with GEM—low staff numbers, budgetary constraints, rostering conflicts—before finally signing on the dotted line. So as Katrina's people squabbled over the same issues, he stared out the window and let his thoughts drift back to AJ.

Five days had passed. Five days of meetings, flights and a hundred other professional commitments that had succeeded in keeping his mind firmly on work. Not on a certain redhead who'd invaded his downtime and strengthened his interest despite her unceremonious rejection.

He shifted in his chair and crossed his arms, his gaze going to the stunning view of Sydney Harbour out the window of the twentieth-floor conference room.

Man, he'd been right, though. AJ *had* changed. She'd gone from a spontaneous free spirit to…what? She'd never talked about her dreams, her wants. Never even mentioned family. Until the wedding he'd had no idea she had a sister. Yet they'd been together six months. Surely they'd talked, right?

What he knew about her could fit on the head of a pin. Prior to working at the local café near his Central Coast house, she'd traveled up and down Australia from northern Queensland to Victoria, doing seasonal fruit picking, waitressing and cleaning. Her nomadic existence fascinated him, given all his plans and constant schedules.

He remembered calling her on his last shift and, no matter what the time, she'd be on his doorstep when he got home. They'd end up in bed, then eat, make love some more, and in the morning she'd be gone. And then there was the way he'd handled their breakup, which was, he admitted, sudden and with little finesse.

No wonder she shut you down.

When the meeting broke up ten minutes later, Matt sighed in relief and headed straight out the door, checking his phone messages as he went. Delete. Delete. Answer. Ignore.

He stopped abruptly, staring at the screen.

AJ was at GEM. He checked the time of his office manager's text, then his watch. She'd been waiting in his office for two hours.

"Now that's interesting," he murmured.

A burst of anticipation quickened his blood, and he frowned. *Forget it. You took a cold shower, spent the rest of the day in a black mood then moved on.*

Apparently not.

* * *

He'd barely got a handle on his curiosity when he pushed through his office door at GEM's Mascot headquarters half an hour later.

He paused, noting her small start before she swiveled in her seat and looked up at him with wide blue eyes. Tellingly, she'd chosen the rigid-backed visitor's chair next to his desk instead of the comfy sofa flanking the far wall.

"Hi, Matt."

He let silence do the talking as he cataloged her appearance, from the worn blue denims, plain white V-neck T-shirt and oversized worn navy jacket to that red hair tightly contained in a low knot.

Man, that was beginning to piss him off.

"What brings you to Sydney?" he finally asked.

"You." She paused, a small frown marring her forehead. "Can you sit? I need to talk to you."

He shrugged and walked over to his desk, lowering himself slowly into the plush leather seat.

Was she here for a do-over?

Pride nipped at his heels, making him frown. He had half a mind to ask her to leave, but at the last moment decided against it. No harm in letting her talk, right? He could always say no.

He remained expressionless as he eyeballed her. She returned his stare.

Damn it, he *wanted* to say no.

Yeah, who're you kidding? If she *was* here to have another go of it, he'd make her stew a little. Then they'd do it his way.

His, imagination went into overdrive as he considered the endless possibilities. He'd take down that ridiculous hairdo for a start. And have her wear something…red. Yeah. A strapless body-hugging red dress that emphasized her delicate collarbone, with those crazy curls falling over her shoulders. And beneath the dress—

"Matt?"

"Yeah?" Her sharp tone snapped his attention back to the

present. When he finally looked at her—really looked—her serious expression set off all kinds of alarms. "What's going on?"

"I need your help with something."

AJ chose her words carefully, instinctively moving to cross her arms before she realized what she was doing. She linked her fingers together in her lap instead.

No, that wasn't right, either. So she recrossed her legs and slid her elbows onto the chair arms, her fingers lightly gripping the ends. Much better.

Her brief composure dissolved under the weight of Matthew's loaded question. "My help?"

"Yes. Well, it's more like a favor. Well, not a favor, which sounds a little trivial, but more like—"

"Take a breath." His smooth, cultured voice flowed over her, bringing the nervousness down a notch. "You flew down to Sydney to ask me for a favor?"

"Yes."

"What's wrong with the phone?"

"This isn't a phone kind of favor."

His mouth suddenly tweaked. "I think I know what this is about."

She blinked. "You do?"

"Yeah. But you used to come right out and say it, AJ. Hesitancy wasn't one of your attributes."

What? She shook her head with a frown. "I'm not entirely—"

"—convinced we should do it?" He leaned forward, planting his elbows on the desk and clasping his hands, an expectant gleam in his eyes. "Wouldn't denial be worse?"

AJ opened her mouth but nothing came out. This was so not going the way she'd planned. Instead of calmly presenting her situation, then laying out the solution in a businesslike manner, she'd let him stall her with one quirk of his sensual lips. Not to mention the heated stare, which melted her senses and sent her body into an anticipatory tingle.

It was déjà vu, except now they were in his office instead of the Palazzo Versace's private cabana. And just like before, that evil little voice echoed: *you have him ready to go—you don't actually have to tell him.*

Yet through the growing tangle of desire another more powerful emotion grabbed hold. Honesty. It's what had stopped her the first time. It's what would always stop her.

"Matthew. I…uh…." She hesitated, casting her eyes over his desk. There was a small mountain of files, a laptop, phone, coffee cup, scattered pens and paper. No family photos, no personal mementoes. The wall behind him held his various diplomas, a crazy-looking yearly schedule, medical diagrams and charts; it was the office of someone who'd had a life plan since he was ten years old. He was Matthew Cooper, work-driven, goal-oriented. He had been—and always would be—a career guy. Ten years later that was still blindingly obvious.

That realization bolstered her courage. "I want a baby."

His sharp inward breath was harsh in the sudden silence and she paused. If ever there was a moment-killer, this was it.

"What?" he choked out.

"I…" She pressed her lips together, working hard to contain the swelling emotion. A few seconds passed, then a few more before she finally got a handle on it. "I'm thirty-two and single. I've met guys but none who—" She swallowed and looked Matt straight in the eye. "I don't want marriage or a husband—just a baby. I've done my homework, even went to a fertility clinic, but my time is running out and it's so expensive and things fell through and—"

"And you want me to recommend a doctor for you?"

"No. I want you to be the donor."

He shot to his feet so fast it made her gasp. She stood, too, even as the ferocity of his expression had her inwardly cringing. "I did have someone lined up," she forged on. "But he—"

"Who?"

"Just some guy. A donor—"

"You thought I was more convenient than 'just some guy'?"

She winced. "That's not what I mean. I've been thinking—"

"Have you?" His lip curled, nostrils flaring. "Since when?"

"Since you called me the morning after Emily's wedding."

He said nothing, just put his hands on his hips and fixed her with such a furious glare that it felt like her face was on fire. "Look, Matt, I know your job is your life. You've invested everything in your career—it's what you live and breathe every day. I totally get that. Don't you see this is a perfect arrangement for us both? I'm not asking you to give anything up because I plan on raising this child by myself."

She paused deliberately, putting on a brave show of outward calm while her insides hammered away like a windup toy. At his narrow-eyed silence, she pressed her point. "This isn't a plan to trap you into marriage or demand child support, and I'll sign anything you want to convince you of that. This would just be a simple…exchange. It wouldn't disrupt your life. Once I'm pregnant, we'd go our separate ways."

She was met with silence.

He crossed his arms, his expression cold. "You have *got* to be kidding."

She bit her bottom lip. "Can we talk about this? I thought—"

"No." He shook his head curtly. "This isn't a favor, AJ. It's a goddamn lifelong decision!"

"For me, yes. Not for you."

His eyes raked her with such ferocity that she nearly flinched. "I was right. You have changed."

Her bravado crumpled but she refused to let the hurt show. "What makes you so righteous? You don't know what my life's been like, Matt."

"No, I don't. I never did, remember? We were just in it for a good time."

Another cheap shot. "Can you tell me what you have to lose? I'm not asking for a piece of your life. I don't expect a relationship or marriage or anything except—"

"Except sex?"

"Yes." She tipped her chin up. "We've done no-strings-attached sex before. Why not now?"

He said nothing as he stood there, hands back on hips, his mouth an angry slash. AJ met his fierce look with one of her own.

Finally, he glanced down at his watch. "I'm due in a meeting in twenty minutes. Sue at the front desk can arrange a cab for you."

"But—"

He cut her off by striding to the door and swinging it wide-open. His expression had all the hallmarks of battered pride combined with tightly wound impatience.

She'd insulted him and now he wanted her gone.

With a dry swallow she cleared her throat, refusing to let the bitter disappointment take the form of tears.

"If you change your mind…" She started then snapped her mouth shut when he fixed her with a chilly glare. She tried not to let that affect her as she straightened her shoulders and walked out the door. It was only when she strode down the corridor and retreated to the cool privacy of the bathroom that everything inside her collapsed.

She leaned against the closed stall door, choking back her abject disappointment. *It's not the end. You still have the clinic.* And Emily would help her, as much as she loathed asking for money. She'd just have to swallow her pride and her tightly held beliefs and ask.

Yeah, she really was Charlene's daughter, wasn't she? Begging for money, expecting a handout. The only difference was she'd honor her debt, not do a runner in the middle of the night to avoid it.

The bitter irony of it all made her heart ache.

Six

Matt paced his office, swinging from outrage to indignation then back again. He paused at the wall, did an about turn then continued pacing.

Damn room was way too small. He scrubbed at his chin, then his cheek, before running a hand into his hair.

What the hell had just happened?

He was insulted. No, more than that—he was deeply offended. Did she really think he was that kind of guy? He snorted, hands on his hips. These past few days all made sense now: AJ's initial coldness, then suddenly agreeing to his invitation. She wanted a convenient stud. Not *him*—just what he could give her.

His hands curled into fists as fury overcame him.

And yet…

He must be the worst kind of idiot, letting his need lead him around like a dog on a leash because he *still* wanted her. Un-fricking-believable.

He stopped and glared out the window, studying the slow ascent of a Qantas jumbo jet as it climbed into the sky. So she thought he was some kind of mindless workaholic man whore, did she? That he'd jump at her offer then happily walk away when she'd gotten what she wanted?

With a curse, he collapsed into his chair, the leather protesting under the sudden weight. AJ Reynolds was trouble. Not worth the stress. Hell, he could pick up the phone and choose from a handful of willing women for an uncomplicated lay.

Since his divorce it was all he'd been prepared to give. GEM occupied his every waking moment; he'd deliberately made it that way so there'd be no room to dwell on the bitter disappointment of Katrina's rejection.

Yet something stirred inside, reminding him of his deeply buried dreams.

Dragging a hand over his chin, he tapped one finger on his bottom lip.

"Why me?" he muttered, his gaze skimming the blue skyline until it latched on to another plane in the distance. Surely there were dozens of eager guys queuing up for the pleasure. Yet when he tried to picture AJ with another man, doing all those things they'd done, touching her, making love to her, something nasty and painful twisted in his gut.

No.

A firm knock startled him from his reverie and he turned to see a familiar figure in the doorway. "Matt? Got a minute?"

"Sure." He straightened his shoulders and nodded.

"Really?" His head of security, James Decker, tipped his chin down and peered over the rims of his dark aviator sunglasses. "Because it looks like you're thinking hard about something important."

Matt sighed. "I've had an offer. And I'm not sure I should take it."

Decker stepped inside the office, closing the door behind him. As always, he was dressed in black—muscle T-shirt, army pants, boots and gun belt. Matt often teased Deck about his militant vigilante look, and the head of security would always come back with, "At least I save your ass." The black was for show, for his team to project power and confidence to the public. It often meant the difference between success and failure when faced with life-threatening situations.

"What's the offer?" Decker asked, crossing his arms over his broad chest.

"A woman, no relationship strings attached."

Decker's whistle came out low. "Lucky bastard. A hot woman?"

"Oh, yeah."

"And your problem is?"

"She's…an old flame."

Decker's hands went to his hips. "Crazy chick, then?"

"God, no. She's—" Matt paused, his mouth curving in remembrance. "AJ's perfectly sane."

"AJ?" Decker's brow dipped. "Not *the* AJ?"

Crap. He'd wondered when that night would come back to bite him in the ass. A close call in Mexico, the hotel bar, expensive whiskey… He and Deck had gotten comfortably drunk and ended up comparing a handful of regrets.

"I take it from your silence it's the same girl," Decker said, his look knowing. "And you want strings."

Matt grabbed the nearest paper and glared at it, feeling his neck flush. "Forget I said anything, okay?"

"Dude, this is me you're talking to here." Decker grabbed a chair, straddled it and crossed his arms over the back. "I've saved your life a dozen times. We've been in the middle of Vietnam, ass-deep in mud. We've run from Zimbabwean vigilantes, dodged bullets in East Timor." He grinned. "And I wasn't that drunk. I remember everything you said."

Matt sighed. Decker was six feet of contained Yankee firepower, all cocky American attitude and muscle with a huge gun fetish. He also happened to be his best mate, not to mention one of the most brilliant strategists he'd ever met.

"She wants more than just sex," Matt said.

"Marriage?"

"No. A baby." Despite the seriousness of the conversation, Decker's curse made Matt grin. "I knew that'd get you."

"She straight up said she wants you to father her kid?"

"Yep."

"What's the catch?"

"Nothing. I get her pregnant, then I can walk away."

Decker snorted. "Like that's gonna happen." He looked

Matt over. "So tell her no. Unless…" His eyes turned shrewd. "You *want* a kid. With her."

That was the question, wasn't it? Did he want a baby with AJ?

Deck and he had shared some moments, but he'd never told anyone this. It meant he'd have to admit that the complicated wound of losing his brother and Katrina's rejection was still fresh in his mind, even four years on.

"I'll take that as a yes," Decker said.

Yeah, the guy wasn't dumb. Not by a long shot.

Decker drummed his fingers on the back of the chair. "Is it possible she's lying to trap you?"

Matt grunted. "Nope. She was painfully clear she just wants a donor."

"Huh."

"What's that supposed to mean?"

"You still have a thing for her."

Matt's frown deepened. "What makes you say that?"

Decker shrugged. "A, because of what you told me all those years ago, and B, because we're still talking about it. You've never put this much thought into a woman before."

"So I have a problem."

"Not really. Dude, you live for a challenge. We wouldn't have half our clients without your Mister Charm-and-Persuasion routine. And do I need to list all the women who've succumbed to your moody charm?" He ticked them off on his fingers. "Snooty French heiress. Billionaire ice queen. Italian model…"

"AJ's different," Matt interrupted.

"I'm getting that loud and clear. Are you?" Decker gave him a meaningful look. "There's obviously something still there. You won't know if you don't make an effort."

"Yeah, but—"

"I'm just saying that if anyone can convince a woman to fall in love with them, it's you. Who wouldn't want the great and powerful Matthew Cooper?" He grinned and stood. "You know the drill—background, assessment, decision, follow-through. I'll come back later and we can talk about our Italian job."

Long after Decker had left Matt stared at the closed door. Background. Assessment. Decision. Follow-through. "BADFIT" was GEM's standard operating procedure when deciding to take on a new client. Yet this was AJ they were talking about, not another job. It wasn't designed for this kind of situation.

Didn't mean it wouldn't work.

There was only one way to find out.

He reached for the phone and dialed.

"Final call for Flight DJ 512 to the Gold Coast. Would all passengers for Flight DJ 512 please make their way to gate twenty-seven as your plane is now ready for takeoff."

AJ rushed off the moving walkway, readjusted the satchel strap across her shoulders, then broke into a jog, wheeling her suitcase behind her. Her sneakers squeaked on the polished floor as the Sydney terminal windows flashed by. Twenty-four, twenty-five…

Twenty-seven. She ground to a halt, shoving back a loose curl from her ponytail. The line was still a dozen people deep.

With a relieved sigh, she dug in her bag and grabbed the boarding pass. The cheap ticket was nonrefundable and she wasn't about to impose on her brother-in-law's generosity and squat another night in his newly built Potts Point apartment, not when he had potential buyers waiting in the wings.

Just then her phone rang, and after three rings she finally found it at the bottom of her bag.

It was Matthew. She shuffled forward in the line. "Yes?"

"Where are you?"

She frowned, eyeing the moving queue. "Why?"

"We need to talk."

"Please remember all phones must be turned off," the flight attendant politely announced, her gaze lingering on AJ as she reached out for her boarding pass. AJ shook her head and stepped out of line, allowing a man in a business suit to grumble past.

She fiddled with her bag strap. "Look, I'm just about to get on a plane. If you want to yell at me again—"

"I just want to talk about your...proposal."

"Ma'am? Are you boarding?" The flight attendant's respectful smile flickered with impatience.

"AJ?" Matt said in her ear.

AJ wavered as she eyed the cavernous departure tunnel that would take her back to her life. A vaguely unsatisfying life, one that lacked true purpose and follow-through after she'd finally decided what she wanted.

"What do you want to say?" she finally asked.

She heard him sigh. "Can we not do this over the phone?"

"My flight is boarding, Matt. Unless you have a spare ticket to compensate me for my fare—"

"Done. I'll pick you up downstairs in twenty minutes."

"But—"

"You wanted to talk. So we'll talk."

She sighed. That didn't mean he'd say anything she wanted to hear. She wasn't about to get her hopes up to have him crush them all over again: she'd done that once and look where that had gotten her.

"You still there?"

"Yes." She rubbed at the spot behind her ear, tugging on the lobe.

"AJ, you're asking for my help. I need to know details before I commit either way."

"Miss," the flight attendant said, her smile tight. "I'll need to have your boarding pass."

That's when AJ finally made a choice. "Okay," she said into the phone, numbly shaking her head at the attendant and turning away. "Twenty minutes."

Seven

AJ waited in the pickup bay, hesitant anticipation congealing in her stomach. The longer she stood there, the tighter her nerves got. Did this mean he'd changed his mind about her proposal? Surely it did. He wouldn't make her miss her flight just to tell her what a dumb idea it was, right?

Still, it didn't stop her from nervously humming *The Wizard of Oz* theme song under her breath. "Somewhere Over the Rainbow"—a familiar soothing song she used to sing to Emily when they were kids, drowning out their parents on a drunken bender, partying loudly at two in the morning. While strangers passed out in the bathroom or stormed up and down the hall, Emily had crawled into AJ's bed and they'd held each other in the scary dark. And AJ had waveringly sung that song about hopes and dreams and following them to find a better place.

Don't think about them. Think about yourself, about what's happening right here, right now.

By the time she spotted the sleek ash-gray Jaguar purring up to the parking bay, she'd worked herself into a state. Yet she still noticed a dozen pairs of eyes swivel to take in the sporty car, their gaze running over the smooth lines with a mix of envy, joy and blatant lust.

Then Matt eased from the driver's seat and she could swear she heard the appreciative murmurs, even over the general chaos of Sydney airport.

He was dressed for serious business—dark gray suit, white shirt, green tie, mirrored sunglasses. He wore the clothes on his lean frame with such casual elegance, a commanding uniform that befitted the CEO of a national corporation. Then he pushed up his glasses and rounded the car in a few strides, leaning down to grab her carry-on. But when his hand went to her shoulder, she instinctively stepped back.

He frowned. "Can I take your bag?"

Embarrassment made her flush. "Oh, yeah. Sure."

He gently eased the strap down, his knuckles grazing her arm, and she barely had time to get flustered before he was hoisting it over his shoulder, then turning to open the passenger door.

She took the opportunity to note the way his jacket tightened across his back when he leaned in to deposit her bags in the tiny backseat. The touchable skin where collar met neck. And the firm way those long-fingered hands grasped the door as he motioned for her to get in.

AJ took a breath and did just that.

It wasn't often she got to revel in the luxury of a sleek European car. Zac guarded his Porsche like the thing was made of eighteen-carat gold, and her bomby Getz was hardly in the same league. But this…this was heaven: soft suede seats cupping her bottom, the distinct smell of money, new car and leather permeating the air. She sat low, way too low, and the sensation was an odd mix of indulgence and discomfort.

"Since when do you have a Jag?" she asked as he buckled up.

"I got it last year." She barely heard the engine kick in before he glanced over his shoulder, turned the steering wheel and merged into traffic while the radio played softly through the speakers. "The Sultan of El-Jahir was very generous."

She blinked. "El-Jahir? Where's that?"

"Tiny independent island off the coast of Africa. The palace guards staged a coup and GEM treated the Sultan's third wife after a hostage drama."

"And he gave you a Jag."

"He originally offered one of his daughters."

AJ snorted out a laugh. "And you turned him down?"

"I'm not the arranged-marriage type."

Their moment of levity lapsed into elongated silence as they made their way out onto Qantas Drive.

"So you said you wanted to talk," she finally said.

His eyes remained on the road. "Out of all the men you know, why me?"

Her mouth thinned. "All the men I know? How many do you think I *know,* Matt?"

His startled gaze met hers. "I didn't mean it that way. I..." He returned his attention to the road and frowned. "You *were* a free spirit—impulsive, crazy. Up for anything. And," he added when she opened her mouth, "I was the one with the rules and the life plan. I'd always figured you'd end up with a guy more on your wavelength." He flicked her a brief glance. "You didn't meet someone else after me?"

"I met a few someone elses. You didn't ruin me for every other man, if that's what you're implying."

"Good to know."

"You don't sound glad."

"I am." The car purred along the road, dashing past the huge Etihad Airlines billboard and DHL's avant garde cube sculpture. "Me, I got married."

"Yeah, so you said. Let me guess..." She paused, taking the moment to study his profile, unashamedly lingering on the aquiline nose and full lips. "A church wedding with lots of influential colleagues on the guest list. The reception was probably at some swanky Sydney restaurant—Rockpool. Maybe Luke Mangan's place at the Hilton. The bride's dress would've been sleek and classic, something subdued but gorgeously elegant. A society queen—no," AJ amended, "another doctor, someone beautiful and ambitious and parent-approved."

Matt said nothing, the Jaguar purring softly in the silence as they drove.

"Am I right?" AJ probed.

He shrugged. "Pretty much."

Despite everything, the confirmation still stung. Huh. *She'd* never been parent-approved.

She thought back to a night she'd rather forget, a moment when she'd gone against every survival instinct, every ingrained memory from her fractured past and put herself out there, only to have her hopes destroyed seconds later.

She crossed her arms, pushing back into the leather seat. She had to focus on the here and now, not dwell on the past. It was how she survived, how she'd always survived.

"So why do you want a baby?" Matt asked.

A million reasons that she didn't have the time or inclination to discuss because that would mean talking about her past and her emotions. And those two things were off-limits. Instead, she settled on the most urgent one. "Because there's a possibility I can't. Three months ago I had surgery for ovarian cysts and they found extensive scarring. Apparently, I have a less than a thirty percent chance of conceiving."

His brief glance spoke volumes yet revealed nothing. "Why me?"

She turned, giving him her full attention. "Why not you? We know each other, and we're sexually compatible. I won't make any emotional or financial demands. You not only get no-strings-attached sex, but you also won't have the hassle of a baby. Life will go on as normal." She shrugged. "We both win."

What the hell could Matt say to that?

She wanted him to make a baby. Only she didn't want him around afterward. The situation was laughable except he'd never felt like laughing less in his entire life.

He made a quick left turn and they pulled into a side street. After he cranked on the handbrake and cut the engine, he turned to face her.

"Well?" she said, arching her eyebrows. She looked confident, her hands clasped in her lap, her head tilted just so, a firm, almost fierce look in her eyes. He remembered that look. He'd missed it.

He'd missed her.

His gut bottomed out. After all these years, after every turn his life had taken, how could that be? But the truth sat right there in his passenger seat, her flame-red hair pulled back in an efficient ponytail, her lean body inadvertently emphasized by jeans and a fitted T.

She'd made it clear what she wanted, and it didn't include him.

He'd worked hard to get where he was. Whenever he decided to pursue a goal, he committed everything to it. He hated the failure that his divorce had wrought, hated that Katrina had not only ridiculed his suggestion that they start a family but also had refused point-blank to even consider it. And now here was AJ, a ghost from his past, offering up his deepest desire. After Katrina's refusal he'd managed to bury those feelings deep, focusing instead on forging a new career from the tattered remnants.

The irony was that AJ had no idea. She still thought he was some career-driven workaholic robot, motivated by success and money. Yet he was no longer the man she knew from back then, that young, overscheduled, goal-oriented man for whom career and the great Cooper name came first and foremost.

Decker was right. Everything he'd pursued he'd gotten— his position as chief surgeon at Saint Cat's, GEM, various bed partners following Katrina. As a doctor, he'd been acutely aware of human frailty, the crazy ways a person's life could hinge on the actions of others. Yet he was also a big believer in fate. He'd never been able to replicate the magic he'd had with AJ, not even with Katrina. But now, incredibly, he was being handed a second chance.

Fate.

Was he crazy? Maybe. But right now, he had the eerie feeling that if he said no to AJ, if he didn't put in the effort to make another go of it, he'd lose her and she'd have their happy ending with someone else.

You're actually going to make a woman fall in love with

you? He could imagine Paige's incredulity just before she burst out laughing.

This was no laughing matter. He had no intention of walking away—didn't want to walk away. AJ had chosen *him,* had come to him.

Fate.

He eyeballed her as she waited patiently for his answer.

"So there's been no one else?"

AJ slowly slid her sunglasses off, placed them high on her head, then met his direct look with one of her own. "One guy loved going out with his mates more than me. One preferred his collection of *Lord of the Rings* action figures. Another had three girls on the go. And one…" She paused. Those battle scars still stung—no doubt would still sting—for years to come. But their presence also proved she was doing the right thing.

"What happened?"

"He came close." She shrugged. No naïveté for her again. "But then I found out he was married and cheating on his wife." At his gently murmured curse she shrugged. "See? Asshats."

"You're still young, AJ. Only thirty-two. There's still plenty of time to—"

"God help me, if you say, 'you'll find someone,' I am so going to smack you."

He clamped his mouth shut and stared out the windshield, the faint strains of traffic barely discernible in the background. "So you've decided to approach motherhood alone," he said.

"Yes."

He paused, eyebrow raised, waiting for her to elaborate.

She sighed and gripped the seat belt still strapped across her chest. "Given my single status and my low chances of getting pregnant, I'd booked an appointment with a fertility clinic, but that fell through and I have to wait six months for another."

"Which is where I come in."

"Yes. Matt, look. Maybe it was just a coincidence seeing you at Emily's wedding. I'm not a believer in fate—"

"I am."

She paused, digesting that interesting little snippet, then continued. "So if you want me to sign a contract, I will. I will not interfere with your life or your career. No one will have to know."

"Keep us a secret?" His brow went up. "You didn't like that idea last time."

"You remember that?"

"You don't?"

Every single moment I think of you. She swallowed the faint feeling of inadequacy, still there after all these years. "It was a long time ago. I'm older now. And I'm prepared to meet your terms."

He remained silent for a moment, then said softly, "You don't know what my terms are."

She suppressed a shiver as his gaze passed over her face, taking in her features before focusing squarely on her eyes. *Wait, did that mean—?*

Her heart skipped a beat. "What are they?" she asked softly.

"Well, first—you have to be able to financially support a child."

"I can." Her calm response belied the growing butterflies in her stomach.

"Because I get the impression your income could be…" He paused, searching for a word. "Fickle."

The implication stung. "Sometimes. But my bank account is decent. Do you want to check my balance?"

"No, that won't be necessary." His gaze skimmed her again. "And having Zac Prescott as financial backup wouldn't hurt, I'm guessing."

Oh, now she was more than stung. She was irritated. "Yeah, sponging off my brother-in-law is not—and never has been— an option, Matt. What's your next condition?"

"Do you have an apartment? A place of your own?"

"I'm looking."

He nodded.

"Saint Cat's fertility specialist is the best in the state. I can get an appointment for a week Thursday."

"That's quick."

His smile was brief. "The perks of being the former head of neurosurgery."

With a nod she asked, "Is that all?" then immediately hated the way her voice came out all stuttery and unsure.

"No." This time his eyes lingered on her cheek, then her lips. "We're going to do this the old-fashioned way. No clinics, no cups. It'll be just you, me and a bed. Or—" his mouth curved "—maybe not a bed. Depends where we are."

AJ's breath stilled. This was…unbelievable. Amazing.

"So you're saying yes," she said out loud. "We're really going to do this."

Matt nodded. "We are."

He'd said yes. He'd actually said *yes*. Reality struck so hard and with such force that her throat closed up and she had to work to regain control of her overwhelming emotions.

One step. This was just one step.

Yet the yearning, the desperate desire, flickered to life, flaring into hope.

A baby. Her baby. A chubby, squirmy, drooly child who would know every day he was loved and wanted. A child who would never go hungry or thirsty. A child who would always come first. A child she'd hold and cuddle and never abandon to the foster system.

She quickly suppressed those bitter memories, locking them away so they wouldn't taint the moment. "Thank you, Matt," she choked out, her hand going to his arm. "Honestly, I cannot thank you enough. This means…" She blinked like crazy and took a breath as the skeins of control began to unwind. *Don't cry. Don't you dare cry!*

"Do you want me to draw up a formal agreement?"

She stilled as reality jolted her back to awareness. "Can you do that?" At his nod she said, "Oh, okay, then. Sure."

Of course, having something down in writing made total sense. She withdrew her hand and glanced at her watch. "So I guess…well, I'm free right now. When do you want to…uh…"

His cough of surprise made her glance up. "AJ."

"Yes?"

"Let's not get ahead of ourselves. Let's see what Dr. Adams says on Thursday."

She could feel the warmth heat her cheeks.

"And anyway," he added casually, "we're going out first."

"Going out? What, on a date?"

"Yes. Tonight. You, me, dinner. Dessert."

AJ hesitated. "Although I appreciate the effort, you really don't have to do that, you know." She smiled, tempering her refusal. "At this stage, it's safe to say I'm a sure thing."

"But I want to. Big difference."

She met his eyes, holding firm under his loaded gaze. So he was determined to wine and dine her before bedding her? AJ shrugged. "Fine," she said in her best blasé voice. "Dinner."

"Where are you staying?" Matt asked after a brief pause.

"I don't know. I'll have to make a call first." She'd handed Zac's apartment keys over to the building super. She'd have to call him, see if she could stay longer until she could work out something that didn't involve taking advantage of her brother-in-law's charity.

"You can always stay with me."

"No!" she blurted out, then added more calmly, "No, that's not necessary. I can find a cheap hotel someplace."

"In Sydney?" He raised a skeptical eyebrow. "I have a perfectly good apartment in Paddington you can use."

She frowned. Surrounded by Matt's things from his normal life? Bad idea.

"Or…" he added slowly. "There's always my house at Pretty Beach."

Oh, no. She shook her head. She needed her own space

to keep up some emotional distance. His apartment would be bad enough, but being smack in the middle of the place where they'd made love and he'd scarred her vulnerable heart ten years ago?

Not going to happen.

"The apartment sounds fine. It'd only be for one night," she added. "I've been staying at Zac's place in Potts Point."

He nodded. "You'll need it for a few months, minimum."

"A few months?"

"How long did you expect this to take, AJ?"

"Well, apparently the Reynolds women are breeders," she muttered, recalling her mother's irritating, oft-declared statement, which was always followed by a cackle and a wheeze.

With a bemused expression, he said, "We're working with reality here, not a cute homily. Thirty percent is low but not impossible." They stopped at the traffic light and he studied her intently, gauging her reaction. "We'll need to take every single opportunity to ensure you get pregnant."

That meant every possible moment having sex with Matt.

Was it bad that she was incredibly turned on right now? That she wanted nothing more than to lean across the seat, grab his tie and plant a kiss on those sensuous lips?

And just like all the times before, he read her intent as clearly as if she'd scrawled it across her face. His eyes darkened, a slow smile teasing the corner of his mouth. Then he deliberately dropped his gaze to her mouth, resting there for agonizing seconds before dragging it up to meet her eyes once more.

The interior of the car heated up by ten degrees.

The light changed and he abruptly turned back to the road. "I'll drop you off at my place now."

Hurry. "Okay."

Twenty minutes later, when he parked in front of his apartment, gathered her bags and led the way into the lobby, her anticipation took a nosedive.

He placed the bags on the slate floor, pressed the elevator

button and held out a key. "I'm on the fifteenth floor. I'll see you at seven-thirty."

Confused, she took the key, barely registering the brief contact their hands made. "But aren't you…?"

"I have to get back to work."

"Oh. Of course." She bit back her disappointment and re-adjusted the strap on her shoulder. *This is who he is, remember? The guy consumed with work. A perfect arrangement for you.*

"AJ?"

"Yes?" She glanced up, and with a swift movement, Matt looped one finger in the top of her jeans and tugged her forward.

The kiss was brief, a mere millisecond of lips on lips. AJ registered the warmth, the seductive smell of his skin and the slight hitch in his breath. A haunting reminder of what they'd once had. And a promise of more to come.

Then it was over and Matt released her, stepping back with a grin as the elevator doors pinged open. "I'll see you tonight. Wear a dress and heels."

She could only nod numbly as she watched him stride through the lobby, all male efficiency and confidence. In stark contrast, emotion churned wildly in her gut, an annoying response to his kiss.

Get a grip, AJ. Put on your big girl panties and deal with this. With a nod, she yanked her suitcase handle and strode into the elevator, Matt's apartment key firm in her clenched hand.

She would not expect anything more than what it was—a physical union to produce a baby. She'd enjoyed men before without the emotional commitment—she could do the same with Matthew Cooper.

Eight

AJ submerged herself in the huge spa bath so that only her mouth remained above the surface. The warm water lapped around her cheeks and over her eyelids, making her breath echo in her ears.

Matthew Cooper had said yes and she couldn't quite believe it.

The doubt that had plagued her for the past half hour welled up again. This wouldn't be a donation from a stranger—it was Matt. Someone she'd had a physical connection with. Someone whose DNA would form part of her child, someone who'd be reflected in the child's face as he grew up.

A constant reminder of her past.

Was she completely insane or just way too focused on the end result not to have realized that before?

No. She ran her hands through her hair, the soft sodden strands floating around her face. Neither she nor Emily looked anything like her parents. Children were not clones—they were individuals with their own unique personalities.

Though her child would most likely have her curly red hair and blue eyes.

She felt the smile curve her mouth. All hers—no one else's.

"Just concentrate on tonight," she murmured, her voice bouncing off the tiled walls. Because Matt was actually taking her out. In public. On a date.

God, how she hated that word! The last time they'd had anything resembling a date was the night he'd broken up with her. Yes, she remembered it all, even if the edges had grown fuzzy with time and other lovers. She'd ordered Thai from their favorite takeaway, dressed up the table by the pool, then splurged on some fancy lingerie and wrapped herself in a satin robe, waiting for his return.

He'd been exhausted, dark circles emphasizing those poet's eyes, brow furrowed from the pressures of his day. They'd eaten in silence while she practiced her speech over and over in her head, excitement and fear tempering her hunger.

Excitement because she'd never let someone this close before. Fear because…well, she'd never let someone this close before. Every survival instinct, every wrenching past disappointment had made its mark, scarring her subconscious and shaping her into the person she was. It was a sordid, painful minefield and she purposefully avoided that area.

Never count on anyone. Never let your guard down. Never, ever get comfortable.

Despite the walls she'd built, Matt had managed to worm his way in.

Damn right it was scary.

I've been thinking…. No, too cliché. *What do you think about me moving in?* She'd frowned into her pad thai. Too direct. She'd run through a few more, before settling on, *I've decided to stay in town a bit longer. What do you think?*

She'd smiled, taken a breath, then opened her mouth to make that scary leap off the cliff.

Matt had gotten there first.

AJ, I'm sorry, but this isn't working for me anymore.

She abruptly sat up, sloshing water over the side of the tub. She was older now, wiser, with years of experience behind her. She'd thought they had meant something, but now she knew it'd all been in her head. No way would she be that vulnerable again. Ever.

With that thought she wrapped herself in a huge white towel, turbaned her hair in another and padded out into the living room. Late-afternoon sun streamed through the huge glass doors that led out onto a wrought-iron balcony housing a sleek state-of-the art Weber barbecue and a long entertainment area with an unhindered view of Sydney's CBD, Centrepoint and the Harbour Bridge.

Like the rest of the buildings on Matt's street, the 1920s facade was expertly restored. The theme continued inside the lobby, with art deco colors and marble stairs. Even the elevator, though modern, had been designed to reflect the period.

The interior of Matt's apartment was beautiful, too, but in a clean, minimalistic way. She'd gone through every room, unashamedly poked into drawers, cupboards and shelves, yet her curiosity had been far from assuaged. The only art adorning the pale blue walls were black-and-white photographs of famous places—the Colosseum, the Great Wall of China, Stonehenge. As stunning as they were, they lacked the warmth and life of a painting. The Bondi Beach watercolor she'd done last year would bring things to life—if only it weren't at home in Surfers, along with the majority of her paints and brushes.

And her clothes.

The limits of her shoestring travel wardrobe had obviously occurred to Matt, too, because he called about it ten minutes after she finished her bath. "If you need to go shopping, the concierge can—"

"Don't worry," she replied breezily. "I've got that covered."

"Okay." But he didn't sound sure and his doubt irritated her. Didn't he trust her to choose appropriate attire? They'd never been out, so he had no idea her tastes extended to more than jeans, tiny summer dresses and X-rated lingerie.

"A dress and heels, hey?" She'd hung up and readjusted her towel, tucking it tightly under her arm before tapping on her phone's contacts list. "I'll give you a dress and heels, Matthew Cooper."

He hadn't been so excited about date since…since forever, Matt thought, changing gears as he drove across Anzac Parade.

He barely recalled the details of that afternoon: a bunch of meetings, phone calls and schedule confirmations. Decker's brief of their Italian job next Sunday. Good thing his office manager put it all in his online calendar; otherwise he'd be screwed.

Yes, for a second he'd experienced doubt but he quickly shut it down. Doubt never got him anywhere, and he wouldn't start entertaining it now. This was their second chance and he was going to pull out all the stops to show her he'd changed and that the best thing for her baby was for both of them to be in its life.

A baby. He felt the crazy grin take shape before he clenched his jaw to kill it. A 30 percent chance of conception wasn't a whole lot to work with but at least it was something.

Twenty minutes later he pulled up in front of his apartment building and yanked on the brake. Anticipation accelerated his step as he strode into the brightly lit lobby.

Then he stopped dead in his tracks.

He registered black heels, a long satiny black dress with one strap tied high on her shapely shoulder. Fiery curls tumbled down her back in thick, touchable waves and her generous mouth was coated in shiny cherry-red lipstick.

Wow.

She took a few steps forward and the slinky material rippled around her legs, revealing a smooth calf and dimpled knee. "I didn't know what you had planned so…" She raised her arms a little, a tiny sparkly clutch in her hand.

"You look amazing." He unashamedly took her in.

She smiled despite her skittering gaze. Ah, now he'd thrown her. *Good.*

"Still nervous with compliments?" He raised his brow.

"Yep."

When he extended an arm, she barely hesitated before taking it. A bewitching smell of strawberries and something floral teased his senses, and he took a deep breath. "I like your hair like that."

"I know."

He couldn't help but laugh. "Honest, too."

"I find it makes things less complicated that way."

Yeah, he remembered that about her. So what would she have to say about his subterfuge? That he planned to put everything into seducing her, into making her fall in love with him?

"So, you just had a spare evening gown hanging around in your luggage?" He drew her toward the front door, her heels clicking on the smooth tiles.

"I have a girlfriend who's a fashion buyer for David Jones."

"Handy."

"Indeed." Her lips curved again, matching his smile, and his heart did a little flip at the thought of the coming evening.

Emily stared out the window as they crawled past an unobtrusive town house, light from a subdued neon sign streaming down onto the sidewalk. "We're eating at Maxfield?"

"Yep."

"George Evans's restaurant? The guy who won last year's *Master Chef?*" They turned the next corner.

"Yep."

"And you got a table on short notice?"

"Yep."

"Are you going to say anything else other than 'yep'?"

"Yep." He gave her a wink before pulling into a spare parking spot. She waited, enjoying the view as he came around the car, opened her door and offered his hand. She took it, swung her legs out and rose fluidly.

They walked hand in hand to the restaurant, the warm intimacy sending a steady thrum of delight over her skin. How could she calmly sit and eat a meal and not succumb to the desire of ripping his clothes off when he was so very close?

She thought back to ten years ago and how she'd sensed his interest the first time he'd come striding into her coffee shop. Lucy and Maz had fallen over themselves to serve him, but he'd focused on AJ, those dark, brooding eyes somehow

detecting her lust concealed beneath her efficient barista facade. The next day he'd asked for her number. That night she'd
ended up in his bed.

Just like tonight. Excitement surged at the thought.

He squeezed her hand, smiling down at her.

"Why are we having dinner again?" she asked, letting out
a breath.

"Because I'm hungry."

"Very funny. But that's not what I meant."

"I know. And we'll get to that soon enough. But right now,
can you just enjoy the evening?"

With a small huff, AJ could do nothing but nod.

The minutes dragged by, painful, boring moments in which
they were seated, given menus and the wine list and then left
to decide.

Matt folded his menu and turned his attention to her. "So,
you have a sister."

"Emily, yes." She rearranged her cutlery, aligning it perfectly with her plate.

"Older or younger?"

"Younger."

"And your parents? Are they—?"

"Not in the picture. Ever."

When she put her elbows on the table and leaned forward,
his gaze latched on to the tiny butterfly pendant at her throat
as it swung gently, glinting in the light. "Matt, look, I'd prefer we don't talk about my past."

He brought his eyes back to her and frowned. "I'm just trying to get a conversation going here."

"I know. But those people are off-limits."

Those people? Matt's brow ratcheted up but he said nothing. *Take your time. You deal with setbacks and plan devia-
tions every day. This one is no different.*

"You and Emily are close."

He heard her small sigh before she laid her arms on the table, cupping her elbows. "Now, yes."

"And before?"

"We hadn't talked in years. But we're good now." She waved a casually dismissive hand, but the deliberateness of the gesture sent up a red flag. He stored that snippet away for future reference.

"So where did you grow up?"

"Lots of places. Look, Matt—"

"Sydney? Brisbane?"

"Perth. I don't think—"

When he leaned in he didn't miss the way she ever so slightly leaned back. "Humor me, AJ. I just want a little background."

"Why?"

"Because I really know nothing about you."

"You know enough."

"No, I don't." He focused on repositioning his wineglass in order to give her time to work out an answer without feeling the pressure of his scrutiny. "For example, where did you go to school? Did you have any pets when you were a kid? What's your favorite movie? Book?"

When he finally glanced up, she was staring at him so hard, it almost felt like a rebuke. Yet he held firm and finally she said, "I stopped counting schools after six. We couldn't afford to feed ourselves, let alone any pets. I must've seen *The Wizard of Oz* a hundred times. And my favorite book? *The Magic Faraway Tree*."

"Enid Blyton?"

She nodded. "I always wanted a tree like that."

"Didn't every kid?" He smiled.

AJ remained grim. "No, I *really* wanted one."

Before he could reply, a waitress appeared. "Are you ready to order?"

He clamped his mouth shut and gave the waitress a neutral smile.

They ordered. When they were alone again, silence reigned. Matt watched the way AJ's gaze dropped, her eyelashes fanning down over her cheeks. She tucked her hands under the table and leaned forward, forearms pressed against the table edge. She still didn't meet his eyes, instead focusing solely on the fractured light streaming through the blue glass water bottle centered on their table.

"So." He poured a glass of water. "You're an artist."

She glanced up. "You could say that."

"People buy your stuff, right? So I'd say that makes you one." He pointed to her glass, and she nodded. They both watched him pour, the awkward tension punctuated only by the soft glug of water filling the glass. "What medium do you work in?"

"I don't mind oils but much prefer watercolors." She wrapped her fingers around her glass and pulled it across the table. "They dry quicker and the customers don't have to wait long."

"Did you study art at uni?"

"No. All self-taught." She took a sip of water. "Story of my life, really."

He was ready with a dozen more questions but he clamped his mouth shut instead.

A few more moments passed, moments in which she refused wine, then casually cast her eye around the restaurant, observing the diners, the staff, the decor. And he, in turn, took his time and studied her with leisurely pleasure. The curve of her cheek that he knew was just as soft as when he'd first touched it. The delicate earlobe full of sensitive nerves that made her alternately shiver then gasp. The stunning hair that curled around his fingers with a life of its own.

When her gaze finally returned to him, his expression must have given him away.

"What?"

He couldn't help but smile. "Nothing."

"Tell me," she persisted, a cautious, curious smile matching his. So he crooked his finger, beckoning her closer.

"Ten years has made you more beautiful." Startled, she pulled back, looking down at the table. "Angel, are you blushing?"

"I don't blush."

"I think you are."

She snapped her gaze back to his, eyes sparkling. "Fine. I am."

"I never knew a woman to take such offense at being called beautiful."

"Oh? So you're free and easy with your compliments, are you?"

"Women like compliments."

"I'm sure they do," she replied archly.

He grinned. "But you are…unique."

"Thanks. I think."

"You're welcome, Angel."

He heard her tiny intake of breath. "Can you stop calling me that?"

"Why? You liked it once."

She tightened her grip on the glass and glared for a few seconds. Then she shrugged and took another sip of water. "Fine, whatever."

Oh, he was getting to her, all right.

"Matt," she started casually, steadily focused on rotating her wineglass by the stem.

"Yes?"

She paused, then shook her head. "It's none of my business."

Matt leaned in. "I'll tell you if that's the case. Ask me anyway."

Her shoulders straightened, then she gave a little head tilt. "Why did you quit Saint Cat's?"

He cupped his glass in his hand, swirling the contents. "Jack—my younger brother—died four years ago."

Her gaze softened as she looked into his eyes. "Oh, Matt, I'm—"

"It's okay." He raised a hand, shaking his head. "It's fine."

It wasn't. It never would be. But she didn't need to know that.

"What happened?"

"He fell while climbing the Taurus mountain ranges in Istanbul. If emergency response had been quicker, he probably would've made it."

"Is that why you set up GEM?"

"After I dropped off the grid for a year, yeah."

"Where'd you go?"

"Nepal. China. Europe." He automatically slid the butter tray across the table as she broke her roll apart.

"How'd your parents take it?"

"Like I'd committed professional suicide."

That year consisted of a bunch of strung-together blurry memories, not much more. He'd experienced a life other than his perfectly mapped out one, drifting around on a whim, helping where he could, getting dirty and frequently drunk without having to think about the consequences. The world was huge and there'd been so many places he'd tried to lose himself.

"But did you enjoy it?" AJ asked.

"Yes. I met people, made friends." He paused, remembering. "One good mate who's now head of security at GEM. I did some amazing stuff."

"Like?"

Lord, when she smiled like that the tight ache in his heart eased. "I hiked the Andes, backpacked the Greek Islands. Biked around France, joined a rebuilding project on some dilapidated castle in southern Italy…"

Her sigh was envious. "See, that's my only problem with Australia—we're too far from the rest of the world."

He watched her methodically butter her roll then take a bite, releasing a small murmur of delight as her teeth tore into the bread. "Still love bread, huh?"

She nodded with a sheepish grin, demurely placing the rest of the roll on her side plate. "I'm surprised you remember. Most men I know have this innate ability to delete great chunks of information from their brains." She grinned, taking the edge off.

"Not me." He leaned in, extending one arm so his hand rested a bare millimeter from hers.

AJ tried—but failed—to ignore that hand so dangerously close to hers. "That's right. You're the only guy I know with total recall."

"Now *that* was a great movie. The original, not the remake."

She quirked her eyebrows. "I didn't know you were an Arnold fan."

"Oh, there's a lot about me you don't know."

"Like…?" It was out before she could stop it, before she could remind herself of her three rules.

Never count on anyone. Never get close enough to care. Never, ever get comfortable.

But she did care. She was only human.

He reached out, tracing one finger over her knuckles. "I sang at the Opera House once."

"Get out! You did not."

"Did so. It was a statewide school thing, with the best from each primary school choir performing for two nights."

"So you can sing."

He shrugged. "Not spectacularly, but yeah."

"Are you trying to impress me?" She smiled as the waitress arrived with their meals.

"Is it working?"

"Maybe."

He threw back his head and laughed, and the rich deep sound warmed her from the inside out. Lord, she'd missed that laugh. Missed the way his eyes creased at the corners, the way that sensuous mouth curved into something sinful.

She settled into eating her meal. The chicken was delicious, cooked in a creamy sauce with just a hint of rosemary and oregano. She took another mouthful and murmured under her breath.

"Good?" Matt asked.

She nodded. "You should try this." She'd already cut off a piece, offering her fork, when the memory hit. Another time, another place. Sharing one of many meals, getting through only a few bites before they'd given in to another craving. The food had been stone cold by the time they'd returned, flushed and physically sated.

He leaned in to take her offering. With a grin he chewed, eyes never leaving hers. "Delicious. Do you want to try mine?"

Yes. "Okay."

She was fully aware of his scrutiny as she parted her lips, slipped the steak in, then let the fork slowly ease from her mouth. The peppery sauce hinted at a few familiar herbs— pesto, basil, a little garlic. She nodded, swallowing. "Wow."

"Yeah."

The seconds lengthened, intimacy warming the moment. Shadows and light flickered over them and suddenly his eyes turned way too serious.

AJ broke his gaze and focused on her plate instead.

They finished their meals and the waitress arrived to take their plates. "Would you like to see the dessert menu?" she asked, stacking everything expertly on one hand.

Matt raised an eyebrow at AJ in silent question. She shook her head. The meal had dragged on long enough and her nerves were at breaking point.

"Coffee?"

She shook her head again, but Matt said, "An espresso would be good."

She glared at him as the waitress left but he just smiled. "Always in a rush, Angel. I remember that about you."

She leaned back in her chair and huffed out a breath. "You're doing this on purpose."

"Doing what?"

"Making me…" *Impatient. Aroused. Frustrated.* She clenched her teeth. "You know, you can be irritating sometimes, Matthew Cooper."

He leaned in. "*I* can be irritating? Let's see. I remember one particular night in my pool—"

"Stop."

"—when you performed a particularly frustrating striptease for me and—"

"Stop!" she hissed through her teeth. "Are you trying to embarrass me?"

"Ah, Angel. The fine art of teasing was never your strong point. At least," he added, his eyes glinting, "not verbally, anyway."

What could she say to that?

"I'm going to the bathroom." She grabbed her clutch and rose.

Teasing? I'll give him teasing. She deliberately put a sway in her hips, knowing Matt was watching every step she took. *Serves him right.*

She pushed open the door to the ladies' room with an exasperated huff. Was he punishing her—was that it? But why? Because she'd asked him to father her child? Because he was attracted to her and…what, he was angry about that?

Or was it something deeper? Something older…maybe ten years old?

AJ strode over to the long vanity and paused in front of the mirror. With one expert finger she smoothed her eyeliner, then dug around in her bag for her lipstick. *He'd* broken up with *her. He'd* moved on, gotten married.

Her reflection blinked back at her. If he could compartmentalize this, so could she.

Her heart contracted as she swept the Revlon lipstick across her mouth, then pressed her lips together. He'd not only gone through a demanding childhood, but he'd also had to deal with the death of his brother, turning that loss into the motivation for creating GEM, a major global rescue company. Drive and determination were two qualities that defined Matthew Cooper, no matter what he did in life. He wanted something, so he pursued it; his medical degree and GEM were proof of that.

Well, she was determined, too.

AJ capped the lipstick, smoothed her hair down, then scrunched the ends to boost the curl. "Time to move this thing along," she murmured, taking one last look at her vampy reflection before turning to the door.

She strode back across the crowded dining floor, ignoring the handful of men watching her progress. Only one guy was in her sights right now, and he was downing his coffee with the smooth efficiency of someone impatient to be somewhere else.

Alrighty, then.

When she stopped at their table, Matt glanced up.

"Are you ready to go?" she said. He took her in for only a second, maybe more, but it was enough to send a shiver over her skin.

"Yes." He abruptly stood, and she had to take a quick step back as he invaded her personal space. Then he reached for her hand, linking his fingers through hers, and her insides sent up a little cheer.

This was it. The moment she'd been waiting for all night.

She was ready.

Nine

They barely made it to the car before he pushed her against the passenger door and kissed her.

The cool metal seared through her dress, a stark contrast to the warm hardness of eager male. He was in her senses, her every breath, her very blood. His kiss was so good, so hot. She had missed this, missed the familiarity of his touch, the way he boldly took control. She'd spent too many years controlling herself and having the chance to release that burden— even for a brief time—was such a welcome relief. And yes, he knew exactly what he was doing, from his hands cupping her bottom, to his mouth sliding across hers, to his questing tongue parting her lips and diving deep inside.

She moaned. Yes. *Yes.* So very good. So good she could hardly take the time to breathe for fear she'd miss something.

"Let's do this in the car," she whispered against his mouth.

He groaned. "Angel. We can't—"

"Of course we can," she said. Her hands went to his belt then crept lower, and she gasped when she encountered the hard bulge.

With an oath he wrenched his mouth from hers. "Not here."

"Why not?"

He sighed, gently placing his forehead on hers. "Because it's a public place and I don't want to get arrested."

Oh, yeah. She grinned. "Then let's go."

"Hello, Matt. Are you coming or going?"

AJ couldn't miss the way Matt's entire body suddenly tensed.

Then he inhaled, deliberately relaxed and turned. "Hi, Katrina. We're just leaving, actually."

Katrina. His ex-wife. AJ glanced past Matt, taking in the Amazonian ice blonde with amazing cheekbones. She was all legs, flat stomach and slim boyish hips, dressed in an oyster-colored knit dress and matching shoes, setting off her tan and thin arms to graceful perfection. Her bright green eyes returned AJ's stare.

She wondered what the other woman could see, whether she felt as gauche as AJ suddenly did.

Highly doubtful. She didn't appear to have a single unsure bone in her body as she stood there on the sidewalk.

"Who's your friend?" Katrina said now, offering a long-fingered hand. Soft skin, firm handshake, AJ noticed.

"AJ Reynolds, this is Katrina Mills."

"Nice to meet you," AJ lied smoothly, suddenly feeling way too loud and dramatic next to this elegant vision.

"Same here. Well." Her smile returned to Matt. "I have a date. Have a nice night."

"You, too." He nodded, watching her go with his hands deep in his pockets.

Finally, he turned back to AJ. "Sorry about that. I honestly didn't know she'd be here."

AJ shrugged, going for nonchalance. "It doesn't bother me. You said you were over, right? So you've got nothing to apologize for." She glanced back at Katrina as the woman disappeared into the restaurant. "She's gorgeous. I can see why you married her."

"Hmm."

What kind of answer was that? Stung, AJ slid into the passenger seat without a word, the mood well and truly broken.

They drove back to Matt's apartment, faint music from the radio filling the silence.

This was awkward. Way more than awkward—excruciating.

Was he thinking about Katrina? Was that why he'd suddenly gone from white-hot to cold? Worse, was he comparing them? And if so, did she come out the winner or the loser?

Matt jabbed a button on the radio and the music changed to some crazy club tune, heavy on the bass and light on originality. AJ stared out the window, her thoughts becoming grimmer.

When they finally drove into the parking garage, AJ turned to him. "What's wrong?"

He turned off the engine. "Nothing. Why?"

"Do you usually drive around in ominous, brooding silence? I'm a pretty good judge of mood, and you, Matthew Cooper, are in a pissy one. Is it your ex-wife?"

He swung open the door and threw a look over his shoulder just before he got out. *Bingo.* She followed suit, slamming the door and rounding the front of the car. "So it wasn't an amicable split?"

He clicked on the car alarm before turning to the elevators. AJ hurried to match his stride. "Oh, it was perfectly amicable." He sighed, punching the button. "Katrina is all about appearance, and our divorce was nothing if not polite and quick."

"So why—?"

"I have to deal with her on a monthly basis, which is once a month more than I'd like. She's Saint Cat's admin director," he added as the elevator doors opened and he walked in. "And my company depends on a mutual arrangement with their doctors and staff."

"I see." She followed him in and the doors slid closed.

"She's damn good at her job." He waved his key at the sensor and the elevator began to move. "My parents were thrilled when we got married. But she and I..."

"Weren't a good match."

"Not really, no."

She couldn't imagine Matt with someone like Katrina. He was too...passionate. Intense. Sensual. And Katrina looked like she could freeze an ice cube off her perfectly sculpted cheekbones.

So what had happened? Curiosity burned yet she let it simmer instead of putting it all out there. She didn't want to know. Talking meant sharing, sharing meant intimacy and intimacy meant...

No. Think about your goal. That's what you're here for.

Never count on anyone. Never get close enough to care. Never, ever get comfortable.

She shifted from foot to foot. Living by those three rules had protected her from the worst of everything—heartbreak, disappointment, setback. Yet after she'd reconnected with Emily and had started to put down tentative roots, those rules had begun to fray around the edges. Her sister had gradually earned her trust until she'd become the one person she loved more than anything in the world. Plus, she'd been sharing a three-bedroom house in Mermaid Beach with a corporate lawyer and her personal trainer cousin for two years, which, she had to admit, was pretty comfortable.

But those were anomalies.

The elevator doors slid open, and she followed Matt into his apartment.

She'd dated a psychologist for a while and apart from the annoying way he'd never bite back when they argued, he'd taught her a lot about the intricacies of human behavior and what drove people to do what they did. Yet knowing that, people still surprised her. Like now. Matt had been so into her at the restaurant, but now... He walked in, loosened his tie and headed straight for the kitchen without a backward glance.

Invisible much?

She sighed, suddenly at a loss. *And I even waxed...*

"Do you want a drink?" he called while she stood in the middle of the living room, contemplating her next move.

"Tea would be good." She glanced at the pristine chocolate-brown corner lounge and the smoked-glass coffee table. She'd been in his apartment less than a day and had already made her chaotic presence known with a water ring and a handful of smudges on the glass top.

"Do you have a cleaning service?" she called.

"No, why? Do I need one?"

She cast her eye around with a frown. "Not at all," she muttered. "You just—"

He emerged from the kitchen, tie askew and top button undone, revealing the inviting vee of his neck. She glanced away.

"What?"

Filter, AJ, filter. She sighed. "You need a little color to brighten up your walls is all."

He glanced around. "You don't like my place?"

"Well, it's nice. Elegant," she added. "I mean, I'm no Picasso, but I have a painting that would—" She suddenly snapped her mouth shut.

"What?"

She shook her head. "I can't believe we're discussing your decor right now."

His brow went up. "What would you rather be discussing?"

Her breath quickened and her eyes zeroed in on his neck again, then went back up to meet his eyes. "Nothing. I'd rather be *doing*."

Man, he'd forgotten how direct this woman could be! After years of office politics, international red tape, playing nice and pretending with the best of them, Matt had missed that directness. She told it like it was, one of the things that had drawn him to her.

"C'mere."

She was in his arms quicker than he could blink, lips tilting up, eager for his. With a groan, he obliged, slowly covering her mouth.

Yes. She welcomed him inside, teasing his tongue as she wrapped her arms around his neck, pulling him closer. The warm press of her breasts against his chest, her lean body and gently curving hips as they bumped urgently into his groin sent his pulse racing.

She murmured something low and encouraging, firing a spark deep inside his belly. Her thighs pressed into his, her arms tight around his neck as she angled her mouth so he could take her deeper.

And just like that, he was hard and ready to go.

"Matt," she gasped, pulling back to stare at him through passion-heavy lids. "Take me to bed."

Then she took his hand and placed it on her breast. The guttural growl came from deep in his throat, wrenching out one word. "Angel…"

He could barely think when her pebble-hard nipple pressed eagerly into his palm. Damn it, he wanted to take his time, seduce her the right way so she'd begin to trust him. A quickie in the middle of his lounge room was not a good place to start, even if it would satisfy his lust.

But it was hard to stop when she was rubbing up against him, the firm globe of her breast in his hand, her nipple erect and ready. His fingers convulsed and he let out a groan, curling them for one agonizing second around that wonderfully soft mound, then slowly dragging his palm across the engorged nipple. She whimpered, sighed and stretched her head back, exposing her long neck.

Furious need thundered through every vein, and he took a deep breath to steady his racing thoughts. Then another.

Plans had a way of derailing, and if he didn't put a stop to this he'd lose the ground he'd already gained. Even as his body screamed in protest, he released her and took a step back. Her eyes sprang open and the dark desire in those depths coupled with a soft moue of disappointment speared him right in the groin.

You can do this. "AJ, we need to—"

A sharp, familiar tune suddenly echoed in the heated silence.

AJ groaned. Her phone.

He frowned. "Is that…?"

"'Young Turks' by Rod Stewart. My sister's choice."

"Then you'd better get it," he said, taking another step back.

Are you insane? AJ gave him an incredulous look. "It can wait."

"Could be important." His expression was shuttered and the distance he'd created spoke volumes. She blinked, watching Matt stride back into the kitchen, undoing his tie as he went, and her confusion was magnified a thousandfold. Still, Rod continued to sing, and with a sigh she reached into her clutch.

"Do you know what time it is?"

"What, did I interrupt you getting ready to go out, Miss Party Queen?" Emily said.

"No." She turned toward the windows with a scowl. "And shouldn't you be doing something more interesting on your Paris honeymoon than calling me?"

"Zac and I had a bet. I thought my carrier had canceled my international roaming and he disagreed."

"You know you can check that in your settings, right?"

"And deny myself the pleasure of hearing your voice?"

AJ felt a reluctant smile form. "Well, tell Zac congrats, he won. Won what, I don't think I want to know."

"You hear that, darling?"

"Smart girl," she heard Zac murmur, then came a pause, followed by a giggle. AJ's heart twisted briefly before she brushed it off.

"If you've quite finished flirting with your husband, Mrs. Preston—"

"Hang on. You left a message about the apartment. How long do you need it for?"

"Not sure. A few months?" She toed off her heels and let her feet sink into the plush carpet with a sigh.

"What?" She heard her sister shift then mumble something to Zac. "What's keeping you in Sydney that long?"

AJ paused, then finally said with a wince, "A...man?"

"You don't sound too sure."

"I am. I think." She couldn't help it—she flicked a glance toward the kitchen. The man in question was exiting with two steaming cups, tie dangling loose and hair still sexily rumpled. She glanced away and shoved a stray lock of her own hair behind her ear.

"What about your stall?" Emily said.

"I can set one up at The Rocks."

"Hmm."

"*Hmm*—what?"

"Oh, nothing. But Zac's planning on having an open house so we'll need the apartment by October third."

AJ did a quick mental calculation. "Seven weeks away?"

"If you say so…" She ended on a gasp, then the phone clunked ominously in AJ's ear.

"I'm hanging up now," AJ called. "Bye, Zac!"

"Bye, AJ," came her brother-in-law's deep voice on the other end before the line cut out.

"Having a good time, are they?" Matt asked, placing her cup on the coffee table.

AJ nodded. "They're in Paris. Who wouldn't have fun?"

"How did they meet?"

AJ eyed him, tapping the edge of her phone gently on her chin. "He was her boss."

"An office romance, hey?"

"Something like that." Emily deserved to be happy. And Zac was perfect for her, despite their rocky start. Clandestine affairs didn't always turn out well, but theirs… Well, you only had to see them together to know they were completely and totally in love. "Emily planned the perfect wedding and the perfect honeymoon." She gave a small smile. "She's such an organizer—unlike me. She likes things just right. She's a true believer in love and romance and all that 'hearts and flowers' stuff."

"And you're not?"

AJ shrugged. "Oh, I believe in attraction, in passion. Love, sure. But fidelity? Soul mates?" She shrugged.

He frowned. "That's a bit cynical. What about the millions

of couples who've been together and stayed faithful over the years?"

"I didn't say it doesn't work. Just not for me."

"Why not? What makes you so different from anyone else, AJ?"

She scowled. "Our past defines us," she said tightly. "It makes us into the people we are."

"So you're saying you have no free will? That you'll let an event or person tell you how to think and feel?"

"No!" She scowled. "But people are conditioned for self-preservation. We're either in pursuit of things that make us feel good or protecting ourselves from hurt. And growing up, it was always the latter. My mother—" She abruptly clamped her mouth shut. That subject was a major mood killer. "Look, are we going to talk about my past or have sex?"

He took her in through hooded eyes as he slowly placed his cup on the coffee table.

She swallowed, realizing she'd said entirely the wrong thing.

"I have some work to do. I'll probably be up awhile."

Yep. Wrong thing. Flustered, AJ couldn't hide her disappointment, yet he didn't say a word, just pulled his tie free. "I'm leaving for Italy on Sunday."

"Italy?" she said, trying to ignore the sudden feeling of loss. "Lucky you."

He shrugged, folding his tie slowly and precisely. "It's for work. I don't have time to sightsee."

"Right." Work. It would always come first. She'd known from the start she'd have to fit in around his work schedule. But was it foolish to be just a little disappointed?

"Good night, AJ." He picked up his coffee then turned and strode toward his office.

She glared at the door as he closed it behind him. If that wasn't a rejection, she didn't know what was.

It was obvious that he wanted her. So why weren't they naked on his couch right now?

"Work," she muttered in the cool, dark silence. "Or the ex." Really, what other explanation could there be?

She stared at the carpet, hands on her hips. She had no reason to be angry, not when she'd actively pursued this arrangement. Hell, she should be thankful he was so work-focused because didn't that just make everything easier?

She huffed out a sigh and stared at the closed door. "Cold shower, I guess," she muttered, then turned toward the bathroom.

AJ rolled over in bed and stared at the faint light coming under her door. Was Matt still working? She grabbed her phone and squinted at the time. 1:17. Surely the man had to sleep sometime.

As she lay there in the darkness, surrounded by unfamiliar scents and silence, her mind sluggishly kicked in. Pretty soon it was full of too many questions, too many thoughts.

Too many doubts.

With a grunt, she tossed off the bed covers then grabbed her robe. When she eased her door open, the subdued living-room lamp cast shadows across the room, but it was Matt's office she focused on. She padded across the carpet, then placed her hand on the closed door.

Inside, she could hear his clear deep voice followed by another male voice that was slightly muffled and tinny. Skype? She heard Matt say, "Thanks. See you Sunday." Then nothing.

The gentle clack of fingers on keyboard punctuated the silence. She grabbed the doorknob and slowly turned it.

Matt was at his desk, a laptop open in front of him, the rest of the surface strewn with papers, pens, a file or two. He'd rolled up his shirt sleeves, revealing lean tanned forearms sprinkled with dark hair.

"Did I wake you?" he said suddenly, his focus still on the computer.

"I'm a light sleeper."

He reached for a paper, scanning it with a frown. "You should go back to bed."

She shoved a hand through her hair. "So should you. It's late."

He paused, placed the paper into a folder, then slowly swiveled his chair to face her. "In Rome it's twenty past five in the afternoon."

Rome. "Nice to know."

"Don't worry, I'll be back for our appointment."

"That's not what I was thinking." When he raised an eyebrow, she continued, "It's Rome. Home of the Trevi Fountain, the Sistine Chapel, the Vatican. All that wonderful history and art…"

He studied her, looking all comfortable and relaxed in his office chair, a curious smile on his lips. "You've never been to Rome?"

"I've never been outside Australia. Too expensive."

His gaze held her firm, revealing nothing. "Come here."

She eyed him back. "Why?"

"Why not?"

She took one step forward, then another, until she was standing barely a foot away. He reached out, snagging her robe and dragging her to him until she was trapped between his thighs.

She reached out to steady herself and when her hands met his shoulders, she felt him tense. Like an old motor starting up, her pulse began to pound, but this time it was panic of a different kind.

She waited, heart in her throat as his eyes held hers for long, agonizing seconds. Then, without breaking contact, he slowly, almost reverently, untied her robe, gently peeling it back like he was unwrapping a wonderful new gift. When his knuckles briefly grazed the curve of her waist, her breath stuck and her eyes widened. Then he slid his hands over her hips and glanced down.

He snorted, mouth curving. "Nice jammies."

"I happen to like Hello Kitty," she said in mock offense. "And they're comfy."

"Yeah, they look it. Very…" His gaze returned to her low neckline, to her breasts barely contained by the soft tank top. "Well-worn." And then he shocked her by reaching out and gently brushing his thumb over her peaking nipple.

Her breath hissed in. Their eyes met.

"I thought you said we should wait until after our appointment," she managed to say.

His eyes darkened. "Do you want me to stop?"

The air suddenly became too warm, too thick.

She started to lean in the exact moment he pulled her down. They met halfway, an eager joining of lips and breath. When Matt kissed her, the outside world dissolved.

With a groan, she closed her eyes and put all she had into that kiss. She welcomed his tongue when it roughly invaded her mouth. She murmured her acquiescence when his hand cupped her breast then teased her aching nipple into eager hardness. And she offered no resistance when he fisted his other hand in her hair, pulling her down. His roughness excited her, making her groin ache. Already her breath was coming out heavy, and as she went to her knees on the carpet, she reached for his shirt, fumbling for the buttons.

After a second—a long-drawn out, painful second—she muffled a curse and instead, ripped his shirt open. The buttons went flying but she didn't care. She just needed to feel his skin, trail her hands along his smooth chest, then follow it with her mouth.

He sucked in a breath when her questing fingers found his nipple. "Matt…" she purred, her smile widening at his guttural response. "Take me to bed."

Matt groaned. When had she managed to turn the tables on him? He was supposed to be in control, making the decisions here. He had a plan, a damn good one. Yet one kiss from AJ's lush mouth and he was panting like a dog in heat, prepared to let everything fall to pieces.

"We need to—"

"What, Matt?" She tweaked his nipple and he gasped, lust exploding in his belly. "What do we need?"

"We should—" He squeezed his eyes shut as her other hand descended, cupping his hard manhood.

"We should…" Her mouth parted again and he leaned down to take it like a thirsty man. She was so very hot, scorching him with her hands and lips and sweet body. He cupped her breast again, marveling at the lush curves on such a lean frame before pulling aside her tank top and releasing the glorious fullness.

He ripped his mouth free from hers and fastened his lips on her nipple with a satisfied groan.

Her gasp echoed off the walls as he tongued the nub, gently using his teeth and lips until it hardened beneath his ministrations. "You taste so sweet, Angel. So very sweet," he muttered, dragging his mouth across the soft globe, then rubbing his stubbled chin over her nipple.

He was rewarded with another gasp, and with lust thundering through his veins, his groin painfully hard and every sense eager and ready to go, he finally gave in.

He hooked his thumbs in her pants and swiftly pulled them down.

After a brief caress and an appreciative murmur, he gently spread her knees, his hand diving between her legs.

Her gasp sent hot, urgent desire flooding his senses, and when he felt her wobble, he placed a steadying hand on her, while with the other he parted her folds and firmly eased one finger into her damp warmth.

She trembled so sweetly, it was hard to get control, but he did, and when he slid his finger deeper, making deep circular motions inside, her voice gurgled in her throat.

"You like that?" he murmured, tipping her forward so his lips met her neck. She nodded her agreement, squeezing him inside.

He paused. "More?"

"Yes." It was a plea and they both knew it, but they were past the point of caring right now. He slowly pulled out before easing back in with two fingers this time.

The tightness made her gasp, her eyes widening as she stared right into his. They were dark like an abyss, passion bleeding them black.

Then he started to move, to glide in and out, and the delicious friction overtook everything else.

He gave himself over to pure sensation, to the smell of their passion, her gentle murmurs and heavy breath, to the way she rocked her hips as he gradually coaxed her higher and higher.

"Matt," she finally managed to gasp. "Please…faster!"

He did as she asked, diving deep, building the moment, teasing and arousing until inevitably, she was right there on the edge.

"Yes," he muttered, his mouth going to her breast again, teeth grazing her nipple.

And then he gently bit down and she exploded with a wrenching cry.

Matt clung to the last remnants of control as she enveloped him, the sensual beat pulsating, filling him to bursting. And then there it was, that gloriously sweet release when she came for him, when she was finally and irrevocably vulnerable beneath his hands. He'd done that and, damn, he felt like he could take on a whole army right now.

Except he was barely holding on and his erection was killing him.

With his hand still intimately holding her, he tried to undo his pants with one hand.

With a soft curse, he sighed. AJ shifted and suddenly her hands were at his belt, undoing it with deft fingers.

His grin matched hers until she hesitated, teeth nibbling her bottom lip as wide eyes met his.

"I can't do this with you…with me…" She shifted then and Matt got it. "Right."

Slowly, gently, he withdrew, and the sweet sound of her

breath hissing out and the sudden musky scent of sex permeating the air made his blood race. They exchanged a knowing look, a look of lovers who knew exactly what was to come.

He took in her passion-brightened eyes, the way her lips curved as she silently yanked down his pants and boxers. He kicked them off, peeled away the tattered remnants of his shirt then reached for her.

They both sighed, lips exploring each other for a brief moment until Matt guided her backward to the desk. Cradling her firm bottom in his hand, he lifted her up, sliding her across the top and scattering the papers and pens in the process. Then he eased her leg around his waist and sure enough, she knew exactly what he wanted her to do. She swiftly brought her other leg around, linking her ankles at the small of his back. Her heels dug into his butt and he repositioned himself, eyes locked on hers. Her breath puffed over his cheek as she leaned in, eager and ready, and his lips caressed the careening pulse in her neck, breathing in the glorious scent of her damp skin.

And then he plunged in and it felt like the whole world skidded to a standstill.

Thrum-thrum-thrum-thrum. The beat throbbed hard and loud in his ears as her wet tightness completely surrounded him, a sweetly painful yet glorious sensation that grew as he struggled for control.

He grabbed her thighs, fingers digging into her pliant flesh as he shuddered. In the back of his mind he registered the odd thought—*this desk is a perfect height*—until she reached up and kissed him.

He devoted a few moments to her mouth, then finally began to move, slowly at first, then with a steady rhythm she quickly picked up on. Her hips thrust to meet his. With a groan he tipped her, angling deeper.

Their shocked gasps came out as one.

"Yes," she murmured, her hot breath in his ear, lips nipping his jaw. "Yes."

Sweat slicked them as they slid together, skin on skin. Muscles stretched and moved harmoniously until slowly a familiar tightness gripped his belly. Matt gritted his teeth, thighs clenching, but still he kept going, blinded by AJ's passionate words in his ear, her sweet breath on his neck and her soft, pliable lips tilting up to receive his mouth. He kept going until he began to feel the swell of orgasm build, rushing closer and closer the more he sank into her hot, welcoming core.

"Angel…" he got out through gritted teeth. "I think—"

"Me, too," she panted, her eyes tight, face straining. "Please, Matt, I need…"

He knew. He knew because he needed it, too. Time stood still and all he could do was suck in a thick breath and focus on her glorious expression as she finally, sweetly, came for him a second time. With a triumphant cry Matt let himself go, breath exploding like a drowning man coming up for air as he spilled into her.

Everything vibrated, pulsated, and his skin felt like someone had ripped a layer off. He shifted, wincing as his calf tightened painfully.

"You okay?" she murmured.

Oh, yeah. "Just a cramp." He stretched his leg, careful not to disrupt her afterglow. He loved seeing her this way, all pouty and languid, her eyes heavy and mouth curved in a satisfied grin. Her belly slid across his, slick with sweat, and he gently skimmed a hand over her damp flesh.

"You've filled out," he said, cupping her hip, taking pleasure in the warm skin.

"Are you telling me I've put on weight, Matthew Cooper?"

His gaze snapped up to her teasing expression and he returned her grin. "Yeah, but it looks good. A few more curves here," he stroked her hip, then trailed back to her belly. "And here. I like it."

She smiled, that luscious top lip teasing him. "You sure know how to flatter a girl." Then she winced and shifted. "I think my butt has fallen asleep."

He glanced over to the clock on his laptop. "Smart butt. It's past two. We should follow its example."

"Okay."

She moved again and Matt gritted his teeth, stilling her with a hand on her thigh. "Wait." As he slowly eased from her, she hissed through her teeth. "Did I hurt you?"

"No. It's just…" She ducked his gaze, demurely drawing her legs together. "A bit tender."

When he stepped back and reached for his clothes, AJ took the moment to regain her composure, sliding off the desk and grabbing her pants from the floor. She didn't embarrass easily, yet she felt that annoying flush creep up her neck.

No other guy could make her blush like Matt could.

With her robe resecured and her pajama pants dangling from her fingers, she paused, watching him pull on his tattered shirt. The lean muscles in his shoulders shifted as he pushed one arm through a sleeve, then the other. She drank in the view, dragging her eyes across his smooth chest and dark nipples, down to his trim waist and abdominal ridges, to finally stop at his belly button where that tantalizing line of hair disappeared into his pants.

Her mouth went dry and she quickly snapped her gaze away. "I'm going to take a shower."

He nodded then said softly, "Sleep well, AJ."

You're not coming with me? She bit down on that presumptuous question and instead managed a smile. "You, too."

She waited until he turned back to the desk and, feeling incredibly out of sorts and oddly dismissed, she withdrew.

The discontent grew as she padded down the hall, offsetting the still-present throb of their lovemaking.

There was no reason to be annoyed, none at all. She'd pursued this and now she was getting exactly what she wanted.

With that thought firm in her head, she pushed open the bathroom door and turned on the light. A shower would go a long way to making her feel normal, even though she suspected this was just the start of many abnormal days ahead.

Ten

Matt leaned back in his chair, rubbed his eyes and reached for his third cup of coffee in two hours. Bright afternoon sun speared through the dark clouds outside and he winced, grabbing the remote to angle down the blinds.

As the shadows lengthened in his office, he relaxed a little. He'd been at GEM since eight and, amazingly, he'd managed to block out last night and focus on his schedule, completing his work in record time.

Until he paused and let his thoughts wander.

Lips...hair...soft sighs...

He swallowed his now-cold coffee, determinedly ignoring the way his body stirred. AJ was like a drug, seeping into his blood and arousing him to that point of almost painful ecstasy. Sure, they'd always been pretty explosive together but not like this. This was something more, something hotter, more intense.

Something deeper.

He shoved his cup across the desk. And now that he had the taste for her again, he wanted nothing more than to explore every new curve, kiss every inch of skin and bring her to climax over and over.

His phone rang, breaking off those dangerous thoughts, and he reached for it with a relieved sigh.

"Hello, darling."

The familiar, oh-so-proper English voice washed over him.

"Hi, Mum." He stuck the phone in between his shoulder and ear and turned back to his computer. "What's up?"

"Katrina tells me you're off to Italy on Sunday."

"Did she?"

"Yes." Alicia Cooper ignored his irritation with practiced ease. "Could you call into Ferragamo and pick up a package for me?"

"More shoes?" He grinned, clicking on his computer screen then glancing over at his iPad as it synced.

"A woman can never have enough shoes," she replied loftily.

As his chuckle petered out, she said, "Katrina also tells me she saw you last night."

"Yeah."

"With a redhead."

His hand stilled on the mouse. "Yep," he said cautiously.

"What happened to that other one…the dark-haired publishing assistant…Lilia, wasn't it?"

"Nothing happened. We just went our separate ways."

Matt ignored his mother's silence, clicking the mouse and closing all the windows until only his schedule remained.

"What's her name?" Alicia finally said.

Ah. There it was. "AJ."

"Excuse me?"

"AJ. As in Angelina Jayne." His computer trilled, indicating his office manager was updating his schedule. "Look, Mum, I'm a bit pushed for time, so…"

"What does she do?"

He swallowed a sigh. God spare him from his mother's dogged determination to interfere in his life. Though Paige would tell him to give the woman a break. She'd lost one son already and Matt had chucked in a career she'd been heavily invested in since he was born. Maybe she just wanted to stay connected.

More like provide unwanted criticism.

"Well, Matthew?" she demanded now. "What does this woman do for a living?"

"She's an artist." The pause on the other end of the line told him so much, none of it good. "Look, Mum, I really have to go—"

"Fine," she replied coolly. "Have a safe trip." Yeah, she was pissed. Matt rubbed his forehead, smoothing out the frown lines.

"I will."

He hung up, his good mood now laced with irritation. He glanced through his emails, forwarding a few, saving some, deleting the rest, before finally pushing away from the desk with a sigh.

This would not do. With a firm set to his jaw, he reached for his phone and dialed.

"Dinner again?" AJ glanced at the clock on the wall above the dining table—twelve-fifteen—then at a muted Dr. Phil on the massive TV screen. She stretched her legs, placing them carefully on the coffee table and crossing them at the ankles, then leaned back into the couch. "You really don't have to, you know."

"Wear something for the water."

"What, a bikini?"

"No." She heard the amusement in his voice. "Something for an ocean breeze. I'll send a car for you at five."

She hung up and tossed her phone onto the couch cushion. Everything still pulsed from last night, a dull ache that had her staring at the ceiling with a goofy, self-satisfied grin.

He was wooing her. Why?

She rolled her neck, wincing as she felt the muscles pop and stretch. Because that's what he did. Along with his passionate intensity, this attentive treatment was part of his charm. For all his faults, she had to admit being the sole focus of Matt's attention when they were together was incredibly flattering, not to mention a massive ego boost.

Amazing he was still single, despite his breakneck work ethic.

She scrolled through her phone messages, answering Emily's, deleting a couple of spam. "Maybe he likes being single," she said aloud to the TV. Dr. Phil nodded sagely. "Maybe he's just not interested in marriage." No, that wasn't right—what about Katrina? "Maybe she ruined it all for him." Hmm. Yes, that sounded plausible. The woman looked as if she could give a guy ice burns in all sorts of awkward places.

"Or maybe…" She deleted a few more texts. "He's just shut it all down." Despite his declaration to the contrary, she'd seen his expression twist into a brief flash of grief and regret when he'd mentioned his brother. Her stomach clenched. Matthew Cooper with emotional baggage? That was a new one. He didn't seem the type to regret anything; he simply plowed through life, single-minded in his focus. He was a man of science, of medicine. Of cold hard facts. The kind of driven, ambitious guy the movies and TV portrayed with eerie accuracy. Yet he was also a guy with hidden depths, who believed in something as ephemeral as fate.

Huh. So they did have one thing in common, besides the sex thing—past hurts equaled an avoidance of attachment.

She didn't have a chance to think more on that because the very last text caught her attention.

Miss you. C U tonight?

Huh. Jesse had texted her at one-thirty last night. "Not a chance in hell," she murmured as she typed in her reply.

No. I don't date married guys.

She sent the text, then glanced back at the TV. Dr. Phil was talking to two teens and it was apparent they both had very different opinions about raising their child.

"Good ol' Dr. Phil," she said, swinging her legs to the carpet. "Where were you when my parental unit needed your sensible advice? Not that she would've taken it, mind you."

Her phone pinged.

2morrow then?

Ass. She scowled at the Android smiley, but the little green face merely grinned back at her.

Only if Nirvana get back together.

Resisting the urge to hurl her phone to the table—not good, considering it was made of glass—she instead gently placed it on the edge and stood. Jesse James Danson. Oh, how he'd loved playing up his outlaw persona, charming her with his wit and boyish smile one afternoon at her stall. And she'd been sucked in all right, recklessly promising to hand deliver her painting to what turned out to be his single guy apartment in Mermaid Beach. Her delivery had turned into coffee, then a week or two of phone tag, then suggestive texts, then finally, a month later, he'd coaxed her into bed.

She grabbed her phone and turned off the ringer for good measure. She wouldn't give that guy any more of her time. She had a date to get ready for.

The sleek white Commodore arrived dead on five, pulling up in front of the apartment as afternoon light bled into early evening. The uniformed driver got out and opened her door with a smile.

"How are you this evening, ma'am?"

"I'm good." She smiled and slid into the soft bucket seat, her stomach somewhere in the region of her throat. Nerves again? After last night? How could that be? Yet the butterflies, the absent tapping of her toe, the familiar song under her breath all pointed to one thing.

She buckled up as the driver got in and met her eyes in the rearview mirror. "To the Quay, is it?"

"I think so. Sorry, what's your name?"

"It's Kim, ma'am."

"Hi, Kim. I'm AJ. And please, no 'ma'am.'"

He smiled and nodded as he pulled away from the curb and switched on the stereo.

AJ watched the traffic as they made their way along Parramatta Road, the University of Sydney on her right, the former Grace Bros. building, which now housed the shiny Broadway shopping center, on the left. The last time she'd been in Sydney, she'd been working in a Pitt Street Mall coffee shop and house sharing with two surfers, a German backpacker and a sex phone worker. Yet as memorable as that time was, the music coming through the car speakers overshadowed it. The songs curled softly into her brain and took her further back, to the times when she'd been crazy, full of youthful recklessness and eager for seduction by a wicked smile and a pair of serious brown eyes.

When the third song came on she sucked in a breath and leaned forward. "Is this your CD?"

"No. Mister Cooper supplied it."

"Oh."

"You want me to turn it off?"

"No, it's fine." She tried to focus on the peak-hour traffic outside but it was no good. "I don't believe it," she muttered as "Sway" by Bic Runga finished and Collective Soul's "Run" began. It was the same playlist her boss at Arabelle's had piped through their system that summer ten years ago, playing it over and over until her coworker Maz had laughingly threatened to strike unless he played something—anything!—else. AJ ticked off the songs, drowning in the past as the car cruised down George Street: "How Will I Know" by Jessica Sanchez, "With or Without You" by U2, "Put Your Arms Around Me" by Texas and, yes, even Cliff Richard's "Miss You Nights."

Her sudden grin was reflected back at her in the car window. Her boss had been a huge Cliff Richard fan. And Matt had remembered.

He couldn't have known that that CD had become her soundtrack of misery, every single song either speaking of lost love, unfulfilled desires or new passion—"Heart & Shoulder" by Heather Nova, "Here We Are" by Gloria Estefan, "Always the Last To Know" by Del Amitri.

She smoothed back her hair and put those thoughts from her mind. Instead, she tried to focus on how much she'd enjoyed working those twelve months at Arabelle's, the casual camaraderie the staff had shared, the fun they'd had spending all their days off at the beach, then partying all night.

Melancholy rose. Hearing this music again made her miss them, a bittersweet emotion considering they'd all moved on with their lives and started their own families.

"In the Air Tonight" by Phil Collins came on and her smile returned.

God, she loved this song. The sexy, mournful guitar, the smooth, haunting lyrics. Then that heavy drum solo that seemed to come from nowhere. It was a hot, provocative song, designed for lovemaking.

Perfect for tonight.

She squeezed her thighs together and breathed deep, the music curling seductively in her belly until the car finally pulled to a stop.

When Matthew swung the door swung open, she couldn't stop her heart from tripping over itself. Just like last night, he offered his hand and she took it, letting him help her from the car with a smile.

He swept his gaze over her, taking in her strappy silver heels, long wraparound red dress with the plunging neckline and soft black cardigan she'd topped it with. "You look great." But when his eyes went to her hair, he frowned.

Her hand went to her careful coiffure. "What?"

"What's with your hair?"

"What do you mean?"

He nodded. "Why do you tie it back like that? Doesn't it give you a headache?"

"No." She smoothed it back, tucking a nonexistent strand behind her ear. "It's more efficient this way. Less annoying."

"You should leave it loose." And before she could reply, he had a hand in her hair and was digging out the hairclips she'd painstakingly positioned.

She twisted away. "Matt! No!" She patted the back, fiddling with the now-messy strands. "Damn it." She scowled at him. "You've ruined it."

"Then take it down."

A soft growl of frustration rattled in her throat. "Fine." She plucked out the pins, then undid the elastic. Her hair came tumbling down, the soft, freshly washed waves falling over her shoulders, making her shiver. With a scowl, she unclasped her clutch and dropped the pins inside. "Happy now?"

"Yes." When he gently rearranged the strands, fingers brushing her cheek, her irritation faltered, then fizzled out. He linked his fingers through hers and led her across the sidewalk.

They were at the Man O' War steps, a long jetty just around the corner from the Opera House. The sun had set behind them, leaving the Botanical Gardens in shadow. She nodded to a sleek cruiser tied to a berth as they walked down the wooden jetty. "Did you hire a boat?"

"No. It's mine."

"You own a *boat?*"

"Sure. It's normally moored at my house but I got my captain to bring it on down."

"Your captain." Boy, this night was getting more surreal by the moment. "Nice music in the car, by the way. You have a good memory."

"Comes from years of study. Good evening, Rex." He nodded to the captain, impressive in his white uniform and brimmed cap. "This is Miss Reynolds."

"Mr. Cooper. Miss Reynolds." Rex inclined his head, smiling. "Are you ready to cast off, sir?"

"We are."

AJ made her way tentatively across the drawbridge, Matt's steadying hand at her back, before finally stepping onto the deck. It was like being on one of Sydney Ferries' JetCats, but where the JetCat was equipped for public service efficiency, carrying hundreds of commuters per trip, this vessel was decked out purely for luxury.

She slowly walked into the cabin, marveling at the opulence. The huge interior was obviously for serious entertainment, from the wraparound glass windows displaying Sydney Harbour in all its glory to the polished wooden floors. A couple of inviting couches huddled around a huge plasma screen to her left, and to her right was an eating area with dining table and bar.

She turned back to Matt and nodded to the unset table. "I thought we were eating."

He smiled. "We are. Aft. And—" he glanced at his watch "—it should be ready now. Come."

He led her to the door at the rear of the cabin, one firm hand on the small of her back.

They emerged into the cold night as the rumbling engines overtook the gentle sound of waves slapping the hull. A glass partition extended along the aft rail, shielding them from the wind, and dead ahead a small table was decked out for two, complete with white plates, oversized wineglasses and candles flickering in huge glass lanterns. A long food warmer sat on one side, and on the other, a huge patio heater emanated a comforting glow.

Wow. The chauffeured car pickup, the music, the boat. And now this. He'd gone all out when she would have been satisfied with takeout on the sofa. Yet something inside her did a little dance at the effort he'd put in.

It was the little things, right?

The engines surged and the boat abruptly picked up pace,

cleaving through the harbor with a whoosh of water and spray. The deck listed beneath her feet and he took her arm, steadying her.

"You like?" His smile was perfectly enigmatic.

She nodded. "I do."

"Great. Let's eat."

If someone had asked her later what the meal was like, she'd be hard-pressed to remember it. Matt's presence overshadowed every bite. She barely felt the cold wind whipping around the boat as he served their meal, all the while keeping up a comfortable commentary about the history of Botany Bay and Fort Dennison, Sydney's first convict island.

When she finally emerged from her little bubble to glance down at her plate, everything had miraculously gone.

"Dessert?" He smiled, holding his wineglass gently by the stem.

"What do you have?"

His smile deepened. "Crème brûlée, strawberries and a decadent mocha mousse."

"The way to a girl's heart." AJ sighed dramatically. "But you know," she went on, tapping a finger on her chin, "I don't remember you ever offering *three* choices before."

"I was a struggling student."

"Matthew Cooper, struggling? Rubbish." Her grin took the sting out of her words and he answered it with one of his own. They sat like that for ages until her phone rang.

She dug it from her bag, glanced down at the screen, scowled, then switched it to mute.

Matt watched her but said nothing.

"No one important," she supplied, dropping it back into her bag. "So. Italy, huh?"

He nodded. "My plane leaves at seven in the morning."

"Your plane? As in your own personal plane?" At his nod, her eyes rounded. "Wow. I am so in the wrong job."

He shrugged. "It's a necessity. That way GEM isn't bound

by commercial airline schedules. I can leave within half an hour if I need to."

"Must be nice to take off on a whim."

He lifted his eyebrows. "Says the Queen of Impulsiveness."

"Yeah…" She sighed. "But not so much anymore. Tell me, Matt." She leaned in, her elbows on the table. "After all the places you've been, having your own private boat and plane… is there something you haven't yet achieved? Some particular goal that's always eluded you?"

"Of course."

"Name one."

He paused, his expression giving nothing away. "I've never backed a winner in the Melbourne Cup."

She snorted. "Winning a horse race is not a dream."

"Speak for yourself!" He looked affronted. "It's not just a horse race—it's *the* horse race."

AJ shrugged. "See, I never really got the whole racing thing. Just seems like you're throwing away good money."

"So you don't drink or gamble," he murmured, eyeing her over the rim of his glass. "I'm learning all sorts of things about you."

Her eyebrows went up. "What's there to learn? What you see is what you get, right here."

"Angel, you are one of the most secretive women I know."

"Oh, know a lot of women, do you?"

He made a moue of indifference. "Right now…? I can't remember a single one."

She felt her face flush again, and when he smoothly rose and offered his hand she didn't hesitate. As she stood, her thigh inadvertently brushed across his groin and he sucked in a breath.

"Sorry," she mumbled.

He shook his head. "Don't be."

Damn it. Why him? Why this instant and intense lust? She had absolutely no clue.

Then he kissed her and she stopped thinking.

They stood there, leisurely exploring each other's mouths, tongue and skin, while the slow burn of desire steadily curled higher and the hint of cold night teased everywhere their bodies didn't touch.

"Matt..." she got out, her breath racing across his mouth. "I need to—"

"I know."

"—use the bathroom."

His crestfallen look was so comical she had to bite back a grin. But when he nodded and stepped back, the keen sense of loss she felt chased away any amusement.

"Inside, to the left."

She nodded. "I won't be long."

Come on. Get it together. Palms flat on the polished vanity, AJ stared at her reflection in the huge bathroom mirror. This gut-sucking passion, this breathless rush of being swept along by something bigger, was all familiar territory. He affected her with every single kiss, every single touch. He had magic hands—magic Matthew hands.

Surgeon's hands, so familiar with the human body, so familiar with healing, with giving life.

So familiar with her.

She straightened the towel on the rack. This was a good thing. It meant she could relax and enjoy herself, which was highly conducive to baby making. Stressing about it would be counterproductive.

Okay, so go out there and have a good time.

With a nod at her reflection, she smoothed the ends of her hair, tweaked the edges of her bra to plump up her breasts, then rubbed her lips together, the smooth glide of lipstick a time-honored confidence booster.

She left the bathroom, her heels ringing boldly on the polished wood. But when she walked outside, her confidence dissolved under the weight of Matt's loaded gaze.

"Your phone rang again," Matthew said as she walked over to the table. "Someone called Jesse?"

"The married ex," she supplied when she noticed his too-casual, I'm-not-going-to-ask look. "He's—" Her phone vibrated and AJ glanced down. "Speak of the devil." She grabbed it and pivoted, stalking to the railing for privacy. Unshielded by the partition, the cold night air blasted over her skin, whipping her hair. She flicked on the phone, then shoved a hand through the whirling mass, shoving it from her eyes. "What do you want?"

"Jay-jay! How are you doing, sexy legs?"

"Stop calling me that—it makes you sound like an idiot." His deliberate twist on her initials and that little pet name had been mildly cute when they were dating. Now it just made her want to smack him.

"So, I thought we could grab a drink tonight."

"Look, I told you we're over. Stop calling me," she hissed, shooting a glance back at Matt, who was leaning over the opposite railing, his attention seemingly absorbed by the dark water below. "Go back to your wife."

"Aww, babe, if we really were over, why're you still taking my calls?"

"Because you keep calling me, dumbass!"

His laugh rumbled down the line. "I miss that mouth! Especially when you did—"

She hung up. With a frustrated growl she stalked back to the table, then slowly, deliberately put her phone down when all she wanted to do was hurl it into the ocean.

She put a cold hand to her cheek and sighed. Her face was burning.

"Why do you still have your ex on your phone?"

Matt had turned back to her and she eyed him, cupping her other cheek. "So I know when to ignore his calls."

"He calls often?"

She shrugged. "Once or twice a month."

"Why don't you tell him to piss off?"

She gave him a look. "I have. He keeps calling."

"So get him blocked. There are laws against stalking, AJ."

"Yeah, I know." She sighed. "But then I'd have to visit the police, file an official report—" That was the biggie. Her parents had screwed with her psyche so well, drumming in that irrational fear of the cops so deep it had taken her years—and a good therapist—to overcome their conditioning.

Plus, there was the small matter of her criminal record....

Her phone rang again but this time, Matt beat her to it. "Jesse? Yeah, this is AJ's phone. Listen, you need to stop calling her," he said in that cool, clipped tone. He ignored her silently mouthed protest and turned his back on her. "She's not interested in jerks who cheat on their wives. So get over it and move on." He paused. "Me? Dr. Matthew Cooper, former head of neurosurgery at Saint Catherine's."

"Oooo, a *doctor!* And *British,* too!"

Oh, Lord, she could hear Jesse's mocking comeback from here! And judging by the way Matthew's expression turned carefully blank, he was not impressed, either. His eyes locked on hers as Jesse let fly with something she couldn't quite make out.

Finally, Matt said softly, "Yeah, okay. I'd be careful who you're threatening, if I were you." Another pause, then a slow smile bloomed, his direct gaze still on her. "Because my best mate is ex-CIA and he really, really loves his guns. So be a good boy and lose AJ's number."

With that, he hung up and handed her phone back.

Honestly, she should be furious he'd butted in, but all that came to mind was... "Do you really know someone in the CIA?"

"He's my head of security."

"Right. But he wouldn't really shoot him."

"Who knows? Decker's been in some tight situations where force was the only option. We both have."

"So your job is dangerous then?"

"It can be." He reached for her hand and drew her close. "Why? Are you worried?"

"No."

She glanced away but Matt, damn him, had her measure. He pulled her flush against him, his heat searing into her, his laugh a soft breath against her cheek.

"You'd miss me, Angel. Admit it."

"Well, I wouldn't miss your huge ego, that's for sure."

"Ahh, but you'd miss this, I bet." Then his lips swooped down to meet hers and she just about melted on the spot.

They kissed until they were both breathless, until she felt her legs go wobbly and Matt gently drew her toward the cabin doors. Then they were inside and after a few more agonizing kisses, AJ felt a soft pressure on the back of her legs.

The sofa.

Matt nudged her and she sank into the cushions, taking him with her. He sprawled across her lap, his thighs hard against hers, his arms against the backrest on either side of her head.

"The windows—"

"Tinted," he got out, nipping her jaw.

"But the crew—"

"Topside. With instructions not to interrupt."

"But—"

"Angel, do you want to keep talking or would you rather I do this?" And with one smooth movement, he swept aside her dress and brought his mouth down to her breast.

Her back arched as he tongued her nipple to painful erectness through the black satin bra. Then he dragged the cup down, exposing her fully to his careful ministrations. His teeth latched on to that swollen nub and her breath hissed out in glorious ecstasy.

Oh, yes. She'd miss this. He was so very, very good at arousing her, whipping her into a bundle of aching, raw nerves until she was begging him to take her. Like now. She squirmed, eager for more of his lips, his tongue, his hands.

Pinned by his thighs, the bulge between them only frustrated her, fueling her desperation.

"Just so you know," she began, "this…ah…is going to be…" Another small groan escaped her as he dragged her dress off one shoulder and flicked his tongue along the exposed flesh. "It's just a simple matter of…"

"Want." There was no triumph, only complete conviction in his reply. Then he lifted his head, grasped her face firmly in his hands and silenced her with a kiss.

It was the best kiss she'd had in her life, and it just went on and on.

Finally, when they were both breathless, he released her mouth and returned to her breasts, gently sucking one nipple as he slowly massaged her other breast with his hand.

She groaned. "Matt…I need to move."

He shifted his weight, allowing her to wrap her legs around his waist.

"Would you miss this, Angel?" he murmured against her breast.

She muttered her ascent, too consumed with sensation to form a coherent word.

"And this?" He squeezed her other breast, kneading, caressing.

"Mmm." Her head lolled, eyes closing, and she heard his soft chuckle, full of male satisfaction.

"Or maybe this?" His hand went to her thigh, dragging her dress up. "You're so warm."

Their gazes locked. A wolfish smile gradually transformed his features, and AJ marveled at the sight. He was so beautiful. So totally and utterly seductive. So—

He pulled aside her knickers and dove into her folds, his thumb brushing over the hard nub.

Enough thinking. She let sensation take her. With every touch of his tongue on her nipple, every stroke of his fingers between her legs, her body jerked, pleasure sparking then fanning out, following the path of her blood as it chugged through her veins.

"Matt!" Ripples of desire sensitized her skin. "Please!"

"You seem to be doing a lot of begging lately, Angel." His voice practically purred as his fingers continued their excruciating work. "What would you say if I did...this?"

One finger slid into her slick heat and she gasped. *Oh, yes.* She waited...waited...

He'd stopped.

What the hell...? She groaned, wriggled around, trying to get him to move. Yet he remained still, his other hand flat on her belly, firmly holding her in place. Her breath raced, blood throbbing as she snapped her head up to meet his glittering gaze.

"Or maybe..." he said, his mouth kinking up into a wicked smile. "This?"

And in one smooth movement he slid down her body, removing her underwear as he went. Then he replaced his fingers with his lips and she nearly bucked off the sofa. White-hot sensation exploded as his tongue began lavishing attention on the most intimate part of her, licking, sucking, loving.

Desire throbbed through every single vein, every muscle in Matthew's body. AJ surrounded him—her skin, her scent, her soft moans of pleasure. It made him want to rip off his clothes and take her hard and fast on the floor. Yet instead of giving in to that desperate need, he took a jagged breath, gathered the threads of his shredded control and focused on loving her with his mouth.

He nibbled her inner thigh, dragging his chin across the sensitive skin. His fingers dug into her skin as he lifted her hips to him and feasted on her sweetness, running his tongue slowly up, then down, loving the way she tasted, loving that her scent and arousal were in his every breath. And when he felt her trembling slowly increase, felt her thighs tense around him, he knew she was heading to the edge.

He left her there, legs spread with her dress rucked around

her waist, one breast exposed, head flung back in a familiar arch of ecstasy while he quickly pulled off his clothes.

It took too long, way too long.

When he was finally naked, he positioned himself between her legs, his hands splayed on her rib cage, feeling her deep panting breath, the ripples of passion across her skin.

"Angel," he ground out. "Look at me."

She did, slowly, languorously, and the arousal in her eyes blew him away. With a groan, he plunged deep inside her.

He made love to her that way, his hands gripping her waist, their eyes locked, as he slid deeply in, then slowly out.

His pounding heartbeat echoed in his head, his chest. Damn, it felt so good! Better than anything he'd ever experienced in his life. He groaned again as she tipped her hips, and when she reached up and wrapped her arms around his neck, he let her pull him down. She kissed him, deeply, passionately, using her tongue to tease, taste, toy. His breath galloped, matching hers, the throb of their hearts pounding in unison as he plunged into her. And gradually, everything built, sweeping closer and closer until he couldn't stand the mix of agony and ecstasy any longer.

He thrust a hand between them, where their bodies were slick with passion and friction, his fingers seeking her tight bud. When he found it, she shuddered, eyes wide, as he flicked it over and over.

"Matt!" She gasped, her breath coming out in tight little puffs as her legs squeezed his waist. "I think…"

"C'mon, Angel," he crooned in her ear, his lips against her damp hair. "Come with me."

When she did, it was the most glorious thing he'd ever seen. It was so intense, so powerful, that his teeth clenched, jaw grinding as waves of pleasure rushed him, tossing him up then quickly dumping him down, down, so deeply down.

Everything screamed, every muscle, every vein, every inch of his skin. *Hot. Too hot. I can't…* Then sensation took over and with a wrenching groan he spilled into her hot warmth.

"Angel," he groaned, her slick heat surrounding him, accepting him, taking all of him.

Glorious.

Eventually, when he slowly began to return back to earth, his other senses kicked in. He took in her racing breath, her musky skin, the aftermath of her orgasm still pulsing around him. He'd done that, brought her to the peak of ecstasy, had made her beg for him, before taking them both over the edge. And man, he felt like leaping up and punching the air like some macho alpha, smug in the knowledge he'd thoroughly pleasured a woman.

Not just a woman. *This* woman. His arms tightened around her, skin still moist with sweat. Her chin was tilted up, her eyes shut, hands provocatively splayed across her neck, just above her breasts.

He dropped a gentle kiss on one peaking nipple and she started. He grinned as she glanced down to meet his eyes.

"You okay?"

Man, that smile undid him every time: languorous and thoroughly sated, full of warm pleasure. "Oh, yeah."

He bathed in the satisfied glow and let the silence surround them, a silence punctuated by the faint hum of the engines and the gentle rocking of the boat as it cleaved through the choppy Sydney waters.

"What time is it?" she finally asked, then suppressed a shiver.

He glanced over to the entertainment unit at the glowing DVD clock. "One. Why?"

"Shouldn't you be getting some rest before your early flight?"

"I can sleep on the plane." He looped his arms around her waist to gather her close but stilled when he felt her gentle tug of resistance.

Okay. That was odd.

Smothering a frown, he eased back, then slowly, regretfully, slid from her.

Whatever she was thinking, it wasn't good, given the prolonged silence while he gathered up his clothes.

When he'd dragged on his pants and turned back to her, she'd fixed her clothes and was now sitting demurely on the couch, knees pressed together, staring thoughtfully at her hands. Almost as if by meeting his scrutiny she'd inadvertently divulge something she'd rather keep private. And judging by her expression, she'd rather make a swim for the shore than tell him what she was thinking right now.

Steady on. This isn't some kind of race. And this was AJ—a woman who heated up his bed, gave herself so completely to their lovemaking, yet managed to keep a part of herself untouched.

The desire to break down her walls had never been as intense as it was right at this moment.

"You know," she finally said, meeting his eyes. "I never did get that dessert."

His sudden bark of laughter made her lips curve in response, and the tension leeched out.

"Then we shall have to fix that."

He offered his hand and she took it without hesitation.

Eleven

AJ awoke slowly in her darkened room, checked the time—nine—then rolled onto her back to stare at the ceiling. She'd left the curtains open last night and now the gathering storm clouds were obvious. A perfect start to a dingy day.

Matt had been gone for hours and he hadn't even said goodbye.

At six she'd heard him turn on the shower, then turn it off barely five minutes later. He'd moved around in the kitchen, then she'd finally heard the front door gently close at half past.

He was under no obligation to say anything, even if she was his houseguest. Even so, his absence of manners nettled her.

"Oh, for heaven's sake, stop with all this emotional stuff," she said sternly in the cool silence. "This is what we want, right? Matt to remain work-focused and you to concentrate on making a baby."

A baby. Her hand slipped down to the flat plains of her belly. It was way too soon, of course. She wasn't even ovulating yet. Still…she gently palmed her stomach, forbidden excitement rising as she glanced down. "Just don't take too long, okay?" she whispered. "Because I'm really not sure how much of Matt I can handle when he gets all focused and intense."

She lay there for a few more minutes, bathing in last night, flushing at certain memories and grinning at others. Finally she sighed, tossed off the covers and headed for the shower.

Today was the perfect day to move back into Zac's apartment. And no doubt Matt would be happy to reclaim his space, too.

* * *

Two hours later she shoved the key in the door to Zac's apartment and stumbled through. Everything about this twenty-fifth-floor penthouse suite drew her in, from the huge panoramic view of Potts Point, Centrepoint, the Harbour Bridge and Rushcutters Bay to the vibrant sunflower yellow interior walls, sleek blond furniture, colorful cushions and tangerine rug in the center of the polished wooden floor. But it was the massive living room that drew a smile every time.

Zac had framed and strategically hung her paintings along the huge feature wall there. She remembered every gentle, colorful mark of her watercolor pencils, the damp brush strokes that brought the scenes to life—Coogee Beach with its beach towels, umbrellas and crashing azure waves. A Sydney cityscape bathed in an orange and purple sunset. And Circular Quay, complete with busy ferries and peak-hour commuters against a Harbour Bridge backdrop.

"Hello, gorgeous things." She grinned as she dropped her bags inside the door and kicked it shut. "Miss me?" She cocked her head, her gaze going from one picture to another. "Of course you did. Well, the good news is, I feel like painting. The bad news? No paints." She dug around in her shoulder bag and plucked out her sketch pad, then a pencil. "Still, better than nothing, right?"

After fixing herself a cup of Earl Grey, she dragged the blanket off the couch arm, wrapped it around her shoulders, then padded to the patio doors. With a whoosh and blast of cold air, she walked out onto the balcony, settled in a comfy chair and began.

AJ formed a routine of sorts for the next few days —she rose at eight, swam a few laps in the heated rooftop pool and lifted weights for half an hour in the fourth-floor gym. Then she had breakfast, followed by sketching, and lunch from one of the many restaurants that occupied the ground floor. After lunch she went walking, undeterred by the weather's sudden return to midwinter temperatures. She made her way down William Street, poking around in the funky boutiques and secondhand stores, admiring the baubles and handmade clothing, then crossing over Crown Street and heading toward Hyde Park. Turning right on College Street, she headed east, toward the New South Wales Art Gallery.

She spent all afternoon soaking up the rest of the amazing art and doing a few sketches before heading back, only detouring for her usual Starbucks grande latte and a chicken sub.

On Tuesday night, Matt called.

"So what have you been doing the past few days?" Just hearing that low, cultured voice in her ear was enough to make her body quiver.

"Oh, you know, living the life of luxury. Sketching, walking. I missed the Van Gogh exhibit at the art gallery by a day."

"Bummer."

"Yeah. He's one of my favorites." She started to sharpen a pencil. "When are you back?"

"I fly in late Wednesday night."

"Okay." She added the finishing touches to her drawing—a view of the sunset-strewn Queensland hinterland from the seventy-eighth floor of the Q Tower. "Oh, by the way, I'm at Zac's apartment."

A small moment of silence passed, way too long to blame on the time delay.

"Why?" Matthew finally said.

She paused and stared out the window, watching a slow-moving ferry glide along Botany Bay. "Because that was my plan, remember? Besides," she added lightly, "I make a lousy houseguest, leaving my wet towels on the floor and hogging all the bathroom bench space."

Another too-long silence. "I wouldn't know. You never stay long enough for me to notice."

Her breath came out sharp. "Wow. That was a bit harsh."

She heard him sigh down the phone. "Sorry. Look, it's been a long trip and I just want to get home. I'll send a car to pick you up tomorrow and I'll meet you at Saint Cat's for our appointment."

"Matt—"

"I have to go. See you on Thursday." And he hung up.

She slowly clicked off her phone, head churning. What on earth was that about? Again he'd brought up their past, which meant it must be bothering him more than he cared to admit.

It's just not working for me, AJ.

Despite the passage of time, that statement still made her wince. He'd made the decision to break up and there was nothing more to be said. So of course, retreat had been her best course of action. She'd simply nodded, risen on unsteady feet and left.

And he'd let her go.

But she needed to stop analyzing this and focus on her appointment. Emily was the deep thinker of their little family; her endless pros and cons list was something AJ ribbed her about all the time.

Sadness bloomed for one second, making her sigh. God, she missed her sister, missed her overwhelming optimism, her unique outlook on life. Her logical advice.

What would she say about this arrangement?

AJ scowled. Eventually she'd have to tell Emily what was going on. That is, if Zac hadn't already.

At any rate, she had a two-week reprieve to practice before they returned. With that thought, she picked up her abandoned pencil, turned the page and began a new sketch.

True to Matt's word, a car arrived at eight-thirty the next morning and took her across the Harbour Bridge to Saint Catherine's Hospital, set in the exclusive north shore suburb of Kirribilli.

The hospital still looked shiny and new even though it was almost twenty years old. She'd read about the amazing leaps in medicine and research they'd made there throughout those years, along with all the other achievements: best heart surgery team in Australia, a crack cancer research facility. And of course, the addition of a new wing, opened by the Prime Minister herself—the Alicia Cooper Neurosurgical Unit.

Matt met her at the entrance with a smile, and before AJ could steel herself, her heart did a little skip. Then he removed his sunglasses. "Hi, Angel. How've you been?"

"Nervous." It was the truth. She'd been riddled with worry all the way across town, and a lot of it had to do with Matt. Despite all that inner talk, all that "this is just a deal, nothing personal" stuff, she was genuinely elated to see him again. Giddy almost.

"Don't be," he said, laying his hand gently on her elbow as they walked to the bank of elevators. "Dr. Adams is the best. Which reminds me, I have to tell you something before we go in."

"Yes?"

"It's going to come up in the consult. I had leukemia when I was seven but I've been in remission for close to thirty years. Don't worry," he added, misinterpreting her shocked expression. "This strain isn't hereditary."

"That's not what I was thinking." *Holy crap.* He had *cancer?* She paused, searching for something, anything, to say. "Are you okay?"

"Never better."

"Good." *He's okay. No reason to panic.* Then in the next moment she felt a small stab of hurt—why hadn't he told her this before? Still, her expression must have given her away because he glanced at her and frowned.

"Don't look at me that way."

"What way?"

"It's not a big deal. I don't need your pity."

"It's not pity."

He said nothing, just reached into his jacket, checked his phone and shoved it back.

It's okay, AJ. He says he's clear. She fiddled with her hair, tightening the knot at her nape. Leukemia was serious. Should she ask how—?

"AJ? Are you listening?"

Not when you drop that bomb in my lap, I'm not. But just as she was opening her mouth, he shut her down.

"Look, it's over, I'm healthy and let's just move on, shall we?"

He wanted to move on. It's what she did, right? It's what she was an expert at. With a sigh, she shifted gears, her mind reluctantly clunking into second as she focused on the long corridor, her loud footsteps as they made their way to the elevators dragging her away from the scary thought of Matthew's mortality. He'd put his hand on her back, and the contact was reassuring. Almost natural.

Of course, there was nothing natural about this arrangement, but she didn't want to dwell on that. All her nervous anticipation took a backseat when they were given forms and she had to switch her focus to the barrage of personal questions: about her parents, their parents, Emily, their health, her health, allergies, drug use. A vague feeling of disquiet rose until a door opened and Dr. Adams arrived to take them through to her office.

As the doctor talked, AJ felt herself warming up to the friendly, middle-aged woman sporting a shock of closely cropped white hair and a wonderfully calming disposition. She skimmed both their forms, then went through the list of tests AJ needed, including an ultrasound and laparoscopy. Then she did the same for Matt.

Dr. Adams had just booked AJ in for her tests when Matt's phone rang. He excused himself and went outside to take it, leaving AJ with the doctor. She didn't mind, not when she had so many questions. She was only halfway through when Matt walked back in.

"I'm sorry," he said, his brow dipping. "I have to leave."

"Everything okay?" AJ asked.

"Auckland was hit by another quake. I'm flying out in an

hour." He turned to Dr. Adams and they shook hands. "Email me the report, Sandi, and let me know when I need to schedule my tests." Then he turned to AJ, leaned down and, to her surprise, kissed her cheek. "I'll be back on Saturday."

She nodded, not trusting herself to speak. It was pointless to feel cheated but damn it, she couldn't stop herself from going there. Then Matt was gone and she was left with a vague feeling of loneliness congealing in her belly.

"Well." She turned to Dr. Adams with an overly cheerful smile. "Where were we?"

Twelve

When Matt returned on Saturday, AJ had given herself a serious talking-to, boxed up all those stupid fears and returned them to their dark corner. She'd spent Friday being poked, prodded and scanned, having blood drawn and being quizzed endlessly about her medical history. Then she'd spent the rest of the night researching the drugs Dr. Adams had mentioned, downloading a fertility schedule and checking her favorite boards and forums for updates. Her situation was not unique: lots of women were forgoing the "fairy-tale family" scenario to embark on single parenthood, and she'd connected with a few via a private chat room months ago. She'd read so many incredible stories and felt such wonderful support from these women that she was almost tempted to go into more detail about her own situation. But something always held her back, even when she'd met up with one of the mothers from the chat room for a long lunch in the Queen Victoria Building earlier that day.

As they'd said their goodbyes on the Town Hall steps at four, AJ's phone rang.

Matthew. Her heart did a weird little skip and suddenly, their evening on the boat came surging up again. It'd been foremost in her dreams the past few nights.

She stopped in her tracks, George Street commuters flowing around her. "Hello, Matt."

"Hi, Angel." His voice caressed her, made her all crumbly inside.

She squinted into the slowly spreading sunset and tried to rein everything in. Her first fertility injection had kicked in, creating havoc with her emotions.

"Hi," she repeated.

"Where are you?"

"Town Hall." She glanced around at the bustle and scurry of people. So serious, so focused on their phones, their destination, their purpose. "Where are you?"

"About twenty minutes away. Wait there—I'll pick you up. I want to show you something."

"Is it dinner again? Because I'm not dressed for it."

"Not dinner," he replied. "See you soon."

She hung up, anticipation quickening her pulse. He was back and she felt like doing a little jig right there in the middle of the street.

It's just the hormones. Her chat room friends had been brutally honest: increased desire was one topic that always cropped up. Her body ached for Matt like he'd been gone for months, not days, and she could acknowledge that fact and proceed accordingly, or make herself crazy worrying about the emotional implications.

Except the doctor had advised against sex, so that avenue of release was no longer a consideration.

She growled under her breath and glared at the passing people as irrational anger swelled inside.

Last week had been wonderful but also incredibly tense, leaving her with way too many raw emotions. Not a good thing. On the scale of importance, she ranked well below his career. She certainly didn't want to spend the rest of her life with him, not when she would never come first.

But what—?

No. She needed to focus on the plan, not poke holes in it. Provided they still *had* a plan. Given the doctor's recommendation, Matt could very well decide to change his mind.

She adjusted her scarf and shoved her hands deeper into the pockets. Well, she'd know soon enough.

* * *

Fifteen minutes later, she spotted Matt's car approaching. When the lights changed and the traffic stopped, she quickly threaded her way through the pedestrians and got in.

"Hi," he said with a grin.

"Hi, yourself." She slammed the door and buckled up, trying hard to ignore the giddy catch to her voice. "So, how was your trip? I was watching everything on the news."

"It went well. We recovered most of the missing and worked out a long-term rebuilding plan with the local services." His gaze returned to the road as the lights changed. "How did the meeting with Sandi finish up?"

"Did you get the report?"

"Not yet."

"Right." She tipped her head as he pulled to a stop at the lights at George and Bathurst. "So you don't know Dr. Adams said we should—mmmmmph!"

He cut her off with a rough kiss.

It was unexpected but definitely not unwelcome. He just put a hand behind her neck and pulled her in, the move shockingly arrogant yet incredibly sexy.

She'd missed him. Despite the stern talking to she'd given herself, she'd actually missed him.

Or maybe she just missed this.

When he palmed her cheek with his other hand, her breath stuttered.

Yeah, that was it.

Finally—regretfully, it seemed to her—Matt pulled back, gave her a lingering look then returned his attention to the lights. They changed a second later and he turned into Bathurst Street.

"How are you feeling?"

"Hot."

His mouth curved, teasing out the dimple. "I meant that as an inquiry into your general well-being."

"Oh. Still hot." *And excited. Aroused. Wanting to—*

"Has Sandi started you on hormone injections?"

Someone blasted a car horn and Matt smoothly avoided a car braking in front of them. AJ nodded. "Yes."

"And I'm scheduled for some tests on Monday, correct?"

"That's right. And Matt…"

"Yeah?" They turned right on Elizabeth, heading west.

"She also said artificial insemination was our best option." The brakes tamped for one jerky second before they pulled into the Liverpool Street merge lane. AJ forged on. "Given my low chances of conception, apparently it's better to do this in a controlled environment. So there's nothing left to chance."

"Of course."

Another moment passed. "Which means after insemination, we can't have sex."

He pressed his lips together. "I know what it means."

They merged into the traffic and her heart began to pound. He wasn't happy and she couldn't blame him. But did that mean he'd go back on their deal?

She huffed out a breath and turned to stare directly ahead. "Matt, I have to ask…does this change things for you?"

"In what way?"

"Well, it's not exactly what you signed up for."

"You think I'd back out because we can't have sex?"

"I…don't know."

He sighed, his disappointment clear in that small exhale. "The answer is no." He shot her a look, then turned back to the traffic. "I gave my word, AJ. You can trust me."

"Okay." She nodded, taking a few slow breaths while she waited for her heart to calm down.

Silence spread until they stopped at another red light.

"Do you have a passport?" he asked suddenly.

She raised her brow. "No, why?"

"How do you feel about Portugal?"

"How do I…?" AJ frowned. "I don't know. They speak Portuguese? They're part of the European Union? Oh, and I've heard the Algarve Coast has a stunning coastline—"

"I'm due to fly out to Faro next Saturday." The lights changed to green, Matt eased into First and they turned left on College. "I'd like you to come with me."

What? "But I don't have a passport."

"I know some people. I can get one for you in a few days."

Of course he knew people. That shouldn't be a surprise. But what stunned her more was the fact that he was asking her to go with him.

"Isn't this a business trip?"

"Yes. But I'm the boss, so I can do whatever I want." His brief glance had her heart rate picking up most alarmingly. "You've never been overseas. So let me take you."

"But your work—"

"—will be finished in a day or two, max."

AJ shook her head, jamming a lid on her swelling excitement. "I don't want to interfere."

"You won't be." The traffic slowed and they crawled past Hyde Park. "The flight leaves at eight on Saturday morning. We refuel in Singapore, fly on to Rome, then land at Faro airport Sunday night. My meeting's Monday afternoon, so we can fly back on Friday. Is five days enough?"

Enough for what? "What are we going to do for five whole days?"

"Oh, I'm sure we'll think of something."

"Matt, I don't think we should—"

"This isn't about…that." She saw his jaw tighten almost imperceptibly as he kept his eyes on the road. "Look, if you don't want to go, just say so."

"I do!" she blurted, then more calmly added, "I do. But…"

"But what? You get to see another country, catch some sun, charge room service and relax by the pool. All good for your stress levels. Which, in turn, increases our chances of getting pregnant."

Our chances. Not *your*. AJ swallowed a small moan. Deliberate? Or a completely innocent slip?

Think about it. Five whole days in his company, sharing

meals, sightseeing and doing touristy things. Normal holiday couple things. Things she'd never pictured him doing, let alone with her. The Matthew Cooper she knew would never allow anything to interfere with his work schedule.

Maybe he's not the Matthew Cooper you remember.

She gazed contemplatively out the windshield. No, that wasn't right. Sure, he was no longer head of neurosurgery at Saint Catherine's, but a man like Matt didn't just turn off that blinding drive and determination to achieve. It made him who he was, and his company was tangible proof of that.

"Five days—" She suddenly broke off to stare out the window. "Wait, are we going to the art gallery?"

"Just wait and see."

"Matt. It's kind of obvious. Unless..." They drove down Art Gallery Road, the expansive grassy Domain parkland on their left, the familiar columned majesty of the art gallery entrance on the right. "There's nothing at the end of this road except Mrs. Macquarie's Chair." When she'd been a Sydney sider, she'd frequently enjoyed the stunning harbor views from that historic chair, which had been specifically carved from a rock ledge for Governor Macquarie's wife.

He found a vacant spot and smoothly pulled the car in. "You were right the first time."

"But it's closing in—" She glanced at the clock on the dash. "Ten minutes."

"Not for us it isn't."

He switched off the engine and turned to face her, sliding up his sunglasses. His expression was casually neutral, but she sensed something else in those dark, hooded eyes. A question? No, he was *waiting* for her. She could feel the expectancy heat the air, spreading gently as his gaze held hers.

She hadn't given him an answer to the Portugal thing.

A small bubble of excitement rose inside her. *An actual trip overseas!* She'd finally get to see another country, another culture, experience the sights, the smells, the tastes. She'd have a chance to observe color and movement, to stretch her drawing skills.

How could she pass this up?

She nodded, biting down on her lip to stop a goofy grin from forming. "Okay. I'll go."

His expression transformed for a brief second, his smile widening as he pulled the keys from the ignition. "Good."

She hadn't missed that look: a flash of elation before he'd glanced away. He was happy she'd said yes, and boy, that thrilled her way more than it should.

She swung her door open. "So are you going to tell me why we're here?"

He shook his head and reached into the back of the car. "First, you'll need these."

Odd. With a curious smile, she opened the paper bag he offered, then stuck her hand in.

She gasped, slowly pulling out a thick, A5-sized leather-bound journal, then a set of Derwent sketch pencils, followed by a box of top-quality HB leads.

"Matt," she breathed, taking in the wonderful smell of new paper and wood before refocusing on him. "You don't have to buy me stuff."

He shrugged but AJ could see the satisfaction in his smile. "There's more."

"What?"

"I'll show you."

AJ stood in front of Van Gogh's famous *Sunflowers* painting and let the beauty of the moment wash over her in stunned silence.

A private showing. For her. That was just… He was…

For the first time in her life, someone actually *got* her.

It was way too much.

She quickly blinked away a sudden well of tears, then took a deep breath while her heart kept on pounding.

"The Starry Night," she said softly, staring at the gorgeous

swirl of blue night sky scattered with yellow stars. "Oh, the self-portrait. *Irises.* Oh, wow, that's *Café Terrace at Night!*" She gave a small clap and surged forward until she was standing right in front of the painting, taking in the bold strokes and rainbow colors.

"I have a poster of this on my bedroom wall at home. This is amazing. How did you manage to pull this off?"

He shrugged. "I know people."

"Well, thank you *so* much."

"You're welcome."

She knew she was grinning like a crazy woman but she couldn't help it. Joy welled up, overwhelming her, propelling her forward.

A second later she wrapped her arms around his neck and hugged him.

His arms automatically went around her, pulling her deep into his warmth, and when she eased back, the kiss was inevitable. A breathless, hot kiss that AJ wasn't sure she'd initiated. Either way, she welcomed it, welcomed his mouth, his hands, his chest pressed up against hers. And when he finally broke away with a soft groan, her disappointment echoed his.

"Take your time," he said thickly, taking a step back and shoving his hands in his pockets. "We have two hours."

She nodded, unable to speak, then quickly turned to the journal she'd left on the leather lounge. She fumbled with the pencil box, but she finally managed to get one out. He'd not only bought her art supplies, but he'd also had the freaking art gallery open just for her.

Whoa, hold on a second. She suddenly panicked.

This was just Matt being thoughtful. She'd mentioned it days ago and he'd remembered. That was all. Yet she still couldn't stop a thread of delight spreading through her belly. Something that felt this good couldn't possibly be bad, right?

Right.

She pressed her lips together and opened the journal,

smoothed out the unlined pristine page and switched her focus to the amazing art before her.

The next few days passed in a blur, and by the time Saturday rolled around again, AJ felt like she was about to explode from the anticipation.

After the art gallery, they'd eaten a late dinner at the Quay, then he'd dropped her off at Zac's apartment. His gentle good-night kiss seared her lips, and she'd practically floated to the top floor.

The routine was set for the next few days: Matt would call in the morning to let her know what time he'd be by, then when the time rolled around, he'd pick her up and they'd go out to dinner. AJ asked about his travels and his job, listening with single-minded attention, determined not to stare at his mouth, those expressive hands. A couple of times she must've lapsed because he'd suddenly stop midsentence and give her such a heated look that it made her skin go all prickly.

The first few days they'd been the picture of restraint. He'd taken her back to Zac's apartment, kissed her on the cheek and left. But after the third night, his patience had obviously worn thin. She'd turned to say good-night and found herself caught up in a rush of lips, eager fingers and panting breath. When Matt finally stepped back with a groan, his frustrated expression echoed her own.

"A suggestion, not an unbreakable rule," AJ muttered in the cool silence now, staring at the shadowed bedroom ceiling. Dr. Adams had confirmed it today. She was due for her first procedure in two weeks' time and a lapse beforehand certainly wouldn't ruin her chances.

So what was the problem?

With a grunt, she rolled over on her side and punched the pillow.

She liked spending time with him. Liked holding his hand. Liked ending the evening with a kiss that left her wanting more. This time, their relationship wasn't just about sex, even if the desperate need for it was killing her.

And he hadn't pushed.

Now here she was, about to spend a week with him, and suddenly all she could think about was his slow smile as he pushed her hair behind one ear. His warm mouth as he kissed her.

"Damn it!" She groaned and pressed her thighs together.

Five days. It'd probably kill her. And after her first procedure, her opportunities to make love would be zero.

She sighed. She'd drawn a line and unless she crossed it herself, she was pretty sure Matt wouldn't.

It was up to her.

They boarded the plane an hour before takeoff. AJ was introduced to Carly, Matt's assistant, then his head of security, James Decker, a brash American dressed all in black with a charming grin and biceps the size of an off-season bodybuilder's.

"Nice to meet you, AJ," he said before glancing past her to his boss. "So…" He waggled a finger between her and Matt. "How'd you two meet?"

"I—"

"We need to board so the pilot can do his checks," Matt interrupted, picking up AJ's suitcase. "You have everything?"

Decker's grin lingered. "*I* do. Do you?"

"Yep."

A cold wind screamed over the tarmac, and AJ shoved her hands deep in her pockets. There was subtext there, but she couldn't work out exactly what.

"So let's go." Matt nodded for her to head up the steps first and she eagerly ascended, the brand-new Australian passport burning a hole in her jeans pocket.

Whatever she was expecting was nothing compared to the reality of Faro. Bustling, colorful Faro with its outdoor markets, cobblestoned streets and friendly locals. Sure, the five-star eighteenth-century Monte Do Casal country house with its pristine walls, sparkling pool and expansive gardens had all sorts of indulgent offerings, from poolside service to massages and facials. But she was more interested in what was going on outside, eager to experience the sights and sounds and smells of the town. Dressed in a loose knee-length skirt and tank top, she managed to secure a table at a café on a busy main road and spent a few hours sketching before she decided to explore.

Discovering a new city alone was a familiar routine, one she'd done since she was seventeen. Yet as she wandered the streets, soaking up every little detail, a niggling thought struck. *Matt should be here to see this.*

She paused at a bodega, peering into the smoky darkness with a frown. That was silly—he'd probably seen this city a dozen times before. Probably not alone, either. Her frown deepened, only to freeze a second later.

Was she jealous? But she wasn't the jealous type. Because that would mean...

"*Senhorita* would like to see our pretty gold rings?"

Her train of thought broken by the swarthy street vendor, she politely declined, shaking her head with an apologetic smile.

No. Getting attached was not part of the plan.

Not ever.

On the second day Matt declared his business concluded, gave Decker and Carly the rest of the week off and they moved out of their hotel.

They drove out of the city in a hired car and headed west on the A25 toward Lagos. The road hugged the coastline, and the view was nothing short of spectacular, with sheer cliff faces, sparkling blue water and lush vegetation. AJ practically hung out the window, engrossed in the breathless beauty of it all.

They got to Lagos in less than two hours. To her surprise,

Matt had booked them into a *pensione* instead of a flashy hotel. They took the top floor while the owners occupied the ground level.

The house was clean, with a private bathroom and a balcony with stunning rooftop views and a view of the main marketplace a couple of streets away. And just like the expensive Faro hotel, it had separate beds.

When AJ saw this, she was both relieved and disappointed. He'd booked both places and couldn't have sent a clearer message than separate beds.

Matt hired a motorbike and they spent the next four days sightseeing. They drove up into the mountains to a small church high in the hills. They explored the street sellers, visited the local Lagos museum. On their fourth day, they spent hours on the beach in comfortable silence, where she sketched the glorious sunset while he lazed on a blanket next to her. When the light finally waned, she glanced up to find him studying her so intensely that her mouth suddenly went dry.

The streetlights flickered on, casting them in a hazy glow as AJ slowly replaced her pencils in her case and snapped the lid shut with a sigh. "That's it. Light's gone."

Matt nodded and stood, brushing off his pants, then offering his hand. Without hesitation she took it, and his warm fingers wrapped around hers, an intimacy that never failed to make her blood quicken.

"Angel…"

"Hmm?" She looked up, waiting, but he said nothing, just devoured her with those dark eyes until finally he glanced away.

"We should go and eat. Our flight's early and you still haven't packed."

When they got back to the *pensione,* she changed into a strapless white cotton dress with buttons from neck to the knee-length hem. She paired it with an azure cardigan, knowing the color made her eyes pop. Her hair was up this time, casually messy and drawn back at the nape. A pair of dangly blue stones—a birthday present from Emily—hung from her ears and her butterfly necklace rested at her throat.

From the look in Matt's eyes, she'd made the right choice.

He offered his hand and she automatically took it, taking pleasure in that small contact as they walked to a restaurant on the corner. The place was decorated as a rustic street, with cobbled floors, skillfully painted stone hacienda walls and overarching olive trees in huge earthenware pots. Tables were scattered throughout, circular booths ringed the outer edges, and at the far end, a fully stocked bar was seeing a brisk trade.

They were led to a secluded booth, their only light two candles on the table. She slid in first and Matt followed until they were hip to hip. His warmth scorched her thigh, and despite her hunger, she wanted nothing more than to touch him, run her fingers over that long smooth forearm, knead the muscle beneath his skin.

"Does the butterfly mean something?"

She blinked. "Hmm?"

"Your necklace." Her hand went to the pendant. "You always wear it. Is it special?"

"Yes." She stroked the edge of one wing with her finger. "Emily gave it to me for my thirtieth birthday." She paused. "It means reinvention. Regeneration."

"The metamorphosis from caterpillar to butterfly."

She nodded.

"I like it." He reached out and gently ran his thumb over the mother-of-pearl wings. "Did you reinvent yourself often?"

"A few times. I—" She stopped.

"Let me guess," he said softly, finally releasing the necklace. "Your past is off-limits, right?"

She nodded, feeling foolish even though she knew that wasn't Matt's intention.

Tell him.

She glanced away, skin prickling under his silent scrutiny. "My mother was sixteen and pregnant with me when she was kicked out of her home. We lived off welfare until she hooked up with my stepfather, a delightful man who got her addicted to booze and drugs." She stopped, face flaming. *Too much. Way too much.* Yet something in his face, in that open, non-judgmental expression, made her forge on. "Parents are supposed to look after their kids, not make them lie and steal and dread every knock on the door. But we survived." She managed a shaky smile. "Well, I guess Emily's doing better than just surviving. She always was the big believer in the glorious fairy-tale of love."

He arched an eyebrow. "You don't believe in love?"

"Of course I do. Just not the whole Prince-Charming-riding-in-to-sweep-me-off-my-feet thing." When he remained silent, she added a little defiantly, "I spent a lot of years on my own. It tend to makes you a realist."

He studied her for an age, almost as if he were waiting for something more. She met his scrutiny head-on, and as the seconds passed, an uncomfortable panic began to leech in. "Don't look at me like that."

"Like what?"

"Like you're sad for me. I don't need it. I don't—" *Need you.* No, that felt wrong and she managed to stop the words before they formed.

She heard him sigh and the mood suddenly changed. "Look, AJ, I understand your need for control, I really do. But closing yourself off to possibilities isn't the right way to go about it."

She scowled and leaned back in the seat. "Why are we even talking about this again?"

"Because talking is what people do."

She huffed out a breath. "I knew this would happen. I'd mention my past and you'd…"

"I'd what?" Matt's expression was a mix of sadness and understanding. Not disgust. Not pity. Yet somehow, his sympathy did something to her insides and she had to glance away. "You can let your past define you, let it keep chipping away at who you are, or you can make a decision and take control."

"Like you did after your brother's accident?"

His mouth tightened for one second. "Yeah."

AJ flushed and clamped her mouth shut. Where on earth had that cheap shot come from? Yet as she studied him, she sensed something behind that smooth expression. What would it take to relieve him of that burden?

More than she could offer. Certainly nothing she could say because hadn't she already stuck her foot in it?

So instead, she placed a hand over his, leaned in and kissed him.

It was a gentle kiss, devoid of ulterior motive. It wasn't a precursor to passion. It was a kiss with the full brunt of her emotional state behind it, and for one second she felt him go still beneath her mouth, almost as if she'd shocked him and he was unsure of what to do.

She let her eyes close, moving slowly, testing the swell of his full bottom lip between hers. His sigh, when it came, shuddered into her and that's when she knew she'd done the right thing.

They kissed for ages, leisurely exploring each other in the dim restaurant light, pressed together from shoulder to thigh. When they finally broke apart, Matt glanced down at the table, then laughed.

AJ followed his gaze. While they'd been lip locked, their waiter had discreetly left their meals, topped up their glasses and added some cutlery.

"This place has excellent service," AJ got out.

Matt nodded, his smile matching hers. "I agree."

By unspoken agreement, they sought each other again, but this time AJ felt the urgency behind his kiss. The pressure had changed, going from sweet to insistent. Then his hand slipped under the table to gently rest on her knee.

She momentarily broke the kiss. "Matt?"

"Mmm?" His hand left her knee, stroking as it eased higher to her thigh.

"We can't."

"Why not?"

Her head swam. *Why not indeed?* "For starters, we're in a public place."

"So we are." AJ felt a tremor of excitement as his fingers crept under the hem of her dress, making their way teasingly up. She held her breath, desperate to see how far he would actually go before one of them put a stop to it.

Would she? Would he?

And still his hand went higher.

She met his gaze and held it. He was at her inner thigh now, his fingers creating a warm path ever upward. Then...

She held her breath as he gently stroked her through the thin cotton of her knickers.

"Matt..."

Slowly, regretfully it seemed, he withdrew. "You don't think we should do this." Her nod, when it came, was a little too reluctant. "But do you *want* to?"

She clamped off a groan and murmured something under her breath.

"What?"

She shook her head. "Let's just eat, okay?"

He stared at her for the longest time, until her eyes darted away to her plate. With infinite care, she silently drew it across the table, picked up her fork then proceeded to eat.

"Fine, Angel. We'll eat."

Thirteen

They walked back to the *pensione,* only this time he didn't take her hand, and it made AJ's heart ache.

No, it was bigger than that. Everything inside ached, like someone had come along and stolen a vital part of herself, and that loss only exacerbated the chaos.

"Matt?"

"Yeah?" He pushed the front door open and let her go in first. She mounted the narrow staircase, more than aware of his presence close behind. When they reached the top of the stairs, she turned to face him. "Back at the beach. You were going to ask me something but didn't." His brows dipped but he said nothing. "What was it?"

"Nothing."

He made a move to go past her but she grabbed his arm, forcing him to stop. "Just say it. I want to know."

He huffed out a sigh. "I was going to ask you about the night we broke up."

She dropped his arm and took a step back. "Why do you want to talk about that?"

"How long did it take for you to forgive me?"

"I just—" Wow, what could she say to that? "I didn't blame you." It was true. She'd blamed herself.

"Not even after the way I just dropped it on you?"

"No." She turned and walked down the short corridor toward their bedroom door. Matt followed. "Why are you asking now? The past is past. Going over it won't change anything."

She shoved the door open, went straight to the wardrobe and grabbed her suitcase.

"You don't like talking about the past, do you?"

She snapped her gaze up, irritated by his brusqueness. "Just because I don't blurt out every tiny detail about my life doesn't mean it's wrong." She turned to the bureau, grabbed a handful of underwear and tossed them into the open case.

"I'm not saying that. But you need to give a little, AJ. You can't expect someone to open up to you if you don't do the same."

I don't want to open up. Not to you. "This isn't part of our deal, Matt," she said softly.

He studied her in cool silence before saying, "That night we broke up? I'd just come off a twelve-hour shift. My tardiness and distraction hadn't gone unnoticed those past six months. I'd had 'the talk' from my parents, then my senior resident—"

"Matt…"

"And the second time, I had to step up and make a choice."

She glared at him as he tried to make his point. *The teeny, tiny point.* "Your career came first." When it came, his slow nod only confirmed what she'd thought all along. "And I wasn't Matthew Cooper girlfriend material."

"I didn't say that."

"You didn't need to. You never once introduced me to your family or took me out where someone from your social circle might see us. Or…or…even invited me to your Christmas party," she added tightly.

If he'd really wanted her, he would've found a way to work it out, right? AJ thought.

He gave a short, exasperated sigh. "I thought you were okay with things being casual. I didn't know you wanted to—"

"Well, you never asked!" Her hands went to her hips, irritation surging through her.

He mirrored her stance. "Nor did you!"

She stood there in silence until she couldn't take it anymore. "Fine. You want to know? I'll tell you. I was planning on staying in town and I was trying to work out the best way to tell you."

The shock on his face was almost laughable. Almost. But instead of laughter, a deep burning embarrassment welled up in her throat, scalding her neck, then her cheeks.

"AJ…"

"Please don't, Matt." She whirled and grabbed a dress from the wardrobe, folding it with sharp precision. "It was a long time ago. I got over it." *Oh, you are such a liar.* "I moved on. So let's just—"

The shrill sound of a phone splintered the air and with a soft curse, Matt whirled and grabbed the offending gadget from the dresser.

"Yes, Mum?"

All the fight drained from AJ with those two little words and she left him to his call, walking into the bathroom to gather her toiletries. As she packed her shampoo, conditioner, toothbrush and toothpaste, she couldn't shake the ominous feeling that she'd put her foot right in it.

You're smarter than this.

She couldn't change the past and there was no point arguing with Matt about it. He didn't need to know how much that rejection had hurt, how it had shaped every relationship since him.

The past had no bearing on the here and now. They both understood this was a physical arrangement, not a romantic one. God, what would he do if he knew she'd been fantasizing about their relationship these past few weeks? That sometimes, in the lonely early-morning light when she imagined them being a real couple, it made everything ache like she'd already lost something she'd never get back?

She was so caught up in her turbulent thoughts she didn't realize he was standing in the doorway until she caught his reflection in the mirror.

He was staring at her with an odd, intense look, as if he

wanted to say something yet wasn't sure she'd want to hear it. A look so unlike Matt that it gave her pause.

She took a deep breath and turned around. "Look, this is stupid, us arguing. I made some silly choices the past ten years." Not to mention reckless and downright dangerous ones, too. She'd been crazy, eager to push boundaries, eager to forget. "But they were *my* choices, and I don't regret them." She'd also learned some hard lessons about life and love and for that she'd always be grateful. "You also made a choice and did what you thought was right. Let's just drop it, shall we?"

She hated it when he said nothing. His scrutiny was so focused, as if he was trying to figure out all the dark marks on her heart. "My parents have some spare tickets for a benefit on Tuesday. Do you want to come with me?"

She frowned. "What?"

"You, me, a Saint Cat's fund-raiser. Will you be my date?"

Yes! No! No, wait...

Confusion warred inside her, her resolution to keep Matt at a distance battling with other, deeper desires. "I don't think that's a good idea."

"Why not?"

Her hands went to her hips. "Oh, only about a dozen reasons. Me and your parents, for one."

"They don't bite."

She snorted. "That's not what I meant. You're the one who still has to work with the hospital."

"It's the twenty-first century, AJ. We're allowed to go out in public without a chaperone."

"Don't be obtuse. You know what I mean."

"Oh, I'm sure they're already talking about us." He crossed his arms and fixed her with a direct look. "We went to see Saint Cat's top fertility specialist together. Our names are on forms, computer systems and now tests. You can't keep secrets in a hospital for long."

Of course, he was right. It didn't matter to her, but... "Does it bother you? The fact that people are probably talking about you?"

He shrugged. "They've been doing that all my life."

"I see."

A beat passed. "So you never did answer. Are you afraid of being seen with me?"

"No." She turned and shoved her moisturizer into her toiletries bag.

He stepped inside the bathroom and crossed his arms, eyes glinting as he blocked her exit. She glared back and let her unimpressed expression do all the talking.

He wasn't buying it. "I don't believe it. AJ Reynolds is *afraid* of meeting my parents?"

"Now, listen here—"

"That's just not possible." He advanced slowly, his mouth slanted into a mocking grin. "Not the same woman who shared my bed last week."

No, don't talk about that! "Matt—" She backed up into the vanity, her butt resting on the cool marble as her heart quickened.

"Not the same AJ who kissed me so hard I couldn't breathe." His hands went out, trapping her against the vanity as he leaned in. "The same one who squirmed beneath me," he whispered. "Writhing and panting as I kissed every inch of her skin—"

AJ's eyes drifted closed, the hot memory washing over her, bathing her in desire. A second later his lips went to her neck and she sighed, welcoming, wanting.

"—then demanded I take her hard and fast on my office desk."

Her hands went to his nape and she dragged his mouth to hers with a soft groan. Yet he held back, the muscles in his neck straining under her grip, eyes liquid pools of chocolate. "What are you afraid of, Angel?"

"Nothing." *Everything. You. Me. This.*

"Then come with me."

How much had she wanted this all those years ago? To be the one on his arm, introduced and included in his life. And now the desperate need flared in her yet again. She wanted to see what his life had been like without her, what had shaped him, who he'd been. A life she regretted not fighting harder to be involved with in the first place, if she were brutally honest.

She breathed out slowly. "Okay."

God, that smile. That brilliant, triumphant smile that wounded her so low and deep. He undid her a thousand times over.

Then his mouth swooped down to cover hers.

AJ could never get enough of his kisses, the way he took control, devouring her. The way his breath filled her mouth and her senses, his soft murmurs cranking her desire into a long, slow burn of need.

He swiftly grabbed her bottom, hiking her up onto the vanity, and she wrapped her legs around his waist, urging him closer.

Their week of abstinence was over. He wanted her. And she wanted him right back.

"Matt…" she gasped against his lips. "We…"

"Do you trust me?"

A low groan reverberated in her throat. She loved the way his dark eyes went languid with passion. They bore into her, as if she was his sole focus and he had no place else he'd rather be.

"Do you trust me?" he repeated.

Her heart twisted. "Yes."

"Then we can do this."

"It won't ruin anything?"

"I promise. I'm a doctor, remember?"

She swallowed. Her body felt like it was on fire, so desperate was her need, and it took barely a second to make the decision. She nodded, not trusting herself to speak.

Everything happened in a split second—the frenzy of clothes being shoved up, off or aside. Her legs spreading at his touch, her mouth parting beneath his eager tongue. The hiss of excitement when skin met skin, then an excruciating pause as Matt readied himself.

Then one hard, swift plunge and they were engulfed in the scorching, familiar heat, their cries of delight echoing through the bathroom.

Matt pounded into her, his hard thrusts skidding her across the cold marble as his fingers dug into her bottom. She groaned and crossed her ankles so her heels bumped on the delicious curve where his lower back met his butt. He was deep, so very deep and it felt so very right.

"Yes," she murmured, urging him on. He filled her completely, his thick length sliding intimately in, out, in, out, his tongue an erotic echo in her mouth. They tangled, they battled, they took. And they shared, too—from breath and kisses to the slick, damp heat intimately joining them in a familiar dance.

AJ climaxed and threw her head back with a cry, losing herself to the bursts of light behind her eyelids. She felt Matt spill into her, his deep groan of satisfaction echoing as everything inside contracted and shuddered.

"Matt…" she breathed. "I…"

He cut her off with a kiss, his mouth gently searing hers. A tender, almost loving gesture that squeezed at something deep inside, something she'd thought buried long ago, prickling her eyes and sending every sense into meltdown.

She broke off the kiss to lay her cheek against his shoulder, her heartbeat filling every slow second.

She squeezed her eyes shut. They had history and chemistry. That was it. That was all it could ever be.

She would not fall in love with Matthew Cooper because that would be supremely stupid. And she, AJ Reynolds, was not stupid.

By nine the next morning they were miles above the earth, on their way back to Sydney. Matt glanced over at AJ, nose-deep in a book, then to Decker, stretched out and asleep behind his dark sunglasses, then to Carly, who was single-mindedly tapping away on her laptop.

He sighed and returned to the schedule laid out on his iPad, but moments later he gave up.

AJ had opened up, stunning him with that little truth from her past.

She'd been planning to stay. How could he have not seen that? But he'd been blind to anything but his own problems and gotten in first, shot her down, and she'd left.

He rubbed the bridge of his nose and scowled.

Now here they were again, treading familiar ground, coming together and getting lost in that crazy desire just like before. *No, not like before.* His eyes darted to her bright red hair, the gentle curve of her cheek. He knew what he wanted now. And AJ...well, she wanted something, too. And apparently that didn't include him.

He'd felt her withdrawal this morning, the way she didn't meet his eyes, the subtle wall she put between them. He'd reassured her that their lovemaking hadn't stuffed anything up but wasn't entirely sure she believed him.

He cast his mind back to the previous night, and suddenly everything flooded in: AJ writhing beneath him, calling his name as he drove deep inside, loving her until they finally collapsed, sated and spent. And later, in bed, she'd driven him crazy with her hands and body, her shock of hair as it teased his sensitive nipples, brushed over his belly, then lower when she took him in her mouth with bold delight.

Damn. He shifted in his seat, trying to relieve the sudden tightness in his groin. Despite that incredible chemistry, he still had no idea what was going on in her head. Oh, she'd let down her guard a little, allowing a brief glimpse inside, but it still wounded him, the way she'd so grudgingly shared that snippet.

Yeah, and you're an open book, right?

AJ glanced up then, meeting his eyes, and he realized he'd been staring.

She blinked, her bright eyes assessing, searching, a hesitant smile hovering on her lips. That tiny uncertainty—from a woman so very sure of everything else in her life—tore at his heart.

He'd put that uncertainty there and he had a lot to make up for. So he held her gaze and put everything he had into his smile, every remembered kiss, every touch, every breath they'd shared.

Her eyes widened…and then there it was, the lush curve of her mouth, the seductive crease of her cat's eyes before she ducked her head and returned to her book.

There was his Angel.

And just like that, he fell. Totally, completely.

He loved her. Loved everything about her—all those doubts, all those tiny scars on her heart, her fractured past that had shaped her into the strong, independent woman she was now.

But would it be enough? Would *he* be enough?

There was only one way to find out. He had to keep going forward.

AJ refused to let disappointment show when Matt dropped her off at Zac's apartment. Instead, she pasted on a smile and accepted his kiss on the cheek.

"I have to go to work," he murmured, his lips lingering, giving her goose bumps. "I have a meeting tonight."

"On a Sunday?"

"Conference call. I'll call you, okay?"

"Sure."

She watched him go, her gaze drinking in his long stride, the way the expensive suit sat on his lean frame, the shaggy hairline that brushed his collar.

She whirled to the elevator, forcing back inexplicable tears. Lust had never gripped her so surely before, trapping her in tight claws until he was all she could think about.

She furiously pressed the up button over and over, determined to ignore the way her breath hitched. And what of last night? How would that affect her chances of getting pregnant? Surely it had consequences, despite his reassurances.

The elevator doors slid open and she strode in, dumping her bag on the floor before digging out her phone and dialing Dr. Adams's number.

As much as she wanted Matt, burned for him like a bush-fire had taken up residence under her skin, she couldn't jeopardize her chances. She had to know the facts. And if that meant complete abstinence, then so be it.

Ten minutes later, after Dr. Adams had eased her mind, she ran a bath, cranked up her iPod and turned her attention to the novel she'd been trying to read since the flight. But she only managed a few pages before restlessness got the better of her.

"Damn you, Matthew Cooper," she muttered, rising from the water and grabbing a towel. After making herself a cup of tea, she pulled out her sketch pad and pencils and began to work.

Fourteen

It was the night of the hospital benefit and AJ was, quite frankly, scared.

Matt's compliments had briefly warmed her—she'd chosen a red below-the-knee ruffled dress with a tight corset bodice—but trepidation had set in as they drove to the Pullman Quay Grand at Sydney Harbour.

If Matt noticed, he didn't say anything. They parked, then made their way into the fancy foyer, all massive windows and panoramic views of the harbor. AJ barely had time to take it all in before he was guiding her toward the restaurant where a bunch of perfectly dressed people were milling about.

This was it. She was actually doing this. With a deep breath, she straightened, pulling her shoulders back.

"You okay?"

She glanced up at him, at the concern creasing his brow. "Yes, I just…" She paused then said carefully, "I don't like crowds."

"Really?"

"They make me nervous, all those people watching," she lied. Truth was, she'd been assessed, dissected and judged before and it had stopped worrying her a long time ago. No, it was the parent thing that freaked her out. She didn't do parents. They made her nervous.

He eyed the packed gathering inside the restaurant, wall-to-wall people in their designer dresses and suits, the loud murmur of voices, clinking glasses and occasional laughter spilling out, then he turned to her with a reassuring smile.

"Honestly, I don't think they'll notice us."

"Matthew! You're late!"

A woman emerged from the crowd and made her way toward them. She was tall, regal and flawlessly done up in a black shift dress and kitten heels. The family resemblance was obvious.

AJ swallowed as she watched Matt's mother kiss his cheek, then slowly turn to her.

"Hello, I'm Dr. Alicia Cooper." The hand she offered was cool and smooth and AJ shook it with a vague feeling of inadequacy, well aware of every mark and freckle on her own.

Still, she managed a polite smile and greeting.

"Matthew, you know Mason Palmer, chief of oncology?" She swept her hand to the man who had stepped up beside her, a tall, good-looking guy in an impeccable suit. They ran through the mandatory introductions before Alicia turned back to AJ. "So, how do you know Matthew?"

"We're…ah…" She glanced at Matt, then back to Alicia's sharp scrutiny. "Old friends. We go back a long way."

"Really. And what do you do?" Alicia efficiently looked AJ up and down before giving her a polite smile. She was being judged—and probably found lacking—behind that cool, elegant charm.

AJ tipped her chin and stared right back at her. "I'm an artist."

"How interesting. What medium do you use?"

"Watercolor mostly." She glanced over at Alicia's companion, who was looking exceedingly bored with the whole interaction.

"I see. Well, don't monopolize each other all night," she said with a smile. A perfectly fine smile except for the irritation behind it, AJ thought. "Lots of people are here—influential people," she added with a pointed look at Matt. "Make sure you mingle. Have a lovely time."

"We will." AJ returned her smile and, for added effect, looped her arm through Matt's. With another icy smile, Alicia Cooper moved on.

After a moment, AJ slowly slipped her arm from Matt's and stared into the crowd in silence.

"Sorry."

"What for?"

"My mother can be somewhat…abrasive."

"She was perfectly fine."

"Right." He scanned the crowd and muttered something under his breath.

AJ leaned in. "Sorry?"

"I said, I'd rather be at home than at this excruciating party, making small talk and being judged."

Oh. She stared at him. Was it wrong that she was thinking exactly the same thing? And should she even admit that? What would it mean if she did? And—

"Angel." He leaned in, his lips close to her ear. "You creep me out when you're so silent. Just say what's on your mind."

But all she could do was shake her head. It would benefit no one to give voice to the strange longing she'd felt ever since they'd returned from Portugal. Their time together had an expiration date. He had an insanely busy career; that had been painfully clear these past few weeks. They'd even signed an agreement, for heaven's sake. It would do absolutely no good to start wishing for something different.

She wouldn't. She *couldn't*.

"I'm going to the bathroom," she muttered, turning from his loaded gaze before she said something completely stupid and ruined all her careful plans.

She was leaning against her closed stall door, giving herself a little pep talk, when she heard two women come in.

"Did you see Matt's date?"

AJ froze.

"Oh, yes, I've met her." That was Katrina. "Pleasant enough. A bit too...brassy, though."

AJ's mouth dropped into an outraged O. *Brassy?*

"Do you think it's natural?" the other woman went on.

"Looks like it. God knows why you'd want to keep that color, though."

"She's got an arse on her, too."

They both laughed as AJ scowled at the stall door, her anger practically burning a hole in the wood.

"She's obviously punching above her weight," the other woman added. "I mean, look at Matt—rich, gorgeous, talented. It won't last."

Then she heard the door swing open and a new voice declare, "Hi, Katrina. Who are we talking about?"

"Matthew's redhead."

"AJ?" AJ held her breath. The new arrival was Matt's sister, Paige. "Oh, we met her at her sister's wedding—Zac and Emily Prescott? She's perfectly lovely."

"Really."

"Yes." There was a pause, then a hushed whisper. Then, suddenly, thundering silence.

AJ had been in the stall long enough. And the others had obviously worked that out, too. With a sigh, she flushed, pulled her shoulders back, then swung the door open.

Her eyes met Paige's first in the mirror, and the woman gave her a genuine smile as she smoothed back her sleek dark hair. As the ominous silence lengthened, AJ offered a nod and a slightly dimmer smile to Katrina and her cohort, then proceeded to wash and dry her hands.

"I love your hairstyle, AJ," Paige said, flicking a deliberate glance at Katrina. "Very Rita Hayworth."

"Thanks." AJ smoothed the curls around her fingers and let them spring back.

She turned to go, then very slowly glanced back to Katrina. "Oh, by the way, Katrina—if you *are* going to talk about someone, make sure the stalls are empty before you do.

Otherwise you'll come across as a gossipy bitch. Not a good look for the hospital, I should think." She speared her companion with a look. "And for the record—Matt and I are just using each other for sex."

With that hanging in the air, AJ pushed the bathroom door open and made a dignified exit.

This was temporary. So why was she so upset? Face burning, she stalked down the tiled corridor back to the party. Matt was in her bed—albeit briefly—not in her life.

Stupid. *He's been your entire life only for the past...* She mentally calculated. Three weeks. They'd shared a bed, numerous meals. And yes, she'd gradually revealed tiny pieces of her life, stuff no one besides Emily knew. And sometimes, even stuff her sister didn't know.

This was ridiculous. She was comfortable in her skin and all too aware of the world around her. She normally shrugged off negative comments and rude attitudes when she encountered them. So why had that bitch session back there gotten under her skin?

She had no idea. But damn, it hurt.

"AJ! Wait!"

She turned and spotted Paige. Matt's sister snagged two glasses of champagne from a passing waiter, then caught up with her.

"I don't drink." AJ gently shook her head at the proffered glass.

"Oh, well." Paige shrugged, then downed half a glass in a few gulps. She grinned at AJ, finished it off, then shoved the empty glass on another passing waiter's tray.

AJ said nothing, just studied Matt's sister in silence. She was tall and lean, with big brown eyes and dark hair pinned back with a diamante Kylie band. Paige was a female version of Matt, dressed in a seventies-style tunic dress tied with a thin belt and accessorized by a heap of silver chains with dangly charms.

"So you're seeing my brother," she began, tipping the second glass to her lips.

"Not really."

Paige's eyes creased in thoughtful scrutiny. "That's not what I hear."

AJ shrugged. "I don't listen to gossip."

"Oh, everyone *listens*." Paige tapped her be-ringed finger against the glass. "Doesn't mean you have to pay attention to it. For instance, I also heard Matt took you to Portugal on a job."

When AJ remained silent, Paige smiled. "Diplomatic silence—that's good. I like you already." Then she shocked AJ by linking her arm through hers with a bright smile. "And anyone who can ruffle Katrina's feathers is okay by me. Let's have a chat."

From his vantage point near the bar, Matt had a perfect view of the restaurant. He glanced past the pristine tables, the mingling guests working out their seating arrangements, to the rest of the crowd milling around the bar and the glorious view of the harbor sunset. Still no sign of her shock of red hair or her fire engine–red dress.

He waved off a passing waiter as he continued his search. When he finally found AJ at the far end of the room, deep in conversation with Paige, he frowned. His sister was incredibly nosy, incredibly determined and a hopeless romantic. She also had a tendency to grill his dates and weed out at least one flaw, no matter how deeply it was buried.

What would she find with AJ?

As he contemplated going over there, he felt someone come up behind him.

"So you brought your date from Maxfield with you?"

He glanced over his shoulder at Katrina. She wore a sleek, sleeveless green gown, her eyebrows raised.

"Yes."

"That was weeks ago."

"Yep."

She followed his gaze, eyes narrowed as she studied AJ more closely. "Pretty enough, I suppose. In a brassy, wild kind of way."

"Careful, Katrina. Your inner bitch is showing."

Her brows ratcheted higher. "And you are acting oddly devoted to one woman."

He said nothing.

"So, I heard some interesting gossip about you visiting Sandi the other week."

He schooled his expression into casual blankness. He didn't have to explain himself to anyone, especially not Katrina. Yet behind the intrusive question and her cool study, he detected a genuine interest. He'd been married to the woman for eight years and no matter how it had ended, they'd still been through a lot. He let a small breath go. "We're trying for a baby, yes."

For one second Matt thought he detected something flash behind Katrina's cool green eyes before she said drily, "Well, good for you."

"Thanks."

They both glanced back to AJ, still in conversation with Paige.

"Your sister seems to like her."

"Looks like," Matt said neutrally. Paige had hated Katrina and they both knew it.

"Well, I'll leave you to it." She placed a hand on his arm. "Enjoy the night, Matt." Then she leaned in, deposited a kiss on his cheek and said softly, "Be happy."

In stunned silence he watched her go, her long, tanned frame cutting a striking figure as she confidently made her way through the crowd.

Wow. That was odd. Totally out of character.

When a waiter offered him a drink, he took it, taking a swig without tasting it.

Be happy.

He was trying.

* * *

Paige had moved off to get another drink, leaving AJ temporarily alone. With a glass of ice water in her hands, she casually scanned the room, noting everything and everyone with a keen eye before moving on.

Ahh. Right there. Her insides did a little dance. He was so tall and lean, whatever he wore always looked good. But Matt in a suit was truly devastating. The charcoal suit, white shirt and tie were a perfect foil to his shaggy hair and stubble. An intriguing mix of bohemian and professional, a look she knew was entirely accidental on his part.

He was watching someone or something and she followed his gaze across the room to where a familiar figure stood in conversation with a handful of people.

Katrina.

She looked away, but the damage was already done. Bitter and unwanted jealousy rattled her composure, leaving her angry and frustrated.

Sure, Matt had a past, but so did she. It was stupid to be angry.

She took a chug of water then palmed the damp base of the glass. Yeah, if you looked at it *logically*. But when she was around Matt, logic just flew out the window.

"Hey, AJ, come and meet some people."

She squared her shoulders, sighed and turned to a smiling Paige. "Sure."

So for the next few hours, AJ threw herself into perfect date mode, smiling, making small talk and generally charming the pants off everyone she met. An aching face and sore feet were a small price to pay because when they finally left, Matthew's satisfied smile made her glow.

"Did you have a good time?" he asked as they waited for the valet to bring his car around.

She nodded. "I really like your sister."

"Yeah, you two chatted for ages."

AJ nodded. "We made a date for the Powerhouse next week.

The Harry Potter exhibit," she added, eyeing the sleek Jaguar as it emerged from the underground parking lot.

"She asked you to go with her?"

She glanced up at him. Had she crossed a line? "I can cancel if you think it's not—"

"No, no." He nodded to the valet, then eased into the car. AJ followed, closing the door softly behind her. "I'm just surprised. Paige's never liked anyone I went out with."

"No one? Not even Katrina?"

"Especially not Katrina."

That confirmed it then. AJ's estimation of Paige Cooper increased a notch.

They drove down the road, both buried in silent thoughts as the thin traffic streamed around them.

Paige Cooper had been refreshingly, painfully forthcoming about the Cooper family, and once AJ had gotten over the shock, she'd been hooked. By the end of their conversation, AJ had been battling serious tears.

"Matt…"

"Yeah?"

She stared out the windshield at the car headlights and the brightly lit road as they made their way toward the Harbour Bridge. She contemplated her next words all the way across the bridge, down York Street and through Sydney's central business district.

It was only when they pulled up to her apartment that she finally settled on what to say.

"I know about Jack."

Oh, how quickly those shutters came down. *Remind you of someone?* "What do you know?"

"I know he was conceived so he could save your life." He frowned and cursed under his breath, but she ignored it. "That must've been tough."

He returned his gaze to the road, his knuckles flexing as he gripped the steering wheel. "Jack struggled with it for years."

"I meant for you."

He said nothing, just tightened his jaw.

"You were the favorite," she added.

He flushed. "I wasn't—"

"Yes, you were—are," she countered gently. "I only had to see your parents tonight to see it. The firstborn, the child genius, the youngest ever to graduate from UTS, the talented intern. And you had a baby brother whose entire existence was meant to save you."

He blinked slowly, his focus still out the window. "Jack called himself a 'harvest baby.' He…" He trailed off, blinked again.

"That's a lot to carry."

"He never really came to terms with the whole 'savior sibling' thing."

"Again, I meant for you."

AJ's heart ached as she watched his silent struggle, until his stormy eyes met hers, betraying the too-calm expression. "Jack had been living with Paige in London since he was seventeen. I'd only seen him once or twice before he died on that mountain."

Alarmed, she put a hand on his arm. "Oh, I didn't mean you should tell me—"

"No, I want to." He took a shuddering breath and seemed to draw strength in, as if he was letting something go in the retelling. "Since I can remember, my career has been carefully planned. Of course I would be a doctor, just like my mother and father, just like their parents and their parents before them. No other choice was considered. It motivated and drove my mum and dad, consuming everyone's lives." His mouth twisted briefly. "It didn't matter that Paige was an incredibly talented artist or that Jack had a way with animals. I was the important one. The Coopers have a lineage; our ancestors had titles and land and commanded power and respect. We're also academic high achievers and I was expected to be no different."

AJ nodded calmly.

"I was six years older than Jack but it felt like twenty. And my insane hours left no time for a life, let alone a baby brother who'd been told he was my only compatible donor, the reason I lived, ever since he could talk."

He paused suddenly, and AJ waited, her heart aching for him.

"After he died I lost it," he said quietly, hands tight on the wheel and his face half covered in shadow. "I escaped to a remote monastery in the Tibetan mountains, a place they opened up to Westerners only once a year for twenty days. The monks left me in peace for five days, even though I could hear them whispering behind the door. Then the priest put me to work assisting the goat herder." He paused, studying his knuckles. Then he slowly released the steering wheel and smiled. "You would've loved it. Think sweeping snow-topped mountains, vast green pastures, craggy outcrops, clean air and you'd be halfway there. It made you feel about an inch tall, surrounded by the massive majesty of nature. And in the middle of that— in the middle of a herd of goats," he added with a shadowy smile, "I finally had my answer."

"Give up Saint Catherine's."

He nodded. "I was working myself to death in a career I was beginning to hate." He gave a self-deprecating snort. "Hell, to be honest I'd never really enjoyed it, not the way I should've."

She nodded. Everything was beginning to make more sense. She'd thought he'd had the perfect family, the perfect career, but beneath that polish lurked so much more.

Just like her, really. AJ blinked and opened her mouth to say something, but he beat her to it.

"So, I'll pick you up tomorrow."

Tomorrow? What…? Oh. Her first appointment. "You're coming with me?"

A small frown creased his brow. "Why wouldn't I?"

"But I thought… What about..?" He confused her! He'd rearranged his schedule to be with her?

"This isn't something you should do alone." His gaze held hers. "I'll see you tomorrow," he said firmly, kissing her for one second, two, then getting out of the car and coming around to open the door for her and walk her inside.

From the foyer AJ watched him return to the car, then drive away, and the aching loss bit so deep her insides felt like they'd crumpled in on themselves. Which meant...

It meant she cared. Otherwise why had she gotten so riled about Katrina's attitude? Why had she been so affected by Matt's retelling of his past?

She cared what other people thought about her, about her relationship with Matt. She cared how other people saw him.

Her heart raced, breath catching painfully in her throat. She was falling for Matthew Cooper all over again.

Unbelievable. Absolutely unbelievable. What the hell was she supposed to do now?

With a sigh she tipped her gaze to the foyer ceiling and closed her eyes.

You'll do what you always do—suck it up and get through it. Because confessing her feelings? Making herself that open, that vulnerable again only to have Matt reject her?

That would kill her.

Fifteen

AJ had no idea how on earth women went through IVF over and over again. Every hope, every emotion was right there on the surface, raw and vulnerable. Handling all of that, plus the actual physical intrusion of the procedure, was way more than she'd bargained for. Thank God Matt had insisted on coming. His presence soothed her, his touch and low murmur of encouragement calmed her as the doctors efficiently went through the motions. His thumb gently stroked her knuckles, a rhythmic reassurance that gave her enough strength to suck everything up and ignore the pain, the uncertainty, the growing wave of doubt that battered her heart.

Hours later, aching and emotionally spent, she let him take her back to his apartment, remove her shoes and settle her on the sofa with a blanket and a cup of tea.

And when he made a move to leave, she grabbed his hand. "Stay with me."

They sat in silence on the sofa, his arms wrapped around her, her head on his chest as the familiar heat seeped into her very bones. Beneath her cheek his heart beat out a comforting rhythm, lulling her into a dangerous sense of contentment.

When the tears came, she didn't bother to wipe them away. He said nothing, but as his shirt slowly dampened his arms tightened around her, which only made the tears flow faster.

She had no idea why she was crying, but she did it silently, without movement, pretending he didn't know and couldn't feel the spreading wetness beneath her cheek. And he didn't let on, just held her, his hand gently stroking her arm over and over until, finally, she fell into an exhausted sleep.

AJ woke the next morning with gritty eyes and a dull ache in her gut.

She blinked, shifted and suddenly realized she was in a strange bed with a warm body pressed up against her back. A cozy lean body, his arm wrapped around her waist, his chin resting at the back of her neck.

Matt.

She vaguely remembered him guiding her into his bedroom, taking off her jacket and then her jeans, before putting her to bed dressed in just her knickers, bra and a blue tank top. A top that had shifted during the night and was now riding high on her rib cage.

A soft breath feathered across her shoulder and everything tightened, a crazy burst of desire and joy welling up in her throat. The reaction was so sudden, so shocking, that it floored her.

You want this. You want him.

Not just for now, not just for a limited time. Despite knowing who he was, how he lived his life and their checkered past, she wanted Matthew Cooper forever.

Her eyes squeezed shut as she tried to block out the tidal wave of emotion flooding in, tossing her high into the air only to leave her floundering as the waters receded.

You can't do this. You approached him. You started it. And now you have to deal with it.

He shifted suddenly, his thigh brushing against her bottom, and she felt another pang of yearning.

How desperately did she want this child? And was that desire enough to give her the strength to keep doing this for as long as it took, knowing that once she was pregnant, she and Matt would cease to be?

She had absolutely no clue.

He stirred again and this time his groin settled in the small of her back.

Oh, no. He was aroused, pressing firmly into her, and she was liking it too much.

His arm tightened around her waist, one hand splaying across her belly, and the intimate gesture short-circuited her brain. She couldn't move, couldn't think, just lay there stunned, her heart going crazy. Then she heard him suck in a deep breath, blowing it out slowly across the back of her neck.

"Angel."

That one sleepy, sexy word did her in.

She couldn't resist. She squeezed her eyes shut, then gently pushed her bottom back into his hardness and was rewarded with a soft groan. Slowly, she moved again but this time, his hand went to her hip, stilling her.

"Angel…" She loved the sound of his rough voice, the remnants of sleep still clinging to it.

"Matt."

"Could you not…?"

"Not what?" She shifted again but he had a firm grip. She couldn't move.

"Not do that."

"Why not?"

"Because you're killing me."

"You don't like it?"

"It's not that."

"Then what?"

She felt him sigh against her nape, the warmth stirring her hair and giving her goose bumps. She waited but he remained silent, and after a few agonizing seconds, she gently removed his hand from her hip and rolled over to face him.

He propped his hand under his cheek, studying her, and the pure vulnerability of the picture he presented had her entire body aching with longing. She leaned in and kissed his cheek, welcoming the roughness, the delicious, just-woken smell of his skin. He remained still, giving no indication of encouragement. But no rejection, either. That emboldened her to keep going, to trail soft kisses down his jaw then back up the other side, until she got to the corner of his mouth and she couldn't resist any longer.

AJ kissed him. Their lips were the only place their bodies touched and she called on every strand of patience not to jump on him. Instead, she seduced him using only her mouth: skimming his bottom lip, stopping briefly to nibble, before heading over to the other corner of his mouth. She traced the gentle curves with the tip of her tongue, a feathery lick that explored the erotic swell of his bottom lip until his warm breath began to pick up.

Oh, she still had it. With a triumphant grin she gently drew his bottom lip between her teeth and sucked. She was rewarded by a strangled moan. Her pulse kicked up and she kept going, languidly giving his mouth all the attention it deserved when what she really wanted to do was strip him naked and lick him all over.

Yet he remained still, letting her command the moment. Lips slid across lips, tongues mingled, at first gently, then with much more insistence. Finally, she eased back, belly pooling with heat as his languid eyes sought hers.

His dark, expressive eyes thrilled and aroused her every time he looked at her that way. Her breath raced and suddenly everything inside melted into a mess of tangled emotion.

"Angel…" His voice was thick and low. "I don't think we should—"

"Let me do this. Please."

She shifted, placing a hand on his shoulder and nudging him back. He went and she followed, bringing them together in a melding of skin and pounding blood. He was naked except for a pair of boxers, and she took untold satisfaction in having his hot flesh against hers. Firm chest, taut belly, lean waist. And his groin, now hard with arousal, pressing into hers.

She brought herself up so she was sitting on his thighs, leaning in.

Such a lean, compact body, without an inch of fat to mar the perfection. She swept her hand across his smooth chest, her palms brushing over first one dark nipple, then the other.

There it was, his swift intake of breath, dragging first in through his nose, then slowly exiting his parted mouth. She loved the way she, AJ Reynolds, had so much influence, knowing if she moved a certain way, kissed him in a particular spot, she could send his pulse racing or have him groan in pleasure.

He had the same effect on her.

Trailing her fingers over the smooth ridges of his abdomen, she went farther down, ringing his belly button then taking the path of the thin hairline that disappeared into his boxers.

He was aroused all right. She cupped him through the cotton, welcoming the thick, throbbing heat beneath her palm. When she glanced up to meet his gaze, those dark eyes were half-mast with passion, a muscle in his jaw working.

"You okay?"

"Yeah." It sounded like he'd been gargling sand and with a slow smile, she looped her thumbs into his waistband and slowly dragged his boxers down.

He sprang free, every hard, beautiful inch of him, and she was suddenly so overwhelmed with emotion that she had to bite her lip to gain control. She wrapped her hand around his thick length and was rewarded by Matt's sharp gasp.

He was hot and hard and she reveled in his velvety length, running her hand along it, pausing at the base, her fingers brushing the springy curls, before continuing back up.

"Angel…" Matt muttered, clenching a fist in the bedsheets. She stroked him again, her hands working magic on his aching manhood.

"Look at me."

At her soft command his eyes sprang open, focusing unsteadily on the ceiling, then slowly, down to where AJ was sprawled across his body.

He took in her disheveled red hair, pale skin, wide blue

eyes, the sensual curve of lips as she firmly and rhythmically kept him at full arousal with her hand.

Then her smile spread and slowly, deliberately she slid him into her hot, wet mouth and he nearly lost it right there.

His eyes rolled back in his head as the excruciating sensations flooded in, removing all thought, all feeling except her mouth, her tongue, her hand. His hips bucked involuntarily, pushing himself deeper, and she obliged, taking all of him, increasing her pace slowly, then with more authority, until he was on the edge in record time.

Finally, he tensed, tightening in one final thrust, and for one drawn-out second he couldn't breathe, couldn't think. Then with a deep guttural groan, he let himself go.

"Angel." She was on his lips, in his breath, under his skin. Everywhere.

It was as it should be.

He'd gone again. That much was obvious. AJ had woken to find a letter, then proceeded to torture herself with the many different ways she could say "I told you so."

He'd be gone at least ten days. Three days in Norway, followed by a side trip to Indonesia and China.

Ten long days.

So for her it was back to business as usual—walking, sketching, living a seemingly idyllic existence. The days dragged, agonizing days of worry and anticipation as she studiously followed Dr. Adams's advice and waited for a sign that the first procedure had taken. Thanks to a combination of hormones and her now-undeniable feelings, her head was a mess, always thinking, always worrying. Desperate to focus on something else, she sketched a bunch of pictures, managed to secure a stall at the Rocks Markets and then threw herself into organizing it. On the upside, it gave her a legitimate reason to distance herself from Matt when he finally returned, ensuring that her crazy, impossible thoughts were kept to a minimum.

He came back on a Saturday, and they spent a perfectly decent time having dinner at a small Italian restaurant in Concord. And as if their last night together had never been, he dropped her off without even once trying to make a move.

It was…a relief. And also frustrating.

And then he was gone again and she kept right on obsessing.

The day soon arrived when Zac's apartment was to be sold and Matt insisted she move back into his place. With no other choice available, she reluctantly agreed.

Just as she was about to walk out the door, Emily called to remind her the time for the open house tomorrow night had changed. AJ's hand was tight on the phone as she sat on a lounge chair arm and listened to her sister's usual enthusiasm with ever increasing gloom.

"So," Emily finally said. "What have you been up to? How's it going with that guy you mentioned?"

To AJ's horror she burst into tears. Then, when she stopped blubbering and attempted to gather at least some dignity, she ended up blurting everything out, from the surgery, to her fertility clinic issues, to Matt's involvement, to the wait for the results that were due later that day.

They both cried. After Emily alternately apologized for not knowing and scolded her for keeping secrets, she finally said, "Well, of course, you'll have to bring Matt to the showing."

AJ stared out the window at the bright afternoon sun piercing the white clouds, then at the Sydney skyline. "There's no 'of course' about it."

"Oh, my God, AJ, you have *got* to be kidding! The man is going to be the father of your child and we haven't even met him. He is a part of your life, regardless of this whole deal thing…which I think is ridiculous, by the way. You will damn well bring him, okay?"

AJ sighed. "He's in Tasmania right now, Em. But fine, I'll ask." She glanced at the clock. "I have to be downstairs. Talk later?"

"Sure. You call him now, okay?"

"Em…"

"Call him. I'm going to hang up then call you back. If your phone is not engaged, I'm going to be so pissed off."

AJ sighed. "Fine."

She clicked off, then dialed Matt's number.

The ease with which he said yes stunned her. "Shouldn't you check your schedule and get back to me?" she said, jamming the phone under her ear as she stared out onto the street, watching the slow-moving midafternoon traffic.

"I'm back tomorrow, AJ. What time?"

"Seven."

"Good. I can come straight from the airport."

So it was done. She placed the phone into her back pocket as a thousand different emotions rushed in to swamp her. Thanks to his work and her avoidance techniques, she hadn't seen him in… She calculated. A week. A whole entire week of not seeing those dark eyes, the softly curling hair she always itched to touch. His lean, capable body perfectly clad in a sharp suit. His smile and the way his eyes creased and that dimple emerged.

She swallowed and collapsed into the foyer sofa. God, her body ached.

It wasn't fair. None of it. She'd gotten over Matthew Cooper once before, but it seemed her luck had run out. No way would she escape the second time.

With a sigh she focused on getting her things back to Matt's apartment, determinedly shoving the inevitable clinic phone call to the bottom of her mental to do list. Matt had wanted to be there when she called but work had dictated otherwise. Instead, she'd promised to wait until he returned that night.

She couldn't wait that long.

Half an hour later, she stood in Matt's apartment, on the phone with Dr. Adams.

When she finally hung up, she collapsed into the sofa,

overwhelming loss choking off her breath, crushing her tiny sliver of hope.

She wasn't pregnant.

Dr. Adams had assured her they would try again and had made an appointment for next week.

She cast her eyes over her meager belongings in the middle of the room. A case, a shoulder bag, a folder full of sketches and a box of perishables—an echo of her former life, aeons ago, when she'd picked up and moved on a whim. A life wandering, searching. She'd done so much yet so little, avoiding commitment, connection, heartache. Yet she'd come full circle and returned to the one man who'd managed to make her feel, make her care. The only man who'd gotten under her skin.

She tipped her head down, tears prickling behind her eyes as her heart swelled with a deep, aching hunger.

Oh, God. I don't want to do this anymore. I can't.

She wasn't that strong, no matter how much Emily said she was. She desperately wanted a baby, more than anything she'd ever wanted before, but she couldn't break her own heart to get it. And if it was Matt's baby, she'd always be wanting something more, something she could never have.

Making a baby was all they'd agreed to and he'd never indicated it could be anything more. He wasn't hers, however much she wanted him.

She just couldn't do it anymore.

Matt arrived at Zac's apartment at six-thirty with a giddy sense of anticipation.

A week. Seven whole days. Sure, he'd been occupied with his crazy schedule, new clients and staff drama, but AJ was always in the back of his mind and surged to the front whenever there was downtime. Like on a long flight with only his thoughts for company. Or alone at night, when sleep refused to come.

In all the time he'd been away, she'd only called once. It

was obvious she was avoiding him and he knew exactly why. For all her bravado, all her tough outer shell, she was scared.

Yeah, he was, too. After his divorce, work was what he knew how to do and do well. Okay, so more than well. He knew how to give life back to those on death's door. Better, he gave hope, faith. Belief.

Yet he still didn't know how to break down the last of AJ's walls.

When he walked into the apartment and spotted her standing alone and to one side in the living room, Matt drank her in—heels, short black shirt, sheer bright blue top that draped off one shoulder—and fleetingly wondered what she'd do if he tossed her over his shoulder and just left.

Then she glanced up and a brief flash of something passed over her features before her mouth stretched into a smile. "Hi," she mouthed.

When she smiled like that…

He demolished the distance in seconds. "Hi yourself." Even though he'd decided not to push, he couldn't help leaning in to place a kiss on her mouth. He'd missed her too much.

Her surprised gasp warmed his lips. He smiled and pulled back. "Miss me?"

She blinked. "No."

He grinned. "Sure."

And suddenly, he was very much looking forward to tonight.

He looked good. Way too good. AJ didn't want to stare but she couldn't help herself, cataloging each feature: rough stubble dusting his chin, lean body in an impeccable black suit, skinny black tie and a sky-blue shirt.

Her heart began to beat a little faster when he smiled, hands jammed in his trouser pockets. He was…a rogue. That was it, a rogue with his rumpled sexy charm. He undid her a thousand different ways and she'd fallen all over again.

The conflict she'd been steadily building up all afternoon

suddenly became unbearable. Why hadn't she waited to call the clinic like she'd promised? She hated this, hated being the sole bearer of important news. It was exhausting. And because it was Matt, it made it a thousand times worse. Now she had to work out what she was going to say, pick the right time, then deal with his disappointment.

God, could this day get any worse?

He must have sensed something from her expression because his brows suddenly took a dive.

"AJ?"

The sound of someone clearing her throat had them both turning. Emily stood behind AJ, looking awkward. "Sorry, AJ, can I have a word?"

She opened her mouth to refuse, but something made her pause. Emily looked…weird. That was the only word for it. With a small frown, AJ nodded. "Sure."

Emily gave Matt a smile and said, "Hi, you must be Matt. Drinks are in the kitchen. We won't be long." Then she motioned for AJ to follow.

"What's up?" AJ asked when Emily led her into the bedroom and gently closed the door.

Emily took a breath, shoved a lock of curly brown hair behind her ear and threaded her fingers. "This is going to shock you…."

"What?" AJ wasn't sure she could take any more bad news today.

"I got a call from our parents today."

"What?"

Emily winced. "They want to meet us."

"Like hell!" AJ yelled. "After all these bloody years—"

"Shh," Emily hissed, her gaze darting to the door.

"After all these years," AJ continued in a furious whisper. "After *nothing.* Not a single call, email, letter, whatever, and they make contact now? What, did they see your photo in the paper and think you're a convenient ATM now that you're married to a billionaire?"

At Emily's twisted expression, AJ knew the thought had occurred to her, too. She shook her head as fury bubbled its way to the surface. "Tell them they can go take a running jump. No—" she swallowed a thick breath "—I'll tell them myself."

"AJ," Emily said softly, grasping her hand. "I told them the decision was up to you. And if you want to do it, then I'll go with you."

A wave of fierce protectiveness swept over her. She'd rather walk on hot coals than see those two people again, but damned if she'd let them invade Emily's life. "Fine," she choked out and grabbed the door. "I need a drink. You call them, then let me know when and where."

With that, she swung the door wide and blindly stalked down the hall. This could not be happening! Just like that, the tainted memories surged, ripping into those solid walls she'd built around her past.

She stormed into the kitchen, startling Matt.

He turned, glass of wine in his hand, but with one look at her expression his smile disappeared. "What's wrong?"

Oh, God, where to start? Her eyes went to the ceiling. "Nothing."

"AJ, look at me." She reluctantly met his eyes, then just as quickly looked away. "Tell me what the problem is."

She couldn't. She just…couldn't. She could share her body with him, maybe even admit her feelings, but her past? Those awful, shameful years she'd tried her best to forget, burying them under a lifetime of parties, partners and spur-of-the-moment decisions?

No.

Instead, she fell back on the one thing that had been front and center up until ten minutes ago.

"I called the clinic today. The pregnancy didn't take."

A mixture of emotions passed over his face—shock, disappointment, sadness. Everything she'd experienced and more. It didn't make it any easier knowing he was affected by this, too.

"You didn't have to be alone for that."

Nausea welled in the face of his concern, the deep thread of guilt overshadowing everything.

She glanced over his shoulder, at the slowly growing gathering, and felt claustrophobia claw at her chest. "I need some air. I should—"

"AJ." She gasped when he grabbed her arms. "That's not all, is it?" His gentle tone, instead of soothing, only served to restoke her anger.

She twisted out of his grip. "It's nothing."

"Then why are you so angry?"

She glared. "That is none of your business, all right?"

He pulled back as if she'd slapped him, his eyes going wide before they suddenly narrowed. "Right. Because I'm only good for one thing."

"I didn't… You're—"

"Oh, no, I get it. Everything's off-limits except what you want and the occasional times we end up in bed," he ground out, his hands going into his pockets with a disgusted snort. "Frankly, I'm getting a little sick of it, AJ."

She stilled. "What are you saying?"

"I'm saying I'm sick of the restrictions. That I'm only allowed to have a part of you. That I'm not supposed to ask questions or bring up the past or even bloody well care about you! *That's* what I'm saying."

She blinked. "You care about me?"

"And that comes as a surprise? AJ, you have no clue, do you?"

"Why? Why would you care, Matt? You don't know me—"

"I know you better than you think."

"Oh, you do? You know nothing." She choked down a sob. "You don't know about my life, about my crappy parents, their drunken binges, their—"

"Can you stop that? You're *not* a sum of your childhood." He sighed. "AJ. Look, I know the news about the pregnancy is disappointing. But we can try again."

Her heart broke, and she felt the force of it reverberate

through every bone. She couldn't do this, not on top of everything else. "I need you to go."

"Why?"

Because I am totally in love with you and you're killing me. "Just go. Please."

His eyes held hers, furious and confused, until she was sure she'd burst into tears any second.

"Fine," He finally sighed. "I'll talk to you at home."

She shook her head. "No, I'm going to get a hotel room."

She'd stunned him and for a second he absorbed the blow, his eyes creasing in confusion. He looked as if he was about to say something but broke off with a disgusted snort.

Then he spun on his heel and stalked out the front door.

Sixteen

It was three on Sunday afternoon and AJ sat with Emily at City Extra in the Quay, both silently watching the bustle of Sydneysiders and tourists passing by on their way to ferries or the Museum of Contemporary Art or simply strolling around and enjoying the sun.

AJ's gut pitched, matching the churning waves in the pier opposite the restaurant. Apprehension, fear and anger all played a part in her emotional turmoil, yet her focus was on her argument with Matt, not on the impending family reunion.

Damn, it was just like before. No—way, way worse. Because now she knew him better and despite every wall she'd built, every warning, she'd gone and fallen in love and now her heart was breaking.

No, that wasn't right. How could her heart break when it was never whole to start with? She was damaged, scarred. She'd done far too much and seen far too many things to be anything other than a product of her broken childhood.

"AJ?"

She turned her attention from her untouched coffee to look up into Emily's concerned blue eyes.

"Are you sure about this?" Her sister reached for her hand. "After everything that's happened, you don't have to do this now. I can just—"

"Oh no." Her fingers wound around Emily's and she winced. "Sorry. But there's no way I'd leave you to do this on your own."

"You had a negative result," Emily pointedly reminded her. "Your body needs to rest."

AJ lifted one eyebrow. "Do you honestly think lying in bed is going to work for me?"

Emily was silent for a second before she shook her head. "We need to do this, don't we?"

"Yeah. But I wish—"

Emily's gaze slid past her shoulder. Her eyes widened, and her face went pale. A sudden roar of blood pounded in AJ's ears as a female voice cut through the chatter of the Sunday crowds.

"Emily! Baby! It's you!"

AJ jumped to her feet and whirled around so fast her chair flew back.

It was their mother, no doubt about it. She was painfully skinny, poured into a pair of white jeans and a leopard-print tank top. Her outfit only emphasized her thin arms and nonexistent waist. But what was more noticeable, past the frizzy red hair, huge gaudy diamante sunglasses and a dozen gold rings and bangles that jangled alarmingly, were the deep grooves bracketing her thin, pink-painted mouth.

"And Angelina Jayne!" Charlene Reynolds declared loudly, raising her sunglasses to her hair and placing her hands on those bony hips. "Girls, you both look absolutely gorgeous!" Her eyes briefly skimmed over AJ before snapping back to Emily, and when that sharp, assessing gaze lingered a little too long on Emily's curvy hips with a brief frown, AJ felt the anger simmer in earnest.

Then she glanced past their gaudily clad birth mother and her gut pitched alarmingly. "Keith?"

"Hi there, Red."

AJ's eyes met Emily's, reflecting her surprise. "You two are still together?"

"Amazing, right?" Her stepfather looked downright respectable in his chinos, checkered shirt and loafers but she knew he was anything but. He'd always reminded AJ of a stereotypical car salesman, a guy whose eyes never met yours, whose oily grin grated on people's nerves, whose fast talk and cheap ways made him more enemies than friends. No wonder they'd had to move so often.

When his arm snaked around Charlene's waist and he planted a kiss smack bang on her mouth, AJ wanted to gag. "Me and Charl, we're just meant to be."

AJ looked back at Emily, who'd been silent and pale for too long. Now she coughed and indicated the table. "Will you sit?"

Charlene nodded her approval and took the seat on AJ's left—which left Keith directly to her right.

"So, girls," she began with a wide smile, arms crossed on the table. "It's wonderful to see you two again after all these years."

"How…?" AJ cleared her throat, then started again. "How did you find us?"

She ignored Emily's frown and instead focused on the woman who had made her life hell for the first twelve years of her life.

The years had not been kind to her mother, with the creases continuing around the older woman's eyes and forehead—not lines born from laughter, sun and joy, but ones AJ knew were the product of drugs, alcohol and awful life choices. Her blue eyes looked tired, yet her assessment of AJ was shrewd and she knew Charlene was forming an unflattering opinion behind that silent scrutiny.

"Well, sweetheart, we saw Emily's wedding photo in the paper, didn't we?" She barely glanced at Keith for confirmation. "What a beautiful dress! And that new husband of yours…" She paused theatrically. "Well, if I were ten years younger—"

"Look, what do you want, Charlene?"

Charlene blinked and focused on AJ, her mouth pursing. "That's not very polite, Angelina."

"My name is AJ."

"Your birth certificate says Angelina, sweetheart." She

blew out a scoffing chuckle, glancing at Emily, then Keith. "What kind of a name is AJ?"

"One I *like*."

Charlene's eyes narrowed. "Well, I *don't*."

"Well, I *don't care*."

Charlene's hand suddenly twitched and even though it had been more than fifteen years, AJ felt the familiar burn of fear and defiance in her stomach. She braced herself, back straightening even though her head screamed *Move!*

Her vision narrowed, focusing on that one small movement, ready for the blow that would come, would always come.

"Charlene," Keith said hastily, putting a hand on the older woman's clenched fists. "This isn't the best way to start our reunion, not after all these years."

Charlene's eyes sparked, throat working as the anger lines thinned her mouth. AJ glared her down, furious flames banking in her belly. *I'm not ten anymore. She can't hurt me now. I'm not about to back down.*

"You're right, Keith," Charlene finally said, dripping saccharine. She gave AJ a death glare before turning her overly bright smile on Emily. "Sweetheart, I can't tell you how proud I am—how we both are—that you've done so well for yourself. Who would've thought my little Emily would end up marrying a *Preston?*" She reverently breathed out the last word, her hand to her throat.

"You want money," AJ blurted out.

Charlene's eyes snapped back to AJ. "What?"

"I said, you want money." AJ leaned back in her chair and crossed her arms. "This isn't some impromptu reunion. You saw Emily's photo, saw who she'd married and thought you could score a freebie."

Charlene's mouth opened, then quickly slammed shut. "That's not a very nice thing to say."

"True, though."

AJ eyed Charlene's hands as they slowly curled into fists, then just as slowly flattened on the table.

"No, Angelina, it's not. Look, you want the truth?" She leaned in, her expression earnest. "I've been looking for both of you for years. I even have my name on a bunch of registers to find you. You can check if you like."

AJ saw a mix of confusion and disbelief in Emily's wide blue eyes and felt protective anger burn the back of her throat. Emily never could hide her feelings. And they'd see that confusion and play on it. Even now, Keith was studying her with a cool calculation that made AJ furious.

"What. A load. Of crap," AJ said succinctly, taking no small satisfaction as everyone's eyes darted back to her.

Charlene took a deep, aggrieved breath. "Listen, Angelina—"

"No, *you* listen." AJ leaned in, fury making her entire body shake. "You abandoned us. I was in the hospital, recovering from surgery, and you *left me there*. Emily was ten years old and had to catch public transport on a Saturday night to find me."

"Angelina, if you'd just—"

"Oh, are you going to tell me it wasn't your fault? That you can't help yourself, that it's the booze, the drugs or whatever loser friends you had at the time?" She raked her gaze over Charlene. "Why don't you just admit you're a pathetic woman and an awful mother and save us both the effort?"

"I never said I was perfect!"

AJ snorted. "I would've settled for decent."

Charlene's expression twisted, her gaze contemptuous. "Yeah, well, I never did want either of you in the first place," she spat. "And you—you're just as bad as your father. That selfish bastard had a mouth on him, too."

AJ glared at the woman who'd given birth to her, the same woman who should have loved and protected her but instead had used and abused her power. She'd conditioned AJ to lie and steal to support Charlene's drug habit. She'd abandoned them both in a public hospital with no clothes, no home and no money.

Finally, after all these years drifting, searching, secretly wishing for something, someone who could make her believe she deserved much more than she'd been born into, she had her answer.

I'm free.

AJ stood, suddenly desperate to leave. "You don't know me, Charlene. You never have." She shoved her chair under the table, noting with satisfaction that Emily was following suit. "Nothing you could say could hurt me because that'd mean I care what you think—and I don't." She dragged her gaze from Charlene's furious expression to her sister. "Em? Shall we go?"

"Sweetheart." Charlene placed a hand over Emily's and squeezed, making her wince. "If you would just hear me out—"

God bless her sister because she yanked her hand away and stood staring down at their mother with a look that could only be described as pity. AJ sent up a silent cheer when their eyes met over Charlene's teased hair and they both gave an imperceptible nod.

AJ grinned. *Love you, Em.*

Emily grinned back. *Love you more, AJ.*

"Wait!" Keith grabbed AJ's wrist. "You can't—oooof!"

AJ's elbow connected with his chest and she couldn't deny the deep satisfaction his yelp gave her. "You, Keith, are a slimy douche bag who can't keep his hands to himself, either above or below the table."

And with that, she took Emily's hand and they walked out into the sun.

Someone was knocking.

AJ paused in her packing and glanced at her hotel door. It came again.

With a sigh she went over, placing her eye up to the peephole. Instantly, she pulled back with a soft murmur.

"AJ, open the door."

She shook her head silently.

"I know you're there."

Still she waited, her cheek on the cool door as she held her breath.

"Please, Angel."

Oh, God. She bit down on her lip, choking off a groan. She'd booked a late-afternoon flight, had rehearsed what she was going to say when she called him from the airport. Yet all that preparation felt somehow inadequate, like she wasn't giving him her full attention.

You can't leave it like this.

With a deep breath, she gathered her composure, pulled her shoulders back and slowly unlocked the door.

He stood there, gorgeous as always in his business suit, and for one second she wanted to launch herself at him, kiss him senseless and confess everything.

She couldn't.

"Paige called me," he said. "Your phone's been off and you missed your date."

Oh, damn. AJ rubbed the bridge of her nose. "I forgot."

"She's worried about you." He tipped his head, dark eyes searching her face. "So am I." He glanced past her. "Can I come in?"

She stepped back, allowing him entry. When he strode past she managed to suck his smell deep into her lungs before reluctantly breathing out again.

You can do this. You have to do this.

He turned in the middle of the room but not before he took in her open suitcase on the bed. Instead of grilling her about that, he said, simply, "Emily also called me."

"Oh?"

"She told me you met your parents yesterday."

What? She clenched her jaw. "Why would she do that?"

"Because she's worried about you, too."

AJ sighed. "I just… I think—" She broke off with a frown, stuck her hands in her back pockets and released a slow breath.

She didn't have to tell him, but she'd come too far now *not* to tell him. She was sick of keeping all this crap inside, sick of having it affect everything she did.

She sighed and slumped into the sofa. "My mother was awful. She partied, drank, took drugs. She and whatever guy she was with were neglectful and selfish, moving from one housing commission to another, trashing the places before skipping out on the rent. They also took great delight in training my sister and me to steal from a very early age. I was arrested a few times."

Shame ripped through her body, the very action of verbalizing it tearing her from the inside out. But something made her continue.

"I was sixteen when my appendix burst. I came out of surgery to find my sister clinging onto the bed rail with child services trying to drag her away.

"Thanks to the Young Offenders Act, it didn't go through the courts—there was mediation, liaison, all that stuff. My parents sat there like contrite model citizens, nodded sagely and expressing their desire to change and be better, while a DOCS worker outlined the issues. They had everyone fooled. Except..." She swallowed, the sting of embarrassment still familiar after all these years. Yet Matt's concerned expression forced her to go on, to finally air the dirty little secrets she'd kept so close to her heart. "One cop. He suspected something was wrong. And when they realized he was digging around, they did a runner."

"They left you?"

She nodded. "A warrant was issued, but because it wasn't considered a major crime, the police had to wait until they crossed back over to Western Australia. Which they never did."

"So what happened?"

AJ shrugged. "Emily went into foster care and I moved to Sydney. Did lots of jobs up and down the coast. Met you. Then I found Emily years later and we reconnected. I..." She scowled, recalling the stupid beliefs that had kept her from her sister for so long. "I thought she'd be better off without me. Plus I couldn't deal with the guilt of leaving her, the questions she'd ask. It was just too much and I didn't want to face it."

She fell silent, studying her nails with determined scrutiny as the memories washed over her. But when the silence stretched, she glanced up. Matt was staring at her, those dark eyes so direct, so firm that she felt the urge to just blurt everything out, put it all out there.

Then he glanced over at her suitcase and the moment was gone. "So you're leaving, then."

She nodded.

His face was expressionless. "I see."

"Don't you want to know why?"

He shoved his hands in his pockets. "Obviously, you've changed your mind about having a baby."

Oh, how easy if that was the true reason. She searched his face with a growing sense of desperation. *Get angry. Yell at me. Anything that would justify my decision.*

He just stared back, waiting.

Instead, he ran his hand through his hair, his eyes softening. "AJ, I'm sorry about yesterday's results. But we can try again—"

"No." She shook her head. "I'm done."

He looked confused. "But this was just the first time. Why—?"

"Because I can't do it anymore."

"Again, why?"

God, she wished he wouldn't look at her that way.

"AJ, just tell me."

Her eyes darted away. "Look, I just don't think it's fair on you to keep doing this. You have a career, a life. One day you'll want to get married again and I don't—"

"Don't you do that. Don't make me the reason, AJ. That's not fair. You tell me what you want without making me the excuse for walking out."

Matt's heart pounded as a terrible fear coursed through his blood. She stood there, still and small with the burden of truth he'd laid on her, and for one heart-stopping second everything teetered on the edge, threatening to crash and burn.

She took a deep breath. "Fine." She crossed her arms, the protective gesture revealing the depth of her doubt. "In a perfect world I want what anyone wants. A baby. A partner. A life full of laughter and love and joyous moments. But it's not a perfect world. I have to face the reality that I'll probably never have kids. I don't want to spend months—years—being poked and prodded only to have the results turn out negative every time. It..." She stared at the floor for the longest time. "It's breaking me and I can't do it."

"AJ..." His voice croaked and he coughed to clear it.

"What do you want, Matt?" She addressed the floor still, and the vulnerability of her stance, in her soft words, wounded him.

This was it. His moment of truth.

He'd rehearsed it over and over in his head. It all came down to this. A terrible fear froze his lungs. *Don't stuff it up.*

But when he opened his mouth, all that came out was, "I want you to stay."

She looked up cautiously.

"You had your clarity six months ago. I had mine when Jack died." He moved closer and she tipped her head up, her eyes wide and riddled with confusion as she met his gaze. "I spent years building a career. I married someone exactly like me and we were driven by success and the need to achieve. But after Jack died, I realized I couldn't do it any longer. I wanted more. I wanted a life. A family. When I asked Katrina, she refused point-blank to consider it." The memory made his jaw clench, but he quickly brushed it away. "I—"

"Are you saying you want a *baby?*"

When he nodded, she crossed her arms and leaned back, staring and openmouthed.

"You've known this all along," she said tightly.

He nodded again and this time she shook her head, one hand pushing away a stray curl. "And these past few weeks have been...what? A way to seduce me?"

"Not exactly..."

She blinked slowly, her eyes never leaving his. "Why, Matt? Why would you do that?"

"Because I was an idiot ten years ago and I let you go. I didn't want to make the same mistake again. AJ..." He took a step toward her. "I haven't stopped thinking about you. Even in the middle of a job, I've been thinking about you."

A soft sound gurgled in her throat as her eyes widened.

"I love you, AJ," he continued, then took her hands, holding them between his warm fingers. "I've always loved you. And I don't want to lose you again."

It felt like the world had stopped spinning in that moment, that everything depended on what she said next. He held his breath, waiting, until her eyes closed briefly, as if it pained her somehow. His heart raced, hanging on the edge, waiting for her response.

"But why...?" She cleared her throat. "Why didn't you just say something?"

He snorted. "Oh, yeah. Sure. You ask me to father a child without strings and I tell you I love you? You would've hit the door running."

AJ couldn't think. Couldn't breathe. Through her deafening heartbeat, through every muscle, every vein screaming in joy, she realized her fingers were trembling.

If she cried now, she wouldn't know how to stop.

Damn it. She was crying.

Matt's expression softened as he stood and she felt the tears flow even faster.

"Angel..." he choked out, stroking a tender thumb across her cheek. "Does this mean you're sad?"

She pressed her lips together, vehemently shaking her head. "I just...I just..."

"Shhh," he squeezed her hands. "Take a breath. Start again."

She did as he suggested, dragging air into her lungs once, then twice, as he brushed the tears from her other cheek.

Then he cupped her face and she became completely, totally undone.

"Do you know how long I've been waiting to say something?" she finally whispered. "All the times we were together, it killed me but I didn't want to stop because I needed to see you again."

He went still, his wide brown eyes searching hers.

"Matt, I didn't want to. I told myself not to. But I fell in love with you and I—"

His mouth cut off the rest of her words.

Yes. His lips slid across hers in a searing kiss. AJ met the full force of his passion and need and gave him back more, wrapping her arms around his neck, bringing him closer, as her heart swelled with total and complete joy. This was too much. She didn't deserve this.

And yet here it was. He wanted her. Matthew Cooper *loved* her.

When they finally broke apart, hot and breathless, AJ sighed. "Matt...are you sure? I mean, really, really sure?" She glanced away from his silent study. "Because you know my chances of having a baby aren't good."

"Angel, just because you might not be able to physically bear a child doesn't mean I don't love you any less. If you want to keep trying, I'll support you. If you want to adopt, I'll support you. Okay?"

Again with the tears. And when he leaned in and placed a tender kiss on her mouth, her heart collapsed.

God, she loved this man! Loved every frustrating, intense, wonderful inch of him. She covered his hands with her own and leaned into the kiss, wanting more, wanting everything.

"I love you, Matt."

She felt his mouth curve against hers. "And I love you, too,

Angel. You're more important to me than anything else. I'm
going to delegate some of my work so I can spend time with
you building our family. And if I have to travel anywhere to
serve my clients, you'll be with me. As my wife."

Wife?

Her surprise must've shown because his soft laugh suddenly broke the silence.

"I want to marry you," he murmured. "Is that so surprising?"

Totally. But instead, she just shook her head. "Not at all."

"Liar. You are totally surprised."

She shook her head with a small smile. "A little."

"Well, believe it. Angelina Jane Reynolds…" He looped his
arms around her waist, his expression deadly serious. "Will
you marry me?"

For this decision, she didn't even need to think. "In a heartbeat."

Epilogue

Three months later, AJ stood at the entrance to the wedding marquee in the Palazzo Versace's private function area, silently panicking inside. A thousand different emotions competed for attention, yet it was overwhelming joy that gripped the most tightly.

Emily handed her the white rose bouquet as Paige busily adjusted her skirts. The cream wedding dress fit to perfection, with its sweetheart neckline, the tight beaded bodice that accented her waist and the skirts that swept down to the floor, parting in front to reveal rich sky-blue satin decorated with starbursts and sequined butterflies.

It was beautiful. She felt beautiful.

When she glanced up, she found herself the entire focus of the crowd and her heart suddenly started to beat double time.

"Don't worry," Emily whispered. "You look gorgeous. And your soon-to-be husband doesn't look too bad himself."

AJ's gaze automatically went down the aisle, where the celebrant and best man stood. But she had eyes only for Matt.

He was dressed in an old-style sandy-colored smoking suit, a pristine white shirt and a shiny blue cravat that matched the lining of her dress. His hair brushed his collar, and his chin was dusted with thin stubble. When those dark eyes fixed on her, then creased in appreciation, everything disappeared.

God, she loved him.

She wanted to sprint down that aisle, grab his hand and run away with him. Instead, she focused on his face, the breathless emotion in his eyes, the grin that spread as she put one foot in front of the other, surely and steadily, until they were finally side by side.

It felt like hours, but in reality, it only took a few seconds to reach him.

He leaned down, lips close to her ear. "You look amazing."

She smiled back, linking her fingers through his when he offered his hand. "So do you."

"Are you ready for this?"

"Yes." She glanced around at their small party, then back to him. "And I hope you're ready for next month, too."

He gave her a quizzical look. "What's next month?"

She bit her lip, unable to contain her cool composure any longer. "Elise from the adoption agency called. They've approved us. This time next week, we'll be parents."

His smile got even wider, to the point where it nearly blinded her. Ignoring all the guests, the celebrant, the hotel staff and a handful of onlookers, he swooped down for a kiss.

"Matt!" she laughingly protested against his mouth. "We haven't said our vows yet."

"I don't care. This is a kissing moment and I'm taking it."

And in that one moment, with the sound of the crowd's laughter ringing around them, AJ had everything she could possibly want.

* * * * *

STAKING HIS CLAIM

BY
TESSA RADLEY

Tessa Radley loves travelling, reading and watching the world around her. As a teen, Tessa wanted to be an intrepid foreign correspondent. But after completing a bachelor of arts degree and marrying her sweetheart, she became fascinated by law and ended up studying further and practicing as an attorney in a city firm.

A six-month break spent traveling through Australia with her family rewoke the yen to write. And life as a writer suits her perfectly—travelling and reading count as research, and as for analyzing the world. . .well, she can think "what if?" all day long. When she's not reading, traveling or thinking about writing, she's spending time with her husband, her two sons or her zany and wonderful friends. You can contact Tessa through her website, www.tessaradley.com.

For all my fabulous readers—
it's always wonderful to write a new book for you!

One

"You've decided to do *what?*"

It was Friday afternoon, the end of a grueling workweek, and Ella McLeod desperately wanted to put up her swollen feet…and relax.

Instead, from the depths of the sofa in her town house living room, Ella bit back the rest of the explosive reaction that threatened to erupt. She hoped wildly that her sister's next words would settle her world back on its axis so that the nasty jolt of shock reverberating through her system might just evaporate.

As if the sight of Ella's swollen belly prodded her conscience, Keira's gaze skittered away and she had the good grace to look discomforted. "Dmitri and I have decided to go to Africa for a year."

Ella shifted to ease the nagging ache in her lower back that had started earlier at the law chambers. Keeping her attention fixed on her sister fidgeting on the opposite end of the sofa, she said, "Yes, I understood that part—you and Dmitri plan to work for an international aid charity."

Her younger sister's gaze crept back, already glimmering with relief. "Oh, Ella, I knew you'd understand! You always do."

Not this time. Clearly Keira thought this was a done deal. It was rapidly becoming clear why Keira had dropped in this evening. And Ella had thought her sister's anticipation about the baby's imminent arrival had driven the surprise visit....

How wrong she'd been!

Gathering herself, Ella said slowly, "I don't quite understand the rest. What about the baby?"

The baby.

The baby in her belly that Keira had been so desperate for. Keira's baby. A baby girl. Keira and Dmitri had been present at the twenty-week ultrasound when the baby's sex had been revealed. Afterward the pair had gone shopping to finish buying furnishings for a nursery suitable for a baby girl.

Yet now that very same baby girl suddenly appeared to have ceased to be the focus of her sister's universe.

"Well—" Keira wet her lips "—obviously the baby can't come with."

It wasn't obvious at all.

"Why not?" Ella wasn't letting Keira wriggle out of her responsibilities so easily. *Not this time.* This wasn't the course of expensive French lessons Keira had grown tired of...or the fledgling florist business that Ella had sunk money into so that Keira would have a satisfying career when the one she'd chosen had become impossible. This was the *baby* Keira had always dreamed of one day having.

When Keira bit her lip and tears welled up in her eyes, a familiar guilt consumed Ella. Before she could relent—as she always did—she said, "Keira, there's no reason why the baby can't go with you. I'm sure you'll find people in Africa will have babies."

The tears swelled into big, shiny drops. "What if the baby becomes ill? Or dies? Ella, it's not as if this is a five-star beach resort. This is aid work in a poverty-stricken part of Africa."

Refusing to be drawn into her sister's dramatics, Ella leaned forward and tore a tissue from the box on the glass coffee table in front of the sofa, then passed it to Keira.

"Do you even know what kind of infrastructure exists? You could ask whether a baby would be safe." But Ella suspected she was fighting a losing battle when Keira failed to answer. She tried again. "If it's so unsafe, then what about your own health? Your safety? Have you and Dmitri thought this through? Do you really want to be living in a war zone?"

"It's not a war zone," Keira denied hotly. The tears had miraculously evaporated without a dab from the tissue that drifted to the carpet. "Credit me with some sense. It's Malawi. The country is stable—the people are friendly. It's poverty and illiteracy that we will be fighting."

So much for Keira's claim that it would be impossible to take a child there. But Ella knew she'd lost the battle; Keira had already made up her mind—the baby was not going with her.

"So what will happen to the baby?"

Silence.

Keira's eyes turned pleading, just like those of Patches, the beloved spaniel from their childhood.

"No! It is not staying with me." Ella made it a statement. A *firm* statement. The kind she used when delivering an ultimatum to opposing counsel.

Keira opened her mouth.

The baby chose that moment to kick.

Ella squeezed her eyes shut and suppressed a gasp at the hard jab against her ribs. Perspiration pricked at her forehead. She rubbed her side.

Thrusting the pain away, she opened her eyes and said to her sister, "Have you spoken to Jo about your new plans?" Ella suspected Jo Wells, the social worker who had been involved in helping arrange the paperwork side of the adoption for Keira and Dmitri, would be as floored as she was by Keira's change of heart.

"Dmitri is right. We're too young to become parents," Keira

said, sidestepping Ella's question. "We haven't even been married a year."

Drawing a deep breath, Ella said slowly, "A bit late to come to the conclusion that you're not ready to be parents."

Nine months too late to be precise.

Ella patted her own swollen stomach and watched mercilessly as Keira flushed.

"This baby is due next week. All your life you wanted to get married, start a family…that's why you did an early childcare course." It was why Ella was now stuck across the sofa from her sister like a stranded whale with a bulging belly. "How can you walk away from your child now?"

She had a nasty suspicion that she knew what—or rather, who—was behind the change of heart. Dmitri's big brother. Yevgeny Volkovoy.

Bossy big brother. Billionaire. Bigot.

Ella couldn't stand the man. He'd been furious to discover that Dmitri had gotten married without his say-so. He'd caused poor Keira endless tears with his terrifying tirades. Only by signing a post-nuptial agreement that allowed Keira the barest of maintenance in the case of divorce, and skewed everything in favor of the Volkovoy dynasty had Keira escaped his ire. Ella'd had a fit when she'd learned about the contract—and her alarm had grown when she read the terms. But by then it had been too late. The marriage was a done deal.

And Keira hadn't asked her for her expertise…or her help.

Of course, Yevgeny hadn't been in favor of the baby plan, either. Ella had known from the moment he'd switched to Russian. Dmitri had gone bright red—clearly he'd been less happy with Big Brother's opinions.

Now it sounded like Big Brother had finally gotten his way and managed to persuade Dmitri that he wasn't ready to become a parent.

Shifting again to ease her body's increasing discomfort, Ella tried to stem the emotions that were swirling around inside her. Disbelief. Confusion. The beginnings of anger. None of this cocktail of emotions could be good for the baby. And, even though Ella had never had any intentions of having her own child, she'd taken great care of this one. She'd eaten well—going to great lengths to cut out her four-cups-a-day coffee habit—she'd even shortened her workday and made certain she'd been in bed by ten o'clock each night. She'd even taught herself to meditate so that the baby wouldn't be contaminated by her stressful workday thoughts.

All because she'd wanted to make sure the baby was perfect. Her gift to Keira.

A gift Keira was now returning. Unborn, rather than unwrapped.

How did one return a baby, for heaven's sake? A baby that was a week away from becoming a live person?

Which brought Ella to…

"You're not leaving for Africa before the baby is born." She made it a statement. "There will be decisions that have to be made before you go."

Panic turned Keira's eyes opaque. "No! I can't."

"What do you mean you *can't?*"

"I can't handle those decisions. We've already booked our tickets. You'll need to make the arrangements."

"Me?" Drawing a deep shuddering breath, Ella went cold. "Keira, this is a baby we're talking about—you can't just walk away."

Her sister's gaze dropped pointedly to Ella's very round stomach. "You're still the legal mother—the adoption doesn't kick in until twelve days after the baby's born. You know that, Ella. Because you told me so yourself."

Of course she knew it. Knowing stuff like that was part of her job as one of the most respected family lawyers in Auckland. But the knowledge was only just starting to sink in that Keira was planning to leave her holding the baby!

"Oh, no!" Shaking her head, Ella said emphatically, "The only reason I lent you my body was so that you could have the baby you always dreamed of having. This is *your* dream, Keira.

Your baby." *My nightmare.* Then, in case it hadn't sunk in, she added pointedly, "Yours and Dmitri's."

"It's *your* egg."

"Only because you can't—" Ella bit off the words she'd been about to utter.

Too late.

Keira had gone white.

Driven by remorse, Ella propelled her colossal self from the sofa and reached for Keira. Her sister was as stiff as a wooden block in her arms. "I'm so sorry, sweetheart, I shouldn't have said that."

"It's the truth." Keira's voice was flat. "I don't have eggs or a uterus—I can't have children."

"So why—" Ella almost bit her tongue off. She tightened her hold around her sister.

"Don't worry, you can ask. No, I'll ask for you. 'Why are you doing this? Why are you going to Africa without the baby?' That's what you really want to know, isn't it?"

Ella inclined her head.

"I'm not sure I can explain." Keira shrugged out of her hold.

Given no choice, Ella let her sister go.

While Keira gathered her thoughts, Ella became aware of the stark silence that stretched to the breaking point between them across the length of the sofa. A silent divide. It might as well have been the blue-green of the Indian Ocean that stretched beyond Australia all the way to Africa that yawned between them…because her sister had already retreated mentally farther than the arm's length that separated them.

Then Keira started to speak. "This is something both Dmitri and I have to do." The blank, flat stare she fixed on Ella was a little unnerving. "I have to find myself, Ella. Find out who I am. All my life I wanted to teach little children—and have my own houseful of kids at home." Her eyes grew more bleak. "But things didn't go according to plan."

"Keira—"

"I loved my job at Little Ducks Center—"

"Keira." The pain in her sister's voice was unbearable. "Don't!"

But Keira carried on as if she hadn't heard. "I couldn't work there after the car accident…after I found out the truth—that there never would be any babies."

"Oh, honey—"

Keira ducked away from Ella's enfolding arms.

An unwelcome sense of rejection filled Ella. Followed by emptiness. Instantly she scolded herself for her selfishness. She shouldn't feel hurt. Keira was suffering.

Yet, despite all her empathy for her sister, the most important question still remained unanswered: What about the baby? *The baby I helped create to fulfill your dream?* "But Keira, you will have a baby now—and you have a husband who loves you."

Wasn't that enough?

Eyes softening, Keira admitted, "Yes, I was very, very fortunate to find Dmitri."

Ella hadn't been so sure of that in the beginning. In fact, she'd foreseen nothing but heartbreak ahead for her sister. The arrival of Yevgeny Volkovoy in Auckland had been big news. Not satisfied with inheriting millions from the hotel empire his father had built up, the Russian had expanded the dynasty by building up the best river cruise operation in Russia. In the past few years he'd expanded into ocean cruise liners. With the planned expansion of Auckland's cruise ship terminal, it was not surprising to learn that Yevgeny intended to secure Auckland as a voyage destination. What had been surprising had been learning through the newspapers that the Russian had fallen in love with New Zealand—and planned to relocate himself permanently. He'd sent his brother to New Zealand to secure corporate offices and staff them for Volkovoy Cruising's new base. At first Ella had been less than impressed with the younger Volkovoy. With all the Volkovoy money Dmitri threw around, Ella had considered him spoiled and irresponsible. Nothing fortunate in that. Yet there was no doubt that he loved her sister…and thankfully he'd lost that reckless edge that had worried Ella so much at first. But heading off to Africa without the baby was not the right thing for Keira.

The baby...

Ella's hand crept to her stomach.

Mindful of how much her sister hated it when she nagged, Ella tempered her outrage. "You can't just leave a baby for a few months...or even a year...and hope it will be there when you get back."

"I know that, Ella." Keira's brows drew together. "Don't try to put the guilts on me. I'm not ready for a baby—neither of us are."

Ignoring her sister's unfair accusation, Ella tried to fathom out what Keira's response meant. Did she intend to give the baby up for adoption? Shock chilled Ella. Had her sister thought this through? She would hate to see Keira suffer when it one day came home to her what she'd lost. Perhaps Keira needed to be reminded of that.

"If you're thinking about giving the baby up for adoption, just remember it's not going to be easy to find a surrogate again if you decide you want a baby when you come back from Africa."

She certainly wouldn't be doing it again. She shouldn't even have done it this time. Dumb. Dumb. Dumb decision. That's what came of making decisions with her heart rather than her head.

Keira flicked back her pale silver hair. "We can do what Yevgeny suggested when we first talked about you being our surrogate—put our names down to adopt a baby."

She'd known Dmitri's high-handed brother was behind this!

The ache in her lower back that had been worsening all day, intensified. It wasn't worth arguing with Keira, pointing out that putting down your name didn't guarantee a baby because so few became available for adoption. And when one did, the legal mother had the final say. She alone could choose whichever couple she wanted—there was no waiting list, no way to predict who she would choose.

But right now Keira's future plans were not her concern.

"And what about this baby?" Ella knew she sounded angry. But, damn it, she *was* angry. Yevgeny made her blood bubble— even when he wasn't present. Just the mention of the man was enough! "You can't just dump it—"

"I'm not dumping it— You're the legal mother. I know you'll make the best decision for the baby." There was an imploring expression in her sister's eyes that caused the hairs at the back of Ella's neck to stand on end.

Oh, no! Keira *had* planned to leave the baby with her and come back to claim it. Panic prickled through her. "I *can't* keep the baby."

Keira's eyes teared up again. "I know I shouldn't have expected you to. But you always wanted the adoption of the baby to us to be an open one. So I hoped you would consider…"

"No!" Panic swamped Ella. "We have a surrogacy arrangement—"

Keira was shaking her head. "But Ella, you explained we can't actually adopt the baby until after you sign the consent to give her up on the twelfth day. As the legal mother, you're entitled to change your mind—but so are we."

She'd explained the legalities too well to her sister. Ella swallowed a curse. "You can't change your mind—because I can't keep this baby."

A wave of sick helplessness engulfed her.

Keira sighed. "We already have. We're not ready to raise a child. I don't even want to think about the decision you're going to have to make, but you have to do what you feel is right, Ella. It's your body, your b—"

"Don't tell me it's my baby!"

Keira looked doleful. "I think I always knew deep in my heart that you wouldn't agree to keep her, and I've made peace with that. Even though I had so hoped…" Her little sister's voice trailed away.

Dear God.

Did Keira not know how much this *hurt*? What she was asking? The pain that pierced her chest was sharp and unforgiving. And guilt made it worse. Ella wished she could burst into tears…weep and wail. But she couldn't. Instead, she fought for composure.

She'd always been the adult in their relationship. No doubt Keira had known all along she would agree to sort everything out.

Her heart was racing, and her head had started to pound. The ache in her back seemed to be growing worse by the minute. Ella knew all this couldn't be good for the baby. She had to calm down. *Think of the baby.* She drew a shuddering breath… counted to five…and exhaled slowly.

Pulling a cloak of assumed indifference around herself, Ella said with every bit of dignity she could muster, "I have a job—a demanding job. I don't have time for a pet, much less a baby." Ella would've loved a pet—a cat. But she didn't have time to care for any living thing.

Keira was staring at her again, her bottom lip quivering.

Ella refused to feel one bit guilty. She was *not* going to be left holding the baby; she couldn't keep it. That had never been the plan. The baby had been conceived for Keira—and Dmitri—to parent. This was not her baby.

Lifting her hand from her belly, she said, "Then we're in agreement. I have no choice but to give your baby up for adoption."

"If you see no other way out."

Before she could reiterate that this was not her preference, that the baby was Keira and Dmitri's responsibility, to her horror Ella felt the warm, wet flood as her water broke.

Keira's baby girl was not going to wait another week to be born.

Night had already fallen by the time Yevgeny Volkovoy strode into the waiting room set aside for family visitors on the hospital's first floor. He didn't notice the calming decor in gentle blues and creams lit up by strategically placed wall sconces, or even the soft-focus photographs of Madonna-like mothers cradling babies that hung on the wall. Instead, his focus homed in on where his brother sprawled across an overstuffed chair while watching a wide-screen television.

Fixing startlingly light blue eyes on Dmitri, he demanded, "Where is he?"

"Who?" Dmitri swung a blank look up at him.

"The child."

"It's not a boy…it's a girl," his brother corrected him even as the soccer game on the television recaptured his attention. "I told you that after the ultrasound."

Yevgeny suppressed the surge of bitter disappointment. He'd been so sure that the ultrasound had been read wrong. He should've known! For almost a century his family had produced boys…there hadn't been a girl in sight. How typical of Ella McLeod to give birth to a girl. Contrary creature.

He waved a dismissive hand. "Whatever. I want to see her."

Retracing his steps out of the family room he emerged in time to see his sister-in-law appear through the next door down the carpeted corridor. Yevgeny strode forward. Nodding at his startled sister-in-law as he passed her, he entered the private ward beyond.

Keira's icicle sister was sitting up in the bed, propped up against large cushions.

Yevgeny came to an abrupt stop. He had never seen Ella McLeod in bed before.

The sight caused a shock of discomfort to course through him. Despite the fact that she barely reached his shoulder when she was on her feet, she'd always seemed so formidable. Stern. Businesslike. Unsmiling. Even at family occasions she dressed in a sharp, formal fashion. Dark colors—mostly black dresses with neck scarves in muted shades.

Now he allowed his gaze to drift over her and take in the other differences.

No scarf. No oversize glasses. No makeup. Some sort of ivory frilly lace spilled around the top of her breasts. She looked younger…paler…more fragile than he'd ever seen her.

The icicle must be thawing.

Yevgeny shook off the absurd notion.

As though sensing his presence, she glanced up from the screen of a slim white phone she'd been squinting at. Antagonism snaked down his spine as their eyes clashed.

"What are you doing here?" she demanded.

"Where is the baby?"

He'd expected to find the child in her arms.

He should've known better. There wasn't a maternal bone in Ella McLeod's frozen body. No softness. No tender feelings. Only sharp, legal-eagle eyes that she usually disguised with a pair of glasses—and from all accounts, a steel-trap brain. According to the rumor mill her law practice did very well. No doubt her success came from divorce dollars siphoned off men with avaricious ex-wives.

Ella hadn't answered. A haunted flicker in her eye captured his attention, but then the fleeting expression vanished and her focus shifted beyond him. Wheeling about, Yevgeny spotted the crib.

Two strides and he stood beside it. The baby lay inside, snugly swaddled and fast asleep. One tiny hand curled beside her cheek, the fingers perfectly formed. Her lashes were impossibly long, forming dark curves against plump cheeks. Yevgeny's heart contracted and an unexpected, fierce rush of emotion swept him.

It took only an instant for him to fall deeply, utterly irrevocably in love.

"She's perfect," he breathed, his gaze taking in every last detail. The thatch of dark hair—the Volkovoy genes. The red bow of her pursed mouth.

A smile tilted the corners of his mouth up.

Reaching out, he gently touched the curve where chin became cheek with his index finger.

"Don't wake her!"

The strident demand broke the mood. Turning his head, Yevgeny narrowed his gaze and pinned the woman in the bed.

"I had no intention of waking her," he said softly, careful not to disturb the infant.

"It's only a matter of time before she wakens with you hovering over her like that."

"I never hover." But he moved away from the cot—and closer to the bed.

Ella didn't respond. But he'd seen that look in her eyes before. She wasn't bothering to argue…not because she'd been swayed by his denial, but because she was so damn certain of the rightness of her own opinion.

The woman was a pain in the ass.

The polar opposite of her sister, she was the least motherly woman he'd ever encountered—with the single exception of his own mother.

Maybe it was as well she wasn't cradling the baby; she'd freeze the little bundle if she got close enough. Ella was ice to the core—he'd been mistaken to imagine a thaw.

"Dmitri called to tell me you're planning to give up the child for adoption?" No discussion. No consultation. She'd made a life-changing decision that affected all of them, by herself. It was typical of the woman's arrogant selfishness.

"Then you must've heard that your brother and my sister have decided not to adopt the baby."

Was that irony buried in her voice? He couldn't read her expression. "Yes—Dmitri told me at the office."

"At the same time that Keira was visiting me."

This time he definitely detected an edge. But he was less concerned about her annoyance than discovering the fate of the oblivious newborn in the cot. "So it's true? You intend to give up the baby just like that?"

Her chin shot up three notches at the snapping sound his fingers made. "I will take care of the arrangements to find a new set of parents as soon as I can." Ella glanced down at the phone in her lap, then back at Yevgeny. "I've already left a message for the social worker who's handling the adoption proceedings for Keira and Dmitri, notifying her of their change of mind and requesting that she get in touch with me ASAP."

"Of course you have." It certainly hadn't taken her long to start the process to get rid of the baby. Anger sizzled inside him. "You never considered keeping her?" Not that he'd ever allow the child to stay in her care.

She shook her head, and the hair shrouding her face shimmered like the moonlit wisps of cloud outside the window. "Not an option."

"Of course it isn't."

She stared back at him, managing to look haughty and removed in the hospital bed. So certain of the rightness of her stance. "Identifying suitable adoptive parents from Jo Wells's records is the only feasible option."

"'Feasible option?'" Was this how his own mother had reasoned when she'd divorced his father and lied her way into sole custody, only to turn around and abandon the same sons she'd fought so hard to keep from their father? "This is a baby we're talking about—you're not at work now."

"I'm well aware of that. And my main concern now is the best interests of the child—exactly as it would be if I was at work."

Yevgeny snorted. "You're a divorce lawyer—"

"A family lawyer," she corrected him. "Marriage dissolution is only a part of my practice. Looking after the best interests of the children and—"

"Whatever." He waved an impatient hand. "I'd hoped for a little less *business* and a little more emotion right now."

From the lofty position of the hospital bed she raised an eyebrow in a way that instantly rankled. "You don't transfer skills learned from business to your home life?"

"I show a little more compassion when I make decisions that relate to the well-being of my family."

She laughed—a disbelieving sound. Yevgeny gritted his teeth and refused to respond. Okay, so he had a reputation— well-deserved, he conceded silently—for being ruthless in business. But that was irrelevant in this context. He'd always been fiercely protective of those closest to him. His brother. His father. His *babushka*.

He studied Ella's face. The straight nose, the lack of amusement in her light brown eyes—despite her laughing mouth. No, he wasn't going to reach her—he doubted she had any warmth to which he could appeal.

Giving a sharp, impatient sigh, he said, "You've got blinkered vision. You haven't considered all the *feasible* options."

For the first time emotion cracked the ice. "I can't keep the baby!"

Two

Ella's desperation was followed by a strained silence during which Yevgeny looked down his perfectly straight nose at her. Something withered inside her but Ella held his gaze, refusing to reveal the fragile grief that lingered deep in her most secret heart.

But she wasn't going to keep the baby.

And she'd hold firm on that.

For her sanity.

Finally he shook his head. "That poor baby is very fortunate that you will not be her mother."

The contempt caused Ella to bristle. "I agreed to be a surrogate—not a mother."

"Right now you're the only mother that baby has—you're the legal mother."

God.

This was never supposed to have happened. She stuck her hands under the bedcovers and rested them on the unfamiliar flatness of her belly. After so many months of having a mound, it felt so odd. Empty.

And, with the baby no longer moving inside, so dead.

Why had she ever offered to donate her eggs—and lend her womb—to create the baby her sister had so desperately wanted?

The answer was simple. She loved her sister...she couldn't bear to see Keira suffer.

Ah, damn. The road to hell was paved with good intentions. Now look where it had landed her—in an entanglement that was anything but simple. Ella knew that if she wasn't careful, the situation had the potential to cause her more pain...more hurt... than any she'd ever experienced before. The only way through the turbulent situation was to keep her emotional distance from the baby—not to allow herself to form that miraculous mother-baby bond that was so tenuous, yet had the strength of steel.

But there was no need to offer any explanation to the insensitive brute who towered over the hospital bed.

Rubbing her hand over her strangely flat stomach, Ella pursed her lips. "I'm well aware that I'm her legal mother."

Mother. Just one word and her heart started to bump roughly. She couldn't keep the baby. *She couldn't.*

Carefully, deliberately she reiterated, "It was never the plan for me to remain her mother. This. Is. Not. My. Baby."

It felt better to spell it out so firmly.

The surrogate agreement had been signed, the adoption proceedings had been started. All that needed to happen to formalize the situation had been to get through the twelve-day cooling-off period the New Zealand adoption laws provided. Once that period had passed, and the mother was still sure she wanted to give up the baby, the adoption could go ahead. But Ella had never contemplated reneging on the promise she'd made to her sister. And she'd certainly never expected Keira to be the one to back out!

"She was created for your brother and my sister—to satisfy their desire for a family. By assisting with her conception and bringing her into the world I've kept my part of the agreement." Damn Keira and Dmitri. "In fact, I've gone way beyond what was expected of me."

His mouth slanted down. "That is your opinion."

"And I'm entitled to it." Ella drew a steadying breath, felt her stomach rise under her hands, then calmness spread through her as she slowly exhaled. "You shouldn't expect me to even consider keeping the baby. Keira and Dmitri changed their minds about becoming parents—not me." She'd had enough of being blamed for something that wasn't her fault. And she was furious with Keira, and Dmitri, for landing her in this predicament—probably because the man standing beside the bed had caused it with his initial resistance to the baby in the first place.

But before she could confront him with his responsibility for this mess, he was speaking again, in that staccato rattle that hurt her head. "Stop making excuses. It tells me a lot about the kind of person you are—that even in these circumstances you can abandon the baby you've carried for nine months...the baby you've just given birth to."

What was the man's problem? Hadn't he listened to one word of what she'd been saying? She drew a shuddering breath. "Let's get this straight. Regardless of the position in law, this is Keira's baby, not mine." Where was her sister? She'd landed Ella in this mess, now Keira had disappeared. She'd been here a few minutes ago, but now Ella couldn't even hear her voice in the family room next door. The loneliness that seared her was as unexpected as it was alien. For once in her life, she could do with her younger sister's moral support. But of course, that was too much to expect. "I *never* intended to have children."

"Never?"

"That's right. Never." Under the bedcovers she clenched her hands into fists.

He shook his head and this time the look he gave her caused Ella to see red.

"And what about your precious brother?" It burst from her. "What about his part in this? He's the baby's biological father. Why don't you harangue him about his responsibilities? Why pick on me?"

For the first time, his glance slid away. "This has nothing to do with my brother."

Her anger soared at the double standard. "Of course not. He's male. He gets to donate his seed and walk away scot-free from all responsibility. It's the woman who carries the baby—and the blame, right?"

Yevgeny shot her a strangely savage look. "I'm not discussing this any further. I will absolve you from all blame and responsibility—*I* will adopt the baby."

"She will become my responsibility," continued Yevgeny, rather enjoying seeing cool, icy Ella looking uncharacteristically shaken. "And *I* do take care of my responsibilities."

Her mouth opened and closed, but no sound came out. Yevgeny's pleasure grew. How satisfying to discover that the always eloquent Icicle Ella, like other mere mortals, could suffer from loss of words.

"You...you live in a penthouse. Y...you're not married..." she finally stuttered out. "A baby ought to be adopted by a couple who will care for it."

It was a great pity she couldn't have remained speechless for a while longer.

"I can buy a house." Yevgeny was determined to ignore the jab about a wife. "And the baby is not an it," he rebuked gently.

Her brown eyes were wide, dazed. "What?"

"You said the baby should go to a couple who love *it*—she's not an it."

"Oh." A flush crept along her cheeks. "Of course she isn't. I'm sorry."

It was the first time he'd ever heard Ella McLeod apologize...and admit she was in the wrong. Yevgeny refused to acknowledge even to himself that he was secretly impressed. Or that it made him feel a little bit guilty about enjoying her confusion.

He studied her. To be truthful her eyes were luminous. Gold-brown with a hint of smoke. Like smoky honey. And the flush gave her pale cheeks a peachy warmth he'd never noticed before. She looked almost pretty—in an ethereal, fragile way that did not normally appeal to him.

In the spirit of reconciliation he felt compelled to add, "And I will care for her."

"A procession of big-bosomed careworkers is not what I had in mind."

Reconciliation was clearly not what Ella had in mind. He suppressed a knowing smirk at how quickly the fragile act had lasted and gave in to the urge to provoke her. "You have something against motherly, homely women?"

The look she gave him would've frozen the devil at fifty feet. "I wouldn't describe a Playboy centerfold model as homely."

This time he allowed himself to smile—but without humor. "I will need some help with the baby…but you may rest assured the criteria for hiring her caregivers will not be physical attributes. I will make sure that the women I employ will be capable of providing her—" he glanced at the baby and realized he didn't yet know her name "—with all the womanly affection the infant will require."

"You will need a wife."

Yevgeny forced a roar of laughter as Ella repeated the ridiculous suggestion. "The child will have far more than a young, struggling couple could ever give her—I don't need a wife to provide it."

"I'm not joking." Ella pressed her lips together. "And I'm not talking about the possessions you can give her—I'm sure you could provide a diamond-encrusted teething ring. But she deserves to have two parents who love her unreservedly."

His laughter ceased. "You're living in a dream if you think that happens simply because a child has two parents." His own mother was living proof of that. To ease the turmoil that memories of his mother always brought, Yevgeny stretched lazily, flexing his shoulders. He noticed how Ella looked away. "She will have to make do with me alone."

That brought her eyes back to him. "Forget it. It's not going to happen—I won't let it."

"It's not only your decision. Fathers have rights, too." He lifted his lips in a feral, not-very-amused grin. "I'm stepping into my brother's shoes."

"As you pointed out, I'm the mother. The legal birth mother." Did she think he'd missed her point? Yevgeny wondered. "I get to make the decisions," she was saying now. "I need only to consider the best interests of the child."

The look on her face made it clear that his solution was not what she considered in "the best interests of the child."

He froze as he absorbed what she was getting at. "How can that be true? This is the twenty-first century!"

"Quite correct. And a child is no longer a chattel of the head of the household."

The eyes he'd been admiring only minutes earlier gleamed in a way that caused his hackles to rise.

"So I have the final say in who will adopt the baby," she continued, "and it won't be an arrogant, unmarried Russian millionaire!"

"Billionaire," he corrected pointedly and watched her smolder even as his own anger bubbled.

"The amount of money you have doesn't change a darn thing. She's going to a couple—a family who wants her, who will love her. That's what I intended when I agreed to be a surrogate for Keira, and that's what I still want for her— I'll make sure the adoption agency is aware of that requirement. You're not married—and you're not getting the baby. End of story."

Her bright eyes glittered back at him with the frosty glare of newly minted gold.

A challenge had been issued. And he fully intended to meet it.

Ruthlessly suppressing his own hot rage, he murmured, "Well, then, it seems I'll just have to get married."

Yevgeny watched with supreme satisfaction as Ella's mouth dropped open.

War, Yevgeny suspected, had been declared.

* * *

Ella did a double take. "You? Get married? So that you can adopt a child?"

She hadn't thought Big Brother Yevgeny could surprise her. She'd thought she had his number. Russian. Raffish. Ruthless. But this announcement left her reeling. What would this playboy Russian billionaire want with a child, a *girl* child at that?

Which led her to say, "But you don't even want a girl."

Something—it couldn't be surprise—sparked in the depths of those light eyes. "What made you think that?"

"I heard you…" Ella thought back to that moment of tension when she'd heard his voice in the family room next door.

"When?"

"As you came in." She searched to remember exactly what he'd said. Slowly she said, "You asked where the *boy* was. You never even considered that the baby might be a girl."

"Aah." He smiled, a feral baring of teeth. "So *obviously* that meant I wouldn't welcome a girl, hmm?"

Sensing mockery, Ella frowned. "Why would you want a child? Any child?" Wasn't that going a little far—even for Yevgeny—to get his own way?

Yevgeny shrugged. "Perhaps it is time," he said simply.

"For a trophy toddler?"

"No, not a trophy."

"Not like your girlfriends?"

That dangerous smile widened, but his eyes crinkled with what appeared to be real amusement. "You yearn to be one of my trophies?" he asked softly—twisting her insides into pretzels.

An image of his latest woman leaped into Ella's mind. Nadiya. One of a breed of supermodels identified by their first names alone. Ella didn't need a surname to conjure up Nadiya's lean body and perfect face that were regularly featured in the double-page spreads of glossy fashion magazines. Barely twenty, Nadiya was already raking in millions as a face for a French perfume, which she wore in copious amounts that wafted about her in soft clouds. Six foot tall. Brunette. Beautiful. With slanting, catlike green eyes, which devoured Yevgeny as though he were a bowl of cream. Enormously desired by every red-blooded man on earth. A trophy any man would be proud to show off. So why should Ella imagine Yevgeny would be any different?

"That's a stupid question," she said dismissively.

"Is it?"

"Of course, I don't want to be any man's trophy." Ella was not about to be dragged into the teasing games he played. She gave him a cool look—mirroring the one she'd caught him giving her earlier—and let her eyes travel all the way down the length of his body before lifting them dismissively back to his face. "Anyway, you're not the kind of man I would ever date."

He was laughing openly now. "That's not an insult. From my observation, there is *no* kind of man you date."

The very idea that he'd been watching her, noting her lack of romantic attachments, caused a frisson to run along her spine. She refused to examine her unease further, and focused back on the bombshell he'd delivered. "You can't adopt this baby."

He came another step closer to the bed. "Why not?"

"I've already told you. You're not married."

"That's old-fashioned." He leaned over her. "Ella, I never expected such traditionalism from you."

His closeness was claustrophobic. He was so damn big. "Everyone knows you're a workaholic—you're never home." Yevgeny had less time for a kitten than she did.

At that, he thrust out his roughly stubbled chin. "I'll make time."

Right.

Somewhere between his twenty-hour workday and his even more hectic X-rated nightlife? The man obviously never slept—he didn't even take time to shave. His life was littered with women—even before his latest affair with Nadiya, she'd seen the pictures in the tabloids. Keira and Dmitri remained fiercely loyal and insisted the news was all exaggerated but Ella ignored their protests. They'd been brainwashed by the man himself. Ella knew his type—she'd seen it before. Powerful men who treated women like playthings. Men who kept their women at home, manacled by domesticity and diamonds, before stripping them of everything—including their self-respect—when the next fancy caught their eye.

"Sure you will."

"Damn right I'll take care of her."

As if the baby felt his insistence, she made a mewing noise and stirred. The pretzel knot in Ella's stomach tightened, yet thankfully the baby didn't wake. But at least it got rid of Yevgeny—he'd shot across to the cot and was staring down into the depths.

Ella breathed a little easier.

"Money doesn't equal care." She flung the words at the back of his dark head.

At her comment, his dark head turned. Ella resisted the urge to squirm under those unfathomable eyes.

"What's her name?"

"She doesn't have one." Ella had no intention of picking out a name—that would be a fast track to hell. Attachment to the baby was a dark and lonely place she had no wish to visit.

"Keira didn't choose one?"

"Not a final name."

It had puzzled Ella, too. Keira had spent weeks pouring over books, searching websites for inspiration. But she'd never even drawn up a short list. Now Ella knew why: Keira had been dithering about motherhood. Choosing a name would've been a tie to bind her to the baby.

To rid herself of that critical, disturbing gaze, Ella said, "I can ask Keira if there's one she particularly liked."

Yevgeny's gaze didn't relent. "You were supposed to be the baby's godmother, yet you have no idea of the names your sister might have been considering?"

She was not about to air her theory about why Keira hadn't picked a name in order to jump to her own defense. She simply stared back at him wordlessly and wished that he would take his big intimidating body, his hostile pale blue eyes and leave.

"Why don't you ask Dmitri what they planned to name the baby?" Let him go bully his brother. Ella had had enough. "Anyway, the baby's new parents will probably want to pick one out. Now, if you don't mind, it's been a long day. I'm tired, I need to rest."

The baby chose that moment to wake up.

At the low, growling cry, Yevgeny scooped her up in his arms and came toward the bed.

No. Panic overtook Ella. "Call the nurse!"

"What?"

"The baby will be hungry. Call the nurse to bring a bottle—they will feed her."

He halted. "The *nurses* will feed her? From a bottle?"

Ella swallowed. "Yes."

Disbelief glittered for an instant in his eyes, then they iced over with dislike. He thrust the waking baby at her. "Well, you can damn well hold her while I go and summon a nurse to do the job that should be yours."

"She's not my baby…" Ella's voice trailed away as he stalked out of the private ward leaving her with the infant in her arms.

Three

The baby let out a wail.

Ella stared down at the crumpled face of the tiny human in her arms and tried not to ache.

How dare Keira—and Dmitri—do this to her?

She'd barely gotten her emotions back under control when, a minute later, Yevgeny swept back into the ward with the force of an unleashed hurricane. Ella almost wilted in the face of all that turbulent energy. In his wake trailed two nurses, both wearing bemused, besotted expressions.

Did he have this effect on every woman he encountered?

No wonder the man was spoiled stupid.

At the sight of the baby in her arms, the nurses exchanged glances. Ella looked from one to the other. The baby wailed more loudly.

"Feed her," Yevgeny barked out.

Instead of rebuking him for his impatience, the shorter nurse, whom Ella recognized from the first feed after the baby's birth, scurried across to scoop the baby out of her arms, while the other turned to the unit in the corner of the room and started to prepare a bottle in a more leisurely fashion. Freed from the warm weight of the baby, Ella let out a sigh of silent relief... and closed her eyes.

They would take the baby to the nursery and feed her there. Ella knew the drill. All she needed to do was get rid of Yevgeny, then she could relax...even sleep...and build up the mental reserves she would need for when the baby returned.

"Do you want the bed back raised higher?"

That harsh staccato voice caused her eyelashes to lift. "If you'll excuse me, I plan to rest."

"No time for rest now." He gestured to the nurse holding the bundle. "You have a baby to feed."

Ella's throat tightened with dread.

"No!" Ella stuck her hands beneath the covers. She was not holding the baby again, not feeling the warm, unexpected heaviness of that little human against her heart. "I am not nursing her. She will be bottle-fed. The staff is aware of the arrangement—we've discussed it."

The nurse holding the baby was already heading for the door. "That's right, sir, we know Ms. McLeod's wishes." The other nurse followed, leaving Ella alone in the ward with the man she least wanted to spend time with.

Yevgeny opened his mouth to deliver a blistering lecture about selfish, self-centered mothers but the sound of light footsteps gave him pause. Ella's gaze switched past him to the doorway of the ward.

"Can I come in?"

The tentative voice of his sister-in-law from behind him had an astonishing effect on the woman in the bed. The tight, masklike face softened. Then her face lit up into a sweet smile—the kind of smile she'd never directed at him.

"Keira, of course you may." Ella patted the bedcover. "Come sit over here."

Yevgeny still harbored resentment toward his brother for the shocking about-face on the baby—not that he'd ever admit that

to Ella—and he found it confounding to witness her warmth
to her sister. He'd expected icy sulks—or at the very least,
reproach. Not the concern and fondness that turned her brown
eyes to burnished gold.

So Ella was capable of love and devotion—just not toward
her baby.

Something hot and hurtful twisted deep inside him, tearing
open scars on wounds he'd considered long forgotten.

To hide his reaction, he walked to the bed stand where
a water pitcher sat on a tray. Taking a moment to compose
himself, he poured a glass of water then turned back to the bed.

"Would you like some water? You must be thirsty."

Surprise lit up Ella's face.

But before she could respond, a vibrating hum sounded.

"That will be Jo Wells. I left an urgent message for her
earlier." Ella's hands dived beneath the covers and retrieved
her phone.

In the midst of perching herself on the edge of the bed, Keira
went still.

And Yevgeny discovered that he'd tensed, too. Given Ella's
reluctance to keep the child, she should've been grateful for his
offer to take the baby. She could wash her hands of the infant.
He'd never contemplated for a second that Ella would actually
turn him down.

Her insistence on getting in touch with the social worker
showed how determined she was to see through her plan to
adopt the baby out. Evidently she wanted to make sure it was
airtight.

The glass thudded on the bed stand as he set it down, the
water threatening to spill over the lip. Yevgeny didn't notice.
He was watching Ella's brow crease as she stared at the caller
ID display.

"No, it's not Jo—it's my assistant," she said.

The call didn't last long. He glanced at his watch—7:00 p.m.
on a Friday night. She'd be charging overtime rates. Ella's tone

had become clipped, her responses revealing little. Another poor bastard was about to be taken to the cleaners.

Ella was already ending the call. "If you wouldn't mind setting up an appointment for early next week I'd appreciate that," she murmured into the sleek, white phone. "Just confirm the time with me first, please."

That caught his attention.

As soon as she'd killed the call, he echoed, "Early next week? You're not intending to go back to work that soon. Have you already forgotten that you have a newborn that needs attention?"

"Hardly." Her teeth snapped together. "But I have a practice to run."

"And a newborn baby to take care of."

"The baby wasn't supposed to arrive for another week!" Ella objected.

Keira laughed. "You can't really have expected a baby to conform to your schedule, Ella. Although, if you think about it, the baby did arrive on a Friday evening. Maybe you do already have her trained."

Ella slanted her sister a killing look.

It sank in that Ella *had* expected the baby to conform. Clearly, she rigorously ran her life by her calendar. Why shouldn't a baby comply, too? Yevgeny started to understand why Ella could be so insistent that she'd never have a baby.

Her selfishness wouldn't allow for it.

The woman never dated. She didn't even appear to have a social life—apart from her sister. Keeping the baby would mean disruption in her life by another person. Ella was not about to allow that. Everything he knew about her added up to one conclusion: Ella was the most self-centered woman he'd ever met.

Except there was one thing wrong with that picture...

Keira must have begged to get her sister to agree to be a surrogate in the first place. Ella carrying the baby for nine months was the one thing that went against the picture he'd built in his mind. Allowing her body to be taken over by a baby she had no interest in was a huge commitment.

But Yevgeny knew even that could be explained—Ella was a lawyer. She knew every pitfall. And she was such a control freak she wouldn't have wanted to risk some other surrogate changing her mind once the baby was born. This way she could make sure that Keira got the baby she and his brother had planned.

Ella was speaking again. He put aside the puzzle of Ella's motivations and concentrated on what she was saying. "Well, that's when I planned my maternity leave to begin," she was informing Keira. "Another week and everything in the office would've been totally wrapped up—I planned it that way."

"Oh, Ella!" The mirth had faded from his sister-in-law's face. "Sometimes I worry about you. You need the trip to Africa more than Dmitri and I. In fact, you should visit India, take up meditation."

"Don't be silly! I'm perfectly happy with my life."

It appeared Ella was not as calm and composed as he'd thought. The brief flare of irritation revealed she was human, after all.

From his position beside the bed stand, Yevgeny switched his attention to the younger McLeod sister. Keira was biting her lip.

"You were going to ask Keira about names." Yevgeny spoke into the silence that had settled over the ward following Ella's curt response.

"Names?" Ella's poise slipped further. "Oh, yes."

Yevgeny waited.

Keira twisted her head and glanced at him, a question in her eyes. "What names are you talking about?"

His brows jerked together. "The names you've been considering for the baby." His sister-in-law shouldn't need a prompt. The baby was so firmly in the forefront of his mind, how could it not be the same for her…and for Ella? What was wrong with these McLeod women?

"I hadn't chosen one yet."

"That's what I told him," Ella added quickly, protectively, her hand closing over her sister's where it rested on the edge of the bed. "Keira, you don't need to think about it if it upsets you...."

Relief flooded Keira's face as she turned away from him and said, "Ella, you're the best. I knew you would take care of everything."

Those words set his teeth on edge.

Shifting away from the sisters, Yevgeny crossed the room. Foreboding filled him.

Keira's confidence in her sister didn't reassure Yevgeny one bit. Because it was clear to him that Ella couldn't wait to get rid of the baby.

And that was the last thing he wanted.

Despite all the drama of the day, Ella surprised herself by managing to get several hours sleep that night.

Yet she still woke before the first fingers of daylight appeared through the crack in the curtains. For a long while she lay staring into space, thinking about what needed to happen. Finally, as dawn arrived, filling the ward with a gentle wash of December sun, she switched on the over-bed light and reached into the drawer of the bed stand for the legal pad she'd stowed there yesterday.

By the time the day nurse bustled in to remind her that the baby would be brought in from the nursery in fifteen minutes for the appointment with the pediatrician, Ella had already scribbled pages of notes. After a quick shower, she put on a dab of makeup and dressed in a pair of gray trousers and a white T-shirt. Then she settled into one of the pair of padded visitor chairs near the window to await the doctor's arrival.

The baby was wheeled in at the same time that the pediatrician scurried into the room, which—to Ella's great relief—meant that she wasn't left alone with the wide-awake infant. The doctor took charge and proceeded to do a thorough examination before pronouncing the baby healthy.

Tension that Ella hadn't even known existed seeped away with the doctor's words. The baby was healthy. For the first time she acknowledged how much she'd been dreading that something might be wrong. Of course, a well baby would benefit by having many more potential sets of adoptive parents wanting to love and cherish her.

After the pediatrician departed, the nurse took the baby back to the nursery, and Ella's breakfast arrived in time to stem the blossoming regret. Fruit, juice and oatmeal along with coffee much more aromatic than any hospital was reputed to produce.

Ella had just finished enjoying a second cup when Jo Wells entered her room. Ella had been pleased when she'd discovered that Jo had been assigned to processing the baby's adoption to Keira and Dmitri. Of course, that had all changed. Now she was even more relieved to have Jo's help.

Slight with short, dark hair, the social worker had a firm manner that concealed a heart of gold. Ella had worked with Jo a few times in the past. Once in a legal case where a couple wanted to adopt their teen daughter's baby, and more recently in a tough custody battle where the father had threatened to breach a custody order and kidnap his children to take them back to his home country.

"How are you doing?"

The understanding in Jo's kind eyes caused Ella's throat to tighten. She waved Jo to the other visitor seat, reached for the yellow legal pad on the bed stand and gave the social worker a wry smile. "As well as can be expected in the circumstances— This is not the outcome I'd planned."

Jo nodded with a degree of empathy that almost shredded the tight control Ella had been exercising since Keira had dropped her bombshell—was it only yesterday?

"I want the best for the baby, Jo."

Focusing on what the baby needed helped stem the tears that threatened to spill. Ella tore the top three pages off the pad and offered them to the social worker.

"I knew you'd ask. So I've already listed the qualities I'd like to see in the couple who adopts her. It would be wonderful if the family has an older daughter—perhaps two years older."

That way the baby would have a bond like the one Ella shared with Keira, but the age difference would be smaller. Hopefully the sisters would grow up to be even closer than she and Keira were. "If possible, I'd like for her to be the younger sister—like Keira is. But above all, I'd like her to go to a family who will love her…care for her…give her everything that I can't."

Another nod. Yet instead of reading the long wish list that had taken Ella so much soul-searching in the dark hours this morning to compile, Jo pulled the second chair up. Propping the manila folder she'd brought with her against a bent knee, she spread the handwritten pages Ella had given her on top.

Then Jo looked up. "I spoke to Keira before coming here. She and Dmitri haven't had second thoughts."

Ella had known that. From the moment Keira had told her of their decision yesterday, she'd known Keira was not going to change her mind. But deep down she must have harbored a last hope because her breath escaped in a slow, audible hiss.

"Is there anyone else in the family who would consider adopting the baby?" Jo asked.

"My parents have just reached their seventies." Ella had been born to a mother already in her forties and Keira had followed five years later. "They've just moved into a retirement village. There's no chance that they're in a position to care for a newborn."

Even if they'd wanted to adopt the child, she wouldn't allow it. Her parents had already been past parenting when she and Keira had reached their teens. She was not letting this baby experience the kind of distant, disengaged upbringing they'd experienced.

"And we have no other close family," she tacked on.

"What about the biological father's family?"

An image of Yevgeny hovering over the bed last night like some angel of vengeance flashed into Ella's mind. His pale, wolflike eyes filled with determination. His expression downright dangerous as she resisted what he wanted.

She dismissed the image immediately and said, "There's no

one to my knowledge—his parents are dead." A pang of guilt seared her. Reluctantly she found herself correcting herself. "He does have an older brother. Yevgeny. But he's far from suitable."

Jo tilted her head to one side. "In what way is Yevgeny not suitable?"

"He's single—for one thing. The adoption laws don't allow single men to adopt female babies." Ella didn't mention Yevgeny's rash vow to marry to flout her plans.

"Except in exceptional circumstances…" Jo's voice trailed away as she bent her head and made a note on the cover of the manila file resting in her lap. "The court may consider his relationship to the baby sufficient."

"It's unlikely." Ella didn't want Jo even considering Yevgeny as a candidate—or learning that he intended to get married for the baby's sake.

But Jo wasn't ready to be deflected. "Hmm. We could certainly consider interviewing him."

Jo would discover that Yevgeny was determined to adopt the baby.

Ella's heart started to knock against her ribs. *No.* This wasn't what she wanted for the baby. Even if he did marry, Yevgeny would farm the baby out to a series of stunning Russian nannies and continue with his high-flying, jet-set lifestyle. Growing up with Yevgeny would be a far worse experience than the distracted neglect she and Keira had suffered.

"He's a playboy—he has a different woman every week."

That assessment was probably a little harsh, Ella conceded silently. He'd been linked to Nadiya for several months and before that he'd been single for a while—according to Keira. Although that hadn't stopped him from dating a string of high-profile women.

"And he's a workaholic," she added for good measure just in case Jo was still considering Yevgeny. Then she played her trump card. "He certainly won't provide the kind of stable home that I always intended for the child. I don't want the baby going to him."

"Being the legal mother, your wishes will take precedence." Jo tapped her pen against her knee. "This is still going to be an open adoption, right?"

An open adoption meant keeping in touch with the new adoptive parents, watching the baby grow up, being part of her life, yet not a parent.

Ella swallowed.

This was the hard part.

"Ella?" Concern darkened Jo's eyes as she failed to respond. "Research has shown open adoptions are far more beneficial because—"

"They give the child a sense of history and belonging, and help prevent the child having identity crises as a teen and in later life," Ella finished. She knew all the benefits. She'd had a long time to ponder over all the arguments. "We'd planned an open adoption with Keira and Dmitri. The baby would always know I was her tummy mummy—" now the affectionate term for a surrogate rang false in her ears "—her birth mother...even though Keira would be her real mother."

"So it will still be an open adoption?"

Ella nodded slowly. "It's in the baby's best interests."

But dear God, it was going to kill her.

Ella was relieved that Jo hadn't asked whether she would consider keeping the baby. She'd already emphatically told both Keira and Yevgeny she couldn't do it. A third denial would've been more than she could handle at this stage.

Jo's head was bent, eyes scanning the wish list Ella had given her.

Finally she looked up. "I have several sets of IPs—intending parents—" Jo elaborated, "who might fit your requirements. I'll pull their profiles out and bring them back for you to look through."

"Thank you." Gratitude flooded Ella. "You have no idea how much of a help it is knowing you are here for support."

"It's my job." But Jo's warm eyes belied the words. "When will you be going home?"

"Probably tomorrow."

"And the baby?"

"The baby will go to a foster carer." Ella was determined not to allow any opportunity for a maternal bond to form.

"I know you probably don't want to hear this, but you should reconsider your decision not to have counseling after you sign the final consent to give the baby up." Without looking at her, Jo shuffled the wish list into the manila file. Getting to her feet she pushed the visitor chair back against the wall before turning to face Ella. "I know you said previously that you didn't feel you'd need counseling because she was never intended to be your baby—that it was your gift to Keira and Dmitri. But given that circumstances have changed, I think it would be a serious mistake. You'll be experiencing a lot of emotions, which you never expected."

Ella resisted the urge to close her eyes and shut out the world. Signing the consent could only be done on the twelfth day. She didn't want to even think about the approaching emotional maelstrom.

So she gave Jo a small smile. "I'll think about it," she conceded. "But I don't think it will be necessary. I'm tougher than I look."

Before Jo could reply, footsteps echoed outside the ward.

A moment later, Yevgeny appeared in the doorway.

Ella's heart sank.

"This is Dmitri's brother, Yevgeny." She made the introduction reluctantly, and hoped that Jo would depart quickly.

To her dismay Jo and Yevgeny took their time sizing each other up. Only once they'd taken each other's measure, shaken hands and exchanged business cards, did Jo finally walk to the door. Ella let out the breath she'd been holding. Neither had even mentioned the baby's adoption.

Disaster averted.

For now.

"We'll talk again," the social worker said from her position in the doorway, giving Ella a loaded look over her shoulder. "I'll be back."

* * *

This morning Yevgeny was wearing a dark gray suit that fitted beautifully.

Towering over the chair she sat on, with the light behind him, Ella could see that his dark hair was still a touch damp—evidence of a recent shower, perhaps.

It was only as he tilted his head to look down at her that she noticed the stubble shadowing his jawline. A dazzling white shirt with the top button undone stood in stark contrast to his dark face.

Ella was suddenly desperately glad that she was not in bed.

Yesterday she'd felt at a terrible disadvantage as he'd towered over her while she'd been clad in a nightdress. She'd felt exposed...vulnerable. Even now, seated, his height was intimidating. But at least she could rectify that...

She rose to her feet. "The baby is in the nursery."

"I know—I have already been to visit her."

Annoyance flared. She had not been consulted. "They let you in?"

The staff would have to be told he was not welcome in the future—she wouldn't put it past him to try and take the baby. This was a man accustomed to getting his own way. But not this time.

Some indefinable emotion glimmered deep in the deceptively clear depths of his eyes. "Keira and Dmitri were with me—they vouched for me."

"Keira's here?"

Had her sister had second thoughts since Jo had spoken to her?

Yevgeny was shaking his head. "They've gone. Dmitri has quite a bit to finalize before I can release him to fly across the world."

All Ella could think of was that Keira hadn't even bothered to come past and say good morning. Hurt stabbed her. Then she set it aside. No doubt Keira was avoiding her because deep down her sister must be experiencing some guilt for the decision she and Dmitri had made.

Ella decided she wasn't going to let herself dwell on the turmoil that Keira's choice had created.

It was done.

Now there was the baby to think about....

But Yevgeny's response caused her to realize that she hadn't even asked her sister when they planned to leave for Africa. She'd been too busy trying to cope with the magnitude of the shock. Keira had said she and Dmitri had already booked the tickets but that's all she knew.

"Do you have any idea when they plan to leave?" It rankled to have to depend on Yevgeny for information but she needed to know.

"I believe they leave the day after tomorrow."

"That soon?"

Ella was still absorbing this new upset when he asked, "What will you be thinking about?"

"Pardon?" For a moment Ella thought Yevgeny had picked up on her earlier hurt at Keira's failure to come say good morning and was asking about her thoughts.

"You told the social worker you'd think about it." Yevgeny had moved up beside her, causing the space in the ward to shrink. "What will you be thinking about?"

Ella frowned as she realized he'd overheard the last part of her discussion with Jo. She had no intention of revealing that Jo thought she needed counseling. The good thing was at least he hadn't detected her hurt over Keira. "It's nothing important," she said dismissively. "It wasn't about the baby."

"Did you tell her I am going to adopt the baby?"

"But you're not." Inside, her stomach started to twist into a pretzel. Ella pursed her lips. "I told her you weren't suitable."

"You did not!"

"Yes, I did."

His gaze blitzed into her. "Because I'm single?"

Ella didn't glance away from his hard stare. "Among other things."

"But once I'm married that will change," he said softly and came another step closer. "You know that."

Ella blinked. And found herself inhaling the warm scent of freshly showered male. This close she could see the crisp whiteness of his ironed shirt.

What was he up to now?

"You should've seen her." His voice took on a husky, intimate tone. "She's so beautiful—"

Ella recoiled. "I don't care what your wife-to-be looks like!"

At her interruption, he looked puzzled, then he smiled. A smile filled with a burst of charm and humor that Ella hadn't wanted to recognize in Yevgeny Volkovoy. It made him all too human. And irresistibly appealing. This wouldn't do at all. She wanted—no, needed—to keep thinking of him as Keira's overbearing, bullying brother-in-law.

"No, not my wife-to-be. The baby." He chuckled. "She was awake…waving her hands and watching them. Smart *and* beautiful. You've seen her this morning."

It was a statement—rather than a question.

Ella squirmed, reluctant to admit that she'd barely glanced at the baby while she was in the ward during the pediatrician's consultation. Then she told herself she had no reason to feel guilty. Keira and Dmitri's actions were not her fault.

Rather than answering his question, she changed the subject. "So you're going through with it? You're really going to get married?"

He nodded. "I want that baby."

God, the man was stubborn. Didn't he ever accept no for an answer? Time for him to learn he couldn't always get what he wanted in life. Sometimes someone else's needs came first.

This time, the baby's best interests were paramount. Not his.

Letting out the breath she'd been unconsciously holding since that first whiff of his male essence, Ella said, "Well, you need to know that you're sacrificing yourself for nothing. I'm not going to change my mind. And it's still my decision. As the legal mother, I get to choose the parents the baby will go to."

He went deadly still. "You will choose me—and my wife."

Was that a threat?

Ella carefully assessed his motionless body, the face with the high Slavic cheekbones, skin stretched taut across them. Yevgeny needed to know she wasn't going to let him bully her.

"Unlikely. This morning I gave Jo a list of the qualities I'm seeking in the prospective parents. Nothing you can offer meets the criteria. She's going to bring me portfolios of prospective parents to look at—and I'll choose a couple from there."

The tension in the air became electric. "When?"

"Shouldn't you be at work doing whatever it is that high-powered billionaires do?" Ella knew she was being deliberately provocative, but she'd never expected him to be this concerned about the baby.

"When?" he repeated, his face tight.

He wasn't going to relent, she realized. "As soon as I'm back home—tomorrow probably."

"And then what happens?"

"The couples have already been interviewed and screened. Police checks have been done. Once I choose a couple and the consent is signed, then the paperwork for the adoption can be filled in and submitted."

"The consent?"

"Yes." Ella explained further, "The legal mother can only sign the consent—that's the formal document where she agrees to give up the baby—on the twelfth day. And yesterday, the day the baby was born, counts as the first day."

From where she stood Ella could sense the intensity of his gaze. He wasn't smiling anymore. He was watching her, his head tipped slightly to one side, his brain working overtime. Yevgeny was busy hatching a fiendish plot. She was certain of it.

There was something curiously exhilarating about being the focus of all that raw, brilliant energy. He might come in a devastatingly well-groomed, freshly scented and well-built male package, but it was his mind that Ella found fascinating. That ability to concentrate with such single-minded intensity. The ability to conjure up solutions no one had come up with before.

She could kind of understand why women might be attracted to that....

"So you can change your mind anytime up until that twelfth day?" he asked.

Ella blinked—and wrenched herself away from her fancies. "In theory. But I wouldn't do it. It wouldn't be very fair to do that to a couple once I've told them they've been chosen."

Determination fired in his eyes. "This baby will be mine—I will do everything in my power to make sure that happens."

Despite the morning sunshine spilling through the windows of the ward, Ella shivered.

It was evening.

The sun was setting beyond the distinctive silhouette of the Auckland Bridge transforming the Waitemata Harbour to liquid gold. Turning his head away from the magnificent view, Yevgeny dropped down onto the king-size bed in Nadiya's hotel suite and gazed contemplatively across at the woman standing in front of the dresser, the woman he planned shortly to reduce to screaming satisfaction.

Yet instead of dwelling on the pleasures of seduction, his mind was already elsewhere.

It was the end of day two. He had only ten days left. Yevgeny knew he needed to act—and fast.

He had to get engaged—and he needed to convince Ella to change her mind about his suitability to be a father.

That was going to take some doing.

It was enough to make him grind his teeth with frustration. Yet he was a long way from conceding defeat. He'd never been the kind of man to back away from a challenge—and this was the most important challenge of his life.

Now or never.

Taking a deep breath, he gave Nadiya his most practiced

smile and patted the bedcover beside him. "Come make yourself comfortable."

Nadiya glided across the room. Kicking off her high heels, she settled herself on the bed beside him. Long fingertips reached for the buttons of her silk shirtdress, and she gave him a pout.

"How do you feel about children?"

"Children?"

Nadiya's eyes widened, and her fingers stilled in the act of undressing. Her lips, still plump with gloss, parted. Yevgeny could identify with her shock. *He* was shocked. This was a discussion he had never before conducted with a woman. It was breaking new ground. But not only had he always desired Nadiya, he'd always liked her, too—even though, for the first time, he struggled to focus on their approaching lovemaking.

She hesitated, and then said, "I've always wanted children."

This was good.

Coming up on his elbow, he propped his hand under his head. "I am pleased to hear that."

From across the pale pink satin comforter, with her long legs folded beneath her, she watched him through those catlike eyes. "So you want children?"

What choice did he have? There was a child…and he couldn't walk away from her. But he wasn't ready to reveal more. So he gave Nadiya the same answer he'd given Ella. "The time has come."

She said, "I do have contractual obligations."

This wasn't what he needed to hear. Talk of contracts reminded him too much of…Ella.

He rolled away and lay back. She, too, was proving to be like the woman he tried never to think about. Keeping his voice level, he said, "You don't have time for children."

"No, no. I'm not saying that!" Nadiya edged closer and placed her hand over his. "But I never expected you to offer—"

She broke off.

Sensing opportunity, he turned his head. "You never expected me to offer...what?"

"What *are* you offering, Yevgeny? You haven't actually said."

This was another thing he liked about Nadiya—she was direct. He chuckled softly, secure that he was about to get what he wanted. The sensation that shot through him was familiar; the dart of adrenaline that signified the successful conclusion of a deal. "I'm offering a diamond ring to the mother of my child."

"Marriage?"

He nodded. For one uncertain instant he considered telling her about the baby girl he planned to adopt...but before he could speak, Nadiya let out a breathy little gasp and started to bounce on the bed. "Yes! Yes! Yes!"

A wave of euphoria swept him. The first step of his plan had been accomplished. Ella McLeod would stand no chance....

But why was he thinking about *her* when he should be focused on Nadiya? Tightening his fingers around his fiancée's, he prompted, "And what about your contract?"

"We will work something out—I do want a baby."

Yevgeny studied her from under hooded eyelids. It might be a good idea to wait...to see how she reacted to the baby before he showed his hand entirely. The brief moment of uncertainty passed. Nadiya was beautiful, no doubt about that. Sexy, too. And beneath the model-perfect exterior she was likable. Everything a man could ever want. Everything he should be desiring....

So why did he keep remembering a pair of outraged honey-gold eyes?

Four

Yevgeny returned to the hospital late the following afternoon—with his supermodel in tow. His face wore no expression as the pair entered the family waiting room where Ella had just met with Jo, and now she tried desperately to match his insouciance. All day, she'd found herself wondering when he would arrive.

Now he was here.

And he hadn't come alone.

Sitting on one of the two-seater love seats, her overnight bag already packed and ready to go, Ella couldn't help wishing that she'd taken the time to blow-dry her hair straight after breakfast instead of wasting time staring out the hospital-ward window for thirty soul-searching minutes. Now, at the end of the day, her hair hung like rats' tails around her face while Nadiya looked absolutely fabulous. Not that Ella should care… but unaccountably she did.

Maybe she couldn't look as if she'd stepped out the pages of *Vogue,* but she wanted to look capable and together—like someone out of a feature on successful women in *Cosmo.*

Brisk. Businesslike. A woman who had achieved every

career goal she'd ever set for herself; not the quivering mass of Jell-O–like uncertainty that she was right now.

Nadiya was glancing around the family room with interest— taking in the large black-and-white photos of mothers cradling babies that decorated the walls. Ella wondered if she'd ever seen inside a maternity unit before. Given the model's whippet-slim figure, pregnancy was not something Ella could imagine the supermodel contemplating with glee.

"Where's the baby?"

Ella managed not to roll her eyes skyward. Of course the baby would be the first thing that Yevgeny asked about.

"Her diaper is being changed."

"The birth went well?" asked Nadiya.

Ella could've hugged the woman for unwittingly preventing Yevgeny from venting the criticism that hovered unspoken on his lips. Clearly he thought *she* should be attending to the baby.

"Yes, very well." She gave the supermodel a small smile. "I've already been discharged."

"That's good. How much does she weigh?"

Ella told her.

"Your sister must be thrilled—she's changing her now?"

Did Nadiya not know that Keira had pulled out of the adoption? Ella's questioning gaze slid to Yevgeny. Perhaps the two weren't as close as she'd assumed…perhaps Nadiya was not the bride he intended to sucker into marriage.

"I—"

"I brought Nadiya to meet the baby," he cut in before Ella could respond. "She has agreed to marry me." He lifted Nadiya's hand to flash a gigantic diamond, and smirked at Ella.

"No!" She realized she'd said it out loud as Nadiya's face reflected shock. "I mean…what a surprise."

The other woman's eyes had narrowed and she was studying Ella in a way that made her feel decidedly uncomfortable. Nadiya's gaze flashed back and forth between Ella and Yevgeny. Her discomfort increased. The conclusion the other woman was drawing about Ella's hasty objection was wrong.

She hastened to correct her. "You don't understand—"

"Let's go visit the baby." Nadiya smiled up at Yevgeny as her fingers walked up his arm then spread out and rested against his suit-clad biceps in an unmistakably possessive gesture. The diamond sparkled. The model turned her head, and her gaze glittered *mine* at Ella.

Nadiya was welcome to the man!

As the pair exited the ward, Ella glared at Yevgeny's retreating back. He was the most devious, cold-bloodedly scheming man she'd ever come across—and she'd seen enough. He'd gone out to find the first woman to marry him—and proposed—without bothering to explain *why* he wanted to marry her.

He was using the young woman.

Deep down, Ella knew she was being unfair. Nadiya might be young but she was far from naive. And what man wouldn't want to marry Nadiya?

But at the back of her mind, worry raged for the baby. Given a choice, a fashion model was hardly the kind of mother she would've picked out. Together, as a couple, Yevgeny and Nadiya were so far removed from her notion of ideal parents. This was a train crash waiting to happen...and the baby would be the biggest victim.

Even as anxiety noodled her stomach into a tangle of nerves, one of the caregivers bustled in. "I've changed the baby. Mr. Volkovoy and his friend are with her in the nursery. The baby is looking well. She'll be fine to leave." She stopped beside Ella and said in a tone of inquiry, "Jo said the adoption is still some time away from being finalized."

Not if Yevgeny had his way....

But Ella was far from convinced that the Russian billionaire and his supermodel fiancée were the kind of parents the baby deserved. The last thing she wanted was to read about the baby in the tabloids and gossip magazines as so often happened with celebrities who seemed to care little for their offspring.

She might not be in a position to keep the baby. But she could damn well make sure it got the best start in life—and that meant the best parents possible.

And she'd told Jo that in as many words.

The five profiles she'd gone through with Jo earlier before rejecting them all had confirmed Jo's statement that there were many parents anxiously waiting to adopt. But Ella had a sinking feeling that Yevgeny's insistence to adopt might still prove a hindrance.

"The baby will stay with a foster family until I choose the final adoptive parents," Ella answered at last.

"That will be one very happy set of parents," the caregiver said, drawing the curtains farther back to let more light into the room.

There was nothing more to say.

Ella knew it was time to pick up the overnight bag she'd packed hours ago and for her to leave the place where she'd given birth—and leave the baby behind.

But before Ella got a chance to gather up her overnight bag and make her escape, Yevgeny and Nadiya returned—with the baby. Wheeling the cot into the middle of the room, Yevgeny bent forward to lift her out.

Ella closed her eyes. Every muscle tensed. *Don't give her to me. Don't give her to me.* The frantic refrain echoed through her head. She hadn't wanted to see the baby before she left. Ella had hoped that the next time she saw her, the baby would be securely in her new parents' home.

A gurgling sound broke into her desperation.

"She's grinning!"

Ella opened her eyes. Yevgeny was holding the baby up, one big hand cradling the back of her neck. Face-to-face with the baby, his strong masculine profile provided a sharp contrast to the baby's swaddled softness. She looked tiny against this big hulk. Ella tensed further. What if he dropped her?

"Careful!"

He didn't even look at her; all his attention was focused on the baby.

"Look, she's laughing."

Nadiya leaned in toward the two of them, resting long slim fingers on Yevgeny's arm, her silky sable hair spilling over his shoulder. "Babies that young don't laugh. She's yawning."

A jab pierced Ella's heart at the sight of the three dark heads so close together. To her horror she felt her throat tighten. She swallowed. The tightness swelled more.

She couldn't have said anything even if she hadn't felt so awful.

"No, that's not a yawn—it's laughter," the billionaire insisted.

Nadiya moved even closer, and Ella was sure that Yevgeny and the baby would be asphyxiated by Nox Parfum fumes.

"This is something I know a lot about," Nadiya said. "I've handled many babies... I've got four sisters and about a dozen nieces and nephews." Nadiya took the baby from him with an easy competence that Ella found herself envying.

Maybe Yevgeny hadn't made such a mistake in picking the supermodel to marry. Clearly Nadiya knew something about babies—despite her glamorous exterior.

Loneliness swamped Ella, dismaying her. To ward it off, she said, "You're happy to adopt her?"

Startled eyes met hers. "Adopt her?"

Yevgeny moved. All too soon he stood between Ella and his bewildered fiancée like some oversize sentinel. He shot Ella a fulminating look.

"Nadiya and I have yet to discuss the specifics."

No...it wasn't possible, he couldn't have been that... arrogant...that dumb. Could he?

Over the head of the oblivious baby, the supermodel's attention shifted to her fiancé. "The specifics of what?"

Yes, he'd been that dumb.

He hadn't told Nadiya.

Now he looked hunted. Then he smiled at his fiancée—a

slow, deliberate smile that oozed intimacy. "We will talk later. In private."

Ella watched as he gave the supermodel a slow once-over that was clearly intended to turn her legs to water. She knew she should've experienced distaste at the obvious sexual manipulation he was using on the young woman. Instead, to her utter dismay, her own stomach started to churn at the blatant sensuality in that hard-boned face. What would it feel like to be the object of this man's desire? To have him gaze at *her* with such unwavering intensity?

Heat, wanton—no, *unwanted*—blazed through her.

To rid herself of the emotional storm she didn't want, Ella said with a coolness she was far from feeling, "Yevgeny intends to adopt the baby."

Nadiya stared down at the wrapped infant in her arms. "This baby?" She lifted her head and turned her attention to her fiancé. "But why?"

"He didn't explain it to you—that I told him he needed a wife?"

Ella couldn't stem the words.

Pity for the younger woman filled her. Yevgeny hadn't taken Nadiya's wishes into account. He'd simply assumed she would fall in with what he wanted. Once again he was putting what he wanted first, not thinking of anyone else. What arrogance! The dislike Ella already felt toward him escalated, not helped by that surge of awareness that he had unwittingly aroused.

But to Ella's surprise, Nadiya was glaring at him. "You asked me if I wanted children..." As her voice trailed away, the frown marring her forehead deepened. "You weren't talking about the future, you were talking about now. About this baby."

"Nadiya—"

But Nadiya held up a hand, interrupting whatever he'd been about to say. A couple of quick steps brought her to Ella's side and she deposited the baby into Ella's lap. The baby started to cry—a gruff, growly sound that caused Ella to freeze. She stared down at the crumpled, red face and panic pierced her.

What the hell was she supposed to do now?

From a distance she could hear Nadiya angrily saying something to Yevgeny, but Ella was in no state to listen. She stroked the baby with a tentative hand. The cries continued. Awkwardly she patted the baby's back…then rocked her a little. There was a pause. The tightly pressed eyelids opened. The baby's eyes were a dark shade of midnight. Ella stared, transfixed.

"You need to support her neck."

The voice came from far off. The words were repeated and a hand with a flashing diamond appeared in Ella's peripheral vision. It cupped her own.

"There. Like that," said Nadiya.

Ella looked up. "Thank you."

But Nadiya had already spun to confront Yevgeny. Ella couldn't look away as Nadiya hissed, "Why this child?" Her hands were on her hips. She shot a quick look over her shoulder at Ella, then moved her attention back to the Russian. "Is it your child?"

"Nadiya—"

"Answer me!"

Holding the now quiet infant, Ella wanted to cheer.

But before she could make any sound, Nadiya's gaze arced to her "…and yours?"

That was taking it too far. It was one thing to needle Yevgeny, but Ella didn't want anyone thinking she'd slept with this bully.

"No!" said Ella. "This is not his child—it's Dmitri's child!"

Confusion misted Nadiya's eyes. "So where is Dmitri?" Her attention swung to Yevgeny. "And why are you talking about adopting your brother's child?"

He really hadn't told Nadiya anything at all.

"Because my brother and his wife have decided they no longer want a baby. She's of my blood. How can I let her go to strangers?"

There lay the key to his behavior—he was prepared to

sacrifice his own freedom for the baby's sake to prevent a person he believed belonged to his family from going to strangers.

Nadiya's gaze moved back to Ella. "And you are the mother, right? Not your sister?"

Why did Nadiya have to put it like that? Ella rocked the baby a little more. "I'm *not* the planned mother—Keira is. Or was supposed to be," she amended. "I'm only a surrogate."

She couldn't help feeling the stab of a traitor's guilt.

"You only carried the baby?"

Ella wriggled uncomfortably before conceding, "The eggs are mine, too."

"So you are the mother." Nadiya cut to the heart of it.

Ella shifted again. The baby mewed. A quick glance revealed that the baby's face had puckered up. Oh, no, she was about to cry again. Ella rocked harder; the puckers relaxed a little. She risked raising her head. "Biologically, yes. Legally, yes. Morally, no."

Over the baby's head, Nadiya gave her a long, searching look. Then she turned to Yevgeny. "You should have told me. You knew I believed you were asking me to have *my* baby."

"It makes a difference?" Yevgeny's gaze was hooded.

"Yes. My career is demanding right now, but I would take time off for my baby. My baby—and yours."

"But not for this baby?"

Nadiya looked tormented.

"That's not fair!" Unable to keep quiet at his hectoring, Ella rose to the younger woman's defense. In her arms the soft body of the baby stiffened. Ella made a mental note to keep her voice level.

"You've already caused enough trouble. You stay out of this," he snarled.

"But she's right. You're not being fair—and I'm not going to do this." Nadiya was tugging the great glittering ring off her finger.

"Wait—"

"No, this isn't going to work. I thought you loved me...that you were talking about us having a baby together. But you were using me!" Fury sparkled in her green eyes. She thrust the ring at him, her fingers shaking. "Take it."

The baby carefully cradled on her lap, Ella drew back into the chair and tried to make herself invisible. Some things deserved privacy. And it was uncomfortable to watch Nadiya's pain as moisture glimmered in her eyes. There was hurt…and anger… and something else that made Ella wince.

It startled her to realize that the model had loved the ruthless Russian. The revelation made Ella furious. Poor, hoodwinked Nadiya.

A woman would have to be incredibly shortsighted to fall in love with him. Yet Nadiya clearly had. Being beautiful and successful hadn't saved her from being devastated by his effortless manipulation.

The tableau playing itself out in front of her brought back old hurts…humiliations…that Ella had hoped were long forgotten….

She never intended to feel like that about any man ever again.

Particularly not a man like Yevgeny Volkovoy.

Nadiya tossed back her head, and her hair rippled like black silk in the light. "No one uses me."

Yevgeny didn't respond. He simply stood there staring down at the woman he'd so recently announced was his fiancée.

"Pah…you're not even prepared to deny it. I feel sorry for you, Yevgeny. You don't recognize the importance of love. But one day you're going to fall in love with someone—real love— and she's going to rip your heart out, just like you've ripped mine out." Wiping the tears away, the supermodel straightened to her glamorous full height. "You're not worth crying over."

"You did that deliberately!" Yevgeny blew out a pent-up breath as the rapid tap-tap of Nadiya's skyscraper heels receded down the corridor.

Ella didn't even flinch at his accusation. "What do you mean?"

Her voice was softer than he expected.

It gave him a strange feeling to see her holding the baby that he already adored. So he looked away from the infant and pinned the most irritating woman he'd ever met under his gaze. "You caused that scene you just witnessed."

"*I* caused it?" Her eyes widened. "I simply told the poor woman the truth. Don't blame me. You should've explained things to her."

Perhaps Ella had a point.

But he'd wanted to assess Nadiya's reaction to the baby first—and it had been more than he'd hoped for. He and Nadiya had never talked much about family…or children. They hadn't shared that kind of relationship. Yet when Nadiya had taken the baby into her arms like a woman created for motherhood, and revealed she was used to her sister's children, Yevgeny had been overcome by relief. He couldn't have gotten a better outcome if he'd planned it for a month. And he'd thought the baby would be safe….

Then Ella had interfered.

He stared blankly at the woman he despised as she moved the baby to and fro in small motions.

Nadiya had made it clear she wasn't prepared to raise someone else's child. In seconds his plan had started to unravel and he could do nothing but watch impotently. It was all Ella's fault. Yet she didn't even want the baby. He could understand Nadiya's stance. It was more acceptable than the distinct lack of warmth that Ella exhibited toward a child she'd carried for nine months. That coldness, that lack of feeling, he would never grasp.

And Ella already had the next step planned—to identify a couple to adopt the child.

Which raised another thought. He'd seen Jo Wells waiting at the elevator when he and Nadiya had arrived. Had the social worker been to see Ella to discuss prospective parents?

Didn't Ella realize it was a waste of time choosing other parents? He was going to adopt the baby. What Ella didn't appear to get was that he was a man of immense financial reserves and infinite patience. Those attributes had made him into the mega-wealthy man he was today. He studied the fake Madonna-child tableau in front of him through narrowed eyes.

From her hesitation, it was clear that Ella had had little to do with babies. She knew as little about them as he did. But he was willing to learn—she wasn't. He wanted this baby…and he wasn't about to let her win this round.

The sooner she got that into her stubborn head, the better.

"Well, I no longer have the prospective wife you considered I need. But I still intend to adopt the baby." He was proud of the lack of emotion in his voice.

Ella's chin came up in a gesture he was starting to recognize. Instantly his muscles tensed.

"I've been looking at portfolios of couples who've already been screened. You have not been interviewed or checked yet."

That answered his unasked question. Jo *had* been here to discuss the baby's future parents. And it was equally obvious that his own proposal had not been on the agenda—because of Ella's prejudice against him.

"Then I'll have to remedy that," he said quietly. "This baby carries the blood of generations of Volkovoys in her veins—she is not leaving my family."

"Not even if it would be better for her?"

"You don't know that." He glanced down at the baby. Her mouth was moving up and down, tempting him to smile. But now was not a time to smile. "You could be letting the baby in for a life of hell."

"That's unlikely. The couples have been assessed and police checks carried out—"

"Who really knows what happens in the privacy of a couple's home? And do you really want to take that risk?"

That silenced Ella.

As color drained from her face, leaving it a pasty shade of white, Yevgeny realized he'd overdone it. Of course, he didn't even believe his own alarmist statement—he and Dmitri might have been better off adopted by a loving couple than ordered by a bamboozled judge to stay with his mother after his parents' divorce. But if his scaremongering changed Ella's mind, then it would be worth it.

The end justified the means; he'd always lived his life by that creed.

Yet unexpectedly, shame lingered within him as unhappiness and worry clouded her eyes. Her fingers had clenched, whitening her knuckles against the Disney print of the baby's swaddling wrap. He glanced away—and caught sight of Ella's overnight bag.

After a beat, he said, "Your bags are packed. You're leaving."

Ella nodded.

"The baby will be going with you."

He told himself she wouldn't walk away now that she'd held...engaged with...the baby. He waited for her affirmation of what he hoped to hear.

She shook her head. "No."

Ella intended to go through with her vow not to keep the baby. She would leave her daughter behind. What kind of woman would do that? Yevgeny still found it hard to believe she could be so callous. "You will leave the baby here?"

"The baby will go to a specially trained foster mother who will look after her until I pick the right family out for her. Jo and I discussed the foster mother earlier—she knows the baby is coming."

Two thoughts filled his head. *She* was made of ice, and how could she not understand that *he* was the right family!

Anger rose like a tidal wave.

Yevgeny reached for his wallet to retrieve the business card Jo Wells had given him the day before. His hands trembled at the emotion swamping him. "That will not happen. I am taking the baby home with me. I will call your social worker and tell her so."

"No!" yelled Ella from behind him. "If you take her, I'll have you arrested for kidnapping."

The baby started to cry.

Yevgeny stopped in his tracks at the sound and whipped around to face them. Ella was frantically rocking the baby—even uttering hoarse hushing sounds.

When the baby quieted, she met his gaze and said in a more even tone, "You need to think about the baby. It's not fair on her to form an attachment with you if she's going to be given to another family."

Angered and frustrated, he snapped, "If you would stop being so goddamned stubborn, you would know that she should stay with me—be my daughter."

"And how will that work?" A note he'd never heard from Ella before filled her voice. "You're never home. You work like a demon—don't deny it. Keira's told me all about how Dmitri's always exhausted."

He bit back the surge of irritation at his sister-in-law. "I'll rearrange my schedule."

"You really believe that?" Ella gazed at him from pitying eyes. "You're a type-A, high-achieving success junkie... You need your daily fix. Staying home with a baby will drive you crazy. You wouldn't last more than two days."

"What makes you think that?"

"Because I know." Her shoulders drooped as she blew out a breath, yet she didn't lower the baby; she continued to rock the bundle back and forth. She gave him a sad smile. "I am exactly the same—and people like us are not made to have children. Babies should be placed in families where they will have a better chance of being loved and living fruitful lives. Taking the baby would be a selfish thing to do. Why not be selfless and allow her the chance to be happy?"

The woman didn't know what she was talking about. He and she were nothing alike. Yevgeny refused to listen to what she was saying.

Yet instead of challenging her claim, he countered, "And you think you're any less selfish?"

"What do you mean?"

"Christmas is coming." He gestured to the small tree standing in the corner of the waiting room. "And you're going to send the baby you gave birth to away to a foster home? Her first Christmas will be spent as an orphan. Alone. I will not allow it. I am calling Jo Wells now—I don't care how she arranges it, but that baby in your arms is going home with me. No baby should be alone at Christmas."

Five

Bringing the baby home was the most ill-considered thing she'd ever done, Ella decided ruefully the following morning.

She'd given up trying to get the baby to sleep an hour ago—after a night spent mixing formula and warming bottles and not a wink of sleep. A glance at the large white clock on the ivory-patterned wallpaper revealed it was already seven-thirty Monday morning. Normally she'd be in the office already, her emails read and answered. She'd be about to fetch the single cup of coffee she'd allowed herself each day during her pregnancy. Made from a fragrant, specially ground blend she favored, it was a must to kick-start her day.

This morning she hadn't even fired up her laptop…much less thought about coffee.

Ella was exhausted.

But it was worth it….

She'd refused to allow Yevgeny to all but kidnap the baby and take it away with him. Once that happened he would never let the baby go. She knew that. The only way to stop that from happening had been to take the baby home herself…and the sacrifice was probably going to kill her.

At the very least, it was going to break what was left of her heart.

She gazed wearily at the tiny girl-monster lying on the plump couch beside her.

"Don't you think it's time for a nap?"

The baby stared back at her with round, wide-awake eyes.

Ella sighed.

She had no idea what she was doing but the few tips from a willing nurse that she'd scribbled down on the legal pad before leaving the maternity unit had been a godsend. At least the baby wouldn't starve—she'd just finished a bottle. Yet it had only reinforced how much Ella didn't know. After all, she hadn't attended parenting classes or read any books on child rearing during the pregnancy because that had been Keira's department. She'd only read the manuals about the dos and don'ts for the period the baby was growing in her stomach, none of which were of any help now.

Thank heavens she'd called an agency to engage a nanny before leaving the hospital yesterday. The agency hadn't been able to send someone at once, and Ella had wished she hadn't been so hasty in telling Yevgeny that she was taking the baby home, but pride hadn't let her back down.

How much trouble could a baby be?

She closed her eyes, thinking about the night past…trouble didn't even begin to describe the experience!

And after today there were still eight days to go before she could sign the adoption consent.

Ella didn't even want to contemplate it.

Opening her eyes, she gazed down at the baby, who was now wiggling her legs. Ella knew her biggest challenge was going to be maintaining a healthy distance from this child. What she didn't need was to form an attachment to a baby she had no intention of keeping. She'd hoped that the baby would spend most of the time asleep—after all, that was what had happened at the maternity unit.

But it certainly hadn't played out like that last night....

Since they'd gotten home to Ella's cozy town house, most of the baby's waking time had been spent in her arms. It seemed to have forgotten what sleep was. Ella had walked her up and down for what seemed like the whole night...to no avail.

Her cell phone beeped.

Ella reached for it and squinted at the hi-tech screen.

The messages had started early this morning—from colleagues and clients who had no idea of the baby's arrival on Friday evening, and thought this would be a normal work Monday. Ella knew she faced a flood of calls and emails...and that she ought to divert them to Peggy, her assistant...but right now she was too tired to move—or to think of anything.

Except sleep...

The baby chose that moment to burp.

As tired as she was, it was impossible not to smile. Ella forced her face straight. This was not the way to maintain a healthy distance. She shifted her attention back to the cell phone. Another message beeped through.

Then it rang.

It was the childcare agency she'd contacted yesterday to let her know the nanny had been dispatched.

Ella sighed with relief as she killed the call. Wrinkling her nose at the child, she said, "Sleep is on its way."

She'd have to summon the energy to call the office, check that Peggy had canceled all her meetings for the day, and then she could crawl into bed. It was the stuff fantasies were made of....

The nanny turned out to be a short, energetic woman named Deb Benson. Within half an hour she'd restored order, unexpectedly leaving Ella feeling inadequate. She was used to making decisions, doing deals, dispensing advice, but as far as babies were concerned, she was a rookie. It was hard to accept how inept she was. Explaining the situation to Deb had also proved to be difficult—so, too, the fact that the baby didn't yet have a name. Yet Deb hadn't even blinked.

It made Ella wonder what it would take to faze her.

A lot more than a baby created for a couple who'd decided to give her up…and a surrogate mother who avoided cuddling her.

But it was for her own protection, Ella reminded herself as she made her way to the sleek white-and-silver home office where she spent much of her out-of-office time. Yet once barricaded in the familiar space, Ella struggled to concentrate. It wasn't the fact that she felt different—heck, it would've been impossible not to! Her stomach felt soft—no more gym-hard abs. Her breasts were swollen, tight and aching.

Having the baby had changed her body—and now, little as Ella wanted to admit it, the infant was changing her life.

Her silver laptop sat on the smooth, white desk. Ella flipped it open. She forced herself to call Peggy.

When she put the phone down she found that her ears were straining to hear what Deb was doing. She stared blindly at the screen in front of her. Against her will she found herself using Google to search "baby names" and faced with pages of websites. Most popular girls' names of the seventies…eighties… nineties…noughties…and beyond.

There were websites for flower names, for foreign names. Her mind boggled.

Lily. Rose. Petunia.

With a click of the mouse the next webpage opened.

Manon. Jeanne.

Another click.

Eleni. Roshni.

Ella clicked back to the first website with the botanical girls' names.

Or Holly.

The sound of the doorbell was an unwelcome interruption. Scant seconds later the door to her office burst open, and an even more unwelcome male presence filled the doorway.

"You've hired a nanny!"

Determined not to give Yevgeny more advantage than surprise had already afforded him, Ella shut the computer lid and rose to her feet. He dwarfed her. She swore silently. Next time she would wear heels.

"Of course I have." She met his outraged gaze as calmly as she was able. "I have a job to get back to."

"You're due maternity leave."

Ella shook her head. "I work for myself, so any leave I take is scheduled long in advance. This time I only allowed myself a few days off." And that had been next week. When the baby was supposed to arrive—not long before Christmas. "Anyway, I wasn't keeping the baby, remember? So I certainly didn't need maternity leave." And now, since Keira's bombshell, Ella knew she definitely didn't want to be sitting around with time to think.

His eyes glittered with disbelief. "And none of that has changed since bringing the baby home?"

She struggled with another wave of weariness and searched for words to explain her feelings to the man watching her as though she were some two-headed alien.

"How can it? I have to work." She stared back at him. *Attack was the best form of defense.* "You employ women—some of them might even be executives." Although she doubted it. Men like Yevgeny Volkovoy didn't take women seriously enough to give them significant responsibility. One only had to look at the women he dated—models, socialites—to see that. Although she had to admit that Nadiya had shown more spunk than Ella would've expected from one of his conquests—certainly more than Yevgeny wanted. "I can only imagine what you'd say about a woman who planned to be back at work, then decided to take several months off instead."

He blinked, and Ella saw the truth of her argument register. He shrugged.

"Maybe." Then he added, "But I would've understood. Eventually." Putting his hands on his hips, he tilted his head to one side. "And that argument doesn't apply here—you are your own boss."

"Which means I can't just disappear from the office—I need to carefully plan the times away and arrange for someone to cover for me." And most important, she wanted to avoid becoming too attached to the child. "I *want* to go back to work."

"So when do you plan to do that?"

"As soon as I can." Ella didn't say "tomorrow," which was what she fully intended—so long as her body obliged and the fatigue that was starting to make her feel dizzy wasn't too much of a factor.

"And dump the child you haven't even given a name on the nanny?"

Ella stifled a yawn. "Holly will be perfectly happy."

"Holly? *Holly?*" He reared back. "You've named the baby?"

"Obviously."

He looked surprised. "Just now? To prove me wrong?"

"Not to prove you wrong! I picked her name earlier." She wasn't admitting to those minutes of scouring websites—after all, she couldn't even fathom what had driven her to do a Google search for baby names. It was all too uncomfortable to absorb. And why did he think she'd done it merely to prove him wrong? Let him think it had been an arbitrary name plucked out of the air. "You shouldn't assume an importance you don't have in my life."

But instead of causing Yevgeny to puff up with annoyance as she'd intended, her comment made him laugh.

"Bravo," he said.

Ella stared. Tiredness must be befuddling her. Because with his white teeth flashing and laugh lines—which she'd never noticed before—crinkling around his eyes, he caused her breath to hook in her throat. In the wickedly sparkling eyes, Ella got a glimpse of his appeal. This must be the reason women hung around him like bees around a honeypot.

The man looked devastating.

And all because she'd tried to put him in his place!

She couldn't help smiling back.

But his next words wiped the smile off her face.

"I came expecting to find you ready to beg me to take her away." His light eyes grew cloudy. "I should've known you'd hire a nanny."

He'd expected her to fail at the first hurdle.

That stung!

Because even though she'd hired a nanny to keep the baby at a distance, deep in her heart she knew he was right. She *had* failed. She was dangerously ignorant about babies, and it didn't help that her ignorance came because she'd never intended to have children of her own. It only served to underscore her secret, deeply held conviction that she would make a terrible parent.

Mostly his criticism stung because the truth of it was Ella wasn't accustomed to failure. Whatever task she undertook she saw through to the bitter end.

And arranging for the baby's adoption would be no different—once she'd had a good-night's sleep and gotten herself back to normal.

But Yevgeny only saw a woman he didn't particularly like, so he wrote her off as useless—like he'd written most of her sex off. He was definitely archaic… She'd dearly love to see him taught a lesson. Tempting as it was to daydream that she might be the woman to do that, Ella knew it wouldn't—couldn't—be her. Some other woman would have to have the pleasure of taking him down a peg or two…one day. How she'd love to see the arrogant Yevgeny grovel.

"Didn't you come to see Holly?" she asked, too exhausted to get drawn into another of their fiery exchanges.

"Thanks to the nanny, she's probably been fed at least."

Annoyance surfaced, exacerbated by the mind-numbing weariness. Did he believe she would neglect the baby? Just because she didn't want a child didn't mean that she'd ever see it harmed. No, not *it…her*. Holly was a little girl. Ella sighed inwardly. It was hard enough to keep her distance to stop an attachment forming; she didn't need his cruel barbs. "I looked after her all night. The nanny only just arrived."

"Then I'd better go check on her."

Ella ground her teeth, and turned her head to stare blindly at her computer screen. Unable to help herself she blurted out, "None of the intending parents' profiles Jo Wells left at the hospital fit what I'm looking for."

It got so quiet, she thought Yevgeny must've already gone, that he hadn't heard her.

That might be for the best.

She turned her head, glanced over her shoulder.

Yevgeny stood as unmoving as a marble statue on the office's threshold, his pale eyes hungry and intent.

Waiting.

This was what he'd wanted to know, wasn't it? But Ella refused to hold out false hope. "Jo has already brought another batch of portfolios for me to look at. There should be at least one set of suitable parents there."

"You're choosing them tonight?"

She shook her head, flinching inwardly at the thought of what lay ahead. Glimpses into the lives of strangers desperate for a baby. And not just any baby—the baby she had helped create.

More hopeful faces would smile out of the pages at her—with carefully picked words detailing their dreams. Each set of parents hoping they would be the chosen ones. And if she liked more than one set, it would only get harder. After meeting the couples, she'd have to choose one couple over the other. Right now she couldn't face the mountain that lay ahead.

"I'll do it tomorrow." She turned away from the intensity that radiated from him, back to her laptop.

A moment later his footsteps receded. After the door closed softly behind him, Ella's shoulders sagged. She could barely concentrate on the letters on the screen in front of her. Giving in, she rose and went to sit on the love seat beneath the window, her computer perched on her stomach. Much more comfortable.

For the next few minutes, she'd see what appointments she could reschedule…then…then, she'd go see what Yevgeny was doing. See if she could hurry him along. Once Yevgeny had departed, she'd be able to relax. She'd go lie down in her bedroom.

And welcome the sleep her body craved.

Yevgeny pushed the door to Ella's office open with the flat palm of his hand and reentered the room. One glance caused him to pause.

The icicle had fallen asleep.

He crossed the room with silent steps, his footfalls muffled by the pile of the pale gray carpet until he stood beside the sofa.

Yet, instead of an icicle's cold clinical perfection, Ella's skin held a very feminine rosy flush. Her hair feathered across her forehead, the sharp-angled bob nowhere in evidence.

She looked younger. Prettier. *Softer.*

Yevgeny shrugged the illusion away.

Her laptop, angled across her midriff, was in danger of toppling off. She'd been working. Of course she had.

What had he expected?

That she'd been mothering? He suppressed a snort of disgust. The baby was where he'd just left her—in the arms of the nanny. His mouth compressing, he lifted the computer gently off Ella's stomach and set it down on her desk. Turning back, he took in the uncomfortable way she was draped over the small couch. Her feet, one hooked over the other, dangled over the edge and her body was skewed so that her bottom cheek was pressed against the white leather cushions. It definitely didn't look comfortable.

Bending over, he lifted her feet and laid them straight along the couch. Instantly they slid back over the edge. He stilled, fearing she might waken. But she didn't stir.

The way her body was twisted suggested she was going to wake with a God-Almighty crick in her neck for sure. Yevgeny didn't know why it was bothering him, but he couldn't leave her like this. When he'd first arrived, she'd looked tired with gray shadows rimming her expressive eyes. Leaving aside her lack of motherly instincts, Ella had been through a lot in the past few days. She'd given birth to the baby that her sister had given up. She'd had to cope with deciding the baby's future.

She must be worn out.

The first flicker of unwilling sympathy for her stirred within him.

He might not agree with the decisions she was planning, but he could appreciate how stressful it must be. He knelt and scooped her up against his chest. She made a tiny mewing sound, and her lashes fluttered. Then she burrowed in against his shoulder.

She smelt of a soft, old-fashioned scent.

Lilacs...

Yevgeny bit back a curse.

Straightening to his full six-foot, three-inch height, he strode out of the glossy white-and-gray office. At the end of the carpeted corridor a door stood ajar. With one foot, he knocked it wide to reveal what was clearly the main bedroom in the town house.

What a difference.

While white once again dominated, it wasn't the glossy white of leather and lacquer that he'd seen in the rest of the house. No reflective glass and silver mirrors in here. This was...

Holding her against him, he let his eyes travel around.

A bed decked out with snowy-white linen was the centerpiece of this pretty, feminine room. In his peripheral vision Yevgeny caught sight of a French-style dressing table with a collection of antique, glass perfume bottles and a set of silver-backed hairbrushes. His gaze stopped on two pairs of ballet shoes suspended by faded pink satin ribbons from an ornately carved brass hook. He started to smile. On the opposite wall hung a large acrylic painting of a dancer in a style reminiscent of Degas.

It was a bedroom filled with nostalgia and romance.

Not quite what he would've expected, given the brisk business exterior Ella McLeod presented to the world.

He entered the bedroom.

Instantly he was enveloped in a mist of that flowery, feminine scent—the scent he was fast coming to associate with the essence of Ella. Gently he laid her down on the pristine white linen of the bed, then stepped back. He could hear her breathing. Deep and even through slightly parted pale pink lips. Pale pink lips that held him enthralled.

Just one kiss…and she could waken.

The idea was ridiculous, but it persisted. Sense warred with temptation. Until, at last, he succumbed to the tantalizing temptation and bent forward. He placed the softest of kisses on her lips then straightened, his color high, feeling unaccountably foolish.

Ella didn't stir.

He'd gotten the legend wrong—she was not Sleeping Beauty—and instead of waking, the Ice Queen slept on.

It was already Tuesday. Keira and Dmitri had departed for Africa—without changing their minds about the baby. It had taken all Ella's willpower not to scream at her sister that she was making the biggest mistake of her life.

To Ella's intense relief, Holly had already survived four full days and nights, and Ella herself had managed to keep from becoming too attached to the newborn.

But this evening Deb was leaving to go to a friend's housewarming party. The party had been planned long before the agency had sent her, and Ella waved aside her apologies.

"Go, enjoy yourself," she said. Holly was sleeping peacefully in her cot upstairs. The speaker for the baby monitor lay on top of a pile of magazines on the low, wide coffee table beside the collection of shopping bags that had been delivered not long ago.

With Deb gone, Ella shut the front door and took advantage of the solitude. She was busily manhandling the huge, cut-pine Christmas tree into the corner of the living room, when the doorbell chimed.

She bit back a curse. No choice but to set the tree down… and undo all the progress she'd made in the past few minutes.

Impatient, she wrenched open the door.

Yevgeny stood on the doorstep, every inch the city billionaire, immaculate in a dark, conservative business suit and a white shirt that still managed to look crisp at the end of the day.

"May I come in?"

Before she could respond, he'd brushed past her. Irritation spiked through her at his high-handedness.

Her voice heavy with irony, she muttered, "Sure you can."

He turned and grinned. "Thank you."

The flash of that wolfish smile, the gleam of wicked laughter in his eyes, indicated that he was fully mindful of her irritation. Ella couldn't halt the unfurling awareness that blossomed through her, starting deep in her chest, near her heart and spreading outward in a glow of warmth. Like a flower following the path of the sun.

The man was dynamite.

And she didn't even *like* him. He was obnoxious, arrogant, inconsiderate. So why the melting heat in the pit of her stomach? Why wasn't she recoiling? What on earth was wrong with her? Didn't she have any sense of self-preservation? Ella drew in a deep breath and was instantly flooded with the woody aroma of his aftershave.

God help her if he ever set himself the task of trying to charm her—she'd be in serious trouble!

With a toss of her head, she blew out the breath she was holding and brushed aside the absurd notion.

No threat from him.

Never.

"Holly is sleeping," she said finally as he brushed past her into the living room.

His response had nothing to do with the baby. "You're putting up a Christmas tree."

Did he have to sound so surprised?

"Yes."

Guilt stabbed Ella. She wasn't about to reveal that it was the first time in the five years she'd lived here that she'd done so. Or that most of the reason why she'd ordered a tree to be delivered stemmed from his barbed comments about Holly enduring her first Christmas alone. Becoming aware of the lack of festive cheer in her home had not been a welcome discovery.

"I almost had it in position…but then the doorbell rang." She gestured to where the tree lay. "Now I'll have to start all over again."

He strode across to where the tree lay. "I'll give you a hand and we'll have it up in minutes."

"Shouldn't you still be at work?" She bit off the bit about "making your next million."

He'd walked around to the far side of the tree. Now he shot one immaculate shirt cuff back to glance at a flat watch on his wrist. "Five o'clock. I've had enough for one day—boss's prerogative. I wanted to see Holly."

She refused to let that sentiment tug at her heartstrings.

Instead, she inspected the dark, formal suit he wore and decided it must be French, while she tried to ignore the effect the broad shoulders tapering down to a narrow male waist had on her. "What about your suit? You'll get resin all over it."

He'd reek of a pine forest for months to come. Ella doubted dry cleaning would get rid of the overpowering smell of pine. It would kill that sexy, seductive scent Yevgeny wore so well.

Her lips tilted up in secret amusement.

"What are you smiling at?"

He sounded so suspicious that her smile broadened. He'd find out soon enough. She slanted him an impish look. "Nothing."

"Somehow I don't believe that. You're plotting."

"Gosh, but you have a suspicious mind."

"Do you blame me? I know exactly what you are."

Her smile vanished and her eyes narrowed.

"There's no point in your staying. Holly's sleeping." Ella had had enough of his unwarranted opinions. Now she just wanted him to leave. Before he tempted her to laugh with him…and then he wounded her again. She wanted him gone.

But before she could turn and walk to the front door to show him on his way, he asked, "Have you reached a decision on the new set of portfolios Jo Wells showed you?"

He'd only come to influence—make that sabotage—her decision.

It was her own fault for giving in and revealing she hadn't selected any parents from the first batch of candidates. She'd been overtired...not thinking properly...reacting with her emotions rather than her head. And look where it had gotten her—Yevgeny hounding her.

Ella headed for the door and opened it. "Once I reach a final decision I'll let you know. Then you can decide if you want to stay in touch with the baby and her new family. Thank you for visiting."

Even from across the room, she saw his face fall.

He really had wanted to see the baby, she realized.

The considerations that had led her to update him about progress on the adoption proceedings yesterday returned. Yevgeny was the only blood relative who was showing any interest in the baby; he deserved to be kept in the picture. This would be an open adoption. Jo was insistent that adoptive children needed ties with their birth relatives. Those ties to family helped children grow up secure, with a healthy sense of self and identity.

Ella recognized that she needed to set aside her own antagonism toward the man...and think only of the baby.

As much as Holly needed contact with her birth mother, it would be to her advantage to know her birth father...and her uncle. Having a clear sense of identity would help her to stay intact as an individual as she grew up.

Even though Ella considered Yevgeny Volkovoy to be the most arrogantly selfish man on the face of the planet, for Holly's sake, she had to recognize that his desire to visit Holly was a blessing.

From her position at the door, Ella relented a little. "You can come back when Holly is awake."

But Yevgeny showed no sign of hearing. He'd already

shrugged off his jacket and put it on the sofa. "I said I'd help you with the tree."

So he was determined to stay—and ignore her wishes. Why had she ever imagined she might persuade him otherwise? He was accustomed to riding roughshod over other people's opinions.

She didn't want to be stuck alone with Yevgeny making small talk. Nor did she want him putting up the Christmas tree she'd bought for Holly. And she certainly didn't want to start thinking that he was helpful. Or, God help her, indispensable.

"You know, I really don't need—" *nor want* "—your help." All too aware of how much more defined the breadth of his shoulders was with his jacket off, Ella didn't dare to allow her suddenly treacherous eyes to linger on the lean narrow hips, the broad chest clad only in the soft, finest cotton shirt with the top button unbuttoned. Far too tempting. "And don't forget to take your jacket with you when you go."

The sooner he put it back on, the sooner she'd be able to visualize him as a corporate Russian bully.

Leaning on the door handle, Ella shut her eyes to block out the image of him standing in her living room rolling up his shirt sleeves. How was it possible to be attracted to a man she detested?

What the hell is wrong with me?

Six

With her eyes shut and her shoulders bowed, Ella looked more vulnerable than Yevgeny had ever seen her as she leaned against the doorjamb of the front entrance waiting for him to leave.

The last time he'd seen her she'd looked exhausted…but this was worse.

Nothing of the Ella he so disliked remained.

No black suit. Instead, she wore a white, sleeveless T-shirt that clung to curves he'd never known she had, while cropped jeans hugged her legs tapering to slim ankles. The simple outfit only served to underline her fragility.

Yevgeny forgot that he'd come to find out whether she'd looked at the portfolios she'd told him Jo would be dropping off today. He even forgot about his plan to convince her that every parent would be wrong for Holly. Except him.

Instead, driven to comfort her, he padded across the room on silent feet to stand beside her.

She hadn't heard his approach—or, if she had, she showed no sign of it. Yevgeny hesitated. Silky blond hair fell onto her shoulders, the style softer, less sharply defined than he remembered. Her scent surrounded him. Lilacs. Sweet…and elusive.

Slowly, oh, so slowly, he reached out a hand and touched the fine strands where they brushed her shoulder.

She started.

Then her head turned. Behind the large spectacles, her eyes had widened, and the summer sun streaming in through the door transformed the light brown irises to lustrous topaz.

As he stared, her lips parted.

He groped for words that made some kind of sense to fill the electric silence. "What do you want me to do first?"

"Do first?"

From this close he could see her pupils darkening.

All thoughts of offering comfort had rushed out of his mind.

Desire—dark and disturbing—grabbed him by the throat. He tried to respond, but his voice wouldn't—couldn't—work. But his body was working…in ways he didn't even want to think about. Whoa, this was Ella McLeod of all people. He didn't like her. *And* the woman had given birth to a child last Friday… He couldn't be feeling desire…where was his sense of perspective?

"What do you want me to do with the tree?" he managed at last in a gravelly rasp.

"The tree?" The dazed, startled look in her eyes faded. With her index finger she pushed her glasses up her nose. "Oh. The *tree.*"

"I told you I'd help. It's too big for you to try and set up by yourself—and you had a baby not so long ago. You shouldn't be straining yourself."

Her shoulders squared. The veil of fragility fell away from her. "I was doing just fine until the doorbell rang."

Yevgeny pressed his lips together.

That was Ella.

Determinedly independent.

Making it clear she didn't need comfort—or help. Maybe she wasn't quite as vulnerable as he'd thought.

"Do you ever accept help from anybody?" he asked with

more than a touch of exasperation, letting his hand drop away. He should be relieved that she'd returned to her usual independent and icy self. At least he could breathe again—and speak. That curious immobilizing spell that had seized his body and paralyzed his vocal cords had started to lift.

Yet he felt a whisper of regret that the moment had passed. God! Had he actually *wanted* to kiss Ella McLeod?

Yes.

The answer shocked him.

He *had* wanted to kiss her, to taste her mouth, to lose himself in her womanliness. Yes, womanliness. There was no doubt about it, Ella was every inch a woman. He would never again be fooled by the lawyer in the black suit again. He'd caught a glimpse of the person—the woman—who lurked behind the legal facade. The lacy night attire. Two pairs of well-used ballet slippers hanging in her bedroom. Even the way she'd held the baby and rocked her in her arms after she'd refused to even look at Holly at first.

She intrigued the hell out of him.

If anyone had told him he'd be hot as a mink in season for lawyer Ella McLeod a few weeks ago he would've howled with scorn. Ridiculous. But now the joke was on him. Only minutes ago he'd been ready to devour her with a desperation that stunned him.

Had he lost all reason?

Could Ella the Icicle really be Ella the Enchantress?

Yevgeny turned away, lest his face reveal the turmoil of his thoughts. Ella was sharp, and he didn't want her recognizing any chinks in his armor that would render him vulnerable to her.

"My parents—when I was younger."

He realized she'd finally answered his question. "They're the only people you accept help from?"

A frown creased her brow. "Probably."

He could see her thinking, trying to come up with other names…and failing. "How about your sister?"

"Keira?" She gave a laugh of astonishment. "She's too young."

"I'm sure you were making decisions at her age."

She shrugged. "Maybe. But Keira always needs help from *me*."

Yevgeny hoarded that nugget of information away, to retrieve and examine later. "What about a mentor…or something?"

Ella immediately shook her head.

He stared then. It was inconceivable to him that she'd never asked for—never needed—help. Even he, who prided himself on his self-made success, had relied on mentors to get where he had so rapidly. How much harder would it have been without the men who had advised him…guided him…helped him?

From slitted eyes he gazed at her with fresh respect. She'd cleaved a way out for herself—amidst fierce competition—and she'd gained a good reputation. He'd seen the recognition and wary respect her name produced. Ella had done it all by herself.

Without anyone to hold her hand.

"Your parents must be proud of you," he said at last.

"They're very much older."

She'd mentioned that before….

And it didn't answer his question. But it prompted another thought. "Don't tell me you look after them, too?"

In response, Ella inclined her head slightly.

"You do!" He blinked in disbelief. She shouldered the burden of her entire family. "And your sister still comes running to you for everything she needs."

"She always has, but I don't mind. We're sisters, after all." She came instantly to Keira's defense. "Your brother does it, too. I know because Keira told me."

Yevgeny bristled. "I don't have your patience. I told him to make a man of himself." And that decision had probably cost him dearly. For a time Dmitri had torn through the Volkovoy fortune while Yevgeny could only watch. He'd been wild—and irresponsible. A spendthrift and a wastrel. He'd run through everything that was handed to him—and then come back to demand more.

That's when Yevgeny had put his foot down—he'd refused... and demanded that Dmitri come with him to Auckland to set up the new headquarters for Volkovoy cruises.

Dmitri had argued that it was a job for a menial manager. But Yevgeny had refused to bow. Do a job, earn a salary or get out.

They'd quarreled. Dmitri had chosen to get out, screeching off to the smell of burnt rubber and Yevgeny had shuddered with fear and regret. For four days his brother had not returned home. Yevgeny had held vigil and waited for news of the worst.

On the fifth day Dmitri had called and sullenly said he was on his way to Auckland. Yevgeny had thanked the gods and hoped his brother wouldn't do anything recklessly stupid.

Yevgeny later learned he had Keira to thank for Dmitri's success in New Zealand.

Meeting Keira had saved his brother—or maybe it had been being cut off from funding for his lavish lifestyle and being forced to work, to be accountable for his actions for the first time in his overindulged life.

Whatever it was, Dmitri had finally started to grow up.

"I'm very proud of what he's done in Auckland. He's hired premises and sourced some excellent staff."

Behind her glasses, Ella rolled her eyes. "Keira said anyone could've done it. That Dmitri felt it was an insult to be given such a menial task to do."

"At least he didn't screw it up." He flashed her a smile.

"You expected him to," she said after a long moment.

"Honestly?" Her eyes demanded the truth, so he gave it. "Yes, I did."

"How could you think he would fail?"

"I didn't think he'd see it through. He's never had any firm idea of what he wants from life." He paused, then turned the focus back on Ella and her sister. "How can you talk. You don't expect anything of Keira. You still take care of her, sort out all her messes. She never needs to take accountability for anything.

You're even sorting out the adoption for a baby she wanted then discarded."

For once Ella had nothing to say. He watched as her mouth opened and closed. Finally she turned away and crossed to where three large store bags sat on the floor. She reached into the closest one and took out a box. She opened it, revealing a tray containing about a dozen shiny, red ornamental balls.

It was a moment of utter emotional devastation.

And Yevgeny felt like a complete toad. It was almost Christmas. It was a time for faith…and family. He'd insisted on helping Ella decorate a tree to celebrate the festivities for Holly—and now he was upsetting her.

That wasn't right. Yevgeny couldn't help thinking that his dearly loved *babushka* would be ashamed of him for ruining Ella's moment of pleasure and forcing her to accept unwanted assistance. She'd already told him to leave—that was what she wanted. If he behaved with the honor that his *babushka* would expect of him, Yevgeny knew he was left with no choice: he must leave….

He came to a decision. "You don't want me to stay and help you with the tree, so I will leave and come back later when Holly is awake."

With an inward sigh of disappointment, Yevgeny made his way to where he'd abandoned his jacket. But before he could lean down to pick it up, Ella spoke from behind him. "You can stay—if you want."

Yevgeny jerked around in surprise.

She wasn't even looking at him, nor did she sound particularly welcoming, yet his heart lifted.

"Thank you." Gratitude welled up inside him. Before she could change her mind, he moved to the tree and hoisted it up with enthusiasm. "The Christmas tree will look good over here, hmm?"

Ella tucked her hair behind one ear, and shifted her glance to where he indicated. "Yes, I think you're right—that's the perfect spot."

His lips curved in a smile and he shot her an amused look through the gap between two branches. "Good. For once we're in agreement."

She met his gaze. Then, after a moment, she grinned back. "Yes. It would appear we are."

Ella McLeod had dimples in both cheeks.

To avoid the confusion the discovery aroused, Yevgeny ducked down and secured the base of the tree. When he'd safely assured himself that noticing Ella had dimples didn't change anything of great consequence, he finally raised his head again.

"Have you got lights for the tree?" he asked. "They will need to go up first."

Ella dove back into the shopping bags and emerged, waving a box of brand-new Christmas lights with a triumphant flourish. Another smile...and her dimples flashed again.

Blood pumped through his veins.

Yevgeny averted his gaze, and busied himself with taking the box from her hands. Her slender fingers brushed against his large ones—an electric connection. He didn't dare look at her as he broke the seal. Once the lid was open, he lifted the coiled rope of lights out. Immediately Ella crowded closer.

He inhaled deeply.

Lilacs.

Yes, he was in danger of becoming addicted to the subtle scent....

Shaking his head in rejection of that craziness, Yevgeny started to weave the lights through the branches while Ella worked alongside him, making adjustments. He'd never been this close to her for any length of time. It felt curiously—he searched for the right word—exhilarating. When she stepped away to shake out the remaining cable and then went to plug it into the wall socket, he found himself sharply aware of the gray void left in her wake.

A flick of the switch and color lit up the room.

Even Ella's white, cropped T-shirt reflected the rainbow wash of Christmas lights. It looked magical. Yevgeny found himself chuckling at the pretty picture she made.

Ella reached down and switched the lights off. "Now we know they work!"

"Are you always so prosaic?"

She glanced at him through the fan of hair that shielded her face. "Always."

Despite her reply, Yevgeny couldn't halt the spreading of awareness. He considered himself a connoisseur of beautiful women—he'd dated some of the world's best. So why hadn't he noticed how well proportioned her features were? The straight nose, the short delicate arch of her upper lip, and the uptilted curve of her smile all combined to create a striking face.

But he hadn't noticed it.

Until now.

He hadn't bothered to look beyond the dark suits, oversize glasses and abrasive manner.

What else had he missed?

"You have lovely eyes, you know," he said abruptly. "But those hideous glasses you wear do nothing to show them off."

Shock flickered in her eyes, and then a flush stained her cheeks. "Thank you…I think."

"It was a compliment—you shouldn't hide your assets."

Without replying, she pushed her glasses up, then tucked her head down and scrabbled around in the shopping bags again. "I bought decorative balls to hang on the tree."

Ella had changed the subject.

His mouth slanted. Had he really expected a different response? Or was it so hard for her to accept a compliment? He was growing more and more curious about a woman whom he wouldn't have glanced at twice a week ago.

He refrained from pointing out that she'd already opened one box and smiled at her as she continued, "I ordered red-and-silver balls from an online catalog." Ella drew out the second box. "They should look very pretty against the dark green foliage."

He let her off the hook. "My grandmother had a collection of antique glass balls."

That garnered her interest. "Your grandmother? Is she still alive?"

Yevgeny shook his head. "Unfortunately not. She passed away two months ago."

Behind those ugly glasses, Ella's eyes were perceptive. "You miss her."

"Very much—she was a loving woman." Unlike her daughter, his mother. But Yevgeny had no intention to brood about the past.

"She was Russian?" Ella was asking.

"No. She was English." He picked up one of the red balls and hooked the silver ribbon securing it over a branch. After a pause during which he could sense Ella bursting to ask more, he said, "She married my very Russian grandfather after the Second World War—and taught him to speak English. In the process, she became more Russian than he was. The handblown glass decorations she treasured belonged to his family."

"Did she ever return to England?"

"No." But his mother had, taking him and Dmitri with her....

"Was she happy living so far from home?"

It took him a moment to shift his thoughts back to their conversation, and pick up the thread again. Ella was talking about his grandmother.

"She loved my grandfather. Her home was with him." And she'd loved him and Dmitri. *Babushka* had brought some degree of normality into their lives, normality that had vanished once his mother had ripped them away from their father. Without *Babushka* their lives had been barren of feminine affection—because his beautiful mother had had little to spare. Every day Yevgeny remembered his *babushka's* legacy of kindness. "She was one in a million."

His words hung in the air as they continued to loop decorations onto the branches.

After a few minutes he added, "My *babushka* collected

wooden decorations, too. She used to say she liked her tree to be a true *yolka*."

"*Yolka?*"

Yevgeny smiled as Ella tried the unfamiliar word out.

"The traditional tree is called the *yolka*," he told her. "The first Christmas tree was brought back to Russia by Peter the Great after his travels. The tradition became very popular, until Christmas was outlawed after the 1917 Revolution. It became known as a New Year's Tree."

"That's sad."

"For most of my life Christmas celebrations have been allowed," he said quickly, lest she feel pity for him, "although people had gotten used to celebrating on the first of January, so changing back to Christmas day came slowly at first." Yevgeny changed the subject. "Your family celebrated Christmas?"

Ella hesitated. "Well, we always decorated a tree—and my parents gave us Christmas gifts each year. But they didn't believe in perpetuating the myth of Santa Claus. They were older," she said with a touch of defensiveness when he stared. "And when Keira was young I used to wrap something of mine for her to find on Christmas morning. I'd tell her it was from Santa."

"My grandmother always made sure the family celebrated Christmas," he said, "even in the Iron Curtain years when it wasn't allowed. Although I don't remember that time—I was very young when the prohibition against Christmas was lifted. We would put our tree up earlier than New Year's Day so that we could have a Christmas tree, and we would decorate it with my grandmother's collection of ornaments and tangerines and walnuts carefully wrapped in tinfoil."

When he'd lived in London, even his mother had followed Western tradition and Santa Claus had visited each year. He and Dmitri had at least had the memories of finding gifts under the Christmas tree on Christmas morning—whatever else his mother had done, she had allowed them that small pleasure. What would life have been like for Ella and Keira? To be deprived of such simple joys? Especially when all their friends must've been visited by Santa's sleigh and his reindeer.

And this Christmas Keira would be on the other side of the world.

"Will you be getting together with your parents this Christmas?"

Ella shook her head. "No, we haven't celebrated together for a number of years."

Yes, Ella would be alone.

Not wanting her to see the compassion in his eyes, he turned away and started to hang the silver balls on the tree. But his mind couldn't let go of the image of Ella stoically wrapping her treasures to give to her sister—so that Keira wouldn't miss out on all the fun that went along with Santa. Was that part of the reason Ella seemed so humorless? Had all the fun been sapped out of her young life?

Perhaps...

All the more reason why this Christmas would be different for Holly.

As he made that vow, Yevgeny hung the last silver ball on the tree then stood back to admire their efforts. "Not bad," he declared. "Let's put the lights back on."

"Before I switch the lights on, there's one more item to go on the tree." Ella was unwrapping dark green tissue paper from the object she held in her hands. "The ornament for the top."

The wrapping fell away.

Yevgeny found himself staring at an angel. His first thought was that he would've expected Ella to choose a shiny silver star for the top of the tree. Nothing as personal—and as touchingly humorous—as this angel.

He reached out a hand to touch the angel.

"She's even more beautiful than I thought she would be from the online picture." Ella placed the angel in his hands, then hit the wall switch so that the tree lights came back on again. "She's handmade," continued Ella, as she straightened up. "What do you think?"

The angel wore a long robe of some kind of shimmery silver fabric. But, as Yevgeny held her up to the light, it was her face that captured his attention. Not beautiful. But full of childlike joy. Chubby and cherubic, the angel's face was brightened by a mischievous smile.

"She's perfect," he replied.

As he reached up and perched the angel on the apex of the tree, Yevgeny couldn't help thinking that in a few years' time, Holly would be itching to be the one to put the angel on top of the Christmas tree.

But Holly wouldn't be here...if Ella got her way.

Green. Yellow. Red.

The wash of light over his face didn't offer any assistance with making Yevgeny's expression easier to read. A mix of pensiveness...and some other emotion that Ella couldn't identify clouded his face.

She hesitated, then blurted out, "Would you like to look through the adoptive parent portfolios that Jo dropped off with me?"

Almost at once she regretted the offer. Already he was frowning. She must be going soft in the head to believe she and Yevgeny could do this without coming to blows. They were polar opposites. They never agreed on anything—this was going to end up in one big battle.

But before she could cast about for a reason to retract the invitation, the cloud cleared from his face, and he said, "Oh, yes! Perhaps I can finally make you see sense."

He flung himself down on the couch beneath the window and stretched his long legs out in front of him. Crossing his arms behind his head as he leaned back, he looked far too sure of himself.

Taking in the picture he made in his suit pants and white business shirt, together with the stubbled chin and rumpled dark hair, Ella wasn't sure whether to be exasperated or amused.

He looked quite at home…and it would probably take a bulldozer to move him out again.

But the truth of it was, if Yevgeny could see what some of these families had to offer a baby, he might even have second thoughts about his rash and selfish demand to keep the baby himself.

If Yevgeny reconsidered his standpoint, and accepted that adopting the baby out would be in Holly's best interests, it would be so much easier for them all. *If* he was involved in choosing a family for the baby, Holly would come out the winner.

Buoyed up with fresh optimism, Ella collected the five profile files Jo Wells had delivered from the dining table, then seated herself beside Yevgeny.

"Those look heavy." Unlocking his arms from behind his head, he bent forward to lift all but the bottom portfolio from her lap and set the stack on the coffee table in front of the couch.

"They are! They hold the whole life story—or at least the pertinent parts—of each couple." Ella opened the first folder. "This is the hardest part for me, the first photo of the couple together. Look at their eyes. They want this baby, they want Holly."

She paused.

Then, when Yevgeny remained silent, she added, "It's the same with each profile. Every time I have to conquer a surge of guilt before I turn the page."

When he slanted her a questioning glance, she said, "In case I don't choose them."

"I see."

From the look on his face, she could tell that he didn't get it.

"In case I didn't see the plea in their eyes, the desperation on their faces," she said to make it clear.

This time he got it.

She knew it by the shock in his eyes.

Maybe it was the word "desperation" that did it.

Ella turned the page. Then the next…and the next…until she reached the end. "This couple has two sons…they live in an apartment in Auckland City. Both parents are professionals—like me." She looked up to find Yevgeny's eyes already fixed on her. Shock jolted through her. She swallowed, then continued in a slightly husky voice. "Being professionals is good—I want Holly to have a career. But I visualized her having an older sister—and a garden growing up. Kids need space to roam. Two boys and an apartment? *And* their parents working long hours? I don't know. It might mean good money and a comfortable existence, but will the parents be able to give Holly—all of them—enough time?"

Yevgeny shook his head.

She set the portfolio aside and reached for the next one. Leaning back she discovered that Yevgeny had rested his arm along the back of the couch, bringing him so much closer. Tingles danced over her skin as her nerve endings went on high alert. A deep, steadying breath only made her more aware of the musky male scent that clung to him.

Hurriedly, Ella flipped open the folder and concentrated on the first photo.

This time the decision was easy. *No.* The family just was not right. But the following profile was much tougher to look through. The family seemed to tick off all the boxes that Ella could ask for, yet she didn't find herself overcome with enthusiasm.

"They do look lovely—they have a daughter already." She tried to fake enthusiasm as she paged through the file. "A garden. And two dogs."

"Her mouth is too set—she's a witch." Yevgeny arched forward and pointed at the mother with the hand that was not settled on the back of the couch.

"Nonsense! She's not a witch. She's smiling!" Glancing up to protest, Ella could see the dark stubble on his chin, the hard angles of his cheekbones.

Yevgeny turned his head. Their gazes tangled. "But her eyes are not. And that dog looks like it can't wait to get off her lap."

Ella couldn't breathe!

Feeling crowded, she glanced away…down…and focused on the photo in front of her.

The little girl wasn't smiling at all.

Ella's heart sank. Did that matter? Was it really significant? With a confused sigh she said, "We may be seeing things that don't even exist."

The instant Yevgeny removed his arm from behind her, the twisted mix of excitement and apprehension that had been fluttering in her stomach like a caged butterfly eased. She watched Yevgeny reach for the previous two portfolios, page through them and jab a finger at the family portraits. "In both of these the parents are touching each other."

Ella looked closer—it was true. She glanced back at the third portrait in the folder still open on her lap. The parents sat far apart—a gaping space yawned between them. Despite their smiles neither of them looked terribly happy. "Perhaps it's the pressure—they know how important this is."

"They're supposed to be selling themselves."

"No!" Ella pulled away a few inches to put some distance between them. "They're trying to adopt a baby."

"All the more reason to put the best—the happiest—picture forward."

She wanted to tell him that he was cynical, that he was oversimplifying the matter. But when Ella stared hard at the three faces in the photo, she realized that it didn't work for her. There was no vibe of joy or intimacy.

Ella made her decision and shut the folder with a snap.

She wasn't letting Holly go to this family. "They may be wonderful people. It may have been a tense day when the photos were taken. But that's a no."

She couldn't take that very remote chance of sending Holly to an unhappy home.

A smile lit up Yevgeny's face.

Was that a glint of triumph? Ella stilled. Suddenly his closeness took on a new aspect. Was the enforced intimacy deliberate? Had his comments been staged?

Was she being manipulated by an expert?

She rejected the suspicion almost instantly. She was no pushover.

Then she paused.

Who had the most to gain if she rejected all the families?

The answer came at once.

Yevgeny.

Ella tipped her head to one side and studied him, measuring and resisting the magnetic pull of that sexy bottom lip, the sculpted masculine features and the clear piercing eyes.

Had he deliberately tried to put her off that last family? "You're not asking me if I'm going to change my mind and keep the baby?"

"I know you won't."

The speed of his response took her aback. Ella realized she'd half expected him to try and persuade her not to give up on the child. "Why've you finally decided that?"

His eyes narrowed. Reaction bolted like lightning forks through her. His gaze drifted over her…down…down…sending shivers in its wake…then returned to her face.

Was *that* calculated, too? A deliberate attempt to ratchet up her awareness of him?

Or was she simply far too suspicious?

Ella forced herself to hold his gaze.

"You're not cut out for motherhood." There was distance between them—as wide as the Pacific and many times as deep. He shrugged. "Some women simply aren't."

All the frisson of awareness froze. The delicious moments of understanding beside the Christmas tree evaporated.

She tensed.

The dismissal implicit in his words, in that careless shrug, needled her.

How dare Yevgeny judge her when he didn't even know what made her tick? How dare he assume who she was…and what she wasn't? But she bit back the fierce tide of anger and said instead with quiet force, "What's that supposed to mean?"

Beneath the question lay a vast sea of unspoken pain.

He looked startled at the challenge. "That your career is too important. That you have other priorities." He shrugged again, in that way that was starting to seriously rile her. "It's not unusual not to want to be a mother. I've known other women like you."

He had?

And had he been as clueless about what made those women tick?

Carefully, through tight-pressed lips, Ella said, "I'm starting to think Nadiya had a very lucky escape."

Yevgeny rolled his eyes to the ceiling. "Of course you do."

Then he reached forward and picked the last profile off the coffee table in front of them. "Let's see if this couple is any more suitable than the rest."

Ella let out the breath trapped in her lungs. This time she was determined to open to the front page and fall in love with the family revealed within. This would be it. Then the search would be over, and Yevgeny would have to live with her decision.

But it didn't happen.

The text accompanying the photo indicated that couple had no children. And they requested a closed adoption.

That request unexpectedly rattled Ella.

Badly.

For the first time she realized what it would mean to never see Holly again—or at least not until her baby was all grown up and legally an adult who could request information about the identity of her birth mother contained in the sealed adoption records. To not know what color her baby's eyes turned out to be. To miss out on news about her first day at school. To never see photos of her first school dance.

Ella hadn't contemplated how much comfort having an open adoption gave her. Until now.

She didn't need to read any further. "No."

In the silence that followed, the thud of the folder landing on the coffee table sounded overloud. Ella flinched.

"At this rate you aren't going to find a family for Holly." Yevgeny sounded faintly smug. "You might find I'll be the only choice left."

"Never!" she vowed. That was not an option.

He smirked. "Never is a very long time."

"I'll ask Jo for the next set of files."

"And when all of those families fall short of your rigorous demands, what then?"

Was Yevgeny right? Was it possible that his manipulation had nothing to do with it, that she had set her standards too high? Ella looked away from him and studied the mountain of portfolios through blank eyes, then dismissed his theory.

No, she knew exactly what kind of parents she wanted for Holly.

They were out there.

Somewhere…

Drawing a steadying breath, she pushed her glasses up her nose and glanced across the couch at Yevgeny. "I'll find a family—and you're right, they will be perfect, absolutely perfect, for the baby."

Instead of the usual cocksure arrogance, there was a glint of something close to sympathy in his eyes. Slowly he shook his head from side to side. "You're not going to find what you're looking for."

"How can you say that?"

"Because I know you, Ella. Better than you know yourself."

Ella rejected that instantly. The man was delusional—he didn't know her. At all. So much for thinking she'd recognized sympathetic understanding in his eyes. All it had been was a different kind of arrogance.

"You're mad," she said.

Yet instead of flaring up in anger as she'd half expected at her accusation, he laughed, showing off dazzling white teeth. His mood had changed again.

"It's day five today. Do you really think you're going to

allow yourself to find a family before Christmas if you carry on being this picky?"

It had nothing to do with "allowing" herself. He had that all wrong. When she saw the right couple…she would know deep in her heart that they were the ones. Ella was utterly certain of that.

"I'm not being unreasonably picky," she argued. "I want the right family. I'm not going to rush this."

Even as she spoke Ella could feel the tension starting to rewind tightly in her stomach. Time was of essence. No one understood that better than she did.

She *had* to find Holly a family.

A week from today would be day twelve, the day she could finally sign the consent to adoption. The sooner Holly could start to bond with her family, the better. Yevgeny was right—if she carried on picking apart every family she would only delay letting Holly go to a family who would love and cherish her.

But on the other hand…it *was* almost Christmas.

How could she push the baby away before Christmas? She paused.

Why not…

Before she could stop herself her mind traveled down the forbidden path. The anguish she'd expected didn't come.

Yes, why not?

Ella came to a decision.

"I don't have to find a family before Christmas. I'm going to wait until after Christmas. That way Holly can spend her first Christmas here." Fearing the blaze of triumph she was certain Yevgeny's face would reflect, her gaze flicked to the corner dominated by the giant tree with its merry flashing lights.

The red-and-silver balls gleamed warmly.

The right family would emerge after Christmas.

Once she'd taken down the Christmas tree that Yevgeny had helped her put up this evening…and finally said goodbye to the baby…she would have plenty of time to reflect—and come to terms with how her life had been unexpectedly changed. And perhaps she would even follow Jo's advice and attend grief counseling.

For now she would take it one day at a time.

In the meantime, she'd take photos—make an album for the baby to take with her to her new life. That way Holly would one day be able to look back and see where her life had started.

And Ella would be satisfied that she'd done everything she could for the baby.

Because Yevgeny was right: she wasn't the kind of woman who wanted to be a mother. She was enough like his own mother to terrify him.

She was determined to choose someone better for Holly.

Seven

Seated behind the desk in her office, a legal pad open in front of her, Ella gazed sympathetically at the young, heavily pregnant woman on the other side of the desk. When Peggy had arrived to start work early this morning, she'd discovered a pregnant, tearful Pauline Patterson waiting in the lobby for the law offices to open. Taking in Pauline's red-rimmed eyes, Ella could see why her paralegal had been worried about the young woman and why Peggy had wasted no time in summoning Ella back to work.

"You're certain divorce is the course of action you want to take?" she asked Pauline.

"I can't afford a lawyer, but my sister said if I didn't retain one my husband would take me to the cleaners."

A few more questions elicited the fact that Pauline Patterson's sister seemed to have a lot of opinions about the marriage— yet some of the problems that were plaguing the couple didn't sound insurmountable to Ella. Especially given the sadness in Pauline's eyes when she spoke of leaving her husband.

Carefully Ella asked, "Have you tried couples counseling?"

Pauline shook her head. "No. My sister said I needed a lawyer—to show Ian I meant business."

Ella ignored the sister's views and explained, "Through the courts you're entitled to six free sessions. I strongly recommend that you try counseling first." Ella couldn't stop herself from glancing down at Pauline's swollen stomach. "It's a good idea to exhaust all alternatives first. Divorce is stressful for everyone... and it can be very final. Sometimes there is no going back."

Fear flared in Pauline's eyes. "I still love Ian. I don't really want to get a divorce—I want to sort this out. My sister says this is the best way to get his attention."

"He's not listening to you?"

"His friends are more important to him than me or the baby." There was a doleful note in the young woman's voice. "I miss my mother—she's back in England. Now that I'm pregnant, I need help." Tears rolled down Pauline's cheeks.

"Have you told your husband you need more help—that you miss your mother?"

Pauline shook her head. "No. His mother and my mother both said we were too young to get married. I've been determined to prove them all wrong. To show everyone—even Ian—that I wasn't too young."

Ella asked a few more questions that revealed that money wasn't a problem. Although both Pauline and Ian seemed to shop more than they should, Ian had a good job with prospects of another promotion soon. Nor, to Ella's relief, was he verbally or physically abusive. It appeared this was a case of both of them needing to grow up quickly now that they had a baby on the way, and learning to talk and listen to each other better.

Coming to a decision, Ella said, "Before you go further down the road with a divorce, why don't you talk to Ian about your unhappiness? I suggest that you both go to counseling and visit a budgeting service. If Ian refuses to go, I think you should take advantage of the sessions for yourself."

Ella reached into a drawer for business cards for a couple of counselors who worked with the court, and another card for a local budgeting service.

She smiled at the young woman as she handed the cards to her. "Sometimes, when you spend more than you earn, financial worries can put a lot of pressure on a marriage—particularly if there's a baby on the way. And if Ian is out with friends all hours of the night when you're tired and pregnant, resentment can breed. These people may be able to help you. If they can't, and you still feel certain that dissolving your marriage is the only way forward, come and see me again. We will put a plan into action."

Pauline glanced down at the business cards she held. "You really think this will work?"

This was a question to which Ella never had a good enough answer. "There are no guarantees. But at least you will know in your heart that you tried everything before you decided that divorce was the only solution. And that will help you when you start the road to recovery. You'll have fewer regrets."

Over the years Ella had learned that often parties who consulted with her determined to secure a divorce wanted nothing more than to be pointed in the right direction to save their marriage. Not in all cases, but enough for her to know that six sessions of counseling were worth trying first.

As Pauline thanked her, tears of hope sparkling in her eyes, Ella's lips curved up into a small smile, and she couldn't help wondering what Yevgeny would say if he saw her now—hardly the hotshot lawyer out to destroy every marriage in town for an outrageous fee.

Yevgeny took in the tearstained face of the young woman exiting Ella's office as he stood aside to let her pass. Then he entered Ella's workspace, shut the door behind him—and pounced. "You're doing her divorce?"

"That's none of your business!"

Ella's light brown eyes were cool. She stood behind the

barrier of a highly polished wooden desk, clad in one of those black power suits he'd come to hate.

"She's pregnant!" The angry words ripped from him.

"That doesn't mean anything. There are times when divorce is the right thing—even for a pregnant woman."

"And what about the baby's father? What if it's not the right thing for him?" Blood pounded in his head. Everything he'd come here to say had evaporated from his mind. Now he could only think about another divorce…another father deprived of his sons. *His* father. "What about the father's rights?"

"Everything in a divorce is negotiated."

"Not if the woman lies." It was a snarl. "Not if she manipulates everything and everyone to get sole custody, and bars her husband from ever seeing the children…I mean, the child," he corrected himself quickly, as he stalked to the front edge of the wooden desk. Ella still stood on the other side. She didn't seem to have noticed his slip of tongue, as she watched him, unmoved. "Both father and child lose then. I ask you, is that right? Is it fair?"

"Yevgeny, it's my job to make certain—"

"Your job is to be a divorce lawyer."

"Family lawyer," she corrected.

"You broker agreements, which keep boys from their fathers and wait like a vulture over a kill."

"What?"

She drew herself up, which wasn't much higher than his shoulder, Yevgeny knew. Her eyes blazed gold fire at him across the expanse of the polished desk.

"I don't do anything of the kind! Divorce is hard on everyone. It's my job to make the arrangements workable after a marriage ends. And that means taking the children's needs into consideration from the very beginning. Sure, the spouses are often furious with each other, but it's part of my responsibility to make sure that the party I'm representing is aware that their children take priority. I don't try to prevent the father's access to his kids—unless there's reason to do so. Violence. A history of abuse." She shrugged. "My job is not always pleasant."

"I'm not talking about instances of domestic violence." Yevgeny refused to back down. "I'm talking about women who manipulate you—and the judge." His voice was thick, his Russian accent pronounced. He drew a deep, shuddering breath and forced himself to relax.

He'd arrived at Ella's house earlier to visit Holly—and discovered Ella had abandoned the baby to return to work. He'd been outraged. He'd come here to tell Ella what he thought of her—not to be dragged into the past.

Her brow wrinkled. "Are we talking about a specific case here?"

He looked away. His stomach tightened. For a moment he could smell the long-forgotten musty smell of another legal office with its wooden-paneled walls and leather chairs. He could see the never-forgotten triumph in his mother's smile as she rose to her feet to shake the lawyer's hand. It had been three years until he'd seen his father again, and only because his mother had walked out of the fancy house his father paid a fortune to maintain, leaving her two sons alone in it. The housekeeper had called his father to advise that his mother had gone—she couldn't have cared less.

When he looked back at Ella, her head was tipped to one side as she inspected him. The brown eyes no longer flamed, they'd warmed to the pale gold of honey behind her glasses. "Did you have a child taken from you in the past?"

He'd never heard that soft, sweet tone from her before.

My God. She felt pity for him! No one ever felt that kind of emotion for him. *Never.* It rocked Yevgeny. He shook his head in a jerky motion, rejecting the very idea. "This is not about me!"

"Isn't it?" Ella stepped around the desk and came toward him. "Are you sure?"

This wasn't about him...this was about...about—

His Holly.

He could feel every muscle in his body growing increasingly

taut with every step that brought Ella closer. He wanted her to stop. He didn't want her coming near enough for him to pick up on her lilac scent. He didn't want her kindness. Not until he could examine why her sympathy caused him to crack wide open inside.

Yevgeny struggled to marshal the anger and outrage that had driven him here. He'd rather remember the side of her he detested—the human icicle, the mother who wanted to send the child she'd given birth to away and abandon her without a second thought.

That was the woman he never wanted near him. And he knew the easiest way to keep that woman—and her questions—at bay....

"What did you advise your young client?" he barked out. "To wangle as much from her husband as she can? To lie to get sole custody?"

Pausing, one foot in front of the other, Ella halted, and Yevgeny exhaled a silent sigh of relief.

Mission accomplished.

Then she said, "You can't expect me to answer that. Any advice I give is subject to legal privilege. But I can tell you that before proceeding with divorce action, I often suggest to clients that they try counseling—"

"Airy-fairy stuff." Yevgeny waved a dismissive hand. "No help at all."

"Or get budgeting advice," she continued evenly as if he hadn't interrupted. But her eyes sparkled behind her spectacles. "I'm sure a financially savvy man like you would appreciate the wisdom of that."

One dark eyebrow shot up. "Budgeting advice so that these women can afford your usurious fees?"

"No!" For the first time Ella sounded annoyed. "Budgeting advice to help them save their marriages!"

He took in the anger on her face. He was angry, too. This was not going to help his position with Holly. Yevgeny let out his breath. "This is not why I came. I will call you when we both have had a chance to simmer down."

Given their previous confrontation, the last person Ella wanted to see when she walked into her home the following evening was Yevgeny. She still had not "simmered down" as he had put it.

To make matters worse, he looked totally at ease sprawled across the carpet of her living room, his gray satin tie loosened, shirtsleeves rolled up and his hair ruffled. Holly lay on her back beside him, looking perfectly content, her bare legs kicking in the air, while the Christmas tree sparkled merrily in the background.

It was all very cozy and festive…a scene from a Christmas card…and Ella felt like a complete outsider in her own home.

"Where's Deb?" she demanded, stopping in front of Yevgeny.

"I told her to take a break while I'm here."

His high-handedness annoyed Ella. Deb reported to her, not to her nemesis. It was something she would have to discuss with the nanny.

Then Ella told herself to lighten up. It was Friday evening, she wanted to relax…but his presence nixed any chance of that.

Holly gave a squeak, and Ella instantly dropped to her knees beside her. The baby appeared to be fascinated with her own hands. She gave another high-pitched shriek.

Ella's heartbeat steadied.

Of course there was nothing wrong!

Except that she was hovering too close to the baby….

She shifted and glanced away.

Straight into Yevgeny's curious eyes.

It was a good time to remember that she hadn't forgiven him for likening her to a vulture circling a kill yesterday.

Which led her to one of the many questions that his visit to her offices had raised….

"I never did find out what you were doing at my offices

yesterday. I take it you didn't simply arrive planning to call me a vulture?" Ella raised a questioning eyebrow.

He looked discomforted. Sitting up, he said, "I ordered in dinner—I thought you might enjoy not having to cook tonight. You could give Deb the entire evening off."

"Then I'd have to look after the baby instead of cook," she pointed out, not sure that she liked the fact that he'd walked in here and taken over her life. She held her breath, waiting for him to accuse her of all the motherly shortcomings he usually did.

A furrow creased his brow, and she tensed. He surprised her by saying, "I intended to play with the baby. I thought you might want to relax. Keira once said you like to take Friday evenings easy."

Ella blinked.

He was trying to be considerate?

Was that possible? Her gaze slid to Holly. The baby was wriggling her fingers and making cooing sounds. She looked wonderfully content. It shouldn't be too difficult for Yevgeny to look after her.

"You ordered dinner in?" she asked in case she'd misunderstood.

"Yes, Italian."

That really got her attention. She loved Italian food. How did he know that? Had he pumped Peggy for information about her yesterday? Or had he been cross-examining Deb? Another thought struck her....

"Should I consider this an apology for your rudeness yesterday?"

A flush seared the high, Slavic cheekbones. "The food is from La Rosa."

The diversion worked. "I didn't know La Rosa does takeout—much less that they deliver."

"They don't."

So he was pulling out all the stops. "But you convinced them?" His sheepish nod confirmed it. "Who told you it's my favorite restaurant?"

"Keira."

"You spoke to Keira today?"

"No—she mentioned it a while ago."

"Before they left?"

"Yes." The word was dragged out of him.

What interpretation was she supposed to put on his reluctant confession that he'd remembered—and acted on—something Keira had most likely mentioned in passing?

Ella grew impatient with herself. It probably meant nothing more than that Yevgeny Volkovoy had a frighteningly good memory.

Something she'd be wise to keep in mind.

True to his word, Yevgeny tended to Holly. He even helped Deb bathe and change the baby before the nanny left. He played with the baby, waving toys and rattles to stimulate her interest. Before she could become too caught up in watching Holly interacting with her uncle, Ella excused herself to express milk from her aching breasts for the baby's next feed and to enjoy a soak in a bubble bath before the meal arrived.

By the time she emerged, dressed in comfortable skinny jeans and a T-shirt, wonderfully relaxed and scented from her fragrant hot bath, Yevgeny had set her dining table for two and, more miraculously, gotten Holly off to sleep. The handset from the baby monitor lay on the table.

Ella was impressed by his efforts—even though her eyes lingered on the second place setting.

Yevgeny intercepted her gaze. "I am staying. I want to assess whether La Rosa's cuisine lives up to your high recommendation. And I have something I wish to ask you. But I think I hear the food arriving. Let's eat first."

To Ella's delight the meal was excellent—well up to La Rosa's high standards, even without the ambience of the restaurant setting. Even better, Yevgeny graciously declared it to be among the best Italian he'd eaten in a long time.

"As an apology, that meal was most certainly acceptable."

Ella set down her dessert spoon after savoring the last spoonful of tiramisu and smiled at him.

Rather than take umbrage at her gentle ribbing, he laughed, but once his laughter died away, an awkward silence settled over the table.

Ella broke it first. Pushing her spectacles up her nose, she said, "Are you ready to tell me why you came to see me yesterday?"

He picked up his half-full glass of red wine and sat back in his chair. "I was annoyed that you'd gone back to work. I intended to confront you."

"You have no right to question my decision. My practice is my livelihood. I don't meddle in your business." Ella leaned forward, determined not to allow him to push her around. For once, the big Russian had the grace to look abashed. "Besides, I made it clear from the outset that I wouldn't look after the baby. I'm giving Holly up for adoption. I don't want to make what is already a difficult situation more difficult by bonding with her." Even by expressing her milk to feed the baby, Ella suspected she was becoming closer than she'd ever meant to be to Holly. Inside she could feel her muscles tensing and the all too familiar anxiety that she took such pains to conceal rising. The sense of well-being that the soak in the tub and the delicious meal had instilled was rapidly ebbing.

"I understand."

"Then why your annoyance yesterday?"

He didn't answer, instead swirling the glass and appearing to be enraptured by the deep ruby glow of the wine. Then he looked up, and the illusion of contentment shattered. His eyes were full of turmoil. "I understand now. I spoke to Jo Wells earlier."

What had Jo said? Ella sought his eyes for answers. But found none to justify the panic that flared inside her.

Jo couldn't have told him anything. Because not even Jo knew.

Unless Keira had told her...

Ella blocked out the possibility of such a devastating betrayal.

"The way Jo explained your decision not to bond with the baby made me realize that it wasn't an act of neglect or selfishness."

Her teeth snapped together. She'd been trying to get that through to him. But he listened to a stranger? "Thanks!"

"She also said that you wouldn't be forsaking Holly—that you intend to keep in close contact with her. She told me that you were always adamant—even when Keira and Dmitri planned to adopt her—that Holly should know that you were her tummy mummy."

Despite her outrage, it was so incongruous to hear him use that term for surrogacy that Ella almost smiled. "It's always been important to me that there should be no deception in this kind of situation—it only hurts the child." She shuddered inwardly as she looked away.

If he only knew…

When she glanced back, it was to find that Yevgeny was swirling the wine again, staring into the rich, red depths.

It must be hard for him to face the fact that he'd seriously misjudged her—and admit it. Many men would've shirked this. Maybe it was time to cut him a little slack.

"You can drink it," she assured him to lighten the mood. "It's a good wine—gold medalist, in fact."

That brought his gaze back to her. "I didn't think you would poison me."

This time it was Ella who laughed. "What makes you so sure?"

"You uphold the letter of the law. I don't see you as breaking it. I'm starting to realize you have plenty of integrity."

The unexpected compliment warmed her.

Her lips tilting up, she said, "Flatterer!"

He shook his head. "No, it's the truth…which I appear to have managed to miss."

"While we're on the topic of truth, what was really going on in my office yesterday? I asked you if you'd lost custody of a child in the past. Tell me about your child, Yevgeny," she invited softly.

A mask dropped into place.

He smiled. But no hint of humor lit his eyes. It was as though a dark thundercloud hung over him. Ella shivered, no longer sure she should pursue this line of questioning. There was pain there…and something else.

"What child? I've never been married."

Ella slanted him an old-fashioned look to lighten the mood. "I didn't think you of all people would believe you had to be married to get someone pregnant."

He chuckled. "Very funny!"

She wrinkled her nose at him, and decided to probe a little more. "So what was it all about?"

"What do you mean?" he stalled.

"There was something else going on."

"You're imagining things."

She stared at him for a long moment. His mouth was flat, there was no hint of the humor that had lit his eyes only seconds before she'd started pushing. "I don't think I am. What's more…I think it has to do with a lawyer—but not me." She thought about her own life, about what had caused her to develop her prickly, reserved shell. "Did a woman do a real number on you?"

He laughed, and she detected a palpable tension beneath the careless sound. "Never!"

"She was a lawyer, wasn't she?"

He laughed again.

This time with relief, Ella suspected. Okay, so she wasn't quite there yet, but she was definitely on the right track. She was certain of it when Yevgeny said, "You're making too much of this—"

"Because you never let anyone in," she interrupted. "No one gets close enough."

His reaction was recognizable. She did the same thing. It was what she'd been doing ever since she was nineteen. She guarded her emotions zealously, only letting Keira past the barricade of her defenses.

"What did she do?"

"Stop trying to psychoanalyze me."

"Why?" She leaned across the dining table, and rested a hand on his arm. Beneath her fingers his flesh was firm, the muscle taut. For a moment she marveled at her brazenness. "Am I getting warm?"

"Warm?" He recoiled from her touch. Ella let her hand fall. The skin stretched across his cheekbones until his face resembled a death mask. "You're as cold as ice."

She got the double meaning at once. Yevgeny considered her cold. It hurt.

Ella swallowed and looked away, determined not to let him see what his words had done to her.

What did it matter that he thought that she was as cold as ice? He wasn't the first to think so, and he wouldn't be the last. It was what she'd wanted, wasn't it? She'd cultivated a cool, distant manner to keep men like him at bay. She certainly didn't want him to feel she was approachable, or God help her, receptive to his compliments and flattery and the advances that would inevitably follow.

Or did she?

That thought was the most horrifyingly painful of all.

Escape became a necessity for survival.

"I think I'll go and check to make sure the baby is sleeping." She stumbled to her feet before he could comment on her sudden maternal urge. "I'm sure you're ready to go. You can close the front door behind you."

It was only after she heard the front door softly close long minutes later that Ella realized that she hadn't discovered what Yevgeny had wanted to ask of her.

Eight

Yevgeny wasn't certain of his reception when he rang the doorbell to Ella's home on Sunday morning. So when she finally opened the door and the warm summer sun fell on her face, he experienced an unfamiliar, giddy surge of relief.

"You never did say what you wanted to ask me on Friday night." Behind her spectacles, her honey-brown eyes were wide with wariness. "I expect that's why you're here today. Or have you come to see Holly?"

It shouldn't surprise him that she'd guessed what he was doing here. But it did. The way in which she was so attuned to his thoughts, his actions, should've driven a stake into his heart. He didn't need Ella of all people possessing the ability to read his mind. There was too much that was private—and some information was not his alone to share.

Yet, instead of bolting in fear as he had on Friday night, he stood his ground.

Nor did he take refuge in half-truths and claim that he'd only come to visit Holly, although the baby did play a big role in his presence here today. But, to be fair, he'd played with her when he'd passed by yesterday. Ella had been out. "I wanted to ask you if you would come with me to look at a house I'm thinking of buying," he said, deciding that directness would be the best policy.

Whatever she'd been expecting, clearly, it hadn't been that. "You're buying a house?"

He nodded. More than a house, a home. For him...and Holly.

With the sun playing across her features Ella looked warm and approachable. For a moment he had a vision of...

Then he pulled himself together.

What was he considering? Was he mad?

He tried to get a grasp on his thoughts...and answer her so that she wouldn't get a whiff of the crazy notion he'd experienced. "It's time. The penthouse apartment has never been more than a place to sleep after a long day's work. I want a building with space around it. A garden. And I'd like a woman's opinion on the house I've seen."

Ella rested one arm against the doorjamb, blocking his entry. "Why not take Nadiya— Why me?"

He gave her a disbelieving look. "Do you think Nadiya would want to come and look at houses with me after the humiliation of our last encounter?"

He didn't want to take Nadiya—or any other woman. It had to be Ella. No one else would understand....

"You haven't seen her since?"

The question jolted him. "Nadiya?"

"Yes, Nadiya."

He shook his head.

Ella hesitated. "I suppose I could join you. Now would be better than later. I'd planned to prepare for a meeting on Monday. So, as long as you give me a few minutes to get ready, I'll come. Holly is taking a nap. I'll need to tell Deb we're going out so that she can get her ready."

"It might be a good idea to leave Holly here."

At the surprised look she shot him, he added reluctantly, "My Porsche is a two-seater." It was becoming clear to him that, along with a new home, he was going to have to purchase a new car, too.

"We can take my car…it's a station wagon," she said wryly.

That amused Yevgeny. Ella didn't have dogs or children yet she drove a station wagon? He kept the observation to himself. "We'll take my car and leave Holly at home. That way the visit will take less time." And as much as he adored the baby, this morning he wanted Ella's undivided attention. It would be easier to assess her gut response to the house without the baby around to distract her. "I'll call the Realtor to arrange access."

"You'd better come in while I get ready." She stepped away from the doorjamb to let him pass, and tossed him a prim smile. "I won't be long."

As Yevgeny followed Ella indoors he told himself it was going to be okay—everything would work out. The sunny morning. Her smile. The fact that Christmas was fast approaching.

All augured well.

He could sense that Ella was beginning to weaken.

As Yevgeny pulled the Porsche to a stop, Ella's breath caught in her throat.

Nestled amidst sprawling gardens, the house was not a multimillion-dollar sculpture comprised of a series of post-modern boxes.

It was a jewel of a home.

With wide lawns and big leafy trees, it cried welcome to a family—not a bachelor billionaire.

Yevgeny unclipped his seat belt and turned to her. "I like the feel of this place. What do you think?"

What did she think? She loved it. But…

Ella stared through the tinted windshield trying—and failing—to imagine Yevgeny living here all by himself. "It looks…big."

"Three stories, garage for half a dozen cars, several reception rooms, a home cinema, an indoor heated pool, staff quarters—and six bedrooms," he recited. "But that's not what interests me."

He climbed out the sports car and came around to open her door before she could ask what *did* interest him—if not the sheer impressive scale of the residence.

"Come."

Ella followed Yevgeny along the path that led up to the house.

Her emotions were all over the place. Why was Yevgeny considering buying such a house? He already had a penthouse apartment—from what she'd heard it was extremely luxurious. Why did he need a house, too?

Unless…

For Holly?

But Ella was not ready to face what the answer to that might mean. For the baby. For her. For everyone. Instead, she paused under the spreading, twisted branches of an old pohutukawa tree, and said, "Ah, a real, live New Zealand Christmas tree. It's made for a tree house."

His gaze followed hers to the beautiful branches loaded with bunches of red flowers. "I'm afraid I know little about tree houses—Dmitri and I never had one."

"This calls out for one." Squinting upward, Ella continued, "In fact, there's enough space for a playhouse up there. It would need to be furnished. Chairs. A table. Kid-size crockery. Keira and I had a tree house growing up—we spent hours in ours."

"What did you do?"

"We held tea parties. And played dress-up. And one summer we even made lemonade from the lemons that grew in the garden and opened a stall." She turned her head to discover a slightly stunned expression in Yevgeny's eyes.

Finally he said, "Then I'll know who to call on to attend to the decor when the time is ripe."

She smiled, but didn't acknowledge the burgeoning certainty that the playhouse would be for Holly. Yevgeny had no intention of disappearing from the baby's life.

It seemed like a huge amount of trouble to go to for a child he would only see for periods agreed to by her adoptive parents. Unless…unless he still believed he could convince her otherwise?

No.

She'd made her position crystal clear—she wanted the baby to go to a family…. Yevgeny would have to accept that once she found the right parents for Holly.

And it was her choice.

Not his.

Hers.

This house was for him—not Holly. Although Ella recognized it would be lovely for Holly to have such a fantasy place to visit from time to time.

He was looking past her at the old tree with its low, sweeping branches crowned with red flowers. "Now, I can see that that bough would be perfect to support a swing."

"A swing?"

Switching his attention back to her, Yevgeny gave her a crooked smile. "Holly would love it."

So it *was* about Holly…not just him.

For a moment Ella allowed herself to imagine him pushing Holly on the swing on a warm summer's eve…she could even hear Holly's laughter ringing out.

Then she pulled herself up short.

No.

This house wasn't for Holly…it was for Yevgeny. Primarily because his penthouse apartment had grown too small for his requirements. Better she keep her mind on task.

"Let's look inside," she said briskly.

The Realtor waited in front of the white front door at the top of the stairs. A smartly dressed woman with dark hair and hungry eyes, she smiled at Ella. "Mrs. Volkovoy?"

Good grief! "No." Ella felt herself flushing. She shouldn't be here. She was starting to feel like an imposter. "I'm not his wife—I'm a lawyer."

The Realtor's gaze arced to Yevgeny. "You didn't mention you were bringing your lawyer."

"Ella is not my lawyer," said Yevgeny through clenched teeth

"Oh." The Realtor's curious eyes darted between them. To Ella's relief the woman didn't ask any of the questions that were clearly burning to escape. "Perhaps I should let you browse— and we can talk afterward?"

"Perfect." Yevgeny gave a grim smile. "We'll catch up later."

Ella couldn't help wondering what the hell she was doing here as she rushed to keep up with Yevgeny's long stride.

"Oh, wow."

Yevgeny stopped at the sound of Ella's breathy exclamation. She was standing in the middle of the living room, staring out the wall of glass sliders leading to a long veranda with a backdrop of verdant gardens and sea beyond.

"One could spend the entire summer living on that veranda," she said, transfixed. Then she gestured to the sleek fireplace in the end wall. "But in winter the fire would make it warm and welcoming inside."

"There's a hot spa at the end of the veranda to make winter even more pleasant," Yevgeny told her.

"How fabulous."

"And a kitchen and dining area made for entertaining on the other side of the dividing wall," he added. "The home theater and wine cellar are downstairs. But come and look upstairs." He wanted her opinion on the bedroom and playroom where Holly would spend most of her time.

"This one. What do you think?" Upstairs he led Ella eagerly to the second bedroom.

As Ella scanned the bedroom from the doorway, taking in the bright sunny light spilling through the high arched windows, he saw her surprise register.

"But this isn't the master bedroom. You wouldn't occupy this room." Her eyes held a question as they met his. "This is for a…" Her voice trailed away.

Yevgeny could see the realization dawning as she entered. He headed in after her.

The room was decorated in shades of rich cream and pale blue. A bed with an intricate white ironwork bedstead was piled high with a collection of soft toys on a patchwork comforter, setting the girlish tone. Overhead, a chandelier winked in the sunlight. There was a window seat beneath the arched windows with space for picture books.

He could imagine Holly seated there paging through her favorite book as she grew up. Perhaps he could even ask Ella to help him furnish the room in a similar style once the house was his.

"This...this room is for Holly, right?" Ella sounded choked up.

Yevgeny came to a stop in front of her. "Yes. Do you like it?"

She shrugged her shoulders helplessly. "What can I say? It's perfect."

For that heartbeat they were in perfect accord, no hint of the animosity that had dogged their relationship since their first meeting. Yevgeny held his breath, loath to say anything lest the instant of harmony shatter into jagged shards of discontent. Seconds passed, and they stood drenched in warm sunlight in the house Yevgeny wanted for a home.

Deep in his chest hope started to build. Ella was starting to see things his way....

At last he moved.

Her eyes squeezed shut.

"Ella?"

At the questioning lilt of his voice, her lids lifted. And she looked straight into his eyes. Yevgeny felt a physical jolt. He was so close that he could see the shades of velvet brown and glittering gold. Desire flared. And something more...something new and fresh.

Again the crazy vision he'd glimpsed on her doorstep earlier and dismissed rose up. It was cemented with how right...how happy...Ella appeared to be in this setting.

Ella fit this place...

He bent his head. His lips met hers...pressed...waiting.

Hers parted.

The kiss deepened.

Closing his own eyes he sank into the softness that was Ella, a softness he'd never expected to discover, and concentrated on imprinting the instant in his memory to pull out and analyze later. To make sense of the inexplicable. For now, he simply absorbed the feel of her body against his. The warmth. The womanliness. The sweet, lilac scent that was the unique essence of Ella.

Finally, when his head lifted, his breath was ragged and he felt dazed and disoriented.

To his enormous dismay, Ella recovered first.

"Well," she said, the bright flush on her cheeks already starting to fade, "I don't think we need to take a look at the master suite after that."

Ella glanced at her watch.

They were back downstairs, standing on the spacious veranda protected from the sea breeze that ruffled the tops of the great trees that flanked the house.

"Need to be somewhere else?" Yevgeny drawled. He leaned against the balustrade, blocking her view of the well-kept gardens below. "Or are you in a hurry to leave?"

Ella looked up at him.

The sun splintered in the gold of her eyes, blinding him for an instant.

Yevgeny blinked.

Ella was speaking, and he struggled to focus on what she was saying.

"No, I was simply thinking that if this was a weekday I'd be in my office working." She made a sweeping gesture with her arm. "Solving other people's problems and missing out on all this beauty."

It was a relief to break away from the spell of her golden

eyes, to swing around and follow where her arm indicated, out over the vista of the gardens to the azure sea and the hazy horizon beyond.

The crazy feeling was back. *Affinity*. A vision of him and Holly and...

He drew a deep, shaky breath.

"I have a proposition for you."

"A proposition?"

Ella lifted a hand and nudged her glasses up. If he'd known better he might have thought she was apprehensive. But this was Ella—she didn't have an apprehensive bone in her body. "Play hooky with me tomorrow."

That gave him twenty-four hours to decide how to broach the topic they most needed to discuss.

Holly...

"Pardon?" She blinked at him.

"Take the day off—we can take Holly out for the day." It would be easier with the baby there. "And enjoy the December sun and fresh summer air. It's almost Christmas, take some time out."

Her brow creased in a frown. "I have a meeting."

"Can you postpone it?"

She shook her head slowly. "It's important."

"Holly is important—nothing else comes close. In five years' time will you even remember what this meeting is about? Because Holly will still be important then."

Ella pushed her glasses up her nose. "I can't—not tomorrow."

"No one else can do it?" he persisted, frustrated. This was important—too important to be overshadowed by work.

Ella shook her head again. "I'm the only one who knows all the fine details."

His frustration bubbled over. "Then you have a problem—you need to learn how to delegate."

"To whom? No one else—"

"Can do the job as well as you?" He raised an eyebrow.

Ella nodded slowly. "I suppose that's what I mean."

"Then you have two problems—maybe more. You've surrounded yourself with the wrong people, you've failed to train them adequately, you don't empower your staff by giving them responsibility. Or all of the above."

"None of the above." Ella's teeth snapped shut. She gave him a "take that" look.

Yevgeny narrowed his gaze. "Then you're guilty of bad planning."

She made a peculiar sound, and stalked to the end of the veranda, where she stood with her back to him, looking out over the garden. Her shoulders were stiff. In the pause that followed Yevgeny found himself watching her...anticipating her next volley. Until he caught himself.

He padded to where she stood, and her shoulders stiffened. This was not what he wanted. "Ella—" He broke off as heels clicked on the tiles behind him.

The Realtor had returned.

Ella still hadn't responded. Yevgeny sighed. "You go to your meeting. I'll take Holly to the park."

To his surprise, she didn't object.

"Are you going to put an offer in on this house?" Ella asked too softly for the Realtor to hear, her back still to him.

He nodded, suddenly tired of the dance around the truth, and then realized she couldn't see his acknowledgement. "Yes," he said. "This will be my home."

Once back at her town house, Ella made a hasty escape on the pretext of checking on the baby, the memory of his unexpected kiss in that wonderful house still numbing her mind.

Ella was in turmoil. Joining Yevgeny for a romp in the park with Holly had been beyond her.

Ella knew that Yevgeny was going to pressure her again.

To try and convince her that he would be the best thing for Holly. She was so confused. Yevgeny offered none of the qualities she wanted in the family who'd adopt Holly.

He was a bachelor. A type-A billionaire. He wasn't even

in a stable relationship. Sure he had a stable full of centerfold supermodels at his disposal, but that was hardly the same thing....

Yet, as she entered the nursery, Ella found herself wondering whether she'd leaped from the frying pan into the fire.

Holly was awake, gurgling happily to herself in the white cot.

Coping with Yevgeny was child's play compared to this....

"She's just woken," Deb told her from the depths of the rocker where she sat surrounded with the Sunday newspapers. "I swear she knew you'd come home. I might go to the kitchen and warm a bottle for her."

"Thank you." Moving slowly across the room, Ella paused beside the cot and glanced down at the baby inside.

Holly moved her head...then chuckled.

Ella told herself it wasn't possible. The baby was too young to be laughing. And she hadn't spent enough time with Ella to form a bond. The baby couldn't possibly recognize her...could she?

Yet Ella couldn't resist.

She bent down and laughed with the baby, an ache in her heart. Her breasts felt hot and tight. Ella tried to convince herself that Deb's mention of the milk bottle had stimulated the need to express. That was better than the danger of the instinctive age-old maternal response at the sight of her child.

Holly kicked her bare legs in the air, and Ella grasped the perfectly shaped little foot. Her fingertips brushed the soles, and the baby crowed with delight.

"You're ticklish! I've discovered your secret." She leaned closer and whispered, "Never fear, it will be safe with me."

Warmth rose within her, fierce and unfamiliar. What spell was Holly weaving about her? Why could she no longer think of the baby without a smile curving her lips? How was she ever going to let the baby go?

This was precisely what she'd fought so desperately to avoid. This...this emotional tug that went all the way to her womb.

As if feeling her straying attention, the baby gurgled and

pumped her legs. Ella smiled again but this time there was a tinge of sadness in the smile.

She would not be privy to all Holly's secrets as she grew up. That would be a role taken by someone else…a woman who could love Holly with all her heart, a mother who wasn't crippled by fear—and pain.

"I'm going to find you the best mother in the world, I promise."

She was so intent on the exchange with the baby, that she didn't sense the arrival of the man in the doorway. Nor did she see him hesitate before exiting, a stormy frown darkening his face.

The Porsche purred as it swept through the bends along Tamaki Drive. On the right, white sails fluttered in the wind in the bay as locals enjoyed the Sunday summer evening, while across the sea the menacing volcano of Rangitoto Island slumbered.

So Ella was going to find his baby the best mother in the world?

Yevgeny braked and geared down for the next curve. He slowed as a pack of cyclists came into sight, throttling back the powerful engine to a throaty roar.

Ella was still determined to give Holly away to strangers. Despite everything he had done to show her that Holly belonged with him….

Watching as one cyclist cut to the center lane, he dropped farther back. A moment later the bikes were bunched up together again, the cyclists in their bright attire pedaling furiously.

Maybe not *everything*.

The time had come to use all the weapons in his armory.

And that meant confronting his brother.

It was not the path he had ever intended to take—for his brother's sake. But Ella's talk of transparency on Friday night had set him thinking.

Ella was right about one thing: Holly came first. The bond—

because that's what it was, a fast, blood bond—that tied him to the baby was as vital to him as breathing. He would not risk losing her.

Tonight, when he announced to his brother what he was going to do, there was a very good chance it was going to cost him their relationship. But Dmitri had Keira.

And Holly had no one…except him.

He already knew his actions were going to alienate Ella. He'd hoped to gain her cooperation by letting her see how much the baby meant to him, but it was finally starting to sink in that Ella would never be swayed from her viewpoint. She was not prepared to recognize what he had to offer Holly.

He had a claim to the baby—one that would secure his place in her life. He had the money and resources to fight Ella and win temporary custody. Up until now, the only thing that had stood in his way of using the brute force of legal muscle had been his brother—or, more accurately, his brother's pride.

The Porsche swung easily into the next curve. Ahead, the group of cyclists had spread into a single file, and he nosed past.

In the previous ten days he'd grown to know and love Holly. He could not walk away. Yevgeny was all too conscious that tomorrow was D-Day, as he'd come to think of it. It would be his last chance to convince Ella that Holly belonged with him. Because the day after tomorrow, Ella would be legally able to sign a consent to allow Holly to be adopted by another couple. Once that was done, the decision would be final.

Sure, she'd said she was going to wait until after Christmas. But Yevgeny could not risk the danger that Ella might change her mind.

Then all would be lost.

Holly would be lost to him.

Forever.

Tomorrow was his best chance.

Tonight he would contact Dmitri far away in Africa to let his brother know of the decision he had made. Because he could not do what he had to do without letting his brother know. He'd left it too long already—because of his misguided confidence in his ability to convince Ella to come round to his point of view.

Time was fast running out....

Nine

The meeting dragged on.

Ella doodled on the legal pad in front of her and wondered what Yevgeny and Holly were doing in the park. Yevgeny had taken Holly alone, giving Deb a sizable block of time off for the first time in over a week. Now Ella was fretting. Had she done the right thing letting Yevgeny take the baby out alone? Of course she had. He was the baby's uncle—he deserved some sort of relationship with Holly. The next worry popped up. Had Deb packed the bag? Would Yevgeny have remembered to take a bottle? To put sunscreen onto the baby's fair skin? Her gaze slid to where her cell phone sat on the conference table beside her legal pad.

She could call him....

"What do you think, Ella?"

The question wrenched her out of her reverie. Ella set her pen down and forced herself to focus. This was important. *But would it be important five years from now?* Yevgeny's lecture came back to her.

Ella gazed around the table. Two unsmiling executives

dressed in pin-striped black suits stared at her. The older executive was the CFO, the younger was the corporation's legal advisor.

Would the outcome of this meeting be important in five years? She considered the radical thought. Work—any work—had always been important. But this time? Ella wasn't so sure. Originally she'd viewed this meeting as an opportunity to gain a toehold in bankruptcy law, and add another specialty to her expertise. But it didn't fit with the rest of her family law practice. She was no longer sure she wanted to do the company's work—she didn't even like the CFO. She'd handled his sister's divorce and received the referral. It had sounded like a great opportunity.

But she didn't want to spend her days filing bankruptcy suits.

So what was she doing wasting precious time on this? Where had her ideals of building a quality practice doing work she loved gone? What was she doing representing corporate sharks? And for what? More money? More prestige? Longer hours?

Was it worth bargaining her soul for?

"Will you be able to do the work?"

"Sorry?" Ella struggled to grasp the implication of the CFO's question. Was he doubting her legal ability? Both men were watching her across the polished expanse of the table. Her stomach knotted. She'd missed a crucial part of the dialogue. Now she was floundering. "I missed the last bit."

"I heard you had a baby." The CFO's tone was patronizing. His gaze dropped to the legal pad in front of her, then lifted to meet hers. His expression said it all. She was losing her edge; her femininity was the problem.

Ella found herself flushing. She resisted the urge to cover the doodles, to deny every thought she read in his face. Then she caught herself.

Why should I feel ashamed?

She had been daydreaming...imaging Holly and Yevgeny out in the sunshine, then fretting about all the things—important things—Yevgeny might forget.

It had taken Holly less than twelve days to change her life.

For the first time in years she was focusing on what she wanted. Evaluating. Choosing.

What had happened to her dreams? When had her desire to only take on work she wanted to do become hijacked by visions of wealth and power? That had been the whole reason she'd left the large, city practice where she'd been a rising star. She'd wanted to be able to take cases that interested her—refuse those she didn't wish to do. Not have her days…weeks…years dictated by billable hours.

It had worked out. She earned a good living…she had a retirement plan…her town house was paid off…she worked for herself and was answerable to no one.

She wanted for nothing.

But along the way she'd become more ambitious. Her schedule had become crowded.

There was no time left for…Ella.

When had she last taken a vacation? She'd always loved movies. When had she last taken the night off and gone to watch a movie and share a tub of popcorn with Keira or a friend? And, for that matter, when had she last actually met up with any of her friends? Ella couldn't even remember. Most of the people she socialized with these days were her work colleagues.

"I don't think I'm the right person for the job," Ella found herself saying. "But I have a colleague who might be a perfect fit. Let me call your office later with his contact details." There was immense satisfaction in watching the CFO sputter for words. Ella rose to her feet, and gave the pair her most gracious smile. "Thank you so much for considering me. I do appreciate it, but I think Mark Stanley will be a much better fit for your company."

And she was going to rewrite her business plan to focus on the work she did best—and enjoyed most. But first she was going to see if she could find Yevgeny and Holly.

She was going out to play in the park.

* * *

Yevgeny spotted Ella approaching long before she reached them. There was something about the way she moved that had clued him in that it was Ella when she'd still been a speck in the distance.

"You were worried about the baby. You thought I'd screw up." Partly annoyed by Ella's inability to give up control but also pleased that she'd been worried enough about the baby to come to the park, Yevgeny grinned at her from where he was sprawled on a picnic blanket on the grass in the shade of an ancient oak.

"I wasn't worried."

Yevgeny didn't believe that for one minute. "So why did you come?"

She glanced away. "I thought it would be nice to be outside on such a lovely day."

He snorted in disbelief.

"I did. Honestly! I—"

She was talking so fast that Yevgeny found his grin growing wider. "Slow down!"

Ella stopped talking abruptly and gave him a sheepish smile. Her dimples appeared. Then she sank down beside Holly, who was sound asleep on the blanket. She touched the baby's cheek with one finger and Holly made a snuffling sound.

Ella quickly withdrew her finger. "I don't want to wake her just yet."

"How did the meeting go?" he asked.

"Fine." Her face tightened.

Not fine, then. His good humor faded. "There was a problem?" He couldn't help remembering his criticism of her priorities. It made him feel guilty.

"No." She paused. "Not really."

"There was a problem." There was no doubt in his mind.

She turned to face him. The bright gold eyes were dulled by specks of unhappiness. Something was bothering Ella. And Yevgeny was surprised by the wave of protectiveness that swamped him.

"What went wrong?"

She hesitated. "Nothing. The meeting went fine. *I* was the problem."

Stretching out beside Ella and the baby, he propped himself on his elbows. Keeping his eyes intent on her face, he asked, "What do you mean?"

"It's hard to explain." She shrugged.

"Try," he prompted, sensing quicksand ahead.

"I'm not sure I understand myself." She looked away.

Yevgeny sensed this was not the time to push her. Above them the wind rustled through the leaves. He could hear blackbirds chirruping.

"Something has changed."

The admission surprised him. "You were treated different than usual?"

She shook her head. "That's not it. It's me—I've changed."

He studied her, seeking signs of the change she was talking about.

The wind caught at her hair. One hand brushed a recalcitrant strand back behind her ear. Except for a mussing from the wind's touch her hair was sleek and styled. The black business suit Ella wore was smart—even though by virtue of sitting on the picnic blanket she was showing far more leg than the designer had ever intended to be revealed in the office.

His eyes traveled down the length of leg encased in sheer stockings. Until he reached her feet. She'd kicked her shoes off. Already scraps of grass clung to the stockinged soles of her feet.

She might look the same...

But he would never have imagined that Ella he'd known before sprawled across a picnic blanket in a suit, her hair wind-tousled, her shoes abandoned.

She *had* changed.

"If you want the truth, I like the change."

Her eyes widened. "You can see it?"

He found himself leaning forward. "You're more relaxed—not so uptight."

"Uptight?" She drew away. "I'm not uptight!"

The quicksand deepened. He drew a measured breath. "I meant that as a compliment, not a criticism."

The look she flicked him was laden with uncertainty. An uncertainty that bothered him far more than he cared to admit. Had he been so critical of her? That she had to examine everything he said for hidden motive? Yevgeny didn't like that thought at all. He always considered Ella opinionated and judgmental. Had he been every bit as bad?

Leaning forward, he brushed the grass cuttings from her stockings.

She wiggled her toes and jerked away. "Don't!"

Acting on instinct, he grasped her foot and pulled it back to him. Then, on a wicked suspicion, he tickled the sole of the foot now resting against his leg.

She gave a shriek of laughter that she quickly bit off.

"You're ticklish." The discovery delighted him.

"Very." She glanced at the still sleeping baby, then mock frowned at him. "Don't you dare!"

"I never could resist a dare."

Or the temptation of revealing this unexpected side of Ella….

She convulsed with laughter as his fingers descended. "I haven't even begun," he protested.

"No, no." But she was laughing.

So he tickled more.

She writhed on the blanket, breathless with mirth. Her body rolled up against him, and Yevgeny went still. He had only a moment to make the decision…it was no decision. His fingers trailed away from her foot, his touch firming as he stroked along her leg.

Her laughter faltered, and her head turned. She must have glimpsed the intent in his eyes because her breath hooked in her throat.

The sudden silence was deafening.

Her lips moved. "Yev—"

Before she could protest he shifted his body and slanted his mouth across hers.

Then he waited.

She made no sound, no move rejecting him.

She gave a little gasp beneath his lips. Then her mouth opened like a flower.

Then a growling wail broke the tension.

"It's Holly, she's awake!" Ella pushed at his shoulders. "Let me up."

Yevgeny rolled away onto his back, one arm flung across his eyes. The baby sure picked her moments....

"My God. Anyone could have seen us." Ella's breath was coming in shallow gasps. "What was I thinking?"

"You weren't thinking...." Yevgeny lowered his arm to gauge her response "You were feeling."

"What's that supposed to mean?" Ella picked up the baby. "That I don't feel? That's what you believe?" She clasped the baby to her chest, rocking her. "That I have no feelings?"

It was hardly the time to confess that he'd considered all her feelings to be entombed in ice. Nor could he lie. He settled for, "I didn't know you."

"So you jumped to conclusions instead of trying to find out more."

There was nothing he could say to refute her statement.

"So much for being someone who doesn't react on impulse."

Having his own words flung back at him was no more than he deserved. He tried not to flinch. "I still believe that is the best way—even though I am perhaps not the best example."

"Well, at least you're honest."

"And you're generous to concede that. Thank you." Her shoulders sagged as she let out a deep breath. She hitched the baby higher.

He reached awkwardly forward. "Let me take her. She must be heavy."

"I can manage."

His arms fell away. For the first time he took in how comfortable Ella looked holding the baby. This wasn't a picture of a woman who couldn't wait to get rid of the child in her arms. Ella looked...maternal.

Surprise jolted Yevgeny.

He blinked. Looked again. Ella still looked perfectly at home. He waited for Holly to regurgitate the bottle he'd given her before she'd gone to sleep over Ella's formal suit. But that didn't happen. Instead, Ella continued looking down at the baby cradled in the crook of her arm with a curiously content expression.

Yevgeny couldn't concentrate on anything except Ella.

Every time he turned his head, those golden eyes ensnared him. The rose-tinted mouth that was so much softer than he'd ever envisaged. The Ella he was discovering behind the professional dark suits and efficient manner was very different from what he'd built her into.

So much more.

Her humor. Her rounded, infectious laugh. The love for her sister. The way her eyes softened like melting honey when she looked at Holly and thought no one was watching.

She even possessed a degree of sensitivity and self-awareness he'd never expected—she knew she was changing.

Like one of his *babushka's matryoshka* dolls where every layer opened to reveal something different. Something unexpected and new. Another layer that entranced him even further.

His chest tightened.

Yevgeny shook his head to clear the confusion. He must be dreaming...having such thoughts, such feelings about Ella.

But Ella was right about one thing: he knew far too little about her. And that was something he intended to remedy.

Starting now.

"What's your star sign?"

Her head lifted, and her attention switched from Holly to him. "My what?"

"Your star sign."

"I heard you, but I can't figure out why you'd want to know. Surely you don't follow astrology?"

He shrugged. "All women know their star signs." Some that he'd dated consulted their horoscopes every day. He couldn't understand why she was fussing about it.

"Because they hope that some vague prediction of good fortune will get them something that usually takes plenty of work."

His mouth quirked up. He suspected that assessment fit a couple of women he had known. "You're talking about finding a husband?"

"No! I'm talking about career and the financial benefits that come with hard work."

"Ah, I should've known." He had known. Of course that's what she meant. But he couldn't resist teasing her. She rose to the bait so beautifully. Every time.

She cast him a suspicious look. "I don't read my daily horoscope."

He didn't grin. "I imagine you read the financial pages."

"What's wrong with that? At least I have a better idea where the real financial advantages lie."

He held his hands up in surrender. "I'm not arguing with that logic."

"Really?" She tipped her head to one side. "Are you saying you actually agree with me?"

"You're surprised?"

Her lips curved up into a smile that attracted his attention to her mouth—her very kissable mouth, a mouth he was rapidly becoming addicted to. But with Holly now awake he had no chance of exploring that new obsession anytime soon.

Better to focus on getting to know what other surprises Ella had in store....

Holly chose that moment to squeak and reach out a hand to tug at Ella's bracelet. As soon as she had Ella's full attention the baby started trying to blow raspberries.

"Oh, Yevgeny, look!"

She laid the baby back down on the blanket and spent the next few minutes playing peekaboo. Holly was wide-eyed with interest.

Ella was laughing.

And Yevgeny knew he needed to get to know this woman better.

"What's your favorite color?"

She stopped giggling at Holly's attempts to blow raspberries and blinked at him. "Why?"

"Just answer."

"Why do you want to know?"

The familiar frustration rose. "Are you always this suspicious?"

"Of you? Yes."

"Why?"

"Because you're not the kind of man who engages in careless conversation. There's always a reason behind everything you say. But I can't figure out why you'd want to know what my favorite color is."

He lowered his voice to a purr. "If you tell me gold, I can tell you it matches your eyes. Or if you say rose, I could compare it to the flush on your cheeks."

Her cheeks flamed. "Why would you want to say such things?"

"You are a beautiful woman—when you allow yourself to be."

"Is this part of the same conversation about my not having feelings?"

He took her hand in his and turned it over. "Rounded nails. Your nails are carefully tended."

She snatched her hand away.

"Wait. I haven't finished." He retrieved it from where she'd laid it back in her lap. "No nail color."

"I'm sorry that displeases you."

"It doesn't displease me, but it tells me plenty about you."

"What? That I'm not trying to capture a man's attention?"

"There are many ways to capture a man's attention. Painted nails are only one." He stroked the back of her hand. "Your skin is soft. That's very attractive. You take care of it."

Her lips parted, but she didn't utter the words that he could see bubbling. Instead, her breathing quickened.

God. He was only touching her hand....

Yevgeny let it go. "When is your birthday?"

"Why? Do you want to read my horoscope? Or do you want to buy me a present?"

"Perhaps—but it would be difficult to choose. I don't know you very well."

"You don't get your assistant to pick out gifts for all your women?"

There was a buzzing in his ears. "Are you saying you're one of my women?"

She paled. "Of course not!" She fussed with the bottle that Holly had discarded. "I can think of nothing worse."

"Nothing?"

Her gaze dropped to the baby and he knew she'd gotten his point. Giving Holly up for adoption was far, far worse than being his woman—or the next step, having a child with him.

Then he spelled it out, "It would be easier to give Holly away, would it?"

Ella went white, and for the first time he noticed the sprinkling of bronze freckles across her nose. "It won't be giving her away. She'll be going to a family who desperately wants a baby to love—and I still intend to see her from time to time." She paused. There was a peculiar light in her eyes. "If you really want to know, my birthday was Friday before last."

It took him only a moment to make the connection. "The day Holly was born."

There was no way in hell he could say any more.

Ella didn't look at the baby on the blanket beside her. Instead, she wrapped her arms around herself. "I better get back to work. I have one more appointment before I'm done for the day."

* * *

"What do you mean you don't care?" Frustration soared as Yevgeny changed the cell phone to his other ear and tried to ignore the crackle that distorted his brother's voice. Yes, it must be the crack of dawn in Africa. Without a doubt, he'd woken his brother out of a deep sleep. But he wasn't sorry. He was too relieved he'd finally made contact, after almost twenty-four hours of trying. He'd pulled the Porsche over to try calling—and gotten lucky. "But you never wanted anyone to know you're sterile. You swore me to secrecy."

Dmitri mumbled something to the effect that Keira already knew—and that was all who really mattered.

Of course Keira knew!

How else had Holly been conceived with Yevgeny's donated sperm?

Which Ella didn't know. She still believed Dmitri was Holly's biological father. And Yevgeny had been so confident that she'd ultimately allow him to adopt Holly without the need to air Dmitri's tragic secret.

He'd sure been wrong about that.

Yevgeny was relieved that the baby wasn't here to experience his raised voice. He never wanted her associating her daddy with anger. He'd left her with Deb only ten minutes ago; soon he would be back at his penthouse.

"But you were so adamant about it," Yevgeny gritted out. Hell, if he'd known his brother had become so casual about who knew about his sterility he'd have told Ella yesterday at that bewitching house. Or earlier today at the park.

He'd had the opportunity.

A year ago it had been a different story altogether…then Dmitri hadn't wanted anyone—except Keira—to know the truth. He appeared to have forgotten all about that.

"Yevgeny, it was you who was so uptight about it." Even over the distorted line he could hear his brother's protest.

"Me?"

That wasn't true. His brother had always been deeply

embarrassed about the sterility that had resulted from his contracting mumps when he was young. During his teen years it had been a shameful secret as he roared around wildly with gangs of girls to prove his virility. Even now the memory of those days, the fights he'd had as Dmitri leaped from one disaster to the next made Yevgeny shudder.

"Yes. You thought it made me less of a man. A sissy."

"I *never* said that!" He struggled with an impotent sense of growing outrage.

"But you thought it."

Never! "Where the hell did you get that screwed-up idea from?" he growled.

"You."

Yevgeny sucked in a breath, counted to ten. Outside the Porsche the street was alive with people hurrying home at the end of the day. "Then you read me wrong."

"*You* were terrified about it getting into the papers. You didn't want anyone to know you'd donated sperm in case *Babushka* found out."

That part was true.

"Maybe I overreacted about that." It was a huge admission to make. Again he was guarding his brother. His grandmother's one shortcoming in life was that she'd always been very conservative—and tended to be too outspoken and hurtful at times. "*Babushka* was probably a lot tougher than I give her credit for being. But it was more than that. I was terrified of the paparazzi stalking you. The stories in the gossip rags would emasculate you." And shame his brother further.

Too late he realized what he'd said. Silence crackled down the line.

"Dmitri?" No answer. More loudly he demanded, "Dmitri?" He was thankful that the Porsche was soundproof. The woman wheeling a pram past the passenger side didn't even turn her head.

An angry grunt told him his brother hadn't hung up.

"I'm sorry." The words came with difficulty. "That was

tactless." And that instinct to protect his brother had been there all his life, started by his mother calling Dmitri a crybaby.

"Tactless?" This time he heard a laugh. His shoulders sagged with relief as Dmitri continued. "My never-wrong brother admits he has been tactless?"

"That's how you see me? Never wrong?" Yevgeny knew he sounded incredulous, but dammit, he'd never heard Dmitri going on like this. Like a sullen child. How long had this resentment been simmering?

"You've always taken charge of everything—there was never any space for me to do anything—you had it all under control."

It sure as hell didn't sound like he had it all under control now! "Dmitri, is everything okay?"

"I'm fine. Better than I've ever been in my life."

"What does that mean?"

"I'm discovering what it means to be myself."

"But you always were yourself." Yevgeny couldn't understand any of this. It was starting to feel as if he'd barged into one of those online gaming sites his brother habitually frequented—a dark, confusing alien parallel universe.

"No." His brother denied. "I was drifting. I wasn't myself. I was living in your shadow."

Yevgeny started to take issue with that, and then stopped to consider what Dmitri was saying. Perhaps he had tried to force choices on his brother, but he'd done it for Dmitri's own good. He had worried Yevgeny with his wild behavior, spendthrift ways, fast cars and equally fast women. Had he unconsciously adopted his mother's attitude that his brother was weak?

His brother was talking again. Yevgeny forced himself to concentrate—to really listen. "Keira's calling. I have to go help in the clinic."

"The clinic?"

"It's a health clinic. Run by volunteers. A nurse comes once every second week—mostly to attend to vaccinations and refer more serious cases to the nearest doctor two hundred miles away. I did a first-aid course in Auckland, so I'm working there."

"You've done a first-aid course?" Yevgeny couldn't keep the surprise out of his voice. "I didn't know."

Dmitri said, "You also don't know that I'm tossing around the idea of going to university to study to become a doctor."

"A doctor?" Yevgeny decided that he must be dreaming.

A laugh came down the line. "There's a whole wide world out there, *braht*—you should see it one day."

But right now Yevgeny needed permission from his brother. "So I can tell Ella?"

"Yes. Keira never wanted to keep it from her. But I thought you didn't want anyone to know your brother was less than a whole man. So I convinced her it was better this way."

Oh, Christ. "I've made a right mess of it, haven't I?"

It didn't matter what he had or hadn't thought. His relationship with his brother was clearly far from healthy.

After a moment his brother came back with, "It's not your fault alone. We always seem to talk at cross-purposes."

"That's going to change," Yevgeny vowed. And his brother wasn't the only person with whom he had a communication issue.

The realization, as he ended the call, was not a pleasant one.

But it had to be faced. His interaction with Ella had been based on quick judgments and half-assed opinions from the start.

No wonder he'd stood no chance of gaining her consent to adopt Holly. But he intended to change that. It was time he put all his cards on the table, and told Ella the truth.

Ella's last appointment took longer than she'd scheduled.

When her cell phone rang, Ella glanced at the caller ID. Yevgeny. Her fingers hovered over the face of the phone. Finally she pressed the button to kill the call and let it divert to voice mail, then looked back at the man sitting in front of her.

Jerry Foster was at the end of his tether.

Two weeks ago he'd received divorce papers. Like many of Ella's clients, he hadn't even known his wife had been unhappy.

Yes, Lois had nagged him to change his workaholic habits a couple of years ago; and, yes, she'd asked him to join the tennis club and play doubles two nights a week but he'd been too busy with the business. He'd told her to find another doubles partner. He'd thought the problem was solved.

Until two weeks ago.

Now he was in a spin. His wife was demanding custody… occupation of the marital home…and worst of all, Jerry was starting to suspect that her new doubles partner was more to her than a fellow tennis player. What Jerry wanted, he'd told Ella, was not a divorce. What he wanted was to keep his wife and kids.

Jerry wanted his life back.

He was ready to do whatever it took to restore his marriage. But his wife wasn't playing ball.

"Why won't she talk to me?" He jabbed his fingers through messed curls, the gold of his wedding ring glinting in the office lighting. "I was doing this for her—for us," he amended.

Jerry owned a multimillion-dollar investment company. It generated enough income to more than meet the family's needs for years to come.

"I wanted her—our family—to be cared for," Jerry was saying. "Not like my mother. My father died when I was ten, a heart attack, and my mother had to scrub toilets to put food on the table."

"Did you ever explain this to Lois?" Ella asked gently.

Jerry looked at her as if she were an alien from another planet. "Of course not. I didn't want her to feel sorry for me. I always played down my roots. My mother died the year before I met Lois—there was no need for her to know all that sordid stuff."

"Do you think she would've loved you less if she'd known about your background?" Ella wasn't a therapist but she'd seen similar versions of this sorry tale played out too many times to count.

A feeling of déjà vu settled over her.

"No!" He looked shocked. "She's not like that. She's the kindest woman I ever met. That's why I love her so much."

The confusion in his eyes made Ella feel like crying.

Jerry didn't need a lawyer—he needed someone who could teach him how to communicate with his wife!

A knock sounded on the door. A moment later Peggy peered around the door frame.

"I have Mr. Volkovoy on the line. He says it's urgent."

Ella gave her cell phone a sideways glance. There were three new messages since she'd killed that call a few minutes ago. Her heartbeat picked up. Holly. Had something happened to the little girl? And if so, wouldn't she have heard from Deb first? Drawing a deep breath she told herself not to jump to conclusions. "Do you know what the matter is?"

"He wouldn't say. But he did admit it wasn't a medical emergency."

Holly was okay!

Ella silently blessed her assistant's unflappable common sense.

"Tell him I'm with a client. I'll call him back in about ten minutes when our meeting is done."

Peggy nodded. "I'll let Mr. Volkovoy know."

Yevgeny found himself pacing the vast black marble floor of his penthouse as he waited for Ella to call him back.

He wasn't sure what childish urge had compelled him to insist it was an emergency. He wasn't used to women not being available to take his calls—and being left to cool his heels. Yet he suspected he'd behaved badly. How often had he been annoyed by women calling and insisting that trivial matters were crises that needed his immediate attention? How often had that led to him backing out of the relationship?

He didn't like the idea that he was acting in a similar, irrational fashion.

In truth, the very idea scared the hell out of him.

Not that he was in any kind of relationship with Ella....

When Ella's call finally came, it came through on his cell phone. He leaped on it.

"You were looking for me?"

Her voice sounded warm and welcoming. He stopped pacing. Something in him responded and he felt the tension that had ratcheted up during his conversation with Dmitri slowly uncoiling. "Yes, I was." He searched for words.

"I called Deb. She says Holly is fine. Is it Keira—has something happened?"

There was a note of fear in her voice now. Yevgeny squeezed his eyes shut. God. Why hadn't he foreseen that his stupidity might cause her to worry needlessly? He opened them again and stared out the wall of glass but, for once, the spectacular view failed to register. "No, no, nothing to do with Keira."

He hesitated.

No, filling her in over the phone about his conversation with his brother was precipitative. He'd talk to her…face-to-face… as he'd planned. Now wasn't the time to go off half-cocked; too much was at stake.

"Then what's wrong?"

"Nothing's wrong."

He shifted his feet. He could feel himself coloring. He felt like a total idiot. It was not a familiar feeling. Against this backdrop he was going to break the news of what he planned to do? He had to pull himself together, or else he was going to end up alienating Ella forever. And that would not be in Holly's best interests.

But the edginess wouldn't leave him. "Uh—I have to go to a charity function tomorrow night."

Today was D-Day.

Was he taking too much of a risk, leaving it until tomorrow? Even though Ella had said she'd only make a decision about Holly after Christmas?

"Yes?"

There was confusion in Ella's voice.

"I accepted several weeks ago." While he'd still been dating

Nadiya. "For myself and a partner. I was wondering whether you would be prepared to come with me?"

His grip on the cell phone tensed.

"You want me to go on a date with you?"

Yevgeny couldn't tell whether she was annoyed or amused. Nor did he want to point out that technically they'd been on two dates already—one he'd orchestrated at her home with food from La Rosa and the second at the park earlier.

"That's what was so urgent?"

The disbelief in her tone made him writhe.

Because he wasn't being truthful.

Turning away from the glass wall, he started to pace again. "The organizer called me to get my partner's name for the table lists— I needed to let her know."

"Urgently?" she asked pointedly.

"Yes— The function is tomorrow." He'd forgotten all about taking a date. Hell, finding a woman had been far from his thoughts these past couple of weeks. The only female that filled his head had been Holly—and Ella. But she didn't really count.

"Why me?"

He hesitated again. He'd reached the silver-and-black open-plan kitchen. He swung around. Then stopped. He drew a deep breath, and let it out slowly. Then he leaned back against the kitchen counter.

God, he was becoming more and more tangled in this deception—even though he'd planned to be honest and put an end to it all.

"Because I can't believe you haven't got someone else in your little black book you could call," she blurted out when he didn't answer.

Yevgeny found himself grinning. "I don't have a little black book."

She clicked her tongue. "The contacts list in your phone, then."

How to admit that none of them stirred his interest enough? His mind skittered away from the terrifying specter that thought raised—the only person he wanted to ask was Ella. Because that had to be wrong. It could never be true.

She was prickly and defensive. Not his type.

She reminded him of his mother.

Or did she? Flashes of Ella laughing with Holly. Of how she looked at the baby. Of her gentle cloying concern for her sister. Of her care for her elderly parents.

For the first time he realized that his assumption was quite untrue: Ella was nothing like the woman who had given birth to him—and then deserted him.

Ella would never desert Holly.

She planned to stay in touch with a baby who was never meant to be hers. She only wanted what she considered the very best for Holly—even though Yevgeny didn't share her views.

"Why me?" she asked again.

"Because you would probably have held it against my proposed adoption if I turned up with a beauty queen from my contacts list."

There was a silence in response to his facetious reply.

Then she said, "I don't think—"

"Please," he said abruptly, kicking himself for not holding his tongue.

"You could go alone, you know."

"I probably will. It's a charity event—I'd feel bad not showing up." With a sigh, he said, "You would've enjoyed the ballet."

"Ballet?"

Yevgeny held his breath.

"Which ballet?"

A vision of two pairs of ballet slippers with faded satin ribbons danced before his eyes. He had her! A smile curved his lips up. *"Giselle."*

He heard as she sucked her breath in. Finally she said, "I'd love to come with you to the ballet."

Ella set the phone down, terminating the connection to Jo Wells.

The day she'd been waiting for had arrived. Yevgeny was

due to pick her up in—Ella glanced at her watch—two hours. She still had to beat the rush-hour traffic home, see that Deb had handed Holly over to the night caregiver, express milk for Holly's night bottle, shower and glam herself up. Now Jo was on her way, too.

Of course, everything always did happen at once.

The social worker had identified a couple whom she believed met every one of Ella's criteria. A professional couple who'd already adopted a two-year-old girl, they had a very good relationship with their daughter's biological parents and grandparents. Their home was located in a rural suburb of Auckland, less than forty minutes drive from where Ella lived. The property abounded with pets and ponies, with a garden that led down to the sea.

They'd flown through the police checks. The family offered everything and more.

Jo was ecstatic. She was bringing the profile file for Ella to view immediately.

The family was so perfect that Jo's biggest concern was that the biological mothers of two other babies currently waiting for adoption might choose this family. But Jo had said that the family was more than happy to let Holly spend Christmas with Ella—if that was what Ella wanted.

Ella knew she should be experiencing profound joy. But she could only feel the heaviness of dread.

When she examined the dark source of that heaviness she concluded that deep down she'd been secretly hoping that Keira would come to her senses and contact Ella to claim the baby. Was that why she'd been stalling? Was that why she'd vetoed every other couple?

Why she'd been so critical of every other solution available to Holly? Even the option Yevgeny offered? She closed her eyes. She didn't even want to think about the house Yevgeny was going to buy. Every nook and cranny of her memory of that place was infused with imaginary visions of Holly running across the lawns, Holly playing on the swing Yevgeny intended to build, Holly curled up in the window seat while a fuzzy feminine figure read her a story—

But this would be an open adoption. No reason why Holly would not still have that… She would visit Yevgeny. This family clearly welcomed full participation for the biological family.

There was no reason to hesitate. Ella knew she had to breach the barrier and take the final, irrevocable step.

But she had to face that it wasn't a case of Keira coming to her senses—Keira had made her own choice. She wanted to find herself—she wasn't ready to become a mother. Keira was a grown-up. Ella could no longer make her decisions—live her life—for her. Keira had already had twelve days to change her mind.

But she hadn't.

Ella knew it was time to stop clinging to a thread of hope that had already snapped.

She had to stop putting roadblocks up. This state of limbo was stressful for everyone. And it was unfairest of all to Holly— Every day that passed was taking away the opportunity for the baby to form a strong relationship with her new mother. Ella knew she had to finally let go of the secret dreams she'd been harboring and start working with Jo Wells to finalize the adoption.

For Holly's sake.

She would look at the profile that Jo was bringing with an open mind…and try not to compare the home with the dream home she'd visited with Yevgeny on the weekend.

Then she would have to face up to Yevgeny himself when he collected her tonight, and tell him what she'd decided.

Applause thundered around the theatre.

The dramatic stage curtains came down as the first act of *Giselle* reached its dramatic conclusion. The lights came up. Around them the audience was already swarming up the aisles to take advantage of the intermission. Yevgeny was in time to

catch the transfixed glow on Ella's face, before she blinked
rapidly.

"Glad you came?"

Ella shivered. "Good grief, of course! Thank you. It's
incredibly powerful."

As Yevgeny got to his feet, Ella gave herself a shake. He
could see her starting to come back down to earth.

"How can they possibly top that performance in the second
act?" she asked as she rose. Her delicate chiffon wrap dropped
from her shoulders, exposing the deep V-shaped back of her
fitted black dress.

Yevgeny tucked his arm around her waist and ushered her
into the aisle ahead of him. She didn't shake his hand away, so
he left it there. Nudged from behind, he pressed up against her,
all at once aware of the warm softness of her body against his.
His gaze lingered on the soft skin exposed by the dress.

He ached to touch that skin, run a finger down her spine, see
the frisson of desire convulse her.

The emotions that had played out on stage in the first act
had heightened all his senses. The love. The despair. And the
intense passion.

His awareness of Ella leaped higher, blazing through him.

Yevgeny swallowed.

This was truly crazy!

As they emerged from the theater into the lobby he murmured, "Let me fetch us a couple of glasses of wine."

She hesitated, then nodded.

In relief he swung away. Surrounded by the din of chatter,
he took a moment to assemble his thoughts, to deal with his
fascination for Ella. A waiter bearing a tray filled with tall,
slim champagne glasses was coming toward him. Yevgeny took
two glasses.

At a touch on his arm, he glanced sideways—and broke
into a smile.

"Jerry, how are you?" Then his smile faded as he remembered

the gossip. Jerry's wife had left him for another man. Awkwardly he held up the glasses. "Sorry, no free hand to shake yours."

An uncomfortable pause followed, and then Yevgeny caught sight of Ella's blond head on the other side of the room. "Good to see you again, Jerry."

"Call me—perhaps we can play golf sometime," Jerry said.

Yevgeny nodded. "I'll do that." Then he made his way over to Ella and handed her a glass.

After a few minutes the bell signaling the end of intermission sounded.

Ella turned away and handed her still-full flute to a passing waiter.

Yevgeny sensed a black hole opening between them. Widening with every second that passed. Yet he couldn't find the words to bridge it.

What to do? To say? Yevgeny wasn't used to floundering for words. He was decisive. A leader.

He wasn't accustomed to this rudderless uncertainty.

Carefully he inched forward. He rested his fingers on her arm. She jumped. He let her go at once.

"Time to see what the second act holds." Ella threw the comment back over one pale exposed shoulder as she made her way back to the theater. "Let's see what the ghosts of jilted brides intend to do to the lying, faithless Albrecht."

That jolted him back to the present.

What was Ella going to say when she learned about the deception Keira, Dmitri and he had been engaged in?

The baby deserved honesty from all the adults around her. Not just from Ella. Holly was the innocent in this situation. Yet, ultimately she would suffer most from any deception.

Shame smothered him.

Ten

"You've booked a table for dinner?" Inside the confines of the cockpit of the stationary Porsche, Ella stared at Yevgeny in horror.

What to do now? How could she possibly tell him about the couple who wanted to adopt Holly amidst a room full of diners having a wonderful time? How could she kill his hopes in such a public arena?

It seemed too callous.

But if she asked him to take her home, and invited him in for a nightcap back at her town house, the night nanny—and Holly—would be waiting....

They needed somewhere private.

"Aren't you hungry?"

"A little." But she wasn't up to enduring two hours of polite pretense in a high-society restaurant while she sat on new information that involved Holly's adoption.

Maybe she should simply insist he take her home...and wait until tomorrow, then ask him to meet at her office? That would

be appropriate. Yet Ella didn't want to leave this any longer—
Yevgeny deserved to know of her decision.

Holly.

It was all for Holly.

Her chest ached, and she felt quite ill. Ella knew her heart
was breaking. Her glasses had misted up. She couldn't possibly
be crying?

Ella ducked her head and fished in her purse for a tissue.
Removing her glasses, she gave them a perfunctory polish then
put them back on. The mist had cleared.

Yevgeny was watching her.

"Don't you feel like going out? Would you prefer to have
something light to eat at my apartment? With a glass of wine?
I have a fabulous cellar."

That was a solution, although wine might not be such a good
idea—not now that Holly was drinking breast milk.

And Ella discovered she was curious to see where he lived,
to find out what lifestyle he would be shedding when he moved
into his new home. The next wave of pain washed over her.

Goodness, she was behaving like a goose.

"That sounds like a good idea—but I had a late lunch so
don't go to any trouble. I'm not that hungry."

"Hold on." The Porsche growled. They started to nose
forward out of the theater's parking lot. "Won't be long now."

Ella pulled out her cell phone to text Holly's night nurse not
to wait up for her.

The talk to come might take a while.

Yevgeny's penthouse apartment was perched high above
Auckland City like an eagle's nest.

From the private elevator, Ella alighted onto a steel mezzanine
bridge spanning the length of the penthouse. Two steps down,
and Ella found herself in the living area with Yevgeny right
behind her.

Black marble floors gleamed under blindingly bright track-
mounted spotlights. The immense space stretched miles to the

left and right. In front of her a wall of glass framed the unfolding cityscape like an enormous, dramatic work of art.

"This is awesome."

Yevgeny touched a panel on the wall and music swelled.

One end of the vast living space was filled with a high-tech kitchen dominated by jet-black marble and the brash shine of stainless steel. In the center of the space, a slab of glass suspended on white marble blocks and surrounded with designer ghost chairs gave a highly luminous, yet strangely floating, transparent take on a dinner table. To her left, a sitting area was furnished with sofas constructed of blocks of black and gray leather artfully arranged to take advantage of the view beyond.

"There's no television." Ella was surprised by the absence of electronics.

"Oh, it's here—you just can't see it."

Yevgeny walked to the sitting area and picked up a sleek object that, had Ella given it a second glance, she would've assumed to be a modern artifact. He pointed it at the glass wall in front of the sofas. With a soft click a narrow panel alongside the window slid open. A second click and the largest, slimmest wide-screen television Ella had ever seen rose out of the floor.

The mind boggled. "Very James Bond."

Amusement flashed in Yevgeny's eyes. "The theater sound system has been built into the walls and ceilings." He moved a finger and the television came on. "There are blinds that roll down to block out the light. Then this becomes a home cinema. The security system is also wired in."

The picture on the television changed and the screen split into a grid of images. As her eyes flicked from one image to the next, Ella could see the Porsche parked underground, the entrance to the private elevator where they'd been minutes before, the concierge desk in the lobby as well as images of rooms she had not yet seen. A huge bedroom with a scarlet bed clearly designed to reflect the passion of the occupant, caused her to glance away.

"There must be cameras everywhere in this apartment. Don't you ever feel…watched?"

"There are no cameras in the guest washroom."

Ella shot him a wary look to see if he was joking. His face appeared to be perfectly straight. With an edge she said, "How very fortunate for your female…guests."

Yevgeny gave her a lazy smile. "All my guests deserve a modicum of privacy."

This…this was a playboy's pad, jam-packed with boy-toys. Ella searched the screen. "What about the guest bedroom? Any cameras in there?"

"There is no guest bedroom—only the master bedroom and bathroom—and a study. I'll show you around if you like."

"The ultimate bachelor's dream," she said, not ready to acknowledge his offer to show her his bedroom. Although her heart had picked up at the thought of standing with Yevgeny in the same space as that wildly passionate scarlet bed….

Her eyes roamed the living area, seeking a distraction.

Minimalist. Glossy hard surfaces. Hardly the kind of place that a child could visit. It belonged on the pages of interior-design magazines and was far removed from the house Ella had visited with Yevgeny on Sunday.

That place—while big—was meant for a family.

"I see why you wanted to go house hunting," she said.

A pang of guilt stabbed her. Ella knew she was procrastinating. It was time to talk to Yevgeny about Holly's future.

The bubble of hope he'd been fantasizing about was about to burst. And it was an unrealistic fantasy— Ella had only to look at the kind of place he lived in to know that his lifestyle was totally unsuited to a child. Buying that dream house wasn't going to change who Yevgeny was.

Even though she'd discovered he was capable of patience and enormous devotion toward Holly, it was not enough.

He could not provide the family Holly needed.

But, Ella told herself, that didn't mean he could have no relationship with Holly. An open adoption allowed that. They would both be able to be part of Holly's life.

Holly would have it all. A wonderful family and plenty of

support from both sides of her biological family. They were all giving Holly the best chance of success in the circumstances.

Yevgeny had opened a panel in the end wall to reveal a bar complete with a fridge below the counter. "Would you like a glass of Merlot? Or I can offer Sauvignon Blanc—or what about a flute of chilled Bollinger?"

About to ask for a glass of mineral water, Ella changed her mind. What the hell, a woman didn't have the chance to drink Bollinger in this kind of place too often in her life. And the effervescence of champagne might clear the sadness that was settling around her like smog at the end of a winter's workday.

With a determined smile, she said, "Bollinger, please."

"Have a seat."

Yevgeny turned back to the bar fridge and extracted a frosted jeroboam. A moment later he popped the cork. Perched on a sofa, Ella listened to the sound of the champagne being poured into two tall flutes and tried to tell herself that everything was working out for the best.

Crossing to where she sat, he handed her a glass, then settled down beside her.

Ella felt her pulse pick up. Partly due to anxiety, she knew, because of the discussion to come about Holly's new family. But there was more to it. Sadness—obviously—because the time with Holly was drawing to an end. And beneath that was another layer: the unsettling edginess that Yevgeny always aroused in her.

She focused on that layer of restlessness. When she'd first met Yevgeny, she'd have identified this feeling as…animosity. Now it had metamorphosized into something else. Still unsettling— but far from unpleasant.

There was excitement…anticipation…and a hint of apprehension, too.

Ella took a small sip of the bubbly liquid then set it down on the highly reflective glass side table. Mistake. Without the drink to focus on, all her awareness centered on Yevgeny.

Her skin prickled and shivers spread through her.

Oh, God.

She shut her eyes.

The music danced along her senses. Sweet. Pleasurable. Ella tried to focus only on that.

It didn't work…because listening to the music led to thoughts of the ballet earlier…which led her to think about the man who had invited her.

Opening her eyes, she found herself impaled by Yevgeny's startling stare. Her heart stopped, then resumed with a jolt.

The silence between them had swelled to an expectant readiness.

When Yevgeny reached forward and cupped her face with one hand, her lashes feathered down and Ella sighed softly.

To Yevgeny's astonishment, the hand that cupped Ella's cheek was shaking.

White-hot emotions chased through him. Emotions so intense, so charged, he did not know what they signaled.

All he knew was that it seemed right to kiss Ella.

With great care he removed her glasses and set them down on the table beside them. Then, moving slowly, he leaned forward. His lips closed over hers. He tasted her gasp, and deepened the kiss. Ella gave a husky, raw moan and relaxed back on the sofa.

Desire burned him.

His heart thundered in his ears as he shifted his body across hers on the black leather and slanted his head to seal their mouths together. Beneath him Ella was soft, incredibly feminine. Still cupping her head, he feasted on the lushness of her mouth, devouring her. He could feel her heart thudding against his chest, and he knew she felt the intensity of this as much as he did.

Ending the kiss, he slid his lips down along the skin of her neck, tracing the V neckline of the sexy dress with open-mouthed caresses until he stopped at the hollow between her breasts. He nuzzled at the lilac-scented valley.

Under him, Ella shivered.

And Yevgeny reacted.

His thigh sank between hers, causing her dress to ruche up.

The temptation was too much. He ran one hand along the soft skin of her inner thigh until he found the lace edge of her panties. He eased his fingers beneath the lace. Lifting his head, he watched her as his fingers roamed closer...closer.

Ella was breathing quickly now, in soft, shallow gasps.

He touched her.

She was slick and already wet. Her back arched off the leather, and her eyes closed tight.

It was his turn to moan.

Withdrawing his hand, Yevgeny shifted off the sofa, so that he kneeled beside her.

"Why are you stopping?" she whispered, her eyes still tightly shut.

"You want me to carry on?"

Gold eyes glinted at him through dark lashes. "Yes!"

Sliding his arms beneath her, he hoisted her up and rose to his feet in one smooth move.

Ella grabbed at his shoulders. "What are you doing?"

"Taking you someplace more comfortable," he murmured. Then he bent his head and licked her ear, his tongue exploring the spiral shape. The moan that broke from her this time sounded wild.

In the softly lit bedroom, he let her slide down his body and as soon as her feet found the carpeted floor, he unzipped her dress. He drew her out of the dress and lifted her onto the bed.

He tore off his shirt and trousers in record time. A moment later, clad only in underpants, he joined her on the bed.

Ella was wearing only wisps of black lace.

Against the red satin of his bedcover, with her blond hair and pale skin, and the skimpy bits of black lace, she looked provocatively sensual.

The low-cut cups of her wicked bra revealed curves he hadn't known she possessed. Until now.

He touched the indent of her waist, and traced the flaring

outline of her hip. His hand rested on the rounded flesh of her bottom, then he stroked up along the groove of her spine. Her skin was like silk. Just touching her aroused him.

"You are lovely."

For a moment uncertainty glittered in her eyes. "Hardly a supermodel. You've dated—"

"Hush." He placed his index finger on her lips to silence her. "Now there is only you. No one else."

It stunned him how right speaking those words felt.

Only Ella?

But he wasn't ready to consider why it felt so right. Not yet. And not now.

He stroked her stomach where only a few weeks ago a baby had rested. The emotions that flooded him were too complex to name.

All he knew was that somewhere in that cocktail was gratitude. He sank his head down and kissed her belly, paying homage to her fertility and femininity.

Then, slipping a hand under her, he unclipped her bra with a deft flick and brushed the lace aside.

His breath caught.

Ella's breasts were full and high. The dark nipples stood proud. He touched them with reverent fingers. "Are they tender?" he asked.

She shook her head.

His index finger traced a light blue vein beneath the taut, pale skin. This was life. This was the very essence of womanhood— and Ella's nurturing of Holly.

Her hands were on him now, stroking up his chest, along the apex of his shoulders and down his arms with soft, feathery caresses.

Immediately he became aware of his body's response to her touch. He was hard and quivering. Ella placed a hand on either side of his hips and pushed his underpants down his legs.

As the full aroused length of him was revealed, he heard her breath catch.

He flung his head back.

Her fingers were sure and clever. She touched him in ways that drove him to the end of madness...then summoned him back.

When he could take no more, he fell back on the bed and pulled her with him, the satin smooth against his skin. Pushing off the last remaining bit of lace, he gently eased two trembling fingers into her slick warmth. Her flesh stretched around him. He moved his fingers, fluttering them, seeking the hard nub that made her breath stop.

When her breathing was ragged, her eyes wild, he shifted over her. With great care, he sank into her, then withdrew. Entered again. And pulled away.

Her arms came round his back, and her fingers dug into his buttocks. "Don't go," she pleaded. "Stay with me."

"Show me what you want," he demanded as passion ripped his heart apart.

Ella didn't hesitate. Within minutes she'd torn any control he'd had to shreds. He felt himself going...going...

As Ella's body clenched around him, he felt the first shudder. She arched beneath him, bucking and twisting, and he could no longer hold on as pleasure flooded them both in a torrent of sensation.

"Will you marry me?"

Whatever Ella had expected him to say on opening her eyes this morning, it was not this.

Her mouth dropped open. "M-marry you?"

His face filled her vision as Yevgeny nodded slowly.

She rolled away from him and dropped her legs out over the edge of the bed. Her naked back to him, she pressed the scarlet cover over her bare breasts and scanned the floor frantically for some sort of clothing.

"This proposal is a bit sudden."

Was this the point of the invitation to the ballet...and the romantic restaurant dinner he'd planned afterward? Had the whole evening been nothing but a staged seduction to get her to do what he wanted?

Except a date to the ballet followed by dinner need not have ended up in bed. *She'd* been the one to veto dinner. In all fairness to Yevgeny, he'd only invited her to his penthouse at her prompting. Ella shook her head to clear the confusion and struggled to focus.

Why had he asked her to marry him?

"Why?"

He didn't answer. But she sensed a distance between them that hadn't been there a moment ago.

The idyll had been shattered.

It had been such a beautiful night.... Ella had felt transported. From the moment the ballet had begun the magic had wound itself around her. As though she'd entered a hidden, undiscovered world of possibilities she'd never imagined. As for the night that had followed...

Not once but twice he'd made love to her.

The beauty of it had called to her. That feeling of exploring an intimate link she'd never dared dream existed. A moment of pure, blistering ecstasy. Then freedom. She'd encountered a facet of herself that she had never known—a facet that fitted perfectly, in fairy-tale fashion with—

She shook her head again, her hair whipping around her face.

There was no such thing as fairy tales—she of all people should know that.

Behind her he spoke in a low voice that breached all the barriers she was rebuilding. "Come back to bed."

Oh, she was tempted. To give in, to give up all her tightly held defenses and surrender to pleasure.

To the vision he offered.

"Say yes, Ella. Come lie with me again. Make love. We have time."

That seductive purr...

Then reality snapped in.

He had time. She didn't.

She was supposed to be meeting Jo Wells and the family who hoped to adopt Holly in—she squinted at the clock beside the bed struggling to make out the numbers without her glasses— an hour. And all she had to wear was a skimpy black cocktail dress, which she couldn't even find.

She would also have to explain to the night nurse and to Deb—who would be arriving at her town house by now—why she hadn't come home last night. The round-the-clock care she'd hired for Holly would mean the baby was fine.

But she wasn't.

Ella fought the urge to bury her head in her hands and burst into uncharacteristic tears as shame swamped her.

She'd almost fallen for it— This request to marry her could be nothing more than another ploy to get Holly.

This was not about intimate connections. Or profound pleasure. Or even about any feeling for her. This was about Yevgeny getting what he wanted in any way possible.

She'd do well to remember that.

Still clutching the covers to her chest, she leaned forward and scanned the carpet. Finally she caught sight of a puddle of black. Her dress. Her bra and briefs were nowhere to be seen. Ella had a distant memory of Yevgeny taking off her glasses last night; she'd have to retrieve them from the living room in order to locate her underwear.

For now she snagged the black dress with the tips of her fingers. In a smooth movement she pulled it over her head and shimmied it over her torso. It seemed absurd to protect her modesty now, but she no longer wanted to be naked in front of Yevgeny. Not until she'd worked out his motives.

Turning her head, she looked at him, fully looked at him, and her heart contracted.

He reclined against the pillows, the sun slanting through the window revealed his lips curved up in a sensual smile, while lazy appreciation still lingered in those glittering wolf eyes.

Lust bolted through her.

She wanted him.

Again.

Even though she suspected his motives.

How *could* she still desire him?

What kind of black magic had he unleashed on her? How had he managed to reduce her to…this? Never had anything interfered with her ability to think…to reason clearly…until now. He had her tied up in knots.

And no doubt he knew it.

It had been his plan.

Suspicion cooled her ardor like a bucket of icy water.

"No."

"No?" He raised a dark brow. "You don't want to stay?"

She flushed. "No—I can't marry you."

Ella emerged from the master bathroom, her purse under her arm. The transformation from siren to icicle was complete. Her makeup was perfect—and no doubt her underwear was back in place, too.

Instead of looking at him where he lounged in the big bed, she pushed her glasses up her nose and glanced down at her watch. "It's late—I have to go."

"Work. I suppose." Yevgeny resisted the urge to roll his eyes skyward.

"My work is important to me." Her voice cooled. Finally she looked at him. "But this time it's about Holly."

He started to pay attention. "Holly?"

Ella was fiddling with pulling the neckline of the black dress straight. He bit back the urge to tell her it was fine. "I intended to tell you about it last night. But I got…distracted." Her chin lifted a notch, signaling that he wouldn't like what was about to follow.

"Yes?"

"Jo Wells found a couple she thinks will be a perfect fit to adopt Holly."

Yevgeny stiffened at that revelation. "*I'm* the perfect fit to adopt Holly," he said unequivocally.

"I saw their profile yesterday. They offer everything I asked for." Ella swept her hair back behind her ear. "I'm meeting them this morning—" She broke off and glanced at her watch again. "In an hour."

Her stubbornness infuriated him. Fixing his gaze on her, he said softly, "I am absolutely committed to adopting Holly."

"It won't work. We've been through this before." She was talking so fast he didn't even try to get a word in. "You're a billionaire playboy. What do you want with a baby? You haven't thought this through. What will you do with a growing girl? How will you provide the mothering model she requires? What do you know about the needs of teenage girls? This feeling of responsibility will pass."

"I will learn. Whatever Holly needs I will provide," he said fiercely. "Whoever adopts her will also have to develop and learn about the needs she has—no one is a perfect parent from the start." He paused for an instant. "Parenting is about committing to learn about the needs of children." Something his own selfish mother had never made any effort to do.

But Ella was already turning away. "I've got to get to this appointment—and I need to stop by my town house to collect some suitable clothes first."

He could not risk Ella allowing a couple to get their hopes up about adopting Holly—he was taking Holly. Nor could he take the chance that Ella would get it into her head to sign the consent to adoption. Twelve days had passed. She could do it now.

"Then I will have to come with you."

She swung around, her face tight and closed—a world away from the woman who had responded so passionately to him last night...all through the night. A tight band settled around his chest.

"I don't want you to come. This is going to be hard enough without you there making it more difficult for me."

Yevgeny got out of the bed. Ella recoiled. Impatiently he reached for a pair of jeans slung over the blanket box at the end of the bed and dragged them on. Buttoning the fly, he said,

"My intention is not to make it more difficult—but to make it easier—"

"You're not doing that!"

"Ella, you should consider my proposal—"

"No!" She warded off his reaching hands. "No. No. *No.* I'm not marrying you!"

He wished she would stop interrupting him, stop rejecting him and stop pushing him away. She was making it so much more difficult...for both of them.

"Ella. *Listen to me.* I am Holly's father."

Eleven

"What?"

Ella's eyes stretched wide with shock. Finally, anger set in.

"What kind of stunt is this?" He'd tried persuasion, coercion—all with no luck. So last night he'd taken her to bed and, while she still basked in the warm, golden glow of his lovemaking, he'd asked her to marry him. *Now this.* Ella marched toward the bedroom door. "I don't believe you."

His hand closed around her arm.

"Wait!"

Fury broke over her. She yanked her arm loose.

"Don't touch me!"

He put his hands up in a gesture of surrender. "This is no stunt. I am Holly's biological father...I donated the sperm."

Frantically Ella searched his face, seeking something—anything—that would prove his claim a lie. Instead, she saw only calm, unwavering certainty.

Her shoulders sagged.

Holly's father. Not her uncle...

The dizzying discovery changed everything. And explained so much.

Like exactly why he'd slept with her last night. And why he'd asked her to marry him…and why he just refused to give up in his pursuit to adopt Holly.

A heavy weight sank over Ella, until it settled deep in her belly. He wanted Holly so badly—because she was his daughter.

The queasy feeling in Ella's stomach grew. Churned. Nausea rolled over her in turbulent, battering waves.

Vivid images flashed through her mind. Yevgeny demanding to know where the baby was that first day in the hospital. Yevgeny bending over Holly's cot, entranced. Yevgeny producing Nadiya as his fiancée so Holly would have the mother Ella demanded. Yevgeny's fury whenever she'd tried to roadblock his efforts. And the picture that hurt most of all? Yevgeny kissing her…loving her…to get want he most wanted….

Holly.

The next realization struck her.

Yevgeny wasn't going to give up. Ever. Last night's seduction had already proved just how far he would go to get Holly.

As Holly's biological father, he would be eligible to adopt the baby. The prohibition against a single man adopting a girl child did not apply to a father.

Ella's lawyerly brain went into overdrive. Hell, he might already be contemplating the first step: applying for guardianship. Ella knew she could challenge that. After all, Yevgeny had not been married to her—or even in a relationship with her. But there was a chance that a judge would grant the order because Holly's best interests were a stake. Once he'd been appointed joint guardian along with her, Ella suspected he'd waste no time seeking temporary custody of the baby. He was Holly's biological father; the court might look favorably on it. Unless she fought him. When Holly had been born, Ella would have done anything she could to stop Yevgeny getting the baby.

But now?

Ella bit her lip. He loved Holly. How could she stand in his way?

There would be some formalities to go through—paternity tests—not that Ella doubted that what he'd said was the truth. She could hear it in his voice, see it in his eyes. He was Holly's father. Even the hard-nosed, skeptical-lawyer part of her believed it. The court would, of course, demand incontrovertible evidence. But Ella knew the tests would prove beyond doubt he was Holly's father.

And once he'd secured temporary care of Holly he'd launch a formal application to adopt the baby.

"You're going to use the courts to get Holly," she breathed. "This is not—"

"You're not going to give up, are you? Why didn't you tell me this before?"

"I hoped to convince you without having to reveal this."

"You're ashamed of being Holly's father?" But that didn't make sense.

His eyes caught fire. "Never!"

"Of being involved in sperm donation?"

"I'm not ashamed of that—but to be honest, I don't think my grandmother would have been too keen on the idea." He shrugged. "But with her recent death that's not relevant anymore. If Keira and Dmitri had adopted the baby as planned no one else need ever have known the truth."

"Not me." Ella made it a statement. "And not even the person who needed most in the world to know the truth—Holly."

"Of course I knew Holly would have to know one day. Ella—"

She warded him off with blank, blind eyes. "But when Keira and Dmitri decided they didn't want Holly—why didn't you tell me then?" An instant pulsed past.

He took two long steps closer to her, and when she shuddered, he halted. "I was as shocked by the situation as you were. The first day I couldn't think straight." He'd expected Ella to do the motherly thing and keep the baby. But he didn't want to say that now. He wasn't prepared to risk extinguishing the burgeoning understanding that was forming between them. "We were always at such loggerheads. And I couldn't tell you... immediately."

"So when did you intend to tell me?"

By the time it had sunk in that he'd have to tell her, Keira and Dmitri had already flown off to Africa. In his arrogance, he'd believed Ella would be grateful for his offer to take the baby from her unwilling arms; he'd never expected her feisty resistance to his proposition. Well, he'd sure discovered how mistaken he was.

"Once I'd spoken to my brother—"

Ella laughed, a high, hopeless sound that sounded wild and desperate, cutting off his clumsy attempt at an explanation. "Sure. Now you need your brother's permission? You've never waited for anyone else in your life before you act, Yevgeny. Now you want me to believe you needed your brother's permission?"

Strangely enough he could understand her pain, her anger. She'd stood so firm in her conviction to be transparent, to do the very best for Holly. To the point where she was prepared to keep in touch with the baby as she grew older so that Holly would have a fully developed sense of her own identity.

"And why you? Why not Dmitri's sperm?"

The first wave of shock had passed. He could see her brain starting to process the information. "I'm trying to explain."

"Then get on with it."

God, this was hard. Even though he now knew how it must hurt her, Ella had been determined to be honest with the baby to whom she'd given birth.

He'd been less honorable.

Regret ate at him. But he couldn't change his actions, couldn't make them more honest. All he could do was explain what had driven his deception. And be totally honest in his relationship with Holly from now on. "Ella, you need to understand..."

Ella focused on him and the pain in her eyes caused the

words to trail away and his heart to clench. Then she raised her
eyebrows in a way that brought his feisty Ella back. "*I* need to
understand?"

He had to make her understand. "I needed to clear it with
Dmitri—because it involves him."

"Does it? I'd say that the essence of the situation is that it
doesn't involve him—he played no part in Holly's conception."
She dropped her head into her hands. "And all the time I
thought—" Ella broke off and lifted her face. "Keira lied to
me, then—she was part of it."

Ella had gone white.

Yevgeny started toward her, but stopped when she glared
at him.

"Keira had no choice," he told her. "Dmitri didn't want
anyone to know—although he disputes that now."

"I don't believe that she kept this…this…from me. I'm her
sister—I offered to carry the baby she wanted. She owed me
some loyalty…she *and* Dmitri." Her mouth twisted in a rictus
of a smile. "Or perhaps Dmitri never wanted a baby—and he
was just stringing Keira along."

"That's not true!"

"Isn't it? Then why the elaborate charade?"

"Because my brother is sterile!" he announced.

There was a deathly silence.

Then Ella said, "Oh." After a moment she said, "But why
such a big secret? Everyone knew from the outset Keira couldn't
have babies. There was no big secret about that."

"It seems that it is my fault."

That got her attention. "Your fault?"

He sighed and rubbed a hand over his hair. "Yes."

"Was there an…accident?" she asked carefully.

It took Yevgeny a moment to realize that she'd taken
him literally. "I didn't cause my brother's sterility," he said
broodingly. "But apparently I caused him to be ashamed of his
lack of manhood."

Ella stared at him without responding.

He laughed without humor. "So it would appear you are right. I am the big-brother bully. My brother didn't want anyone to know because he feared I would be angry—while I thought he didn't want anyone to know because he would feel…awkward."

"You were trying to protect him."

Yevgeny shrugged. "Except he doesn't see it that way."

"Of course he doesn't. He only sees it from his side—because that's what you've allowed him to do all his life. You've allowed him to be selfish. You created a monster."

He opened his mouth to object to the attack on his brother.

But Ella was already speaking. "Don't worry—I've done the same thing." She lifted her hands and shrugged. "I've indulged Keira so much that she doesn't need to take responsibility for anything. She simply needs to dump it on me and swan off secure in the knowledge that I will take care of it." Ella hitched her purse up. "Whatever 'it' happens to be at the moment."

"And right now it is Holly."

"Exactly."

It took a minute of silence for that to sink in. Yevgeny found himself smiling at her as a newfound sense of truce surrounded them. "We're a fine pair, aren't we?"

Ella glanced at her watch. "Good grief, the meeting. I need to fly."

"I am coming with you—don't even try to keep me away."

Ella was relieved that today was over.

Jo Wells had dropped her home. Ella had been extremely grateful. She had a headache and it had taken all her energy to persuade Yevgeny that she didn't want him taking her home. She needed nothing more than to sleep—which she'd done, while Deb had tended to Holly.

Now she sat curled up in the rocking chair in Holly's nursery, watching the baby sleep in her cot while the night nurse took a coffee break in the kitchen.

This morning's meeting had been unspeakably difficult,

despite the fact that Yevgeny had behaved like a saint. And, to make things worse, Jo Wells had been right.

The family was delightful—everything Ella had once wanted for Holly.

Holly. It was all about Holly.

Only Holly.

Too soon Holly would be gone....

Ella knew she shouldn't be thinking about herself. About how she was going to feel once Holly had gone. But she couldn't help herself.

She'd taken all possible precautions to stop this from happening yet still it had happened. She'd grown attached to the baby lying in the cot only feet away.

One thing had become clear to Ella—Yevgeny wanted to adopt the baby with his whole heart. He might not be listed on the birth certificate as Holly's father, but she didn't need to have blood tests run to confirm his paternity claim. She believed him—even though the lawyerly side of her would force her to cross the *t*'s. His desire to keep Holly wasn't a spur-of-the-moment whim driven by impulse. He loved Holly—he was her father. Holly was his daughter, a part of him.

An ache filled Ella. Holly was a part of her, too. Her daughter. *Their* daughter.

Her heart was telling her Holly belonged with the father who already loved her...even though he was far from perfect.

Could she forget about the plans—dreams—she'd had for Holly to go to the perfect family? And give Yevgeny what all his billions would never buy him?

That way there would be no messy, turbulent court battles... no legacy of bitterness.

Ella rose to her feet and went to stand by the cot. Inside Holly slept peacefully.

"What do you want, my angel?" she asked the baby.

It was Christmas Eve.

Using the excuse that his brother and her sister were both

away in Africa, Ella had invited Yevgeny around for dinner. She hadn't been surprised when he'd leaped at the opportunity to spend time with Holly.

Ella had decorated the table with cheery green-and-red place settings for her and Yevgeny. There was a place for Holly, too, and Ella planned to draw her stroller up to the table for dinner to participate in the event.

This Christmas Eve was special.

It was Holly's first Christmas Eve. And, Ella knew, it would be the only Christmas she would ever spend with the baby. At the moment the baby was lying on her back on the carpet wearing a cute Santa's elf outfit.

She looked absolutely adorable.

Ella had spent the afternoon since returning from work taking photos. One day Holly would be able to look back through the album that Ella would put together for this day. In fact, Ella had decided to keep a duplicate copy of the album for herself...to form an invisible bond between her and Holly.

Forever.

A secret they would share.

The doorbell interrupted her musings.

That would be Yevgeny.

Opening the door, she found him standing outside in the warmth of the evening sunshine, his arms piled high with goodies and gifts.

"You shouldn't have." She laughed, ushering him in. "Put the presents under the tree. Actually, let me help unpack the top items first."

There was a bouquet of flowers, chocolates, an iced Christmas cake...and crackers.

"This wasn't necessary," she scolded.

"What? And deprive me of the opportunity to spoil Holly rotten?" He started to pack the gaily wrapped parcels under the tree. Ella couldn't help noticing how well his black jeans fit his narrow waist and long legs, and how the T-shirt clung to his muscular shoulders.

Oh, my. All he needed was a red bow and some ribbon to be someone's perfect Christmas present.

But she had to remember he wasn't intended for her.

She swallowed. "Can I get you something to drink?"

"There's a bottle of red wine somewhere in here. Or it may still be in my car— I'll go check."

"I'll find it," Ella said. "Look, here it is."

But Yevgeny had already disappeared through the front door. He returned minutes later without the wine—but this time he carried an enormous boxed gift as tall as he was.

Ella did a double take. "What is that?"

"A playhouse—one to set up inside, until I get the one in the tree built."

Ella couldn't help herself. She laughed.

They had eaten dinner. Lazy now, Ella sat on the carpet in the living room leaning against the sofa, her legs stretched out in front of her with Holly cradled in the crook of her arm sucking sleepily at the last dregs of her bottle, while Yevgeny sprawled in front of the Christmas tree with his head propped up on his elbow, watching them both through pale, wolf eyes.

"Holly is almost asleep," Ella said softly, bending her head. The baby was heavy and relaxed in her arms.

For so long Ella had been at pains not to hold or feed Holly, to keep her distance. Yet tonight she was eager for the experience. With Deb gone home to enjoy Christmas with her family it seemed like the right time. Ella knew that she was going to spend plenty of time with Holly over the next two days, and that she'd grow fonder of the baby with every hour, making the final wrench of separation so much harder. But she'd accepted that.

With the pain came immense pleasure. The joy in watching Holly's mouth twitch as she sucked. The satisfaction of stroking a finger along the baby's velvety skin. And these precious days would give her a chance to say goodbye to the baby.

But tonight there were three of them—herself, Yevgeny and the baby.

Almost a family.

To escape that delinquent thought she glanced back at Yevgeny, and asked, "What was your first Christmas memory?"

The flickering red-and-green lights on the tree reflected in Yevgeny's colorless eyes.

"The Christmas season would run from the last day of December to around the tenth of January. When I was a boy, on New Year's Day we would hold hands and form a chain around the tree and call out for Grandfather Frost—not Santa Claus. He would hand out presents helped by his granddaughter, the Snow Maiden. There were always tables laden with food, a total contrast to the food shortages that my parents had grown up with. Things denied us during the rest of the year appeared. A goose. Cakes. Meatballs. Pineapple— My mother queued for hours to get pineapple. I'd almost forgotten about that. And no celebration would be complete without *kutya*."

"*Kutya?*"

"A kind of porridge made from wheat berries, honey, poppyseed and nuts. My *babushka* would make it a few days in advance because that way, she used to say, the flavors had time to develop. But the best part, the part I couldn't wait for, was watching my grandmother hurl a spoonful of *kutya* up at the ceiling in the hope that it would stick."

Ella found herself laughing. "She sounds like a character."

"Everyone did it—it was a tradition. The theory went that if the *kutya* stayed stuck to the ceiling, a successful honey harvest would follow. And that is good for everyone—because honey represents happiness and success." His mouth softened into a smile, and even the hard angles of his cheekbones disappeared as he lost himself in the memories.

"Your grandmother must've been a wonderful woman."

"Oh, she could be a tartar, too." He reached out and grasped the hand resting on Holly's cheek. His fingers tightened around hers. "But she made Christmas special."

Who would make Holly's Christmas special?

The sudden question flitted through Ella's mind with the

speed of light, causing her to stare down at the little angel in her arms. Not her—she wouldn't be around to be Holly's mother. Yevgeny had a wealth of tradition that she would never have expected. But where would the mother figure in Holly's life be?

Yes, she would visit—but would that be enough? Ella shook her head, her throat tight. Why was she worrying? Yevgeny loved the baby, and he'd clearly forged a strong bond with Holly. What did it matter that Holly would have no mother figure? She would have a father who loved her.

"Ella?"

She looked up.

"What are you thinking?" he asked softly.

The tightness in her throat made it impossible for her to speak. She shook her head instead.

"You love her, don't you?"

She hesitated, then nodded. It was true. Holly had crept into her heart against Ella's will and twisted herself around it. She bit her lip, struggling to hold back the tears that threatened.

"You've come to a decision," he prompted.

The tears spilled over. She nodded. Only once. Then her face puckered up. Ella knew she was going to disgrace herself by sobbing all over Yevgeny.

She found her voice. "I think I'll take her upstairs and put her to bed."

His hands clenched hers. "You're running away."

"No!" She simply wanted to get herself under control. Ella rose to her feet, and his hand slipped away. "I won't be long. I'll be back in a few minutes."

When Ella came back to the living room, Yevgeny's gaze fastened to her. He'd settled himself on the sofa, and she hesitated a moment before perching on the opposite end. She turned so that she was facing him, and drew her bare feet up onto the seat.

"You've decided you're going to keep the baby," he said.

Ella blinked at him. There was loneliness in his eyes. Was

he giving up? "No, I haven't changed my mind." At least not about that.

"No?"

This was so hard. "I love Holly."

There, she'd said it. Now for the next bit…

"But my keeping Holly would not be in her best interests." Ella got restlessly to her feet.

"Because you've got your mind fixed on wanting her to be raised by a family?"

Because she'd make a terrible parent. "That's part of it, but not the only reason I can't do it."

She'd reached the Christmas tree. Ella leaned forward and scooped up a wrapped scroll.

"I'd planned to give you this tomorrow, on Christmas Day. But now is as good a time as any."

She handed it to him. He took it with reluctance. "Open it," she said.

He drew out the document she'd rolled up and secured with gold ribbon. "What is this?"

Even as he pulled the ribbon loose, Yevgeny stared across at Ella.

She sighed. "It's my consent to the adoption."

He glanced down. "Why give it to me…"

The moment his voice trailed away Ella knew he'd seen his name. "It's in your favor."

When he looked up, the brilliance in his eyes made her want to cry. But this time with joy…and relief.

She was doing the right thing.

"I can't offer her a big sister—or a mother," he said. "But I can offer her a home, a garden, a place to call her own."

"I think Holly will be very fortunate to call the house we looked at together home."

"But more than a home, I can offer her every bit of love I am capable of giving. And I can offer her an aunt and an uncle—" he hesitated "—and a tummy mummy who are all her family."

The sweetness of his words caused her to smile.

"What about the other family?" he asked.

His concern caused her heart to melt. "I've already told Jo—she promised to let them know." At least she'd never told them they were getting the baby. To hold out hope then snatch it away in such circumstances was more than Ella could bear.

Mixed up with a sense of sadness at the goodbyes she needed to say to Holly once Christmas was over was relief that Yevgeny wouldn't be taking her away. He wouldn't whisk Holly away to Russia—or London. He would be working and living in Auckland. He was buying a house with Holly in mind. She'd seen the room that would be Holly's. She would be able to visualize Holly safe in her home, keep her in mind in the months—years—that lay ahead.

Ella knew she would see the baby and, thanks to Jo Wells, Yevgeny knew how important it was to her that this be an open adoption.

She shouldn't be feeling like this....

So empty.

Like her guts—her heart—had been ripped out.

Get over it. For once, Ella found the bracing words didn't work.

So she tried reason instead. Her daughter would still live in the same city, not across the ocean in another world.

And she would stay in touch with the baby.

That made Ella feel better.

While Holly would not call her mom, she would always be Holly's tummy mummy—Yevgeny had made that clear. She felt a lump forming at the back of her throat. The alternative, cutting all ties to the little girl, would be so much worse. It was not an option—not for Holly.

And not for her.

Yet the night he'd made love to her, Yevgeny had offered more. He'd asked her to marry him. She had said no in a way that had brooked no argument. For one wild, magic moment Ella considered what might have happened if she'd accepted.

Then she shrugged it away. The moment was past. He would not ask again. Why should he? He had what he wanted....

Holly.

Why would he want her? He didn't even like her....

Why could it not have been different?

She quickly stifled that thought. That would mean that she never agreed to act as surrogate for Keira and Dmitri, that Holly had never been born, that she would never have gotten to know Yevgeny better.

And those were things she could not contemplate living without now.

Because she loved Holly.

As for Yevgeny...she was so confused about the swings of emotion he aroused in her. Anger. Passion. Empathy. And something she feared to name.

So when his arms came around her, the lighted Christmas tree, the gaily colored packages, all dissolved in a blur of tears as Ella started to weep uncontrollably.

Twelve

"Hey, don't cry," Yevgeny whispered against Ella's hair, and his arms tightened around her.

She snuffled. "I'm not crying." And she felt him smile.

"Sure you're not." He pressed a kiss to the top of her head. After a moment he added, "Thank you for my Christmas gift. It is without a doubt the best present I've ever received."

"My pleasure." Ella found she meant it. With her tears stanched, she lifted her head and warned him, "But you better make Holly happy."

His expression deadly serious, he said, "My offer is still open. If you marry me and come live with us, you'll be able to gauge for yourself how happy she is."

Ella's heart leaped, and then settled into a rapid beat.

The offer was unbearably tempting. Looking away, she focused on the flickering of the Christmas lights. There was something about the powerful emotions that Yevgeny stirred in her that made her suspect she was falling in love with him. Heck, not falling…fallen.

She was in love.

It had been so long, she'd forgotten how it felt to be in love.

And back then it had been so different. Young love. This time it was deeper…less impulsive. Yet Ella knew if she accepted Yevgeny's proposal she needed to be sure that her love was strong enough for both of them. There could be no going back because Holly would suffer.

Of course, they shared that bond. She loved Holly…and Yevgeny loved the baby, too.

But, despite his proposal, Ella was under no illusion that he loved her. He never had. Could he learn to love her in the future? Was it worth taking a chance on that? Could she love enough for two?

"So what do you think?" he asked at last.

"I'm scared," she said honestly, switching her gaze back to find him still watching her with that unnerving intensity.

"Scared? *You?*" There was disbelief in his voice. "But why?"

Not ready to confess that she wasn't sure about the wisdom of going into a marriage where he didn't love her, she said instead, "I don't know that I'd make a very good mother."

He reared back and looked down at her. "What makes you think that? You're wonderful with Holly. I didn't think that at the start but you've managed to convince me. Your love for her is evident every time you look at her."

"My parents haven't provided the best template, but to be truthful, that's not the only reason I think I'd be a hopeless failure as a mother…and wife."

"Who was he?"

She gave him a startled look. "How did—" Ella broke off. Then, "What makes you think there was a man?" she hedged.

"Your reaction." Yevgeny's brow was creased in a frown of concern, and his hold loosened, giving her more space. "Tell me who he was."

Did she really want to expose herself to the possibility that he might not even understand her pain? Perhaps the time had come to reveal something more. It was the only way to discover if there was substance to this attraction that floated between them.

Her shoulders slumping, she said, "I was eighteen, he was nineteen. We were in love."

A shadow passed across his face.

"You can't imagine it, can you?" Ella pulled a face. "I was besotted. I thought it was forever."

"What happened?"

"I got pregnant."

He sighed, the sound overloud in the living room of Ella's town house. Something cold shriveled in Ella's chest. "It was perfectly predictable," she said. "He disappeared as soon as I told him. All his promises of our future together vanished as he ran for the plane to take him to a new job and new future in Australia. Within weeks I heard he had a new girlfriend, too."

"And you were left holding the baby." Ella could feel the tension that coiled through his body even before he asked, "You had an abortion?"

She gave him a sharp look and broke out of his arms, shifting to sit on the side of the sofa farthest from him. "No!"

"So what happened to the baby?"

"The baby," she said through stiff lips, "died."

This time Yevgeny brooked no resistance as he took Ella in his arms.

Her body was rigid and she felt worryingly cold. He rubbed his hands along her arms, and marveled that he'd ever considered Ella a human icicle.

She was complex, yet kind. And she'd endured more than any woman should need to.

"I'm sorry."

He brushed his lips over hers in a gesture of sympathy. Her mouth clung to his, and Yevgeny kept the contact until she finally broke it.

"Thank you."

He let the silence surround them, not pressing her to tell him more. It was curiously companionable, with no rough edges as she nestled closer. His hands stroked along her back, touching, offering wordless comfort, even as Yevgeny wished he could take the pain from her.

When she did speak, she lifted her face up to him and said, "Make love to me."

"Now?" His hands paused in their stroking. "Are you sure?"

She nodded, her honey-colored eyes pleading. "Yes. Now. Here. I want to feel alive again."

This time their loving held a well of tenderness.

Rather than passion, it was care and concern that Yevgeny expressed with every stroke and touch. Only when her body softened, became increasingly fluid, did he finally pull her over him and let her take him into her.

Then he rocked her.

Slowly and so gently. Until the sensations built to a peak and the passion broke.

When it was over, he pulled her up against him, and held her tight.

A while later, Ella straightened up. "I feel much better." She sounded surprised. "Definitely more alive."

"Good."

She sat up slowly and reached for the clothing she'd discarded. "You've been very patient."

"It's one of my less well-known qualities." He gave her a small smile and was relieved when her eyes sparkled back. After she'd pulled the garments on, Yevgeny reached out his hand and took hers. "I'm here for as long as you need me."

Astonishment flitted across her face, followed by acceptance. "Thank you."

"I'm the one who needs to say thank you," he said, "for giving me Holly."

"The other baby—" Ella broke off.

"You don't need to talk about that if you don't wish to."

"I want to." Her eyes met his bravely. "The other baby was going to be adopted out. It was a closed adoption—my parents thought it would be for the best. I never knew anything about the family she was going to—only that they couldn't have children. Once the baby was gone…I knew I would never see it again."

That's why she'd been so insistent about an open adoption this time around, he realized. "That must have been hard to deal with."

Her eyes had gone blank. She'd retreated into the world of the past. "The morning I went into labor—I changed my mind. I wanted to keep the baby. My parents wouldn't hear of it. We were still fighting when I went into labor. It was a boy."

Yevgeny waited. Nothing he could say would be adequate to comfort her.

"But something went wrong. The cord was wrapped around his neck…and he died. I felt like I'd killed him—by changing my mind and deciding to keep him."

"No!"

"I know. It's not a rational fear. But it took me a long time to come to terms with it."

Yevgeny finally understood why it had been so difficult for her to change her decision to give Holly up to a couple who could love her…to give her to him.

It had taken courage. She'd had to conquer her demons.

"You're the bravest woman I've ever met," he told her.

It was then that he realized how deeply he loved her. But now was not the time to convince her that marrying him would heal them all.

So all he said was, "Come, let me hold you."

When the doorbell rang on Christmas morning, Ella had no idea who could be outside.

She pulled open the door to find Keira and Dmitri on the doorstep, luggage piled up beside them. "You're back!"

Concern instantly settled over her. What had gone wrong? Then she gathered her scattered thoughts.

"Merry Christmas! Don't stand out on the doorstep. Come in."

Ushering the pair into her living room, while leaving the

luggage stacked in the hall, Ella asked, "What happened? Why've you left Malawi?"

Keira came to a halt in the middle of the room and exchanged glances with Dmitri.

"Ella, we've changed our minds."

Something in her sister's tense tone caused adrenaline to surge through Ella's veins. "You've changed your mind? About volunteering in Malawi?"

But she knew…

It was much, much more.

"No, about the baby." Keira's words confirmed what Ella had already sensed. Keira wore a mulish expression. "Dmitri and I have decided we're going to keep Jessica."

"Jessica?" Ella's brain was spinning. "Her name isn't Jessica, it's Holly."

"We've chosen to name her Jessica." Dmitri placed an arm around Keira's shoulders and drew her close.

This was what she'd wanted…wasn't it? Taking in their unified pose, Ella swallowed. She'd hoped for Keira to change her mind and keep the baby. Yet now confronted by the pair who had just announced that's what they wanted, Ella found the idea of losing Holly terrified her.

Then anger set in.

"But you gave her up—you told me to sort everything out."

"We made a mistake."

Her sister's eyes filled with tears. For the first time ever, Keira's tears failed to move Ella. The customary protectiveness failed to materialize. This time it was Holly she wanted to protect.

"You decided you weren't ready for a baby yet."

"That's what we thought, but the time in Malawi made us decide we're ready for parenthood."

"It's too late, Keira—"

"She's already been adopted? You've signed the consent?" Keira must've seen the answer in her eyes. "You should've let me know—"

"You walked away—you made her my problem. Remember?"

"Because I knew you would be able to give her up for adoption—you've done it before. And you did it without any trouble." Keira huddled closer to Dmitri. "I'm not as tough as you, Ella, I couldn't face the pain. I could never have done it."

Tough? A shaft of pain shot through Ella. Was that how her sister saw her? Did no one see how painful these decisions were for her? Ella swallowed. She'd lost one baby—she wasn't losing this one. "I couldn't give Holly up."

"Then why did you imply she's been adopted?"

"Wait, let me get a word in edgewise. I never said she's been given up for adoption. I'm getting married—I'm going to keep her."

"Married?" Keira gave a laugh of surprise. "To who?"

"Your sister is marrying me."

The dark voice came from behind her. Yevgeny. Relief swarmed through Ella as he enfolded her in his arms. She shut her eyes and allowed herself to lean into his strength.

Strength. Comfort. Understanding. That was what he'd offered her through this period of turmoil. He'd been there for her—and Holly—every minute. He'd never failed her or walked away.

He was a man in a million.

A man worth loving. Forever.

It would be so easy to abdicate all responsibility, to let Yevgeny take over. But it wasn't fair.

Ella forced herself to keep steady. And to think. Was this the best course for Holly? She loved Yevgeny but he didn't love her. But he was reliable. He would never leave her…. She knew from what he'd told her about his mother walking out on him and Dmitri he would never do that to his own child. Could she marry him under such circumstances, knowing there was no way out?

"We came back for the baby." Dmitri stood toe to toe with his older brother.

"Until you change your mind again next week?"

"We won't."

"Ella and I are hardly convinced. Until you turned up here today we haven't received one call from the pair of you to find out how the baby was."

"I called," objected Keira. "Only once but at least I called."

"This is true?" Yevgeny spoke into Ella's ear.

She nodded slowly, and waited for him to stiffen, to release his hold and withdraw his support.

But he stayed exactly where he was.

Before she could say anything, Keira started to speak. "Yes, Ella told me she'd hired a nanny, that she was back at work. I felt so guilty. I knew the baby was screwing up her life."

Ella closed her eyes. "Things changed."

She'd changed.

And Yevgeny had noticed the change even as she'd started becoming aware of it herself. She thought back to their visit to that magical house…the day he'd kissed her for the first time.

Ella placed her hands on his forearms, emphasizing their unity in the face of her sister and his brother. What they were doing was right. They both loved Holly.

They would make this work.

It had to.

Her resolve hardened. "I'm sorry, Keira. I got pregnant for you originally. Then you and Dmitri decided you both needed time and space for yourselves. But now I can't give her up. I'm her mother."

Saying those words freed something deep inside her. All the hurt of the past softened, eased and floated gently away.

For the first time in many years, Ella felt…whole. At peace.

"After my first baby died, I thought I'd never smile again…" Her voice trailed away.

Behind her the rise and fall of Yevgeny's chest slowed. His arms tensed into bands of steel around her.

Keira's face crumpled. "None of us could reach you."

"I'm happy now. Holly has brought me happiness. Please be happy for me— I don't want to fight you on this," she said to her sister.

There'd been enough fighting. Against Yevgeny. Against herself. But she would fight no longer.

"Keira, I haven't discussed this with Yevgeny, but why don't we talk about you and Dmitri becoming Holly's godparents? That way, you can both have a significant part in her life." When Keira's eyes brightened, Ella started to think about the old saying that it took a village to raise a child. Holly would never be short of family. She glanced from Keira to Dmitri and finally to Yevgeny. "What do you all think?"

Yevgeny nodded, his expression unfathomable.

"We'll discuss it," said Keira. "But first I want to be matron of honor at your wedding."

Ella knew she should come clean and reveal there might be no wedding—she hadn't yet given Yevgeny his answer, even though she'd told Keira and Dmitri they were getting married.

Ironically, she now desperately wanted to marry Yevgeny—but there was still a stumbling block.

He didn't love her.

Thirteen

Red. Yellow. Green.

The Christmas tree lights lit up Ella's pale face.

Holly was having her afternoon nap, and they'd finally seen Keira and Dmitri off after they'd stayed for Christmas lunch. Yevgeny had given the pair the keys to the Porsche and the freedom to stay in his penthouse. He would've done anything to get rid of them.

Because he needed to talk to Ella.

She'd announced to his brother and her sister that they were getting married—that she was keeping Holly. He should be pumped…everything he wanted was falling into place. But he didn't like the quiet air that had settled around her like a shroud. It was a far cry from the happiness expected of a bride-to-be.

"Ella, are you okay?"

Her hands paused in the act of picking up the shredded wrapping paper that lay on the carpet, left over from the orgy of unwrapping that had taken place earlier. Holly had gotten a treasure trove of gifts. The eyes that looked up at him held confusion—with none of the honey-gold tones that indicated happiness. She pushed her glasses up her nose in the way she had when she was uncertain.

"Do you think I've been too hasty?" she asked. "Holly was born for Keira and Dmitri—should I give her back to them?" The pain in her eyes was blinding. "It would give Keira the gift of happiness I intended all along."

"But what about you?"

She stared at him. "Me?"

"Yes, *you.*" This lay at the heart of the matter, he realized. He came to stand in front of her. "What do *you* want?" Ella blinked up at him. "I think, for once in your life, you need to think about what you want. And go after it."

The bewilderment faded, and a strange expression came over her face. Her eyes flicked to him, then shot away. "That would be selfish."

"You deserve to be happy, too."

"It's not just about me. There are other issues at stake here, too."

He placed his finger under her chin and tilted it so that he could see her eyes. They were guarded. "Like what?"

"Like you."

He tried to read her, started to hope. "What do you mean?"

"I don't want you to feel obliged to marry me because of what my stupid pride caused me to say to Keira."

Had it been pride that had caused her declaration? He'd thought there'd been a lot of honesty—her love for Holly had shone from her.

Yet now doubt shadowed her face.

"You're having second thoughts about giving Holly up?"

She shook her head. "No, she belongs with you."

"You could belong with us, too. If you choose." His finger trailed along her jawline and stroked her hair off her face as he'd seen her do so often in the past. He was no longer sure whether marriage for Holly's sake alone would be enough for him.

In the past few weeks his fears had changed. He no longer dreaded that Ella would abandon Holly someday, as his mother had abandoned his father, himself and his brother. He now feared that she would never be able to love him. Hell, she hadn't liked him that long ago. His own arrogance had cemented that. At least the raw antagonism had diminished. He could make her laugh. He was certain she at least liked him now.

But love?

Not yet.

He didn't want to wait for her to fall in love with him—to live in uncertainty about whether it would come to pass even as he took her to his bed each night.

He wanted her love. Now.

But he didn't want to put more pressure on her, either. This time he had to be selfless, this time he was putting Ella first.

This was about Ella. It was her choice.

"What do you want, Ella? What is your dream?"

Ella bit her lip.

How to tell Yevgeny that her dream lay at the magical home he'd bought for him and Holly. She wanted to share that home with him and Holly—she wanted to share their future.

Because she loved them both…more than anything in the world. Between the two of them, they'd taught her to love again. They'd brought her back to life.

Yevgeny's hands cupped her face.

She met his gaze…and trembled inside.

Could she risk revealing her dream to him? What if he ridiculed it? Or dismissed it? As quickly as they came the thoughts vanished. Once they'd come to an understanding about Holly, Yevgeny had shown her nothing but kindness. And passion. *That* thought swept in from nowhere and caused her cheeks to heat.

"Let me tell you what I never dared dream of." His voice broke into her thoughts. "I never dared dream that I'd one day have a family. You see, my family was a train wreck. My mother and father had a dysfunctional relationship and when my mother left, she used me and Dmitri to get what she wanted—financial support while she swanned around with her new lover."

Ella knew she should have suspected something like this; all the clues had been there. She should have worked out that he was the childhood victim of a bitter divorce.

"Your mother got custody of you both?" she asked slowly.

He nodded, his eyes vulnerable. "She took us away from Russia—to London. Until she decided she wanted to be young and unfettered again and ran off with her toyboy. My father came to fetch us—it was the first time we'd seen him in three years. She'd fed the court a bunch of lies, and he'd been barred from seeing us."

"I'm sorry," she said, and took a step forward. She wrapped her arms around this strong man, and leaned into him. She kissed his cheek.

He dropped his face into the cleft formed by her neck and shoulder, and said so softly that she had to strain her ears to hear, "I never wanted to marry—to risk that happening to my child. I was not ever going to give any woman that kind of power over me."

Ella struggled to absorb what he was telling her. But he'd asked her to marry him. What did that mean? Was this regret for flouting his vow to himself?

Probably.

Ella knew exactly what to do. She had to set him free. Dropping her arms, she said, "And now I've gone and told both our families that we're getting married. I'll tell Keira it was a mistake."

"No!" He raised his head. The expression in his eyes caused her breath to catch in disbelief. "Ella, you don't understand—I *want* to marry you. That's the dream I never dared to dream. I love you."

To Ella's horror, she felt tears prick.

"Hey, I didn't mean to make you cry."

That caused her to smile through the tears. "I'm sorry. I don't normally cry this much. But these are tears of relief—and joy. You see, I love you, too."

At that, Yevgeny's arms encircled her and crushed her to his heart.

"Are you happy?"

"Me?" Ella turned her head to smile at her fiancé. Yevgeny's arm rested around her waist as they stood on the wide veranda of their dream home taking in the view they'd be seeing every day in the new year. "I'm walking on clouds—life couldn't be better."

The sale of the house had gone through. In a few days they would be moving in.

Everything in her world was going right.

Ella glanced down at the stroller beside them, where Holly was quite comfortably ensconced. For now. In years to come Ella knew Holly would tear around the gardens, explore the trees…and play on the swing Yevgeny intended to build. Perhaps there would be a younger sister. Maybe a brother, too.

A hand cupped her chin. Instantly her pulse quickened. Yevgeny bent his head and sealed her smiling lips with a kiss.

When he raised his head, she said, "Did you ever imagine this could happen between us?"

"I'll tell you a secret."

She tipped her head back, waiting for him to continue. "Yes?"

"I used to think you were an icicle. I didn't think the man had been born who could melt you."

"No secret." She laughed. "I knew what you thought of me. But you once told me you never could resist a dare. Was that how you viewed me? A challenge to defrost?"

"It never crossed my mind. I have to say that I must be incredibly blind because you're the warmest, most passionate woman I've ever known." He ran a finger over her bottom lip. "You're not angry?"

"I'd be hypocritical if I was." Ella paused, then grinned.

"You see, I thought you were a bully—I called you Bossy Big Brother."

"I'm not a bully!"

"Ah, but I thought you were. I thought you controlled every aspect of your brother's life, and that was why the poor thing was so irresponsible."

Yevgeny swung round and leaned against the balustrade. Placing his hands on her hips, he drew her closer. "What can I say? I admit it. I did pull him out of too many scrapes."

"I did the same with Keira. It was easier to sort her mistakes out for her than let her learn to do it herself." She grinned at him as she allowed her body to rest against his. "At least we won't make those mistakes with Holly."

"I have no doubt there will be others to make."

Ella looked up at him, aghast. "Good grief. I hope not."

"But don't worry. Like her mother, I know she's ticklish—under her feet."

"How long have you known that?"

He paused. "I'll tell you something else I know."

"What's that?"

"The night I discovered Holly was ticklish, I overheard your promise to our daughter that you'd find her the best mother in the world. If you ask me, I think you've done that."

Her heart stopped. "That's the nicest thing you've ever said to me."

"And it's perfectly true. Come here my wife-to-be. Let me show you again how much I love you."

This time when his mouth closed over hers, he was in no hurry to end the kiss.

* * * * *

A TRICKY PROPOSITION

BY
CAT SCHIELD

Cat Schield has been reading and writing romance since high school. Although she graduated from college with a BA in business, her idea of a perfect career was writing books for Mills & Boon. And now, after winning the Romance Writers of America 2010 Golden Heart Award for series contemporary romance, that dream has come true. Cat lives in Minnesota with her daughter, Emily, and their Burmese cat. When she's not writing sexy, romantic stories for Mills & Boon Desire, she can be found sailing with friends on the St Croix River or in more exotic locales like the Caribbean and Europe. She loves to hear from readers. Find her at www.catschield.com. Follow her on Twitter @catschield.

To my best friend, Annie Slawik.
I can't thank you enough for all the laughter
and support. Without you I wouldn't be who I am.

One

Ming Campbell's anxiety was not soothed by the restful trickle of water from the nearby fountain or by the calming greenery hanging from baskets around the restaurant's outdoor seating area. With each sip of her iced pomegranate tea she grew more convinced she was on the verge of making the biggest mistake of her life.

Beneath the table, her four-pound Yorkshire terrier lifted her chin off Ming's toes and began her welcome wiggle. Muffin might not be much of a guard dog, but she made one hell of an early warning system.

Stomach tightening, Ming glanced up. A tall man in loose-fitting chinos, polo shirt and casual shoes approached. Sexy stubble softened his chiseled cheeks and sharp jaw.

"Sorry I'm late."

Jason Sterling's fingertips skimmed her shoulder, sending a rush of goose bumps speeding down her arm. Ming cursed her body's impulsive reaction as he sprawled in the chair across from hers.

Ever since breaking off her engagement to his brother, Evan, six months ago, she'd grown acutely conscious of any and all contact with him. The friendly pat he gave her arm. His shoulder bumping hers as he sat beside her on the couch. The affable hugs he doled so casually that scrambled her nerve endings. It wasn't as if she could tell him to stop. He'd want to know what was eating at her, and there was no way she was going to tell him. So, she silently endured and hoped the feelings would go away or at least simmer down.

Muffin set her front paws on his knee, her brown eyes fixed on his face, and made a noise that was part bark, part sneeze. Jason slid his hand beneath the terrier's belly and lifted her so she could give his chin a quick lick. That done, the dog settled on his lap and heaved a contented sigh.

Jason signaled the waitress and they ordered lunch. "How come you didn't start without me?"

Because she was too keyed up to be hungry. "You said you were only going to be fifteen minutes late."

Jason was the consummate bachelor. Self-involved, pre-occupied with amateur car racing and always looking for the next bit of adventure, whether it was a hot girl or a fast track. They'd been best friends since first grade and she loved him, but that didn't mean he didn't occasionally drive her crazy.

"Sorry about that. We hit some traffic just as we got back into town."

"I thought you were coming home yesterday."

"That was the plan, but then the guys and I went out for a couple beers after the race and our celebration went a little long. None of us were in any shape to drive five hours back to Houston." With a crooked smile he extended his long legs in front of him and set his canvas-clad foot on the leg of her chair.

"How is Max taking how far you are ahead of him in points?" The two friends had raced domestic muscle cars in events sanctioned by the National Auto Sports Association since they were sixteen. Each year they competed to see who could amass the most points.

"Ever since he got engaged, I don't think he cares."

She hadn't seen Jason this disgruntled since his dad fell for a woman twenty years his junior. "You poor baby. Your best buddy has grown up and gotten on with his life, leaving you behind." Ming set her elbow on the table and dropped her chin into her palm. She'd been listening to Jason complain about the changes in his best friend ever since Max Case had proposed to the love of his life.

Jason leaned forward, an intense look in his eyes. "Maybe I need to find out what all the fuss is about."

"I thought you were never going to get married." Sudden anxiety crushed the air from her lungs. If he fell madly in love with someone, the dynamic of their friendship would change. She'd no longer be his best "girl" friend.

"No worries about that." His lopsided grin eased some of her panic.

Ming turned her attention to the Greek salad the waitress set in front of her. In high school she'd developed a crush on Jason. It had been hopeless. Unrequited. Except for one brief interlude after prom—and he'd taken pains to assure her that had been a mistake—he'd never given her any indication that he thought of her as anything but a friend.

When he headed off to college, time and distance hadn't blunted her feelings for him, but it had provided her with perspective. Even if by some miracle Jason did fall madly in love with her, he wasn't going to act on it. Over and over, he'd told her how important her friendship was to him and how he didn't want to do anything to mess that up.

"So, what's up?" Jason said, eyeing her over the top of his hamburger. "You said you had something serious to discuss with me."

And in the thirty minutes she'd sat waiting for him, she'd

talked herself into a state of near panic. Usually she told him everything going on in her life. Well, almost everything.

When she'd starting dating Evan there were a few topics they didn't discuss. Her feelings for his brother being the biggest. Holding her own council about such an enormous part of her life left her feeling as if a chunk of her was missing, but she'd learned to adjust and now found it harder than she expected to open up to him.

"I'm going to have a baby." She held her breath and waited for his reaction.

A French fry paused midway between his plate and his mouth. "You're pregnant?"

She shook her head, some of her nervousness easing now that the conversation had begun. "Not yet."

"When?"

"Hopefully soon."

"How? You're not dating anyone."

"I'm using a clinic."

"Who's going to be the father?"

She dodged his gaze and stabbed her fork into a kalamata olive. "I've narrowed the choices down to three. A lawyer who specializes in corporate law, an athlete who competes in the Ironman Hawaii challenge every year and a wildlife photographer. Brains. Body. Soul. I haven't decided which way to go yet."

"You've obviously been thinking about this for a while. Why am I only hearing about it now?" He pushed his plate away, abandoning his half-eaten burger.

In the past she'd been able to talk to Jason about anything. Getting involved with his brother had changed that. Not that it should have. She and Jason were friends with no hope of it ever being anything more.

"You know why Evan and I broke up." She'd been troubled that Evan hadn't shared her passion for family, but she thought he'd come around. "Kids are important to me. I wouldn't do what I do if they weren't."

She'd chosen to become an orthodontist because she loved kids. Their sunny view of the world made her smile, so she gave them perfect teeth to smile back.

"Have you told your parents?"

"Not yet." She shifted on her chair.

"Because you know your mother won't react well to you getting pregnant without being married."

"She won't like it, but she knows how much I want a family of my own, and she's come to accept that I'm not going to get married."

"You don't know that. Give yourself a chance to get over your breakup with Evan. There's someone out there for you."

Not likely when the only man she could see herself with was determined never to marry. Frustration bubbled up. "How long do I wait? Another six months? A year? In two months I turn thirty-two. I don't want to waste any more time weighing the pros and cons or worrying about my mom's reaction when in my heart I know what I want." She thrust out her chin. "I'm going to do this, Jason."

"I can see that."

Mesmerizing eyes studied her. Galaxy blue, the exact shade of her '66 Shelby Cobra convertible. He'd helped her convince her parents to buy the car for her seventeenth birthday and then they'd spent the summer restoring it. She had fond memories of working with him on the convertible, and every time she drove it, she couldn't help but feel connected to Jason. That's why she'd parked the car in her garage the day she started dating his brother and hadn't taken it out since.

"I'd really like you to be on board with my decision."

"You're my best friend," he reminded her, eyes somber. "How can I be anything but supportive?"

Even though she suspected he was still processing her news and had yet to decide whether she was making a mistake, he'd chosen to back her. Ming relaxed. Until that second she hadn't realized how anxious she was about Jason's reaction.

"Are you done eating?" she asked a few minutes later, catching the waitress's eye. Jason hadn't finished his lunch and showed no signs of doing so. "I should probably get back to the clinic. I have a patient to see in fifteen minutes."

He snagged the bill from the waitress before she set it on the table and pulled out his wallet.

"I asked you to lunch." Ming held her hand out imperiously. "You are not buying."

"It's the least I can do after being so late. Besides, the way you eat, you're always a cheap date."

"Thanks."

While Jason slipped cash beneath the saltshaker, she stood and called Muffin to her. The Yorkie refused to budge from Jason's lap. Vexed, Ming glared at the terrier. She was not about to scoop the dog off Jason's thighs. Her pulse hitched at the thought of venturing anywhere near his muscled legs.

Air puffing out in a sigh, she headed for the wood gate that led directly to the parking lot. Jason was at her side, dog tucked beneath his arm, before she reached the pavement.

"Where's your car?" he asked.

"I walked. It's only two blocks."

Given that humidity wasn't a factor on this late-September afternoon, she should have enjoyed her stroll to the restaurant. But what she wanted to discuss with Jason had tied her up in knots.

"Come on. I'll drive you back." He took her hand, setting off a shower of sparks that heightened her senses.

The spicy scent of his cologne infiltrated her lungs and caused the most disturbing urges. His warm, lean body bumped against her hip. It was moments like these when she was tempted to call her receptionist and cancel her afternoon appointments so she could take Jason home and put an end to all the untidy lust rampaging through her body.

Of course, she'd never do that. She'd figure out some other way to tame the she-wolf that had taken up residence beneath her skin. All their lives she'd been the conservative one. The one who studied hard, planned for the future, organized her life down to the minute. Jason was the one who acted on impulse. Who partied his way through college and still managed to graduate with honors. And who liked his personal life unfettered by anyone's expectations.

They neared his car, a 1969 Camaro, and Jason stepped forward to open the passenger door for her. Being nothing more than friends didn't stop him from treating her with the same chivalry he afforded the women he dated. Before she could sit down he had to pluck an eighteen-inch trophy off her seat. Despite the cavalier way he tossed the award into the backseat, Ming knew the win was a source of pride to him and that the trophy would end up beside many others in his "racing" room.

"So what else is on your mind?" Jason asked, settling behind the wheel and starting the powerful engine. Sometimes he knew what she was thinking before she did.

"It's too much to get into now." She cradled Muffin in her arms and brushed her cheek against the terrier's silky coat. The dog gave her hand a happy lick.

"Give me the CliffsNotes version."

Jason accelerated out of the parking lot, the roar of the 427 V-8 causing a happy spike in Ming's heart rate. Riding shotgun in whatever Jason drove had been a thrill since the year he'd turned sixteen and gotten his first muscle car. Where other boys in school had driven relatively new cars, Jason and Max preferred anything fast from the fifties, sixties and seventies.

"It doesn't matter because I changed my mind."

"Changed your mind about what?"

"About what I was going to ask you." She wished he'd just drop it, but she knew better. Now that his curiosity had been aroused, he would bug her until he got answers. "It doesn't matter."

"Sure it does. You've been acting odd for weeks now. What's up?"

Ming sighed in defeat. "You asked me who was going to be the father." She paused to weigh the consequences of telling him. She'd developed a logical explanation that had nothing to do with her longing to have a deeper connection with him. He never had to know how she really felt. Her heart a battering ram against her ribs, she said, "I wanted it to be you."

Silence dominated until Jason stopped the car in front of the medical building's entrance. Ming's announcement smacked into him like the heel of her hand applied to his temple. That she wanted to have a baby didn't surprise him. It's what had broken up her and Evan. But that she wanted Jason to be the father caught him completely off guard.

Had her platonic feelings shifted toward romance? Desire? Unlikely.

She'd been his best friend since first grade. The one person he'd let see his fear when his father had tried to commit suicide. The only girl who'd listened when he went on and on about his goals and who'd talked sense into him when doubts took hold.

In high school, girlfriends came and went, but Ming was always there. Smart and funny, her almond-shaped eyes glowing with laughter. She provided emotional support without complicating their relationship with exasperating expectations. If he canceled plans with her she never pouted or ranted. She never protested when he got caught up working on car engines or shooting hoops with his buddies and forgot to call her. And more often than not, her sagacity kept Jason grounded.

She would have made the perfect girlfriend if he'd been willing to ruin their twenty-five-year friendship for a few months of romance. Because eventually his eye would wander and she'd be left as another casualty of his carefully guarded heart.

He studied her beautiful oval face. "Why me?"

Below inscrutable black eyes, her full lips kicked up at the corners. "You're the perfect choice."

The uneasy buzz resumed in the back of his mind. Was she looking to change their relationship in some way? Link herself to him with a child? He never intended to marry. Ming knew that. Accepted it. Hadn't she?

"How so?"

"Because you're my best friend. I know everything about you. Something about having a stranger's child makes me uncomfortable." She sighed. "Besides, I'm perfectly comfortable being a single parent. You are a dedicated bachelor. You won't have a crisis of conscience and demand your parental rights. It's perfect."

"Perfect," he echoed, reasoning no matter what she claimed, a child they created together would connect them in a way that went way beyond friendship.

"You're right. I don't want marriage or kids. But fathering your child…" Something rumbled in his subconscious, warning him to stop asking questions. She'd decided against asking him to help her get pregnant. He should leave it at that.

"Don't say it that way. You're making it too complicated. We've been friends forever. I don't want anything to change our relationship."

Too late for that. "Things between us changed the minute you started dating Evan."

Jason hadn't welcomed the news. In fact, he'd been quite displeased, which was something he'd had no right to feel. If she was nothing more than his friend, he should have been happy that she and Evan had found each other.

"I know. In the beginning it was awkward, but I never would have gone out with him if you hadn't given me your blessing."

What other choice did he have? It wasn't as if he intended to claim her as anything other than a friend. But such rational thinking hadn't stood him in good stead the first time he'd seen his brother kiss her.

"You didn't need my blessing. If you wanted to date Evan, that was your business." And he'd backed off. Unfortunately, distance had lent him perspective. He'd begun to see her not only as his longtime friend, but also as a desirable woman. "But let's get back to why you changed your mind about wanting me."

"I didn't want *you,*" she corrected, one side of her mouth twitching. "Just a few of your strongest swimmers."

She wanted to make light of it, but Jason wasn't ready to oblige her. "Okay, how come you changed your mind about wanting my swimmers?"

She stared straight ahead and played with the Yorkie's ears, sending the dog into a state of bliss. "Because we'd have to keep it a secret. If anyone found out what we'd done, it would cause all sorts of hard feelings."

Not anyone. Evan. She'd been hurt by his brother, yet she'd taken Evan's feelings into consideration when making such an important decision. She'd deserved better than his brother.

"What if we didn't keep it a secret? My dad would be thrilled that one of his sons made him a grandfather," Jason prompted.

"But he'd also expect you to be a father." Her eyes soft with understanding, she said, "I wouldn't ask that of you."

He resented her assumption that he wouldn't want to be involved. Granted, until ten minutes earlier he'd never considered being a parent, but suddenly Jason didn't like the idea that his child would never know him as his father. "I don't suppose I can talk you out of this."

"My mind is set. I'm going to have babies."

"Babies?" He ejected the word and followed it up with a muttered curse. "I thought it was a baby. Now you're fielding a baseball team?"

A goofy snort of laughter escaped her. Unattractive on ninety-nine percent of women, the sound was adorable erupting from her long, thin nose. It probably helped that her jet-black eyes glittered with mischief, inviting him to join in her amusement.

"What's so funny?" he demanded.

She shook her head, the action causing the ebony curtains of hair framing her exotic Asian features to sway like a group of Latin dancers doing a rumba. "You should see the look on your face."

He suppressed a growl. There was not one damn thing about this that was funny. "I thought this was a one-time deal."

"It is, but you never know what you're going to get when you go in vitro. I might have triplets."

Jason's thoughts whirled. "Triplets?" Damn. He hadn't adjusted to the idea of one child. Suddenly there were three?

"It's possible." Her gaze turned inward. A tranquil half smile curved her lips.

For a couple, triplets would be hard. How was she going to handle three babies as a single mom?

Images paraded through his head. Ming's mysterious smile as she placed his hand on her round belly. Her eyes sparkling as she settled the baby in his arms for the first time. The way the pictures appealed to him triggered alarm bells. After his father's suicide attempt, he'd closed himself off to being a husband and a father. Not once in the years since had he questioned his decision.

Ming glanced at the silver watch on her delicate wrist. "I've got seven minutes to get upstairs or I'll be late for my next appointment."

"We need to talk about this more."

"It'll have to be later." She gathered Muffin and exited the car.

"When later?"

But she'd shut the door and was heading away, sleek and sexy in form-fitting black pants and a sleeveless knit top that showed off her toned arms.

Appreciation slammed into his gut.

Uninvited.

Unnerving.

Cursing beneath his breath, Jason shut off the engine, got out of the car and headed for the front door, but he wasn't fast enough to catch her before she crossed the building's threshold.

Four-inch heels clicking on the tile lobby floor, she headed toward the elevator. With his longer legs, Jason had little trouble keeping pace. He reached the elevator ahead of her and put his hand over the up button to keep her from hitting it.

"The Camaro will get towed if you leave it there."

He barely registered her words. "Let's have dinner."

A ding sounded and the doors before them opened. She barely waited for the elevator to empty before stepping forward.

"I already have plans."

"With whom?"

She shook her head. "Since when are you so curious about my social life?"

Since her engagement had broken off.

On the third floor, they passed a door marked Dr. Terrance Kincaid, DDS, and Dr. Ming Campbell, DDS. Another ten feet and they came to an unmarked door that she unlocked and breezed through.

One of the dental assistants hovered outside Ming's office. "Oh, good, you're here. I'll get your next patient."

Ming set down Muffin, and the Yorkie bounded through the hallway toward the waiting room. She headed into her office and returned wearing a white lab coat. When she started past him, Jason caught her arm.

"You can't do this alone." Whether he meant get pregnant or raise a child, he wasn't sure.

Her gentle smile was meant to relieve him of all obligations. "I'll be fine."

"I don't doubt that." But he couldn't shake the sense that she needed him.

A thirteen-year-old boy appeared in the hallway and waved to her.

"Hello, Billy," she called. "How did your baseball tournament go last month?"

"Great. Our team won every game."

"I'd expect nothing else with a fabulous pitcher like you on the mound. I'll see you in a couple minutes."

As often as Jason had seen her at work, he never stopped being amazed that she could summon a detail for any of her two hundred clients that made the child feel less like a patient and more like a friend.

"I'll call you tomorrow." Without waiting for him to respond, she followed Billy to the treatment area.

Reluctant to leave, Jason stared after her until she disappeared. Impatience and concern urged him to hound her until he was satisfied he knew all her plans, but he knew how he'd feel if she'd cornered him at work.

Instead, he returned to the parking lot. The Camaro remained at the curb where he'd left it. Donning his shades, he slid behind the wheel and started the powerful engine.

Two

When Ming returned to her office after her last appointment, she found her sister sitting cross-legged on the floor, a laptop balanced on her thighs.

"There are three chairs in the room. You should use one."

"I like sitting on the ground." With her short, spiky hair and fondness for natural fibers and loose-fitting clothes, Lily looked more than an environmental activist than a top software engineer. "It lets me feel connected to the earth."

"We're three stories up in a concrete building."

Lily gave her a "whatever" shoulder shrug and closed the laptop. "I stopped by to tell you I'm heading out really early tomorrow morning."

"Where to this time?"

For the past five years, her sister had been leading a team of consultants involved with transitioning their company's various divisions to a single software system. Since the branches were all over the country, she traveled forty weeks out of the year. The rest of the time, she stayed rent-free in Ming's spare bedroom.

"Portland."

"How long?"

"They offered me a permanent position."

Her sister's announcement came as an unwelcome surprise. "Did you say yes?"

"Not yet. I want to see if I like Portland first. But I gotta tell you, I'm sick of all the traveling. It would be nice to buy a place and get some appliances. I want a juicer."

Lily had this whole "a healthy body equals a healthy mind" mentality. She made all sorts of disgusting green concoctions that smelled awful and tasted like a decomposing marsh. Ming's eyes watered just thinking about them. She preferred to jump-start her day with massive doses of caffeine.

"You won't get bored being stuck in one city?"

"I'm ready to settle down."

"And you can't settle down in Houston?"

"I want to meet a guy I can get serious about."

"And you have to go all the way to Portland to find one?" Ming wondered what was really going on with her sister.

Lily slipped her laptop into its protective sleeve. "I need a change."

"You're not going to stick around and be an auntie?" She'd hoped once Lily held the baby and saw how happy Ming was as a mom, her sister could finally get why Ming was willing to risk their mother's wrath about her decision.

"I think it's better if I don't."

As close as the sisters were, they'd done nothing but argue since Ming had divulged her intention of becoming a single mom. Her sister's negative reaction had come as a complete surprise. And on the heels of her broken engagement, Ming was feeling alone and blue.

"I wish I could make you understand how much this means to me."

"Look, I get it. You've always wanted children. I just think that a kid needs both a mother and a father."

Ming's confidence waned beneath her sister's criticism. Despite her free-spirited style and reluctance to be tied down, Lily was a lot more traditional than Ming when it came to family. Last night, when Ming had told her sister she was going to talk to Jason today, Lily had accused Ming of being selfish.

But was she? Raising a child without a father didn't necessarily mean that the child would have problems. Children needed love and boundaries. She could provide both.

It wasn't fair for Lily to push her opinions on Ming. She hadn't made her decision overnight. She'd spent months and months talking to single moms, weighing the pros and cons, and using her head, not her emotions, to make up her mind about raising a child on her own. Of course, when it came right down to it, her longing to be a mother was a strong, biological urge that was hard to ignore.

Ming slipped out of her lab coat and hung it on the back of her office door. "Have you told Mom about the job offer?"

"No." Lily countered. "Have you told her what you're going to do?"

"I was planning to on Friday. We're having dinner, just the two of us." Ming arched an eyebrow. "Unless you'd like to head over there now so we can both share our news. Maybe with two of us to yell at, we'll each get half a tongue lashing."

"As much as I would love to be there to see the look on Mom's face when she finds out you're going to have a baby without a husband, I'm not ready to talk about my plans. Not until I'm completely sure."

It sounded as if Lily wasn't one hundred percent sold on moving away. Ming kept relief off her face and clung to the hope that her sister would find that Portland wasn't to her liking.

"Will I see you at home later?"

Lily shook her head. "Got plans."

"A date?"

"Not exactly."

"Same guy?" For the past few months, whenever she was in town, her sister had been spending a lot of time with a mystery man. "Have you told him your plans to move?"

"It's not like that."

"It's not like what?"

"We're not dating."

"Then it's just sex?"

Her sister made an impatient noise. "Geez, Ming. You of all people should know that men and women can be just friends."

"Most men and women can't. Besides, Jason and I are more like brother and sister than friends."

For about the hundredth time, Ming toyed with telling Lily about her mixed feelings for Jason. How she loved him as a friend but couldn't stop wondering if they could have made it as a couple. Of course, she'd blown any chance to find out when she'd agreed to have dinner with Evan three years ago.

But long before that she knew Jason wouldn't let anything get in the way of their friendship.

"Have you told him about your plans to have a baby yet?"

"I mentioned it to him this afternoon."

She was equally disappointed and relieved that she'd decided against asking Jason to help her get pregnant. Raising his child would muddle her already complicated emotions where he was concerned. It would be easier to get over her romantic yearnings if she had no expectations.

"How did he take it?"

"Once he gets used to the idea, I think he'll be happy for me." Her throat locked up. She'd really been counting on his support.

"Maybe this is the universe's way of telling you that you're on the wrong path."

"I don't need the universe to tell me anything. I have you." Although Ming kept her voice light, her heart was heavy. She was torn between living her dream and disrupting her relationships with those she loved. What if this became a wedge between her and Lily? Or her and Jason? Ming hated the idea of being pulled in opposite directions by her longing to be a mom and her fear of losing the closeness she shared with either of them.

To comfort herself, she stared at her photo wall, the proof of what she'd achieved these past seven years. Hundreds of smiles lightened her mood and gave her courage.

"I guess you and I will just have to accept that neither one of us is making a decision the other is happy with," Ming said.

Jason paced from one end of his large office to the other. Beyond his closed door, the offices of Sterling Bridge Company emptied. It was a little past six, but Jason had given up working hours ago. As the chief financial officer of the family's bridge construction business, he was supposed to be looking over some last-minute changes in the numbers for a multimillion-dollar project they were bidding on next week, but he couldn't focus. Not surprising after Ming's big announcement today.

She'd be a great mom. Patient. Loving. Stern when she had to be. If he'd voiced doubts it wasn't because of her ability to parent, but how hard it would be for her to do it on her own. Naturally Ming wouldn't view any difficulty as too much trouble. She'd embrace the challenges and surpass everyone's expectations.

But knowing this didn't stop his uneasiness. His sense that he should be there for her. Help her.

Help her what?

Get pregnant.

Raise his child?

His gut told him it was the right thing to do even if his brain warned him that he was embarking on a fool's journey. They were best friends. This was when best friends stepped up and helped each other out. If the situation was reversed and he wanted a child, she'd be the woman he'd choose to make that happen.

But if they did this, things could get complicated. If his brother found out that Jason had helped Ming become a mother, the hurt they caused might lead to permanent estrangement between him and Evan.

On the other hand, Ming deserved to get the family she wanted.

Another thirty minutes disappeared with Jason lost in thought. Since he couldn't be productive at the office, he decided to head home. A recently purchased '73 Dodge Charger sat in his garage awaiting some TLC. In addition to his passion for racing, he loved buying, fixing up and selling classic muscle cars. It's why he'd chosen his house in the western suburbs. The three-acre estate had afforded him the opportunity to build a six-car garage to house his rare collection.

On the way out, Jason passed his brother's office. Helping Ming get pregnant would also involve keeping another big secret from his brother. Jason resented that she still worried about Evan's feelings after the way he'd broken off their engagement. Would it be as awkward for Evan to be an uncle to his ex-fiancée's child as it had been for Jason to watch his best friend fall in love with his brother?

From the moment Ming and Evan had begun dating, tension had developed between Jason and his brother. An unspoken rift that was territorial in nature. Ming and Jason were best friends. They were bonded by difficult experiences. Inside jokes. Shared memories. In the beginning, it was Evan who was the third wheel whenever the three of them got together. But this wasn't like other times when Ming had dated. Thanks to her long friendship with Jason, she was practically family. Within months, it was obvious she and Evan were perfectly matched in temperament and outlook, and the closer Ming and Evan became, the more Jason became the outsider. Which was something he resented. Ming was his best friend and he didn't like sharing her.

Entering his brother's office, Jason found Evan occupying the couch in the seating area. Evan was three years older and carried more weight on his six-foot frame than Jason, but otherwise, the brothers had the same blue eyes, dark blond hair and features. Both resembled their mother, who'd died in a car accident with their nine-year-old sister when the boys were in high school.

The death of his wife and daughter had devastated their father. Tony Sterling had fallen into a deep depression that lasted six months and almost resulted in the loss of his business. And if Jason hadn't snuck into the garage one night to "borrow" the car for a joyride and found his father sitting behind the wheel with the garage filling with exhaust fumes, Tony might have lost his life.

This pivotal event had happened when Jason was only fifteen years old and had marked him. He swore he would never succumb to a love so strong that he would be driven to take his own life when the love was snatched away. It had been an easy promise to keep.

Jason scrutinized his brother as he crossed the room, his footfalls soundless on the plush carpet. Evan was so focused on the object in his hand he didn't notice Jason's arrival until he spoke.

"Want to catch dinner?"

Evan's gaze shot toward his brother, and in a furtive move, he pocketed the earrings he'd been brooding over. Jason recognized them as the pearl-and-diamond ones his brother had given to Ming as an engagement present. What was his brother doing with them?

"Can't. I've already got plans."

"A date?"

Evan got to his feet and paced toward his desk. With his back to Jason, he spoke. "I guess."

"You don't know?"

That was very unlike his brother. When it came to living a meticulously planned existence, the only one more exacting than Evan was Ming.

Evan's hand plunged into the pocket he'd dropped the earrings into. "It's complicated."

"Is she married?"

"No."

"Engaged?"

"No."

"Kids?"

"Let it go." Evan's exasperation only increased Jason's tension.

"Does it have something to do with Ming's earrings in your pocket?" When Evan didn't answer, Jason's gut clenched, his suspicions confirmed. "Haven't you done enough damage there? She's moving on with her life. She doesn't need you stirring things up again."

"I didn't plan what happened. It just did."

Impulsive behavior from his plan-everything-to-death brother? Jason didn't like the sound of that. It could only lead to Ming getting hurt again.

"What exactly happened?"

"Lily and I met for a drink a couple months ago."

"You and Lily?" He almost laughed at the odd pairing. While Evan and Ming had been perfectly compatible, Evan and Lily were total opposites. Then he sobered. "Just the once?"

"A few times." Evan rubbed his face, bringing Jason's attention to the dark shadows beneath his eyes. His brother looked exhausted. And low. "A lot."

"Have you thought about what you're doing?" When it came to picking sides, Jason would choose Ming every time. In some ways, she was more like family to him than Evan. Jason had certainly shared more of himself with her. "Don't you think

Ming will be upset if she finds out you and her sister are dating?"

Before Evan could answer, Jason's cell began to ring. With Ming's heart in danger and his brother in his crosshairs, Jason wouldn't have allowed himself to be distracted if anyone else on the planet was calling. But this was Ming's ringtone.

"We'll talk more about this later," he told his brother, and answered the call as he exited. "What's going on?"

"It's Lily." There was no mistaking the cry for help in Ming's voice.

Jason's annoyance with his brother flared anew. Had Ming found out what was going on? "What about her?"

"She's moving to Portland. What am I going to do without her?"

What a relief. Ming didn't yet know that her sister was dating Evan, and if Lily moved to Portland then her relationship with her sister's ex-fiancé would have to end.

"You still have me." He'd intended to make his tone light, but on the heels of his conversation with his brother moments before, his declaration came out like a pledge. "Do you want to catch a drink and talk about it? We could continue our earlier conversation."

"I can't. Terry and I are having dinner."

"Afterward?"

"It's been a long day. I'm heading home for a glass of wine and a long, hot bath."

"Do you want some company?"

Unbidden, his thoughts took him to an intoxicating, sensual place where Ming floated naked in warm, fragrant water. Candles burned, setting her delicate, pale shoulders aglow above the framing bubbles of her favorite bath gel. The office faded away as he imagined trailing his lips along her neck, discovering all the places on her silky skin that made her shiver.

"Jason?" Ming's voice roused him to the fact that he was standing in the elevator. He didn't remember getting there.

Damn it. He banished the images, but the sensations lingered.

"What?" he asked, disturbed at how compelling his fantasy had been.

"I asked if I could call you later."

"Sure." His voice had gone hoarse. "Have a good dinner."

"Thanks."

The phone went dead in his hand. Jason dropped the cell back into his pocket, still reeling from the direction his thoughts had gone. He had to stop thinking of her like that. Unfortunately, once awakened, the notion of making love to Ming proved difficult to coax back to sleep.

He headed to his favorite bar, which promised a beer and a dozen sports channels as a distraction from his problems. It failed to deliver.

Instead, he replayed his conversations with both Ming and Evan in his mind. She wanted to have a baby, wanted Jason's help to make that happen, but she'd decided against it before he'd had a chance to consider the idea. All because it wouldn't be fair to Evan if he ever found out.

Would she feel the same if she knew Evan was dating Lily and that he didn't care if Ming got hurt in the process? That wouldn't change her mind. Even if it killed her, Ming would want Evan and Lily to be happy.

But shouldn't she get to be selfish, too? She should be able to choose whatever man she wanted to help her get pregnant. Even the brother of her ex-fiancé. Only Jason knew she'd never go there without a lot of convincing.

And wasn't that what best friends were for?

Fifteen minutes after she'd hung up on Jason, Ming's heart was still thumping impossibly fast. She'd told herself that when he'd asked if she wanted company for a glass of wine and a hot bath, he hadn't meant anything sexual. She'd called him for a shoulder to cry on. That's all he was offering.

But the image of him sliding into her oversize tub while candlelight flickered off the glass tile wall and a thousand soap bubbles drifted on the water's surface…

"Ready for dinner?"

Jerked out of her musing, Ming spun her chair away from her computer and spied Terry Kincaid grinning at her from the doorway, his even, white teeth dazzling against his tan skin. As well as being her partner in the dental practice and her best girl friend's father, he was the reason she'd chosen to become an orthodontist in the first place.

"Absolutely."

She closed her internet browser and images of strollers disappeared from her screen. As crazy as it was to shop for baby stuff before she was even pregnant, Ming couldn't stop herself from buying things. Her last purchase had been one of those mobiles that hangs above the crib and plays music as it spins.

"You already know how proud I am of you," Terry began after they'd finished ordering dinner at his favorite seafood place. "When I brought you into the practice, it wasn't because you were at the top of your class or a hard worker, but because you're like family."

"You know that's how I feel about you, too." In fact, Terry was so much better than her own family because he offered her absolute support without any judgment.

"And as a member of my family, it was important to me that I come to you with any big life-changing decisions I was about to make."

Ming gulped. How had he found out what she was going to do? Wendy couldn't have told him. Her friend knew how to keep a secret.

"Sure," she said. "That's only fair."

"That's why I'm here to tell you that I'm going to retire and I want you to take over the practice."

This was the last thing she expected him to say. "But you're only fifty-seven. You can't quit now."

"It's the perfect time. Janice and I want to travel while we're still young enough to have adventures."

In addition to being a competitive sailor, Terry was an expert rock climber and pilot. Where Ming liked relaxing spa vacations in northern California, he and his wife went hang gliding in Australia and zip lining through the jungles of Costa Rica.

"And you want me to have the practice?" Her mind raced at the thought of all the things she would have to learn, and fast. Managing personnel and finances. Marketing. The practice thrived with Terry at the helm. Could she do half as well? "It's a lot."

"If you're worried about the money, work the numbers with Jason."

"It's not the money." It was an overwhelming responsibility to take on at the same time she was preparing for the challenge of being a single mom. "I'm not sure I'm ready."

Terry was unfazed by her doubts. "I've never met anyone who rises to the challenge the way you do. And I'm not going to retire next week. I'm looking at the middle of next year. Plenty of time for you to learn what you need to know."

The middle of next year? Ming did some rapid calculation. If everything went according to schedule, she'd be giving birth about the time when Terry would be leaving. Who'd take over while she was out on maternity leave? She'd hoped for twelve glorious weeks with her newborn.

Yet, now that the initial panic was fading, excitement stirred. Her own practice. She'd be crazy to let this opportunity pass her by.

"Ming, are you all right?" Concern had replaced delight. "I thought you'd jump at the chance to run the practice."

"I'm really thrilled by the opportunity."

"But?"

She was going to have a baby. Taking over the practice would require a huge commitment of time and energy. But Terry believed in her and she hated to disappoint him. He'd taken her under his wing during high school when she and Wendy had visited the office and shown her that orthodontia was a perfect career for someone who had an obsession with making things straight and orderly.

"No *buts*." She loaded her voice with confidence.

"That's my girl." He patted her hand. "You have no idea how happy I was when you decided to join me in this practice. There's no one but you that I'd trust to turn it over to."

His words warmed and worried her at the same. The amount of responsibility overwhelmed her, but whatever it took, she'd make sure Terry never regretted choosing her.

"I won't let you down."

Crickets serenaded Jason as he headed up the walk to Ming's front door. At nine o'clock at night, only a far-off bark disturbed the peaceful tree-lined street in the older Houston suburb. Amongst the midcentury craftsman homes, Ming's contemporary-styled house stood out. The clean lines and geometric landscaping suited the woman who lived there. Ming kept her surroundings and her life uncluttered.

He couldn't imagine how she was going to handle the sort of disorder a child would bring into her world, but after his conversation with Evan this afternoon, Jason was no longer deciding whether or not he should help his oldest friend. It was more a matter of how he was going to go about it.

Jason rang her doorbell and Muffin began to bark in warning. The entry light above him snapped on and the door flew open. Jason blinked as Ming appeared in the sudden brightness. The scent of her filled his nostrils, a sumptuous floral that made him think of making love on an exotic tropical island.

"Jason? What are you doing here?" Ming bent to catch the terrier as she charged past, but missed. "Muffin, get back here."

"I'll get her." Chasing the frisky dog gave him something to concentrate on besides Ming's slender form clad in a plum silk nightgown and robe, her long black hair cascading over one shoulder. "Did I wake you?" he asked, handing her the squirming Yorkie.

His body tightened as he imagined her warm, pliant form snuggled beside him in bed. His brother had been a complete idiot not to give her the sun, moon and whatever stars she wanted.

"No." She tilted her head. "Do you want to come in?"

Swept by the new and unsettling yearning to take her in his arms and claim her lush mouth, Jason shook his head. "I've been thinking about what we talked about earlier today."

"If you've come here to talk me out of having a baby, you can save your breath." She was his best friend. Back in high school they'd agreed that what had happened after prom had been a huge mistake. They'd both been upset with their dates and turned to each other in a moment of weakness. Neither one wanted to risk their friendship by exploring the chemistry between them.

But in the back of Jason's mind, lying in wait all these years, was curiosity. What would it be like between them? It's why he'd decided to help her make a baby. Today she'd offered him the solution to satisfy his need for her and not complicate their friendship with romantic misunderstandings. He'd be a fool not to take advantage of the opportunity.

"I want to help."

"You do?" Doubt dominated her question, but relief hovered nearby. She studied him a long moment before asking, "Are you sure?"

"I've been thinking about it all afternoon and decided I'd be a pretty lousy friend if I wasn't there when you needed me."

A broad smile transformed her expression. "You don't know how much this means to me. I'll call the clinic tomorrow and make an appointment for you."

Jason shook his head. "No fertility clinic. No doctor." He hooked his fingers around the sash that held her robe closed and tugged her a half step closer. Heat pooled below his belt at the way her lips parted in surprise. "Just you and me."

Something like excitement flickered in her eyes, only to be dampened by her frown. "Are you suggesting what I think you're suggesting?"

"Let's make a baby the old-fashioned way."

Three

"Old-fashioned way?" Ming's brain sputtered like a poorly maintained engine. What the hell was he…? "Sex?"

"I prefer to think of it as making love."

"Same difference."

Jason's grin grew wolfish. "Not the way I do it."

Her mind raced. She couldn't have sex—make love—with Jason. He was her best friend. Their relationship worked because they didn't complicate it by pretending a friends-with-benefits scenario was realistic. "Absolutely not."

"Why not?"

"Because…" What was she supposed to give him for an excuse? "I don't feel that way about you."

"Give me an hour and I'm sure you'll feel exactly that way about me."

The sensual light in his eyes was so intense she could almost feel his hands sliding over her. Her nipples tightened. She crossed her arms over her chest to conceal her body's involuntary reaction.

"Arrogant jackass."

His cocky grin was her only reply. Ming scowled at him to conceal her rising alarm. He was enjoying this. Damn him. Worse, her toes were curling at the prospect of making love with him.

"Be reasonable." *Please be reasonable.* "It'll be much easier if you just go to the clinic. All you have to do is show up, grab a magazine and make a donation."

"Not happening."

The air around them crackled with electricity, raising the hair at the back of her neck.

"Why not?" She gathered the hair hanging over her shoulder and tugged. Her scalp burned at the harsh punishment. "It's not as if you have any use for them." She pointed downward.

"If you want them, you're going to have to get them the old-fashioned way."

"Stop saying that." Her voice had taken on a disturbing squeak.

Jason naked. Her hands roaming over all his hard muscles. The slide of him between her thighs. She pressed her knees together as an ache built.

"Come on," he coaxed. "Aren't you the least bit curious?"

Of course she was curious. During the months following senior prom, it's all she'd thought about. "Absolutely not."

"All the women I've dated. Haven't you wondered why they kept coming back for more?"

Instead of being turned off by his arrogance, she found his confidence arousing. "It never crossed my mind."

"I don't believe that. Not after the way you came on to me after prom."

"I came on to you? You kissed me."

"Because you batted those long black eyelashes of yours and went on and on about how no one would ever love you and how what's-his-name wasn't a real man and that you needed a real man."

Ming's mouth fell open. "I did no such thing. You were the one who put your arm around me and said the best way to get over Kevin was to get busy with someone else."

"No." He shook his head. "That's not how it happened at all."

Damn him. He'd given his word they'd never speak of it again. What other promises would he break?

"Neither one of us is going to admit we started it, so let's just agree that a kiss happened and we were prevented from making a huge mistake by my sister's phone call."

"In the interests of keeping you happy," he said, his tone sly and patronizing, "I'll agree a kiss happened and we were interrupted by your sister."

"And that afterward we both agreed it was a huge mistake."

"It was a mistake because you'd been dumped and I was fighting with my girlfriend. Neither one of us was thinking clearly."

Had she said that, or had he? The events of the night were blurry. In fact, the only thing she remembered with crystal clarity was the feel of his lips on hers. The way her head spun as he plunged his tongue into her mouth and set her afire.

"It was a mistake because we were best friends and hooking up would have messed up our relationship."

"But we're not hormone-driven teenagers anymore," he reminded her. "We can approach the sex as a naked hug between friends."

"A naked hug?" She wasn't sure whether to laugh or hit him.

What he wanted from her threatened to turn her emotions into a Gordian knot, and yet she found herself wondering if she could do as he asked. If she went into it without expectations, maybe it was possible for her to enjoy a few glorious nights in Jason's bed and get away with her head clear and her heart unharmed.

"Having…" She cleared her throat and tried again. "Making…" Her throat closed up. Completing the sentence made the prospect so much more real. She wasn't ready to go there yet.

Jason took pity on her inability to finish her thought. "Love?"

"It's intimate and…" Her skin tingled at the thought of just how intimate.

"You don't think I know that?"

Jason's velvet voice slid against her senses. Her entire body flushed as desire pulsed hot and insistent. How many times since her engagement ended had she awakened from a salacious dream about him, feeling like this? Heavy with need and too frustrated to go back to sleep? Too many nights to count.

"Let me finish," she said. "We know each other too well. We're too comfortable. There's no romance between us. It would be like brushing each other's teeth."

"Brushing each other's teeth?" he echoed, laughter dancing in his voice. "You underestimate my powers of seduction."

The wicked light in his eye promised that he was not going to be deterred from his request. A tremor threatened to upend the small amount of her confidence still standing.

"You overestimate my ability to take you seriously."

All at once he stopped trying to push her buttons and his humor faded. "If you are going to become a mother, you don't want that to happen in the sterile environment of a doctor's office. Your conception should be memorable."

She wasn't looking for memorable. Memorable lasted. It clogged up her emotions and made her long for impossible things. She wanted clinical. Practical. Uncomplicated.

Which is why her decision to ask him to be her child's father made so little sense. What if her son or daughter inherited his habit of mixing his food together on the plate before eating because he liked the way it all tasted together? That drove her crazy. She hated it when the different types of food touched each other.

Would her baby be cursed by his carefree nature and impulsiveness? His love of danger and enthusiasm for risk taking?

Or blessed with his flirtatious grin, overpowering charisma, leadership skills and athletic ability.

For someone who thought everything through, it now occurred to her that she'd settled too fast on Jason for her baby's father. As much as she'd insisted that he wouldn't be tied either legally or financially to the child, she hadn't considered how her child would be part of him.

"I would prefer my conception to be fast and efficient," she countered.

"Why not start off slow and explore where it takes us?"

Slow?

Explore?

Ming's tongue went numb. Her emotions simmered in a pot of anticipation and anxiety.

"I'm going to need to think about it."

"Take your time." If he was disappointed by her indecisiveness, he gave no indication. "I'm not going anywhere."

Three days passed without any contact from Ming. Was she considering his proposal or had she rejected the idea and was too angry at his presumption to speak to him? He shouldn't care what she chose. Either she said yes and he could have the opportunity to satisfy his craving for her, or she would refuse and he'd get over the fantasy of her moaning beneath him.

"Jason? Jason?" Max's shoulder punch brought Jason back to the racetrack. "Geez, man, where the hell's your head today?"

Cars streaked by, their powerful engines drowning out his unsettling thoughts. It was Saturday afternoon. He and Max were due to race in an hour. Driving distracted at over a hundred miles an hour was a recipe for trouble.

"Got something I didn't resolve this week."

"It's not like you to worry about work with the smell of gasoline and hot rubber on the wind."

Max's good-natured ribbing annoyed Jason as much as his

slow time in the qualifying round. Or maybe more so because it wasn't work that preoccupied Jason, but a woman.

"Yeah, well, it's a pretty big something."

Never in his life had he let a female take his mind off the business at hand. Especially when he was so determined to win this year's overall points trophy and show Max what he was missing by falling in love and getting engaged.

"Let me guess, you think someone's embezzling from Sterling Bridge."

"Hardly." As CFO of the company his grandfather began in the mid-fifties, Jason had an eagle eye for any discrepancies in the financials. "Let's just say I've put in an offer and I'm waiting to hear if it's been accepted."

"Let me guess, that '68 Shelby you were lusting after last month?"

"I'm not talking about it," Jason retorted. Let Max think he was preoccupied with a car. He'd promised Ming that he'd keep quiet about fathering her child. Granted, she hadn't agreed to let him father the child the way he wanted to, but he sensed she'd come around. It was only a matter of when.

"If it's the Shelby then it's already too late. I bought it two days ago." Max grinned at Jason's disgruntled frown. "I had a space in my garage that needed to be filled."

"And whose fault is that?" Jason spoke with more hostility than he meant to.

A couple of months ago Jason had shared with Max his theory that the Lansing Employment Agency was not in the business of placing personal assistants with executives, but in matchmaking. Max thought that was crazy. So he wagered his rare '69 'Cuda that he wouldn't marry the temporary assistant the employment agency sent him. But when the owner of the placement company turned out to be the long-lost love of Max's life, Jason gained a car but lost his best buddy.

"Why are you still so angry about winning the bet?" Despite his complaint, Max wore a good-natured grin. Everything about Max was good-natured these days. "You got the car I spent five years convincing a guy to sell me. I love that car."

He loved his beautiful fiancée more.

"I'm not angry," Jason grumbled. He missed his cynical-about-love friend. The guy who understood and agreed that love and marriage were to be avoided because falling head over heels for a woman was dangerous and risky.

"Rachel thinks you feel abandoned. Like because she and I are together, you've lost your best friend."

Jason shot Max a skeptical look. "Ming's my best friend. You're just some guy I used to hang out with before you got all stupid about a girl."

Max acted as if he hadn't heard Jason's dig. "I think she's right."

"Of course you do," Jason grumbled, pulling his ball cap off and swiping at the sweat on his forehead. "You've become one of those guys who keeps his woman happy by agreeing with everything she says."

Max smirked. "That's not how I keep Rachel happy."

For a second Jason felt a stab of envy so acute he almost winced. Silent curses filled his head as he shoved the sensation away. He had no reason to resent his friend's happiness. Max was going to spend the rest of his life devoted to a woman who might someday leave him and take his happiness with her.

"What happened to you?"

Max looked surprised by the question. "I fell in love."

"I know that." But how had he let that happen? They'd both sworn they were never going to let any woman in. After the way Max's dad cheated on his wife, Max swore he'd never trust anyone enough to fall in love. "I don't get why."

"I'd rather be with Rachel than without her."

How similar was that to what had gone through his father's mind after he'd lost his wife? His parents were best friends. Soul mates. Every cliché in the book. She was everything to

him. Jason paused for breath. It had almost killed his dad to
lose her.

"What if she leaves you?"

"She won't."

"What if something bad happens to her?"

"This is about what happened to your mom, isn't it?" Max
gave his friend a sympathetic smile. "Being in love doesn't
guarantee you'll get hurt."

"Maybe not." Jason found no glimmers of light in the shadows around his heart. "But staying single guarantees that I
won't."

A week went by before Ming responded to Jason's offer to
get her pregnant. She'd spent the seven days wondering what
had prompted him to suggest they have sex—she just couldn't
think of it as making love—and analyzing her emotional response.

Jason wasn't interested in complicating their friendship with
romance any more than she was. He was the one person in her
life who never expected anything from her, and she returned
the favor. And yet, they were always there to help and support
each other. Why risk that on the chance that the chemistry between them was out-of-this-world explosive?

Of course, it had dawned on her a couple of days ago that
he'd probably decided helping her get pregnant offered him a
free pass. He could get her into bed no strings attached. No
worries that expectations about where things might go in the
future would churn up emotions.

It would be an interlude. A couple of passionate encounters
that would satisfy both their curiosities. In the end, she would
be pregnant. He would go off in search of new hearts to break,
and their friendship would continue on as always.

The absolute simplicity of the plan warned Ming that she
was missing something.

Jason was in his garage when Ming parked her car in his

driveway and killed the engine. She hadn't completely decided to accept his terms, but she was leaning that way. It made her more sensitive to how attractive Jason looked in faded jeans and a snug black T-shirt with a Ford Mustang logo. Wholly masculine, supremely confident. Her stomach flipped in full-out feminine appreciation as he came to meet her.

"Hey, what's up?"

Light-headed from the impact of his sexy grin, she indicated the beer in his hand. "Got one of those for me?"

"Sure."

He headed for the small, well-stocked fridge at the back of the garage, and she followed. When he bent down to pull out a bottle, her gaze locked on his perfect butt. Hammered by the urge to slide her hands over those taut curves, she knew she was going to do this. Correction. She *wanted* to do this.

"Thanks," she murmured, applying the cold bottle to one overheated cheek.

Jason watched her through narrowed eyes. "I thought you didn't drink beer anymore."

"Do you have any wine?" she countered, sipping the beer and trying not to grimace.

"No."

"Then I'm drinking beer." She prowled past racing trophies and photos of Jason and Max in one-piece driving suits. "How'd your weekend go?"

"Come upstairs and see."

Jason led the way into the house and together they ascended the staircase to Jason's second floor. He'd bought the home for investment purposes and had had it professionally decorated. The traditional furnishings weren't her taste, but they suited the home's colonial styling.

He'd taken one of the four bedrooms as his man cave. A wall-to-wall tribute to his great passion for amateur car racing. On one wall, a worn leather couch, left over from his college days, sat facing a sixty-inch flat-screen TV. If Jason wasn't racing his Mustang or in the garage restoring a car, he was here, watching NASCAR events or recaps of his previous races.

He hit the play button on the remote and showed Ming the clip of the race's conclusion.

The results surprised her. "You didn't win?" He'd been having his best season ever. "What happened?"

His large frame slammed into the old couch as he sat down in a disgruntled huff. A man as competitive as Jason had a hard time coming in second. "Had a lot on my mind."

The way his gaze bore into her, Ming realized he blamed her for his loss. She joined him on the couch and jabbed her finger into his ribs. "I'm not going to apologize for taking a week to give your terms some thought."

"I would've been able to concentrate if I'd known your answer."

"I find that hard to believe," she said, keeping her tone light. Mouth Sahara dry, she drank more beer.

He dropped his arm over the back of the couch. His fingertips grazed her bare shoulder. "You don't think the thought of us making love has preoccupied me this last week?"

"Then you agree that we run the risk of changing things between us."

"It doesn't have to." Jason's fingers continued to dwell on her skin, but now he was trailing lines of fire along her collarbone. "Besides, that's not what preoccupied me."

This told Ming all she needed to know about why he'd suggested they skip the fertility clinic. For Jason this was all about the sex. Fine. It could be all about the sex for her, too.

"Okay. Let's do it." She spoke the words before she could second-guess herself. She stared at the television screen. It would be easier to say this next part without meeting his penetrating gaze. "But I have a few conditions of my own."

He leaned close enough for her to feel his breath on her neck. "You want me to romance you?"

As goose bumps appeared on her arms, she made herself

laugh. "Hardly. There is a window of three days during which we can try. If I don't get pregnant your way, then you agree to do it my way." Stipulating her terms put her back on solid ground with him. "I'm not planning on dragging this out indefinitely."

"I agree to those three days, but I want uninterrupted time with you."

She dug her fingernails beneath the beer label. In typical Jason fashion, he was messing up her well-laid plans.

She'd been thinking in terms of three short evenings of fantastic sex here at his house and then heading back home to relive the moments in the privacy of her bedroom. Not days and nights of all Jason all the time. What if she talked in her sleep and told him all her secret fantasies about him? What if he didn't let her sleep and she grew so delirious from all the hours of making love that she said something in the heat of passion?

"You're crazy if you think our families are going to leave us alone for three days."

"They will if we're not in Houston."

This was her baby. She should be the one who decided where and when it was conceived. The lack of control was making her edgy. Vulnerable.

"I propose we go somewhere far away," he continued. "A secluded spot where we can concentrate on the business at hand."

The business at hand? He caressed those four words with such a high degree of sensuality, her body vibrated with excitement.

"I'll figure out where and let you know." At least if she took charge of where they went she wouldn't have to worry about her baby being conceived in whatever town NASCAR was racing that weekend.

She started to shift her weight forward, preparing to stand, when Jason's hand slid across her abdomen and circled around to her spine.

"Before you go."

He tugged her upper half toward him. The hand that had been skimming her shoulder now cupped the back of her head. She was trapped between the heat of his body and his strong arm, her breasts skimming his chest, nipples turning into buds as desire plunged her into a whirlpool of longing. The intent in his eyes set her heart to thumping in an irregular rhythm.

"What do you think you're doing?" she demanded, retreating from the lips dipping toward hers.

"Sealing our deal with a kiss."

"A handshake will work fine."

Her brusque dismissal didn't dim the smug smile curving his lips. She put her hand on his chest. Rock-hard pecs flexed beneath her fingers. The even thump of his heart mocked her wildly fluctuating pulse.

"Not for me." He captured and held her gaze before letting his mouth graze hers. With a brief survey of her expression, he nodded. "See, that wasn't so bad."

"Right." Her chest rose and fell, betraying her agitation. "Not bad."

"If you relax it will get even better." He shifted his attention to her chin, the line of her jaw, dusting his lips over her skin and making her senses whirl.

"I'm not ready to relax." She'd geared up to tell him that she'd try getting pregnant his way. Getting physical with him would require a different sort of preparation.

"You don't have to get ready." His chest vibrated with a low chuckle. "Just relax."

"Jason, how long have we known each other?"

"Long time." He found a spot that interested him just below her ear and lingered until she shivered. "Why?"

Her voice lacked serenity as she said, "Then you know I don't do anything without planning."

His exhalation tickled her sensitive skin and made holding still almost impossible. "You don't need to plan. Just let go."

Right. And risk him discovering her secret? Ever since she'd decided to ask his help in getting pregnant, she'd realized that what she felt for him was deeper than friendship. Not love. Or not the romantic sort. At least she didn't think so. Not yet. But it could become that sort of love if they made love over and over and over.

And if he found out how her feelings had changed toward him, he'd bolt the way he'd run from every other woman who'd tried to claim his heart.

Ming tensed to keep from responding to the persuasive magic of his touch. Just the sweep of his lips over her skin, the strength of his arms around her, raised her temperature and made her long for him to take her hard and fast.

"I'll let go when we're out of town," she promised. Well, lied really. At least she hoped she was lying. "What are you doing?"

In a quick, powerful move, he'd shifted her onto her back and slid one muscular leg between her thighs. Her body reacted before her mind caught up. She bent her knees, planted her feet on the couch cushions and rocked her hips in the carnal hope of easing the ache in her loins.

"While you make arrangements for us to go away, I thought you'd feel better if you weren't worried about the chemistry between us."

His heat seeped into her, softening her muscles, reducing her resistance to ash. "No worries here. I'm sure you're a fabulous lover." She trembled in anticipation of just how fabulous. With her body betraying her at his every touch, she had to keep her wits sharp. "Otherwise, why else would you have left a trail of broken hearts in your wake?"

Jason frowned. "I didn't realize that bothered you so much."

"It doesn't."

He hummed his doubt and leaned down to nibble on her earlobe. "Not sure I believe you."

With her erogenous zones on full red alert, she labored to keep her legs from wrapping around his hips. She wanted to feel him hard and thick against the thudding ache between her thighs. Her fingernails dug into the couch cushions.

"You're biting your lip." His tongue flicked over the tender spot. "I don't know why you're fighting this so hard."

And she didn't want him to find out. "Okay. I'm not worried about your sexual prowess. I'm worried that once we go down this path, there'll be no turning back."

"Oh, I see. You're worried you're going to fall in love with me."

"No." She made a whole series of disgruntled, dismissive noises until she realized he was teasing her. Two could play at this game. "I'm more concerned you'll fall in love with me."

"I don't think that's going to happen."

"I don't know," she said, happy to be on the giving end of the ribbing. "I'm pretty adorable."

"That you are." He scanned her face, utterly serious. "Close your eyes," he commanded. "We're going to do this."

She complied, hoping the intimacy they shared as friends would allow her to revel in the passion Jason aroused in her and keep her from worrying about the potential complications. Being unable to see Jason's face helped calm the flutters of anxiety. If she ignored the scent of sandalwood mingled with car polish, she might be able to pretend the man lying on top of her was anyone else.

The sound of his soft exhalation drifted past her ears a second before his lips found hers. Ming expected him to claim her mouth the way he had fifteen years ago and kiss her as if she was the only woman in the world he'd ever wanted. But this kiss was different. It wasn't the wild, exciting variety that had caused her to tear at Jason's shirt and allow him to slip his hand down the bodice of her dress to bare her breasts.

Jason's lips explored hers with firm but gentle pressure. If she'd worried that she'd be overcome with desire and make a complete fool of herself over him, she'd wasted her energy.

This kiss was so controlled and deliberate she wondered if Jason was regretting his offer to make love to her.

An empty feeling settled in her chest.

"See," Jason said, drifting his lips over her eyelids. "That wasn't so bad."

"I never expected it would be."

"Then what are you so afraid of?"

What if her lust for him was stronger than his for her? What if three days with him only whet her appetite for more?

"The thought of you seeing me naked is one," she said, keeping her tone light to hide her dismay.

His grin bloomed, mischievous and naughty. "I've already seen you naked."

"What?" Lust shot through Ming, leaving her dazzled and disturbed. "When?"

"Remember that family vacation when we brought you with us to Saint John? The outdoor shower attached to my bedroom?"

"Everyone was snorkeling. That's why I came back to the villa early." She'd wanted the room Jason ended up with because of the outdoor shower. Thinking she was alone, she'd used it. "You spied on me?"

"More like stumbled upon you."

She shoved at his beefy shoulder but couldn't budge him. "Why did you have to tell me that?"

"To explain why you have no need to be embarrassed. I've seen it all before." And from his expression, he'd liked what he saw.

Ming flushed hot. Swooning was impossible if she was lying down, right?

"How long did you watch me?"

"Five, maybe ten minutes."

Her mouth opened, but no words came out. Goose bumps erupted at the way his gaze trailed over her. Was she wrong about the kiss? Or was she the only one who caught fire every time they touched?

He stood and offered her his hand. She let him pull her to her feet and then set about straightening her clothes and finger-combing her hair.

Already she could feel their friendship morphing into something else. By the time their three days together were up, she would no longer be just his friend. She would be his ex-lover. That would alter her perspective of their relationship. Is that really what she wanted?

"I've been charting my cycle for the last six months," she said, uncaring if he'd be disinterested in her feminine activities. "The next time I ovulate is in ten days. Can you get away then?"

"Are you sure you want to go through with this?"

Had he hoped his kiss would change her mind? "I really want this baby. If sleeping with you is the only way that's going to happen, I'm ready to make the sacrifice."

He grinned. "Make the arrangements."

Four

Ming had chosen Mendocino, California, for her long weekend with Jason because the only person who knew it was her favorite getaway spot was Terry's daughter, Wendy, her closest girlfriend from high school. Wendy had moved to California with her husband seven years earlier and had introduced Ming to the town, knowing she would fall in love with the little slice of New England plopped onto a rugged California coast. The area featured some of the most spectacular scenery Ming had ever seen, and every year thereafter she returned for a relaxing long weekend.

That all had ended two years ago. She'd arrived early in September for a few days of spa treatments and soul-searching. Surrounded by the steady pulse of shore life, she lingered over coffee, browsed art galleries and wine shops, and took a long look at her relationship with Evan. They'd been going out for a little over a year and he'd asked her to decide between becoming a fully committed couple or parting ways.

That long weekend in Mendocino she'd decided to stop feeling torn between the Sterling brothers. She loved Evan one way. She loved Jason another. He'd been nothing but supportive of her dating Evan and more preoccupied than ever with his career and racing hobby. Ming doubted Jason had even noticed that Evan took up most of her time and attention. Or maybe she just wished it had bothered him. That he'd tell his brother to back off and claim Ming as his own.

But he hadn't, and it had nagged at her how easily Jason had let her go. She'd not viewed a single one of his girlfriends as casually. Each new love interest had meant Jason had taken his friendship with Ming even more for granted.

In hindsight, she understood how she'd fallen for Evan. He'd showered her with all the attention she could ever want.

Despite how things worked out between them, she'd never regretted dating Evan or agreeing to be his wife. So what if their relationship lacked the all-consuming passion of a romance novel. They'd respected each other, communicated logically and without drama. They'd enjoyed the same activities and possessed similar temperaments. All in all, Evan made complete sense for her as a life partner. But had everything been as perfect as it seemed?

A hundred times in the past six months she'd questioned whether she'd have gone through with the wedding if Evan hadn't changed his mind about having kids and ended their engagement.

They'd dated for two years, been engaged for one.

Plenty of time to shake off doubts about the future.

Plenty of time to decide if what she felt for Evan was enduring love or if she'd talked herself into settling for good enough because he fit seamlessly into her picture of the perfect life.

They were ideally suited in temperament and ideology. He never challenged her opinions or bullied her into defending her beliefs. She always knew where she stood with him. He'd made her feel safe.

A stark contrast to the wildly shifting emotions Jason aroused in her.

The long drive up from San Francisco gave Ming too much time to think. To grow even more anxious about the weekend with Jason. Already plagued by concern that letting him help her conceive a baby would complicate their relationship, now she had to worry that making love with him might just whip up a frenzy of emotions that would lead her to disappointment.

Knowing full well she was stalling, Ming stopped in Mendocino and did some window-shopping before she headed to the inn where she and Jason would be staying. To avoid anyone getting suspicious about the two of them doing something as unusual as heading to California for the weekend, they'd travelled separately. Ming had flown to San Francisco a few days ago to spend some time with Wendy. Jason had headed out on Friday morning. As much as Ming enjoyed visiting with her friend, she'd been preoccupied with doubts and worries that she couldn't share.

Although Wendy was excited about Ming's decision to have a baby, she wouldn't have approved of Ming's choice of Jason as the father. So Ming kept that part of her plans to herself. Wendy had been there for all Ming's angst in the aftermath of the senior prom kiss and believed she had wasted too much energy on a man who was never going to let himself fall in love and get married.

Add to this her sister's disapproval, and the fact that the one person she'd always been able to talk to when something was eating at her was the source of her troubles, and Ming was drowning in uncertainty.

The sun was inching its way toward the horizon when Ming decided she'd dawdled long enough. She paid the gallery owner for the painting of the coast she'd fallen in love with and made arrangements to have it shipped back to her house. Her feet felt encased in lead as she headed down the steps toward her rental car.

She drove below the speed limit on the way to the inn. Gulls wheeled and dove in the steady winds off the Pacific as the car rolled down the driveway, gravel crunching beneath the tires. Silver Mist Inn was composed of a large central lodge and a collection of small cottages that clung to the edge of the cliffs. The spectacular views were well matched by the incredible cuisine and the fabulous hospitality of the husband-and-wife team who owned the inn and spa.

Rosemary was behind the check-in desk when Ming entered the lodge. "Hello, Ming," the fifty-something woman exclaimed. "How wonderful to see you."

Ming smiled. Already the relaxing, familiar feel of the place was sinking into her bones. "It's great to see you, too, Rosemary. How have you been?"

Her gaze drifted to the right of reception. The lodge's main room held a handful of people sipping coffee, reading or talking while they enjoyed the expansive views of the ocean. Off to the left, a door led to a broad deck that housed lounge chairs where waitresses were busy bringing drinks from the bar.

"Busy as always." Rosemary pushed a key toward Ming. "Your friend checked in three hours ago. You're staying in Blackberry Cottage."

The change of plans revived Ming's earlier uneasiness. "I booked my regular room in the lodge."

Rosemary nodded. "After your friend saw all we had to offer, he wanted to upgrade your accommodations. It's a little bigger, way more private and the views are the best we have."

"Thank you." Ming forced her lips into a smile she wasn't feeling.

Why had Jason disrupted her arrangements? Whenever she vacationed here, she always stayed in the same room, a comfortable suite with a large balcony that overlooked the ocean. This weekend in particular she'd wanted to be in familiar surroundings.

Ming parked her car beside the one Jason had rented and

retrieved her overnight bag from the trunk. Packing had taken her three hours. She'd debated every item that had gone into the carry-on luggage.

What sort of clothes would set the correct tone for the weekend? She'd started with too much outerwear. But the purpose of the trip wasn't to wander the trails by the cliffs but to explore Jason's glorious, naked body.

So, she'd packed the sexy lingerie she'd received as a bridal shower gift but never gotten the chance to wear. As she'd folded the silky bits of lace and satin, she realized the provocative underwear sent a message that Ming hoped to drive Jason wild with passion, and that struck her as very nonfriendlike.

In the end, she'd filled the suitcase with leggings and sweaters to combat the cool ocean breezes and everyday lingerie because she was making too big a deal out of what was to come.

Ming entered the cottage and set her suitcase by the front door. Her senses purred as she gazed around the large living room decorated in soothing blues and golds. Beyond the cozy furnishings was a wall of windows that revealed a deck gilded by the setting sun and beyond, the indigo ocean.

To her right something mouthwatering was cooking in the small, well-appointed kitchen. An open door beside the refrigerator led outside. Nearing the kitchen, she spied Jason enjoying the ocean breezes from one of the comfortable chairs that flanked a love seat on the deck.

For an undisturbed moment she observed him. He was as relaxed as she'd seen him in months, expression calm, shoulders loose, hands at ease on the chair's arms. A sharp stab of anticipation made her stomach clench. Shocked by the excitement that flooded her, Ming closed her eyes and tried to even out her breathing. In a few short hours, maybe less, they would make love for the first time. Her skin prickled, flushed. Heat throbbed through her, forging a path that ended between her thighs.

Panic followed. She wasn't ready for this. For him.

Telling her frantic pulse to calm down, Ming stepped onto the deck. "Hi."

Jason's gaze swung her way. A smile bloomed. "Hi yourself." He stood and stepped toward her. "You're later than I expected."

His deep voice and the intense light in his eyes made her long to press herself into his arms and pretend they were a real couple and that this was a magical getaway. She dug her nails into her palms.

"It's been over a year since I've seen Wendy. We had a lot to catch up on."

"What was her take on your decision to have a baby?"

"Total support." Ming slipped past him and leaned her elbows on the railing. As the sapphire-blue ocean churned against rugged cliffs, sending plumes of water ten feet into the air, she put her face into the breeze and let it cool her hot cheeks. "After the week I had, it was a relief to tell someone who didn't go all negative on me."

"I wasn't negative."

Ming tore her gaze from the panorama and discovered Jason two feet away. Attacked by delicious tingles, she shook her head. "No, but you created trouble for me, nonetheless."

"Did you tell her about us?"

Ming shook her head. "We're supposed to keep this a secret, remember? Besides, she never liked you in high school."

"Everybody liked me in high school."

Although he'd been a jock and one of the most popular guys in school, Jason hadn't been mean to those less blessed the way his football buddies had been.

"Don't you mean all the girls?" Blaming nerves for her disgruntled tone, Ming pressed her lips together and redirected her attention to the view. The sun was still too bright to stare at, but the color was changing rapidly to orange.

"Them, too." Jason reached out and wrapped the ends of her scarf around his fists.

He tugged, startling her off balance, and stepped into her space. Her hormones shrieked in delight as the scent of cologne and predatory male surrounded her. She gulped air into her lungs and felt her breasts graze his chest. A glint appeared in his eyes, sending a spike of excitement through her.

"Something smells great in the kitchen. What's for dinner?" she asked, her voice cracking on the last word. Her appetite had vanished in the first rush of desire, but eating would delay what came later.

"Coq au vin." Although his lips wore a playful smile, his preoccupation with her mouth gave the horseplay a sexual vibe. He looked prepared to devour her in slow, succulent bites. "Your favorite. Are you hungry?"

He looked half-starved.

"I haven't eaten since breakfast." Her stomach had been too knotted to accept food.

"Then I'd better feed you." He softened his fists and let her scarf slip through his fingers, releasing her. "You'll need your strength for what I have planned for you tonight."

Freed, Ming couldn't move. The hunger prowling through her prevented her from backing to a safe distance. His knowing smirk kept her tongue-tied. She silently cursed as she trailed after him into the kitchen.

"I found a really nice chardonnay in town." He poured two glasses of wine and handed one to Ming. "I figured we'd save the champagne for later."

Great. He was planning to get her liquored up. She could blame the alcohol for whatever foolish thing she cried out in the heat of passion. She swallowed half the pale white wine in a single gulp and made approving noises while he pulled a wedge of brie out of the fridge. Grapes. Crackers. Some sort of pâté. All the sort of thing she'd served him at some point. Had he paid attention to what she liked? Asking herself the question had an adverse effect on her knees and led to more dangerous ruminating. What else might he have planned for her?

"Dinner should be ready in half an hour." He had everything assembled on a plate and used his chin to gesture toward the deck. "It's a gorgeous night. Let's not waste the good weather."

Early September in northern California was a lot cooler than what they'd left behind in Houston, and Ming welcomed the break from the heat. "It really is beautiful." She carried their glasses outside. "We should take a long walk after dinner."

Jason set down the plate and shot her a look. "If you have any strength in your legs after I'm done with you, we'll do that."

Despite the hot glance that accompanied his suggestive words, she shivered. Is this how the weekend was going to go? One long flirtation? It took them away from their normal interaction. Made her feel as if they'd grown apart these past few years and lost the comfortable intimacy they'd once shared.

"You're cold. Come sit with me and I'll warm you up."

Her scattered wits needed time to recover before she was ready to have his arms around her. "I'll grab my wrap."

"Let me get it."

"It's on my suitcase by the door."

How was she supposed to resist falling under his spell if he continued being so solicitous? This was the Jason she'd glimpsed with other women. The one she'd longed to have for her own. Only this Jason never stayed to charm any one woman for more than a few months, while Ming had enjoyed her fun-loving, often self-involved friend in her life for over twenty years. She sighed. Was it possible for him to be the thoughtful, romantic lover and a great friend all in one?

Was she about to find out? Or would making love with him complicate her life? Was he close to discovering she'd harbored a secret, unrequited crush on him for years? At best he'd not take it seriously and tease her about it. At worst, he'd put up walls and disappear the way he always did when a girlfriend grew too serious. Either way, she wasn't ready for his pity or his alarm.

Jason returned with her dark blue pashmina. "I put your suitcase in the bedroom."

Foolishly her heart jerked at the last word. Every instinct told her to run. Altering their relationship by becoming sexually intimate was only going to create problems.

Then he was wrapping the shawl around her and grazing her lips with his. All thoughts of fleeing vanished, lost in the heat generated by her frantic heart.

She put a hand on his arm. "Jason—"

He put a finger against her lips and silenced her. "Save it for later."

The twinkle in his eye calmed some of the frenzy afflicting her hormones. She reminded herself that he was way more experienced in the art of seduction, having had vast numbers of willing women to practice on. He liked the chase. It was routine that turned him off. And right now, he was having a ball pursuing her. Maybe if she stopped resisting, he'd turn down the charisma.

So, she took half a dozen slow, deep breaths and forced herself to relax. Nibbling cheese, she stared at their view and kept her gaze off the handsome man with the dazzling blue eyes. But his deep voice worked its way inside her, its rumble shaking loose her defenses. She let him feed her grapes and crackers covered with pâté. His fingers skimmed her lips, dusted sensation over her cheeks and chin. By the time they were bumping hips in the small kitchen while transferring coq au vin and potatoes to plates, pouring more wine and assembling cutlery, Ming had gotten past her early nerves.

This was the Jason she adored. Funny, completely present, a tad bit naughty. The atmosphere between them was as easy as it had ever been. They'd discussed Terry's offer to take over the practice. Her sister's decision to buy a house in Portland. And stayed away from the worrisome topic of what was going to happen after dessert.

"This is delicious," Ming murmured, closing her eyes in

rapture as the first bite of coq au vin exploded on her taste buds. "My favorite."

"I thought you'd appreciate it. Rosemary told me the restaurant was known for their French cuisine." Jason had yet to sample the dinner.

She indicated his untouched plate. "Aren't you hungry?" He sure looked half-starved.

"I'm having too much fun watching you eat."

And just like that the sizzle was back in the room. Ming's mouth went dry. She bypassed her wine and sipped water instead. After her first glass of the chardonnay, she'd barely touched her second. Making love to Jason for the first time demanded a clear head. She wanted to be completely in the moment, not lost in an alcoholic fog.

"How can watching me eat be fun?" She tried to make her tone light and amused, but it came out husky and broken.

"It's the pleasure you take in each bite. The way you savor the flavors. You're usually so matter-of-fact about things, I like knowing what turns you on."

He wasn't talking about food. Ming felt her skin heat. Her blood moved sluggishly through her veins. Even her heart seemed to slow. She could feel a sexy retort forming on her tongue. She bit down until she had it restrained. They were old friends who were about to have sex, not a man and a woman engaged in a romantic ritual that ended in passionate lovemaking. Ming had to be certain her emotions stayed out of the mix. She could count on Jason to do the same.

"The backs of my knees are very ticklish." She focused on cutting another bite of chicken. "I've always loved having my neck kissed. And there's a spot on my pelvis." She paused, cocked her head and tried to think about the exact spot. "I guess I'll have to show you when we get to that point." She lifted her fork and speared him with a matter-of-fact gaze. "And you?"

His expression told her he was on to her game. "I'm a guy.

Pretty much anywhere a beautiful woman touches me, I'm turned on."

"But there has to be something you really like."

His eyes narrowed. "My nipples are very sensitive."

She pressed her lips together to keep from laughing. "I'll pay special attention to them," she said when she trusted her voice.

If they could talk like this in the bedroom, Ming was confident she could emerge from the weekend without doing something remarkably stupid like mentioning how her feelings for him had been evolving over the last few months. She'd keep things casual. Focus on the physical act, not the intimacy. Use her hands, mouth and tongue to appreciate the perfection of Jason's toned, muscular body and avoid thinking about all those tiresome longings she'd bottled up over the years.

Savor the moment and ignore the future.

While Jason cleared the dishes from the table, Ming went to unpack and get ready for what was to come. Her confidence had returned over dinner. She had her priorities all in a row. Her gaze set on the prize. The path to creating a baby involved being intimate with Jason. She would let her body enjoy making love with him. Emotion had no place in what she was about to do.

Buoyed by her determination, Ming stopped dead in the doorway between the living room and bedroom. The scene before her laid waste to all her good intentions. Here was the stuff of seduction.

The centerpiece of the room was a king-size bed with the white down comforter pulled back and about a hundred red rose petals strewn across the white sheets. Candles covered every available surface, unlit but prepared to set a romantic mood when called upon. Piano music, played by her favorite artist, poured from the dresser, where portable speakers had been attached to an iPod. Everything was perfect.

Her chest locked up. She could not have designed a better setting. Jason had gone to a lot of trouble to do this. He'd planned, taken into account all her favorite things and executed all of this to give her the ideal romantic weekend.

It was so unlike him to think ahead and be so prepared. To take care of her instead of the other way around. It was as if she was here with a completely different person. A thoughtful, romantic guy who wanted something more than three days of great sex and then going back to being buddies. The sort of man women fell for and fell for hard.

"What do you think?"

She hadn't heard Jason's approach over the thump of her heart. "What I think is that I can't do this."

Jason surveyed the room, searching for imperfections. The candles were vanilla scented, her favorite. The rose petals on the bed proclaimed that this weekend was about romance rather than just sex. The coq au vin had been delicious. Everything he'd done was intended to set the perfect stage for romance.

He'd given her no indication that he intended to rush her. He'd promised her a memorable weekend. She had to know he'd take his time with her, drive her wild with desire. This wasn't some spontaneous hookup for him. He took what they were about to do seriously.

What the hell could possibly be wrong?

"I'm sorry," she said into the silence. Sagging against the door frame, she closed her eyes and the weight of the world appeared to descend on her.

"I don't understand."

"I don't, either." She looked beautiful and tragic as she opened her eyes and met his gaze. "I want to do this."

He was very glad to hear that because anticipation had been eating him alive these past few days. He wanted her with an intensity he'd never felt before. Maybe that was because ever since he'd kissed her, he'd been fantasizing about this moment. Or maybe he'd never worked this hard to get a woman into bed before.

"Being a mom is all I think about these days. I know if I want your help to get pregnant, we have to do it this weekend." Ming lapsed into silence, her hunched shoulders broadcasting discomfort.

"I didn't realize making love with me required so much sacrifice on your part." He forced amusement into his tone to keep disappointment at bay.

Her words had cut deep. When he'd insisted they make her baby this way instead of going to a clinic, he thought this would be the perfect opportunity to satisfy his longing for her. The kiss between them a few days earlier confirmed the attraction between them was mutual. Why was she resisting when the vibe between them was electric? What was she afraid of?

"I didn't mean it that way." But from her unhappy expression his accusation hadn't been far off.

"No?" Jason leaned against the wall and fought the urge to snatch her into his arms and kiss her senseless. He could seduce her, but he didn't want just her body, he wanted... "How exactly did you mean it?"

"Look, we're best friends. Don't you think sleeping together will make things awkward between us?"

"Not possible. It's because we're just friends that it will work so great." He sounded as if he was overselling used cars of dubious origin. "No expectations—"

"No strings?"

He didn't like the way she said that. As if he'd just confirmed her worst fears. "Are you worried that I'm in this just for the sex?" She wasn't acting as if she hoped it would lead to something more.

"Yes." She frowned, clearly battling conflicting opinions. "No."

"But you have some sort of expectation." Jason was surprised that his flight response wasn't stimulated by her question. Usually when a woman started thinking too much, it was time to get out.

"Not the sort you mean." She gave her head a vigorous shake. "I know perfectly well that once we have sex—"

"Make love."

"Whatever." She waved her hand as if she was batting away a pesky fly. "That once we…become intimate, you will have your curiosity satisfied—"

"Curiosity?" The word exploded from him. That's not how he'd describe the hunger pulsing through him. "You think all I feel is curiosity?"

She gave him a little shoulder shrug. Frustration clawed at him. The bed was feet away. He was damned tempted to scoop her up in his arms and drop her onto the softly scented sheets. Give her a taste of exactly what he was feeling.

He pushed off the wall and let his acute disappointment and eight-inch height advantage intimidate her into taking a step back. "And what about you? Aren't you the least bit curious how hot this thing between us will burn?"

"Oh, please. I'm not one of the women you date."

The second she rolled her eyes at him, Jason knew he'd hit a soft spot. Ming overthought everything. She liked her life neat and orderly. That was great for her career, but in her personal life she could use a man who overwhelmed her senses and short-circuited her thoughts. His brother hadn't been able to do it. Evan had once complained that his fiancée had a hard time being spontaneous and letting go. He'd never come right out and said that she'd been reserved in bed. Evan had too much respect for Ming to be so crass, but Jason had been able to read between the lines.

"What is that supposed to mean?"

"Has it ever occurred to you to look at the sort of women you prefer to date?"

"Beautiful. Smart. Sexy."

"Needy. Clinging. Terrified of abandonment." She crossed her arms over her chest and stared him down as no one else did. "You choose needy women to get your ego stroked and then, when you start to pull away because they're too clingy, they fear your abandonment and chase you."

"That's ridiculous." Jason wasn't loving the picture she was painting of him. Nor was this conversation creating the romantic mood he'd hoped for, but he refused to drop the subject until he'd answered her charges.

"Jennifer was a doctor," he said, listing the last three women he'd dated. "Amanda owned a very successful boutique and Sherri was a vice president of marketing. Independent, successful women all."

"Jennifer had daddy issues." She ticked the women off on her fingers. "Her father was a famous cardiologist and never let her feel as if she was good enough even though she finished second in her class at med school. Amanda was a middle child. She had four brothers and sisters and never felt as if her parents had time for her. As for Sherri, her mom left when she was seven. She had abandonment issues."

"How did you know all that?"

Ming's long-suffering look made his gut tighten. "Who do you think they come to when the relationship starts to cool?"

"What do you tell them?"

"That as wonderful as you are, any relationship with you has little chance of becoming permanent. You are a confirmed bachelor and an adrenaline junky with an all-consuming hobby who will eventually break their heart."

"Do they listen to you?"

"The healthy ones do."

"You know, if we weren't such old and dear friends, I might be tempted to take offense."

"You won't," she said confidently. "Because deep down you know you choose damaged women so eventually their issues will cause trouble between you and you have the perfect excuse to break things off."

Deep down he knew this? "And here I thought I dated them because they were hot." About then, Jason realized Ming had picked a fight with him. "I don't want to talk about all the women I've dated." But it was too late.

Ming wore the mulish expression he'd first encountered on the playground when one of his buddies had shoved her off the swings.

"This weekend was a mistake." She slipped sideways into the bedroom and headed straight for her suitcase.

To Jason's bafflement, she used it as a battering ram, clearing him from her path to the front door.

"You're leaving?"

"You thought conceiving a baby should be memorable, but the only thing I'm going to remember about being here with you is this fight."

"We're not fighting." She was making no sense, and Jason wasn't sure how trying to provide her with a romantic setting for their first time together had sparked her wrath. "Where do you think you're going?"

"Back to San Francisco. There's a midnight flight that will put me back in Houston by morning."

How could she know that unless…? "You'd already decided you weren't going to stay."

"Don't be ridiculous." Her voice rang with sincerity, but she was already out the door and her face was turned away from him. "I just happened to notice it when I was booking my flight."

Ming was approaching the trunk of her rental car as Jason barreled through the front door and halted. His instincts told him to stop her. He was reasonably certain he could coax her mood back to romance with her favorite dessert and a stroll through the gardens, but her words had him wondering about his past choices when it came to relationships.

In the deepening twilight, a full harvest moon, robust and orange from the sunset, crested the trees. A lovers' moon. Pity it would go to waste on them.

Jason dug his fingers into the door as Ming turned her car

around. Was giving her time to think a good idea? He was gambling that eventually she'd remember that she needed him to get pregnant.

Five

Ming hadn't been able to sleep on the red-eye from San Francisco to Houston. The minute her car had reached the Mendocino city limits, she'd begun to feel the full weight of her mistake. She had three choices: convince Jason to use a clinic for her conception, give up on him being her child's father or stop behaving like a ninny and have sex with him. Because it was her nature to do so, she spent the flight home making pro and con lists for each choice. Then she weighted each item and analyzed her results.

Logic told her to head for the nearest sperm bank. Instead, as soon as the wheels of the plane hit the runway, she texted him an apology and asked him to call as soon as he was able.

The cab from the airport dropped her off at nine in the morning. She entered her house and felt buffeted by its emptiness. With Lily in Portland and Muffin spending the weekend with Ming's parents, she had the place to herself. The prospect depressed her, but she was too exhausted to fetch the active Yorkshire terrier.

Closing the curtains in her room, she slid between the sheets but didn't fall asleep as soon as her head touched the pillow. She tortured herself with thoughts of making love with Jason. Imagined his strong body moving against her, igniting her passion. Her body pulsed with need. If she hadn't panicked, she wouldn't feel like a runaway freight train. She'd be sated and sleepy instead of wide awake and horny.

Ming buried her face in the pillow and screamed her frustration until her throat burned. That drained enough of her energy to allow her to sleep. She awakened some hours later, disoriented by the dark room, and checked the clock. It was almost five. She pushed to a sitting position and raked her long hair away from her face. Despite sleeping for six hours, she was far from rested. Turbulent dreams of Jason returned her to that unfulfilled state that had plagued her earlier.

If not for the evocative scents of cooking, she might have spent what remained of the day in bed, but her stomach growled, reminding her she hadn't had anything to eat except the power bar she'd bought at the airport. She got dressed and went to the kitchen to investigate.

"Something smells great." Ming stepped off the back stairs and into her kitchen, surprising her sister.

The oven door closed with a bang as she spun to face Ming. "You're home." Lily's cheeks bore a rosy flush, probably put there by whatever simmered on the stove.

Even though both girls had learned to cook from their mother, only Lily had inherited their mother's passion for food. Ming knew enough to keep from starving, but for her cooking was more of a necessity than an infatuation.

"You're cooking."

"I was craving lamb."

"Craving it?" The dish was a signature item Lily prepared when she was trying to impress a guy. It had been over a year since she'd made it. "I thought you were going to be house hunting in Portland this weekend."

"I changed my mind about spending the weekend."

"Does this mean you're changing your mind about moving?" Ming quizzed, unable to contain the hope in her voice.

"No." Lily pulled a bottle of wine from the fridge and dug in a drawer for the corkscrew. "How come you're home so early? I thought you were gone all weekend."

Ming thought of the chardonnay she and Jason had shared. How he'd fed her grapes and how she'd enjoyed his hands on her skin. "I wasn't having any fun so I thought I'd come home." Not the whole truth, but far from a lie. "I didn't get a chance to tell you before you left town last week, but Terry wants to sell me his half of the practice. He's retiring."

"How are you going to manage a baby and the practice all by yourself?"

"I can handle it just fine."

"I think you're being selfish." Lily's words, muffled by the refrigerator door, drove a spear into Ming's heart. She pulled a bowl of string beans out and plunked them on the counter. "How can you possibly have enough time for a child when you're running the practice?"

"There are a lot of professional women who manage to do both." Ming forced back the doubts creeping up on her, but on the heels of her failure with Jason this weekend, she couldn't help but wonder if her subconscious agreed with Lily.

What if she couldn't do both well? Was she risking complete failure? No. She could do this. Even without a partner in her life to help her when things went wrong, or to celebrate the triumphs?

She was going to be awfully lonely. Sure, her parents would help when they could, but Lily was moving and Jason had his racing and his career to occupy him. What was she thinking? She would have her child and the practice to occupy her full attention. What about love? Marriage?

She brushed aside the questions. What good did it do to

focus on something she couldn't control? Planning and orga-
nization led to success, and she was a master of both.

With her confidence renewed, she poured wine from the
bottle Lily had opened. As it hit her taste buds, she made a
face. She checked the label and frowned at her sister.

"Since when do you drink Riesling?"

"I'm trying new things."

"This is Evan's favorite wine."

"He recommended it so I bought a bottle."

"Recently?"

"No." Her sister frowned. "A while ago. Geez, what's with
all the questions? I tried a type of wine your ex liked. Big deal."

Lily's sharpness rocked Ming. Was her sister so upset with
her that it threatened to drive a wedge between them?

Ming set down her wineglass. "I'm going to run over to
Mom and Dad's and pick up Muffin. Is there anything you
need me to get while I'm out?"

"How about a bottle of wine you prefer?"

Flinching at her sister's unhappy tone, Ming grabbed her
keys and headed for the door. "You know, I'm not exactly
thrilled with your decision to move to Portland, but I know
it's something you feel you have to do, so I'm trying to put
aside my selfish wish for you to stay and at least act like I'm
supportive."

Then, without waiting for her sister's reply, Ming stepped
into her garage and shut the door firmly behind her. With her
hands shaking, she had a hard time getting the key into the ignition of the '66 Shelby Cobra. She'd chosen to drive the convertible tonight, hoping the fresh air might clear away all the
confusion in her mind.

The drive to her parents' house was accomplished in record
time thanks to the smoothly purring 425 V8 engine. She really
should sell the car. It was an impractical vehicle for a mother-
to-be, but she had such great memories of the summer she and
Jason had spent fixing it up.

After her spat with Lily, she'd planned to join her parents for dinner, but they were meeting friends at the country club, so Ming collected her dog and retraced her path back to her house. A car sat in her driveway. In the fading daylight, it took her a second to recognize it as Evan's.

Because she and Jason were best friends and she knew there'd be occasions when she'd hang out with his family, Ming had made a decision to keep her interactions with Evan amicable. In fact, it wasn't that hard. Their relationship lacked the turbulent passion that would make her hate him for dumping her. But that didn't mean she was okay about him showing up without warning.

Ming parked the convertible in the garage. Disappointment filled her as she tucked Muffin under her arm and exited the car. She'd been hoping Jason had stopped by. He hadn't called her or responded to her text.

When she entered the house, the tension in the kitchen stopped her like an invisible wall. What the heck? Evan and her sister had chosen opposite sides of the center island. An almost empty wine bottle sat between them. Lily's mouth was set in unhappy lines. Her gaze dropped from Evan to the bowl of lettuce on the counter before her.

"Evan, this is a surprise." Ming eyed the vase of flowers beside the sink. Daisies. The same big bunch he always gave her after they'd had a difference of opinion. He thought the simple white flower represented a sweet apology. He was nothing if not predictable. Or maybe not so predictable. Why had he shown up on her doorstep without calling?

Lily didn't look Ming's way. Had her sister shared with Evan her dismay about Ming's decision to have a baby? Stomach churning, she set Muffin down. The terrier headed straight for her food bowl.

"What brings you here?" Ming asked.

"I came by to… Because…" He appeared at a loss to explain his reason for visiting.

"Are you staying for dinner? Lily's making rack of lamb. I'm sure there's enough for three, or I should say four, since usually she makes it for whomever she's dating at the time."

Evan's gaze sliced toward Lily. "You're dating someone?"

"Not dating exactly, just using him for sex." Ming lowered her voice. "Although I think she's ready to find someone she can get serious about. That's why she's moving to Portland."

"And the guy she's seeing." Since Lily refused to look up from the lettuce she was shredding, Evan directed the question at Ming. "She can't get serious about him?"

"She says they're just friends." The Yorkie barked and Ming filled Muffin's bowl. "Isn't that right, Lily?"

"I guess." Lily's gaze darted between Ming and Evan.

"So, when are you expecting him to show?"

"Who?"

"The guy you're preparing the lamb for."

"There's no guy," Lily retorted, her tone impatient. "I told you I was craving lamb. No big deal."

Ming felt the touch of Evan's gaze. She'd been using Lily's love life to distract him from whatever purpose he had for visiting her tonight. Something about Evan had changed in the past year. The closer they got to their wedding, the more he'd let things irritate him. A part of her had been almost relieved when he called things off.

What was he doing here tonight? She glanced at the daisies. If he was interested in getting back together, his timing was terrible.

"I'm going to head upstairs and unpack," she told them, eager to escape. "Evan, make sure you let me know if Lily's mystery man shows up. I'm dying to meet him."

"There's no mystery man," her sister yelled up the stairs at her.

Ming set her suitcase on the bed and began pulling clothes out of it. She put everything where it belonged, hamper and dry cleaning pile for the things she'd worn, drawers and hangers for what she hadn't. When she was done, only one item remained. A white silk nightie. Something a bride might wear on her wedding night. She'd bought it in San Francisco two days ago specifically for her weekend with Jason.

Now what was she supposed to do with it?

"Ming?"

She spun around at the sound of Evan's voice. "Is Lily's date here?"

His gaze slid past her to the lingerie draped over the foot of her bed. He stared at it for a long moment before shifting his attention back to her.

"I've wanted to talk to you about something."

Her pulse jerked. He was so solemn. This couldn't be good. "You have? Let's go have dinner and chat."

He put up his hands as she started for the door. "This is something we need to discuss, just us."

Nothing that serious could ever be good. "You know, I'm in a really good place right now." She pulled her hair over one shoulder and finger-combed it into three sections. "The practice is booming. Terry wants me to buy him out." Her fingers made quick work of a braid and she snagged a scrunchy off her nightstand. "I'm happy."

"And I don't want that to change. But there's something you need to know—"

"Dinner's ready."

Ming cast her sister a grateful smile. "Wonderful. Come on, Evan. You're in for a treat." She practically raced down the stairs. Her glass of wine was on the counter where she'd left it and Ming downed the contents in one long swallow. Wincing at the taste, she reached into her wine cooler and pulled out a Shiraz.

Over dinner, Evan's sober expression and Lily's preoccupation with her own thoughts compelled Ming to fill the awkward silence with a series of stories about her trip to San Francisco and amusing anecdotes about Wendy's six-year-old daughter.

By the time the kitchen was cleaned up and the dishwasher happily humming, she was light-headed from too much wine and drained from carrying the entire conversation.

Making no attempt to hide her yawns, Ming headed upstairs and shut her bedroom door behind her. In the privacy of her large master suite, she stripped off her clothes and stepped into the shower. The warm water pummeled her, releasing some of the tension from her shoulders. Wrapped in a thick terry-cloth robe, she sat cross-legged on her window seat and stared out over her backyard. She had no idea how long her thoughts drifted before a soft knock sounded on her door.

Lily stuck her head in. "You okay?"

"Is Evan gone?"

Lily nodded. "I'm sorry about what I said to you earlier."

"You're not wrong. I am being selfish." Ming patted the seat beside her. "But at the same time you know that once I decide to do something, I give it my all."

Lily hugged Ming before sitting beside her on the window seat. "If anyone is going to be supermom it's you."

"Thanks." Ming swallowed past the tightness in her throat. She hated fighting with Lily. "So, what's up with Evan?"

"What do you mean?"

"When I came in tonight, he looked as grim as I've ever seen him. I figured he was explaining why he showed up out of the blue." Ming knew her sister had always been partial to Jason's older brother. Often in the past six months, Ming thought Lily had been the sister most upset about the broken engagement. "You two became such good friends these last few years. I thought maybe he'd share with you his reason for coming here tonight."

"Do you think Jason told him that you want to have a baby?"

"He wouldn't do that." Ming's skin grew warm as she imagined where she'd be right at this moment if she hadn't run out on Jason. Naked. Wrapped in his arms. Thighs tangled. Too happy to move. "I know this sounds crazy, but what if Evan wants to get back together?"

"Why would you think he'd want to do that?" Lily's voice rose.

"I don't. Not really." Ming shook her head. "It's just that after I told Jason I wanted to get pregnant, he was so insistent that I'm not over Evan."

"Are you?" Her sister leaned forward, eyebrows drawn together. "I mean Evan broke up with you, not the other way around."

Ming toyed with the belt of her robe. The pain of being dumped eased a little more each day, but it wasn't completely gone. "It really doesn't matter how I feel. The reasons we broke up haven't changed."

"What if they did? What if the problems that came between you were gone? Out of the picture?" Lily was oddly intent. "Would you give him another chance?"

Ming tried to picture herself with Evan now that she'd tasted Jason's kisses. She'd settled for one brother instead of fighting for the other. That was a mistake she wouldn't make again. She'd rather be happy as a single mom than be miserable married to a man she didn't love.

"I've spent the last six months reimagining my life without Evan," she told her sister. "I'd rather move forward than look back."

At a little after 8:00 p.m., Jason sat in his car and stared at Ming's house. When she'd left him in Mendocino, his pride had kept him from chasing after her for a little over two hours. He'd come to California to spend the weekend with Ming, not to pace a hotel room in a frenzy of unsatisfied desire. Confident she wouldn't miraculously change her mind and return to him, Jason had gotten behind the wheel and returned to the San Francisco airport, where he'd caught a 6:00 a.m. flight back to Houston.

He hadn't liked the way things had been left between them, and her text message gave him hope she hadn't, either. After catching a few hours of sleep, he'd come here tonight to talk her into giving his strategy one last shot.

But the sight of his brother's car parked in Ming's driveway distracted him. What the hell was Evan doing here? Had he come to tell Ming that he was dating her sister? If so, Jason should get in there because Ming was sure to be upset.

He had his hand on the door release when her front door opened. Despite the porch light pouring over the couple's head, he couldn't see Lily's expression, but her body language would be visible from the moon.

Ming's sister was hung up on his brother. And from the way Evan slid his hands around her waist and pulled her against him for a deep, passionate kiss, the feeling was mutual.

It took no more than a couple of seconds for an acid to eat at Jason's gut. He glanced away from the embracing couple, but anger continued to build.

What the hell did Evan think he was doing? Didn't he care about Ming's feelings at all? Didn't he consider how hurt she'd be if she saw him kissing Lily? Obviously not. Good thing Jason was around to straighten out his brother before the situation spun out of control.

A motor started, drowning out Jason's heated thoughts. Evan backed out of the driveway. Jason had missed the chance to catch his brother in the act. Cursing, he dialed Evan's number.

"Jason, hey, what's up?"

"We need to talk."

"So talk." Considering the fact that Evan had just engaged in a long, passionate kiss, he wasn't sounding particularly chipper.

"In person." So he could throttle his brother if the urge arose. "O'Malley's. Ten minutes."

The tension in Jason's tone must have clued in his brother to Jason's determination because Evan agreed without protest. "Sure. Okay."

Jason ended the call and followed his brother's car to the neighborhood bar. He chose the parking spot next to Evan's and was standing at his brother's door before Evan had even turned off the engine.

"You and Lily are still seeing each other?" Jason demanded, not allowing his brother to slide from behind the wheel.

"I never said I was going to stop."

"Does Ming know?"

"Not yet."

"She'll find out pretty quickly if you keep kissing Lily in full view of Ming's neighbors."

"I didn't think about that." Evan didn't ask how Jason knew. "I was sure Ming wouldn't see us. She'd gone up to her room."

"So that made it okay?" Fingers curling into fists, Jason stabbed his brother with a fierce glare. "If you intend to flaunt your relationship, you need to tell her what you and Lily are doing."

"I started to tonight, but Lily interrupted me. She doesn't want Ming to know." And Evan didn't look happy about it. "Can we go inside and discuss this over a beer?"

Considering his mood, Jason wasn't sure consuming alcohol around his brother was a wise idea, but he stepped back so Evan could get out of the car. With an effort Jason unclenched his fists and concentrated on soothing his bad temper. By the time they were seated near the back, Jason's fury had become a slow burn.

"Why doesn't Lily want Ming to know?" Jason sat with his spine pressed against the booth's polished wood back while Evan leaned his forearms on the table, all earnest and contrite.

"Because I don't think she intends for it to go anywhere."

If Evan wasn't running the risk of hurting Ming all over again, Jason could have sympathized with his brother's pain. "Then you need to quit seeing her."

"I can't." Despite the throb in his brother's voice, the corners of his mouth relaxed. "The sex is incredible. I tell myself a hundred times a day that it's going nowhere and that I should get out before anyone is hurt, but then I hear her voice or see her and I have to..." He grimaced. "I don't know why I'm telling you this."

"So you two are combustible together." Resentment made Jason cross. He and Ming had great chemistry, too, but instead of exploring some potentially explosive lovemaking, they were at odds over what effect this might have on their friendship.

"It's amazing."

"But...?" Jason prompted.

"I don't know if we can make it work. We have completely different ideas about what we want." Evan shook his head. "And now she's moving to Portland."

Which should put an end to things, but Jason sensed the upcoming separation was causing things to heat up rather than cool down.

"Long-range relationships don't work," Jason said.

"Sometimes they do. And I love her." Something Evan looked damned miserable about.

"Is she in love with you?"

"She claims it's nothing but casual sex between us. But it sure as hell doesn't feel casual when we're at it."

Love was demonstrating once again that it had no one's best interests at heart. Evan was in love with Lily, but she obviously didn't feel the same way, and that made him unhappy. And finding out that her ex-fiancé was in love with her sister was going to cause Ming pain. Nothing good came of falling in love.

"All the more reason you should quit seeing Lily before Ming finds out."

"That's not what I want."

"What *you* want?"

Jason contemplated the passion that tormented his brother. The entire time Evan and Ming were dating, not once had Evan displayed the despair that afflicted him now.

"How about what's good for Ming?" Jason continued.

"Don't you think you did enough damage to her when you broke off your engagement two weeks before the wedding?"

"Yeah, well, that was bad timing on my part." Evan paused for a beat. "We weren't meant to be together."

"You and Lily aren't meant to be together, either."

"I don't agree." Evan sounded grim. "And I want a chance to prove it. Can I count on you to keep quiet?"

"No." Seeing his brother's expression, Jason relented. "I'm not going to run over there tonight and tell her. Talk to Lily. Figure this out. You can have until noon tomorrow."

As his anger over Evan's choice of romantic partner faded, Jason noticed the hollow feeling in his chest was back. He sipped the beer the waitress had set before him and wondered why Ming had chosen to pick a fight with him in California instead of surrendering to the heat between them.

Was she really afraid their relationship would be changed by sex? How could it when they'd been best friends for over twenty years? Sure, there'd been sparks the night of senior prom, but they'd discussed the situation and decided their friendship was more important than trying to date only to have it end badly.

And what they were about to do wasn't dating. It was sex, pure and simple. A way for Ming to get pregnant. For Jason to purge her from his system.

For him to satisfy his curiosity?

Maybe her accusation hadn't been completely off the mark. He wouldn't be a guy if he hadn't looked at Ming in a bathing suit and recognized she was breathtaking. From prom night his fingers knew the shape of her breasts, his tongue the texture of her nipples. The soft heat of her mouth against his. That wasn't something he could experience and then never think about again.

But he wasn't in love with her. He'd never let that happen. Their friendship was too important to mess up with romance. Love had almost killed his father. And Evan wasn't doing too well, either.

Nope. Better to keep things casual. Uncomplicated.

Which didn't explain why he'd offered to help Ming get pregnant and why he'd suggested they do it the natural way. And Jason had no easy answer.

Six

By Sunday afternoon Ming still hadn't heard from Jason, and his lack of response to her phone calls and texts struck her as odd. She'd apologized a dozen times. Why was he avoiding her? After brunch with Lily, she drove to Jason's house in the hope of cornering him and getting answers. Relief swept her as she spied him by the 'Cuda he'd won off Max a few months ago. She parked her car at the bottom of the driveway and stared at him for a long moment.

Bare except for a pair of cargo shorts that rode low on his hips, he was preoccupied with eliminating every bit of dust from the car's yellow paint. His bronzed skin glistened with a fine mist of water from the hole in the nearby garden hose. The muscles across his back rippled as he plunged the sponge into the bucket of soapy water near his bare feet.

Ming imagined gliding her hands over those male contours, digging her nails into his flesh as he devoured her. The fantasy inspired a series of hot flashes. She slid from behind the wheel and headed toward him.

"I think you missed a spot," she called, stopping a couple feet away from the back bumper. Hearing the odd note in her own voice brought about by her earlier musing, she winced. When he frowned at her, she pointed to a nonexistent smudge on the car's trunk.

Since waking at six that morning, she'd been debating what tack to take with Jason. Did she scold him for not calling her back? Did she pretend that she wasn't hurt and worried that he'd ignored her apologies? Or did she just leave her emotional baggage at the door and talk to him straight like a friend?

Jason dropped the sponge on the car's roof and set his hands on his hips. "I'm pretty sure I didn't."

She eyed the car. "I'm pretty sure you did." When he didn't respond, she stepped closer to the car and pointed. "Right here."

"If you think you can do better…" He lobbed the dripping sponge onto the trunk. It landed with a splat, showering her with soapy water. "Go ahead."

Unsure why he got to act unfriendly when she'd been the one to apologize only to be ignored, she picked up the sponge and debated what to do with it. She could toss it back and hope it hit him full in the face, or she could take the high road and see if they could talk through what had happened in California.

Gathering a calming breath, she swept the sponge over the trunk and down toward the taillights. "I've left you a few messages," she said, focusing on the task at hand.

"I know. Sorry I haven't called you back."

"Is there a reason why you didn't?"

"I've been busy."

Cleaning an already pristine car was a pointless endeavor. So was using indirect methods to get Jason to talk about something uncomfortable. "When you didn't call me back, I started wondering if you were mad at me."

"Why would I be mad?"

Ming circled the car and dunked the sponge into the bucket. Jason had retreated to the opposite side of the 'Cuda and was spraying the car with water. Fine mist filled the air, landing on Ming's skin, lightly coating her white blouse and short black skirt. She hadn't come dressed to wash a car. And if she didn't retreat, she risked ruining her new black sandals.

"Because of what happened in Mendocino."

"You mean because you freaked out?" At last he met her gaze. Irritation glittered in his bright blue eyes.

"I didn't freak…exactly."

"You agreed we'd spend three days together and when you got there, you lasted barely an hour before picking a fight with me and running out. How is that not freaking?"

Ming scrubbed at the side mirror, paying careful attention to the task. "Well, I wouldn't have done that if you hadn't gone all Don Juan on me."

"Don Juan?" He sounded incredulous.

"Master of seduction."

"I have no idea what you're talking about."

"The roses on the bed. The vanilla candles. I'm surprised you didn't draw me a bubble bath." In the silence that followed her accusation, she glanced up. The expression on his face told her that had also been on his agenda. "Good grief."

"Forgive me for trying to create a romantic mood."

"I didn't ask for romance," she protested. "I just wanted to get pregnant."

In a clinic. Simple. Uncomplicated.

"Since when do you have something against romance? I seem to remember you liked it when Evan sent you flowers and took you out for candlelit dinners."

"Evan and I were dating." They'd been falling in love.

She picked up the bucket and moved to the front of the car. This time Jason stayed put.

"I thought you'd appreciate the flowers and the candlelight."

Ming snorted. "Men do stuff like that to get women into bed. But you already knew we were going to have sex. So what was with the whole seduction scene?"

"Why are you making such an issue out of this?"

She stopped scrubbing the hood and stared at him, hoping she could make him understand without divulging too much. "You created the perfect setting to make me fall in love with you."

"That's not what I was doing."

"I know you don't plan to make women fall for you, but it's what happens to everyone you date." She applied the sponge to the hood in a fury. "You overwhelm them with romantic gestures until they start picturing a future with you and then you drop them because they want more than you can give them."

The only movement in his face was the tic in his jaw. "You make it sound like I deliberately try to hurt them."

"That's not it at all. I don't think you have any idea what it's like when you turn on the Sterling charm."

"Are you saying that's what I did to you?"

It was the deliberate nature of what he'd done that made her feel like a prize to be won, not a friend to be helped. Another conquest. Another woman who would fall in love with him and then be dumped when she got too serious. When she wanted too much from him.

"Yes. And I don't get why." She dropped the sponge into the bucket and raked her fingers through her damp hair, lifting the soggy weight off her neck and back so the breeze could cool her. "All I wanted was to have a baby. I didn't want to complicate our friendship with sex. Or make things weird between us." Dense emotions weighed on her. Her shoulders sagged beneath the burden. She let her arms fall to her sides. "That's why I've decided to let you off the hook."

"What do you mean?"

"I'm going forward as originally planned. I'll use an anonymous donor and we can pretend the last two weeks never happened."

"I'm tired of pretending."

Before she'd fully processed his statement, chilly water rained down on her. Ming shrieked and stepped back.

"Hey." She wiped water from her eyes and glared at Jason. "Watch it."

"Sorry." But he obviously wasn't.

"You did that on purpose."

"I didn't."

"Did, too."

And abruptly they were eight again, chasing each other around her parents' backyard with squirt guns. She grabbed the sponge out of the bucket and tossed it at his head. He dodged it without even moving his feet, and a smattering of droplets showered down on her.

The bucket of water was at her feet. Seconds later it was in her hands. She didn't stop to consider the consequences of what she was about to do. How long since she'd acted without thought?

"If you throw that, I'll make sure you'll regret it," Jason warned, his serious tone a stark contrast to the dare in his eyes.

The emotional tug-of-war of the past two weeks had taken a toll on her. Her friendship with Jason was the foundation that she'd built her life on. But the longing for his kisses, the anticipation of his hands sliding over her naked flesh... She was on fire for him. Head and heart at war.

"Damn you, Jason," she whispered.

Soapy water arced across the six feet separating them and landed precisely where she meant it to. Drenched from head to groin, Jason stood perfectly still for as long as it took for Ming to drop the bucket. Then he gave his head a vigorous shake, showering soapy droplets all around him.

Ming watched as if in slow motion as he raised the hose in his hand, aimed it at her and squeezed the trigger. Icy water sprayed her. Sputtering with laughter, she put up her hands and backed away. Hampered by her heels from moving fast enough to escape, she shrieked for Jason to stop. When the deluge continued, she kicked off her shoes and raced for the house.

Until she stood dripping on Jason's kitchen floor, it hadn't occurred to her why she hadn't made a break for her car. The door leading to the garage slammed shut.

Shivering in the air-conditioning, Ming whirled to confront Jason.

He stalked toward her. Eyes on fire. Mouth set in a grim line. She held her ground as he drew near. Her trembling became less about being chilled and more about Jason's intensity as he stepped into her space and cupped her face in his hands.

"I'm sorry about California…"

The rest of her words were lost, stopped by the demanding press of his lips to hers. Electrified by the passion in his kiss, she rose up on tiptoe and wrapped her arms around his neck and let him devour her with lips, tongue and teeth.

Yes. This is what she'd been waiting for. The crazy wildness that had gripped them on prom night. The urgent craving to rip each other's clothes off and couple like long-lost lovers. Fire exploded in her loins as pulse after pulse drove heat to her core.

She drank from the passion in his kiss, found her joy in the feint and retreat of his tongue with hers. His hands left her face and traveled down her throat to her shoulders. And lower. She quaked as his palms moved over her breasts and caressed her stomach. Before she knew what he was after, he'd gathered handfuls of her blouse. She felt a tremor ripple through his torso a second before he tore her shirt open.

Flinging off her ruined shirt, Ming arched her back and pressed into his palms as he cupped her breasts through her sodden bra and made her nipples peak. Between her thighs an ache built toward a climax that would drive her mad if she couldn't get him to hurry. Impatience clawed at her. She needed his skin against hers. Reaching behind her, Ming released her bra clasp.

Jason peeled it away and drew his fingertips around her

breasts and across her aching nipples. "Perfect." Husky with awe, his voice rasped against her nerves, inflaming her already raging desire.

He bent his head and took one pebbled bud into his mouth, rolling his tongue over the hard point before sucking hard. The wet pulling sensation shot a bolt of sensation straight to where she hungered, wrenching a gasp from Ming.

"Do that again," she demanded, her fingers biting into his biceps. "That was incredible."

He obliged until her knees threatened to give out. "I've imagined you like this for so long," he muttered against her throat, teeth grazing the cord in her neck.

"Like what, half-naked?"

"Trembling. On fire." He slipped his hand beneath her skirt and skimmed up her thigh. "For me."

Shuddering as he closed in on the area where she wanted him most, Ming let her own fingers do some exploring. Behind the zipper of his cargo shorts he was huge and hard. As her nails grazed along his length, Jason closed his eyes. Breath escaped in a hiss from between his clenched teeth.

Happy with his reaction, but wanting him as needy as he'd made her, she unfastened his shorts and dived beneath the fabric to locate skin. A curse escaped him when she sent his clothes to pool at his feet. She grasped him firmly.

Abandoning his own exploration, he pulled her hands away and carried them around to his back. His mouth settled on hers again, this time stealing her breath and her sense of equilibrium. She was spinning. Twirling. Lost in the universe. Only Jason's mouth on hers, his arms banding her body to his, gave her any sense of reality.

This is what she'd been missing on the couch in his den and on the deck in California. The line between friend and lover wasn't just blurred, it was eradicated by hunger and wanton impulses. Hesitations were put aside. There was only heat and urgency. Demand and surrender.

Her back bumped against something. She opened her eyes as Jason's lips left hers.

"I need you now," she murmured as he nibbled down her neck.

"Let's go upstairs."

Her knees wouldn't survive the climb. "I can't make it that far."

"What do you have in mind?"

His kitchen table caught her eye. "How about this?"

Her knees had enough strength to back him up five feet. He looked surprised when she shoved him onto one of the four straight-back chairs.

"I'm game if you are."

She hadn't finished shimmying out of her skirt when she felt his fingers hook in the waistband of her hot pink thong and begin drawing it down her thighs. Naked, she stared down at him, her heart pinging around in her chest.

There was no turning back from this moment.

Jason's fingers bit into her hips as she straddled the chair. Meeting his gaze, she positioned herself so the tip of him grazed her entrance. Looking into his eyes, she could see straight to his soul. No veils hid his emotions from her.

She lowered herself, joining them in body as in spirit, let her head fall back and gloried at the perfection of their fit.

He'd died and gone to heaven. With Ming arched over his arm, almost limp in his grasp, he'd reached a nirvana of sorts. The sensation of being buried inside her almost blew the top of his head off. He shuddered, lost in a bewildering maze of emotions.

"This is the first time," he muttered, lowering his lips to her throat, "I've never done this before."

She tightened her inner muscles around him and he groaned. Her chest vibrated in what sounded like a laugh. With her fingers digging into his shoulders, she straightened and stared deep into his eyes.

"I have it on good authority," she began, leaning forward to draw her tongue along his lower lip, "that this is not your first time." She spoke without rancor, unbothered by the women he'd been with before.

He stroked his hands up her spine, fingers gliding over her silken skin, feeling the ridges made by her ribs. "It's the first I've ever had sex without protection."

"Really?" She peered at him from beneath her lashes. "I'm your first?"

"My only."

The instant the words were out, Jason knew he'd said too much. Delight flickered in her gaze. Her glee lasted only for the briefest of instances, but he'd spotted it, knew what he'd given away.

"I like the sound of that."

"Only because I am never going to get anyone but you pregnant."

Her smile transformed her from serene and mysterious to animated and exotic. "I like the sound of that, too." This time when she kissed him, there was no teasing in her actions. She took his mouth, plunged her tongue deep and claimed him.

Fisting a hand in her hair, Jason answered her primal call. Their tongues danced in familiar rhythm, as if they hadn't had their first kiss over a decade before. He knew exactly how to drive her wild, what made her groan and tremble.

"I'll let you in on a little secret," she whispered, her breath hot in his ear. "You're my first, too."

Incapable of speech as she explored his chest, her clever fingers circling his nipples, nails raking across their sensitive surface, he arched his brow at her in question.

"I've never had sex on a kitchen chair before." She rotated her hips in a sexy figure eight that wrenched a groan from his throat. "I rather like it."

Pressure built in his groin as she continued to experiment with her movements. Straddling his lap, she had all the control she could ever want to drive him mad. Breath rasping, eyes half-closed, Jason focused on her face to distract himself from the pleasure cascading through his body. In all the dreams he'd had of her, nothing had been this perfect.

Arching her back, she shifted the angle of her hips and moved over him again. "Oh, Jason, this is incredible."

"Amazing." He garbled the word, provoking a short laugh from her. "Perfect."

"Yes." She sat up straight and looked him square in the eyes. "It's never been like this."

"For me, either."

Deciding they'd done enough talking, Jason kissed her, long and deep. Her movements became more urgent as their passion burned hotter. His fingers bit into her hips, guiding her. A soft cry slipped from her parted lips. Jason felt her body tense and knew she was close. That's all it took to start his own climax. Gaze locked on her face, he held back, waiting for her to pitch over the cliff. The sheer glory of it caught him off guard. She gave herself completely to the moment. And called his name.

With his ears filled with her rapture, he lost control and spilled himself inside her. They were making more than a baby. They were making a moment that would last forever. The richness of the experience shocked him. Never in a million years would he have guessed that letting himself go so completely would hit him with this sort of power.

Shaking, Jason gathered Ming's body tight against his chest and breathed heavily. As the last pulses of her orgasm eased, he smoothed her hair away from her face and bestowed a gentle kiss on her lips.

"I'm glad I was your first," she murmured, her slender arms wrapped around his neck.

He smiled. "I'm glad you're my only."

* * *

Taking full advantage of Jason's king-size bed, Ming lay on her stomach lengthwise across the mattress. With her chin on his chest, her feet kicking the air, she watched him. Naked and relaxed, he'd stretched out on his back, his hands behind his head, eyes closed, legs crossed at the ankle. An easy smile tipped the corners of his lips upward. Ming regarded his satisfied expression, delighted that she'd been the one to bring him to this state. Twice.

While her body was utterly drained of energy, the same couldn't be said for her mind. "Now that we have that out of the way, perhaps you can explain why you've been avoiding me for two days."

Jason's expression tightened. "Have you talked to your sister?"

"Lily?" Ming pushed herself into a sitting position. "We had brunch before I came here. Why?"

His lashes lifted. "She didn't tell you."

She had no idea what he was talking about. "Tell me what?"

"About her and Evan." Jason looked unhappy. "They've been seeing each other."

"My sister and your brother?" Ming repeated the words but couldn't quite get her mind around the concept. "Seeing each other…you mean dating?"

Her gaze slid over Jason. Two weeks ago she'd have laughed at anyone who told her she and Jason were going to end up in bed together. The news of Evan and Lily was no less unexpected.

"Yes." He touched her arm, fingers gentle as they stroked her skin. "Are you okay?"

His question startled her. But it was the concern on his face that made her take stock of her reaction. To her dismay she felt a twinge of discomfort. But she'd be damned if she'd admit it.

"If they get married we'll end up being brother and sister." She was trying for levity but fell short of the mark.

Jason huffed out an impatient breath. "Don't make light of this with me. I'm worried that you'll end up getting hurt."

Ming's bravado faded. "But it can't be that serious. Lily is moving to Portland. She wouldn't be doing that if they had a future together." Her voice trailed away. "That's why she's leaving, isn't it? They're in love and my sister can't break it off and stick around. She needs to move thousands of miles away to get over him."

"I don't know if your sister is in love with Evan."

"But Evan's in love with her."

Jason clamped his mouth shut, but the truth was written all over his face.

Needing a second to recover her equilibrium, Ming left the bed and snagged Jason's robe off the bathroom door. She put it on and fastened the belt around her waist. By the time she finished rolling up the sleeves, she felt calmer and more capable of facing Jason.

"How long have you known?" Ming heard the bitterness in her voice and tried to reel in her emotions. Evan hadn't exactly broken her heart when he'd ended their engagement, but that didn't mean she hadn't been hurt. She'd been weeks away from committing to him for the rest of her life.

"I've known they were going out but didn't realize how serious things had gotten until I spoke with Evan last night." Jason left the bed and came toward her. "Are you okay?"

"Sure." Something tickled her cheek. Ming reached up to touch the spot and her fingers came away wet. "I'm fine."

"Then why are you crying?"

Her heart pumped sluggishly. "I'm feeling sorry for myself because I'm wondering if Evan ever loved me." She stared at the ceiling, blinking hard to hold back the tears. "Am I so unlovable?"

Jason's arms came around her. His lips brushed her cheek. "You're the furthest thing from unlovable."

Safe in his embrace, she badly wanted to believe him, but

the facts spoke loud and clear. She was thirty-one, had never been married and was contemplating single motherhood.

"One of these days you'll find the right guy for you. I'm sure of it."

Hearing Jason's words was like stepping on broken glass. Pain shot through her, but she had nowhere to run. The man her heart had chosen had no thought of ever falling in love with her.

Ming pushed out of Jason's arms. "Did you really just say that minutes after we finished making love?"

His expression darkened. "I'm trying to be a good friend."

"I get that we're never going to be a couple, but did it ever occur to you that I might not be thinking about another man while being naked with you?" Her breath rushed past the lump in her throat.

"That's funny." His voice cracked like a whip. "Because just a second ago you were crying over the fact that my brother is in love with your sister."

Ming's mouth popped open, but no words emerged. Too many statements clogged the pathway between her brain and her lips. Everything Jason had said to her was perfectly reasonable. Her reactions were not. She was treating him like a lover, not like a friend.

"You're right. I'm a little thrown by what's happening between Lily and Evan. But it's not because I'm in love with him. And I can't even think about meeting someone and starting a relationship right now."

"Don't shut yourself off to the possibility."

"Like you have?" Ming couldn't believe he of all people was giving her advice on her love life. Before she blurted out her true feelings, she gathered up all her wayward emotions and packed them away. "I'd better get home and check on Muffin."

"I'm sure Muffin is fine." Jason peered at her, his impatience banked. "Are you?"

"I'm fine."

"Why don't I believe you?"

She wanted to bask in his concern, but they were in different places in their relationship right now. His feelings for her hadn't changed while she was dangerously close to being in love with him.

"No need to worry about me." Ming collected her strength and gave him her best smile. Crossing to his dresser, she pulled out a T-shirt. "Is it okay if I borrow this since you ruined my blouse?"

Jason eyed her, obviously not convinced by her performance. "Go ahead. I don't want to be responsible for any multicar pile-ups if you drive home topless." His tone was good-natured, but his eyes followed her somberly as she exchanged shirt for robe and headed toward the door.

"I'll call you later," she tossed over her shoulder, hoping to escape before unhappiness overwhelmed her.

"You could stay for dinner." He'd accompanied her downstairs and scooped up her black skirt and her hot pink thong before she could reach them, holding them hostage while he awaited her answer.

"I have some case files to look over before tomorrow," she said, conscious of his gaze on her as she tugged her underwear and skirt from his hands.

"You can work on them after dinner. I have some reports to go over. We can have a study date just like old times."

As tempting as that sounded, she recognized that it was time to be blunt. "I need some time to think."

"About what?"

"Things," she murmured, knowing Jason would never let her get away with such a vague excuse. Like how she needed to adjust to being friends *and* lovers with Jason. Then there was the tricky situation with her sister. She needed to get past being angry with Lily, not because she was dating Ming's ex-fiancé, but because her sister might get what Ming couldn't: a happily-ever-after with a man who loved her.

"What is there to think about?" Jason demanded. "We made love. Hopefully, we made a baby."

Her knees knocked together. Could she be pregnant already? The idea thrilled her. She wanted to be carrying Jason's child. Wanted it now more than ever. Which made her question her longing to become a mother. Would she be as determined if it was any other man who was helping her get pregnant? Or was she motivated by the desire to have something of Jason otherwise denied to her?

"I hope that, too." She forced a bright smile.

His bare feet moved soundlessly on the tile floor as he picked up her ruined blouse and carried it to the trash. Slipping back into her clothes, she regarded him in helpless fascination.

In jeans and a black T-shirt, he was everything she'd ever wanted in a man, flaws and all. Strong all the time, sensitive when he needed to be. He demonstrated a capacity for tenderness when she least expected it. They were incredible together in bed and the best of friends out of it.

"Or are you heading home to fret about your sister and Evan seeing each other?"

"No." But she couldn't make her voice as convincing as she wanted it to sound. "Evan and I are over. It was inevitable that he would start dating someone."

She just wished it hadn't happened with her sister.

Ming lifted on her tiptoes and kissed Jason. "Thanks for a lovely afternoon." The spontaneous encounter had knocked her off plan. She needed to regroup and reassess. Aiming for casual, she teased, "Let me know if you feel like doing it again soon."

He grabbed her hand and pushed it against his zipper. "I feel like doing it again now." His husky voice and the intense light in his eyes made her pulse rocket. "Stay for dinner. I promise you won't leave hungry."

The heat of him melted some of the chill from her heart. She leaned into his chest, her fingers curving around the bulge in his pants. He fisted his hand in her hair while his mouth slanted over hers, spiriting her into a passionate whirlwind. This afternoon she'd awakened to his hunger. The power of it set her senses ablaze. She was helpless against the appeal of his hard body as he eased her back against the counter. On the verge of surrendering to the mind-blasting pleasure of Jason's fingers sliding up her naked thigh, his earlier words came back to her.

One of these days you'll find the right guy for you.

She broke off the kiss. Gasping air into her lungs, she put her hands on Jason's chest and ducked her head before he could claim her lips again.

"I've really got to go," she told him, applying enough pressure to assure him she wasn't going to be swayed by his sensual persuasion.

His hands fell away. As hot as he'd been a moment ago, when he stepped back and plunged his hands into his pockets, his blue eyes were as cool and reflective as a mountain lake.

"How about we have dinner tomorrow?" she cajoled, swamped by anxiety. As perfect as it was to feel his arms tighten around her, she needed to sort out her chaotic emotions before she saw him again.

"Sure." Short and terse.

"Here?"

"If you want." He gave her a stiff nod.

She put her hand on his cheek, offered him a glimpse of her longing. "I want very much."

His eyes softened. "Five o'clock." He pressed a kiss into her palm. "Don't be late."

Seven

Ming parked her car near the bleachers that overlooked the curvy two-mile track. Like most of the raceways where Jason spent his weekends, this one was in the middle of nowhere. At least it was only a couple of hours out of Houston. Some of the tracks he raced at were hundreds of miles away.

Jason was going to be surprised to see her. It had been six or seven years since she'd last seen him race. The sport didn't appeal to her. Noisy. Dusty. Monotonous. She suspected the thrills came from driving, not watching.

So, what was she doing here?

If she was acting like Jason's "friend," she would have remained in Houston and spent her Saturday shopping or boating with college classmates. Driving over a hundred miles to sit on a metal seat in the blazing-hot sun fell put her smack dab in the middle of "girlfriend" territory. Would Jason see it as such? Ming took a seat in the stands despite the suspicion that coming here had been a colossal mistake.

The portion of track in front of her was a half-mile drag

strip that allowed the cars to reach over a hundred miles an hour before they had to power down to make the almost ninety-degree turn at the end. The roar was impressive as twenty-five high-performance engines raced past Ming.

Despite the speed at which they traveled, Jason's Mustang was easy to spot. Galaxy-blue. When he'd been working on the car, he'd asked for her opinion and she'd chosen the color, amused that she'd matched his car to his eyes without him catching on.

In seconds, the cars roared off, leaving Ming baking in the hot sun. With her backside sore from the hard bench and her emotions a jumble, it was official. She was definitely exhibiting "girlfriend" behavior.

And why? Because the past week with Jason had been amazing. It wasn't just the sex. It was the intimacy. They'd talked for hours. Laughed. She'd discovered a whole new Jason. Tender and romantic. Naughty and creative. She'd trusted him to take her places she'd never been, and it was addictive.

Which is why she'd packed a bag and decided to surprise him. A single day without Jason had made her restless and unable to concentrate.

Ming stood. This had been a mistake. She wasn't Jason's girlfriend. She had no business inserting herself into his guy time because she was feeling lonely and out of sorts. She would just drive back to Houston and he'd never know how close she'd come to making a complete fool of herself over him.

The cars roared up the straightaway toward her once again. From past experience at these sorts of events, she knew the mornings were devoted to warm-up laps. The real races would begin in the afternoon.

She glanced at the cars as they approached. Jason's number twenty-two was in the middle of the pack of twenty-five cars. He usually saved his best driving for the race. As the Mustang reached the end of the straightaway and began to slow down for the sharp turn, something happened. Instead of curving to the left, the Mustang veered to the right, hit the wall and spun.

Her lungs were ready to burst as she willed the cars racing behind him to steer around the wreckage so Jason didn't suffer any additional impact. Once the track cleared, his pit crew and a dozen others hurried to the car. Dread encased Ming's feet in concrete as she plunged down the stairs to the eight-foot-high chain-link fence that barred her from the track.

With no way of getting to Jason, she was forced to stand by and wait for some sign that he was okay. She gripped the metal, barely registering the ache in her fingers. The front of the Mustang was a crumpled mess. Ming tried to remind herself that the car had been constructed to keep the driver safe during these sorts of crashes, but her emotions, already in a state of chaos before the crash, convinced her he would never hear how she really felt about him.

"Wow, that was some crash," said a male voice beside her. "Worst I've seen in a year."

Ming turned all her fear and angst on the skinny kid with the baseball cap who'd come up next to her. "Do you work here?"

"Ah, yeah." His eyes widened as the full brunt of her emotions hit him.

"I need to get down there, right now."

"You're really not supposed—"

"Right now!"

"Sure. Sure." He backed up a step. "Follow me." He led her to a gate that opened onto the track. "Be careful."

But she was already on the track, pelting toward Jason's ruined car without any thought to her own safety. Because of the dozen or so men gathered around the car, she couldn't see Jason. Wielding her elbows and voice like blunt instruments, she worked her way to the front of the crowd in time to see Jason pulled through the car's window.

He was cursing as he emerged, but he was alive. Relief slammed into her. She stopped five feet from the car and watched him shake off the hands that reached for him when he swayed. He limped toward the crumpled hood, favoring his left knee.

Jason pulled off his helmet. "Damn it, there's the end of my season."

It could have been the end of him. Ming sucked in a breath as a sharp pain lanced through her chest. It was just typical of him to worry about his race car instead of himself. Didn't he realize what losing him would do to the people who loved him?

She stepped up and grabbed his helmet from his hands, but she lost the ability to speak as his eyes swung her way. She loved him. And not like a friend. As a man she wanted to claim for her own.

"Ming?" Dazed, he stared at her as if she'd appeared in a puff of smoke. "What are you doing here?"

"I came to watch you race." She gripped his helmet hard enough to crack it. "I saw you crash. Are you okay?"

"My shoulder's sore and I think I did something to my knee, but other than that, I'm great." His lips twisted as he grimaced. "My car's another thing entirely."

Who cares about your stupid car? Shock made her want to shout at him, but her chest was so tight she had only enough air for a whisper. "You really scared me."

"Jason, we need to get the car off the track." Gus Stover and his brother had been part of Jason's racing team for the past ten years. They'd modified and repaired all his race cars. Ming had lost track of how many hours she and Jason had spent at the man's shop.

"That's a good idea," she said.

"A little help?" Jason suggested after his first attempt at putting weight on his injured knee didn't go so well.

Ming slipped her arm around his waist and began moving in the direction of the pit area. As his body heat began to warm her, Ming realized she was shaking from reaction. As soon as they reached a safe distance from the track, Jason stopped walking and turned her to face him.

"You're trembling. Are you okay?"

Not even close. She loved him. And had for a long time. Only she'd been too scared to admit it to herself.

"I should be asking you that question," she said, placing her palm against his unshaven cheek, savoring the rasp of his beard against her skin. She wanted to wrap her arms around him and never let go. "You should get checked out."

"I'm just a little banged up, that's all."

"Jason, that was a bad crash." A man in his late-thirties with prematurely graying hair approached as they neared the area where the trailers were parked. He wore a maroon racing suit and carried his helmet under one arm. "You okay?"

"Any crash you can walk away from is a good one." Leave it to Jason to make light of something as disastrous as what she'd just witnessed. "Ming, this is Jim Pearce. He's the current points leader in the Texas region."

"And likely to remain on top now that Jason's done for the season."

Is that all these men thought about? Ming's temper began to simmer again until she saw the worry the other driver was masking with his big, confident grin and his posturing. It could have been any of these guys. Accidents didn't happen a lot, but they were part of racing. This was only Jason's second in the entire sixteen years he'd been racing. If something had gone wrong on another area of the track, he might have ended up driving safely onto the shoulder or he could have taken out a half dozen other cars.

"Nice to meet you." As she shook Jim's hand, some of the tension in her muscles eased. "Were you on the track when it happened?"

"No. I'm driving in the second warm-up lap." His broad smile dimmed. "Any idea what happened, Jason? From where I stood it looked like something gave on the right side."

"Felt like the right front strut rod. We recently installed Agent 47 suspension and might have adjusted a little too aggressively on the front-end alignment settings."

Jim nodded, his expression solemn. "Tough break."

"I'll have the rest of the year to get her rebuilt and be back better than ever in January."

Ming contemplated the hours Jason and the Stover brothers would have to put in to make that happen and let her breath out in a long, slow sigh. If she'd seen little of him in the past few months since he'd made it his goal to take the overall points trophy, she'd see even less of him with a car to completely rebuild.

"The Stovers will get her all fixed up for you." Jim thumped Jason on the back. "They're tops."

As Jim spoke, Jason's car was towed up to the trailer. The men in question jumped off the truck and began unfastening the car.

"What happened?" Jason called.

"The strut rod pulled away from the helm end," Gus Stover replied. "I told you the setting was wrong."

His brother, Kris, shook his head. "It's so messed up from the crash, we won't know for sure until we get her on the lift."

"Do you guys need help?" Jason called.

Jim waved and headed off. Ming understood his exit. When Jason and the Stovers started talking cars, no one else on the planet existed. She stared at the ruined car and the group of men who'd gathered to check out the damage. It would be the talk of the track for the rest of the weekend.

"Looks like you've got your hands full," she told Jason, nodding toward a trio of racers approaching them. "I'm going to get out of here so you can focus on the Mustang."

"Wait." He caught her hand, laced his fingers through hers. "Stick around."

She melted beneath the heat of his smile. "I'll just be in the way."

"I need you—"

"Jason, that was some crash," the man in the middle said.

Ming figured she'd take advantage of the interruption to escape, but Jason refused to relinquish her hand. A warm feeling set up shop in her midsection as Jason introduced her. She'd expected once his buddies surrounded him, he wouldn't care if she took off.

But after an hour she lost all willpower to do so. Despite the attention Jason received from his fellow competitors, he never once forgot that she was there. Accustomed to how focused Jason became at the track, Ming was caught off guard by the way he looped his arm around her waist and included her in the conversations.

By the time the car had been packed up later that afternoon, she was congratulating herself on her decision to come. They sat side by side on the tailgate of his truck. Jason balanced an icepack on his injured knee. Despite the heat, she was leaning against his side, enjoying the lean strength of his body.

"What prompted you to come to the track today?" he questioned, gaze fixed on the Stover brothers as they argued over how long it would take them to get the car ready to race once more.

The anxiety that had gripped her before his crash reappeared and she shrugged to ease her sudden tension. "It's been a long time since I've seen you race." She eyed the busted-up Mustang. "And now it's going to be even longer."

"So it seems."

"Sorry your season ended like this. Are you heading back tonight?"

"Gus and Kris are. I've got a hotel room in town. I think I'll ice my knee and drive back tomorrow."

She waited a beat, hoping he'd ask her to stay, but no invitation was forthcoming. "Want company?"

"In the shape I'm in, I'd be no use to you." He shot her a wry smile.

As his friend, she shouldn't feel rejected, but after accepting that she was in love with him and being treated like his girlfriend all day, she'd expected he'd want her to stick around. She recognized that he was in obvious pain and needed a restful night's sleep. A friend would put his welfare above her own desires.

"Then I guess I'll head back to Houston." She kissed him on the cheek and hopped off the tailgate.

He caught her wrist as her feet hit the ground. "I'm really glad you came today."

It wasn't fair the way he turned the sex appeal on and off whenever it suited him. Ming braced herself against the lure of his sincere eyes and enticing smile. Had she fallen in love with his charm? If so, could she go back to being just his friend once they stopped sleeping together?

She hoped so. Otherwise she'd spend the rest of her life in love with a man who would never let himself love her back.

"Supporting each other is what friends are for," she said, stepping between his thighs and taking his face in her hands.

Slowly she brought her lips to his, releasing all her pent-up emotions into the kiss. Her longing for what she could never have. Her fear over his brush with serious injury. And pure, sizzling desire.

After the briefest of hesitations, he matched her passion, fingers digging into her back as he fed off her mouth. The kiss exhilarated her. Everything about being with Jason made her happy. Smiling, she sucked his lower lip into her mouth and rubbed her breasts against his chest. As soon as she heard his soft groan, she released him.

Stepping back, Ming surveyed her handiwork. From the dazed look in his eyes, the flush darkening his cheekbones and the unsteady rush of breath in and out of his lungs, the kiss had packed a wallop. A quick glance below his belt assured her he would spend a significant portion of the evening thinking about her. Good.

"Careful on the drive home tomorrow," she murmured, wiping her fingertip across her damp lips in deliberate seduction. "Call me when you get back."

And with a saucy wave, she headed for her car.

The sixty-eight-foot cruiser Jason had borrowed for Max's bachelor party barely rocked as it encountered the wake of the large powerboat that had sped across their bow seconds earlier. Cigar in one hand, thirty-year-old Scotch in the other, Jason tracked the boat skimming the dark waters of Galveston Bay from upstairs in the open-air lounge. On the opposite rail, Max's brothers were discussing their wives and upcoming fatherhood.

"She's due tomorrow," Nathan Case muttered, tapping his cell phone on his knee. "I told her it was crazy for me come to this bachelor party, but she was determined to go out dancing with Missy, Rachel and her friends."

Nathan's aggrieved tone found a sympathetic audience in Jason. Why were women so calm about the whole pregnancy-and-giving-birth thing? Ming wasn't even pregnant, and Jason was already experiencing a little coil of tension deep in his gut. He hadn't considered how connected he'd feel to her when he'd agreed to father her baby. Nor could he stop wondering if he'd feel as invested if they'd done it her way and he'd never made love to her.

"I'm sure Emma knows what she's doing," Sebastian Case said. Older than Max and Nathan by a few years, Sebastian was every inch the confident CEO of a multimillion-dollar corporation.

"I think she's hoping the dancing will get her contractions started." Nathan stared at the cell phone as if he could make it ring by sheer willpower. "What if her water breaks on the dance floor?"

"Then she'll call and you can meet her at the hospital." Sebastian's soothing tones were having little effect on his agitated half brother.

"You're barely into your second trimester," Nathan scoffed. "Let's see how rational you are when Missy hasn't been able to see her feet for a month, doesn't sleep more than a few hours a night and can't go ten minutes without finding a bathroom."

Sebastian's eyes grew distant for a few seconds as if he was imagining his wife in the final weeks before she was due.

"Do you know what you're having?" Even as Jason asked Nathan the question, he realized that a month ago he never would have thought to inquire.

"A boy."

Jason lifted his Scotch in a salute. "Congratulations."

"You're single, aren't you?" Sebastian regarded him like a curiosity. "How come you're not downstairs with Max and his buddies slipping fives into the ladies' G-strings instead of hanging out with a couple old family men?"

Because he wasn't feeling particularly single at the moment. Jason raised the cigar. "Charlie said no smoking in the salon."

"But you're missing the entertainment." Nathan gestured toward the stairs that led below.

Some entertainment. Max might be downstairs with a half dozen of their single friends and a couple of exotic dancers someone had hired, but Jason doubted his best friend was having any fun. Max wasn't interested in any woman except Rachel.

Up until two weeks ago Jason hadn't understood what had come over his friend. Now, after making love with Ming, his craving for her had taken on a life of its own. His body stirred at the memory of her dripping wet in his kitchen. The way her white blouse had clung to her breasts, the fabric rendered sheer by the water. He wasn't sure what he would have done if she'd denied him then. Gotten down on his knees and begged?

Probably.

Jason shoved aside the unsettling thought and smirked at Nathan. "When you're free to hit a strip club any night of the week, the novelty wears off. You two are the ones who should be downstairs."

"Why's that?" Nathan asked.

"I just assumed with your wives being pregnant…"

Sebastian and Nathan exchanged amused looks.

"That our sex lives are nonexistent?" Sebastian proposed. He looked as relaxed and contented as a lion after consuming an antelope.

The last emotion pestering Jason should be envy. He was the free one. Unfettered by emotional ties that had the potential to do damage. Unhampered by monotony, he was free to sleep with a different woman every night of the week if he wanted. He had no demanding female complicating his days.

"Did it surprise either of you that Max is getting married?" Jason asked.

Sebastian swirled the Scotch in his glass. "If I had to wager which one of you two would be getting married first, I would have bet on you."

"Me?" Jason shook his head in bafflement.

"I thought for sure you and Ming would end up together."

"We're close friends, nothing more."

Sebastian's thumb traced the rim of his glass. "Yeah, it took me a long time to see what was waiting right under my nose, too."

Rather than sputter out halfhearted denials, Jason downed the last of his drink and stubbed out the cigar. The Scotch scorched a trail from his throat to his chest.

"I think I'll go see if Max needs rescuing."

They'd been cruising around Galveston for a little over an hour and Jason was as itchy to get off the boat as Nathan. He wanted to blame his restlessness on the fact that the bachelor party meant a week from now his relationship with his best buddy would officially go on the back burner as Max took on his new responsibilities as a husband. But Max had been splitting his loyalty for three months now, and Jason was accustomed to being an afterthought.

No, Jason's edginess was due to the fact that like Nathan, Sebastian and Max, he'd rather be with the woman he was intimate with than whooping it up with a bunch of single guys and a couple of strippers.

What had happened to him?

Only two weeks ago he'd been moaning that Max had abandoned him for a woman. And here he was caught in the same gossamer net, pining for a particular female's companionship.

He met Max on the narrow stairs that connected the salon level to the upper deck, where Nathan and Sebastian remained.

"Feel like getting off this boat and hooking up with our ladies?" Max proposed. "I just heard from Rachel. They've had their fill of the club."

Jason glanced at his watch. "It's only ten-thirty. This is your bachelor party. You're supposed to get wild one last time before you're forever leg-shackled to one woman."

"I'd rather get wild with the woman I'm going to be leg-shackled to." Max punched Jason in the shoulder. "Besides, I don't see you downstairs getting a lap dance from either Candy or Angel."

"Charlie said no smoking in the salon. I went upstairs to enjoy one of the excellent cigars Nathan brought."

"And this has nothing to do with the warning you gave Ming tonight?"

Jason cursed. "You heard that?"

"I thought it was cute."

"Jackass." Swearing at Max was a lot easier than asking himself why he'd felt compelled to tell Ming to behave herself and not break any hearts at the club. He'd only been half joking. The thought of her contemplating romance with another man aroused some uncomfortably volatile emotions.

"And it doesn't look like she listened to you."

"What makes you say that?"

Max showed him his cell phone screen. "I think this guy's pretty close to having his heart broken."

Jason swallowed a growl but could do nothing about the frown that pulled his brows together when he glimpsed the photo of Ming dancing with some guy. Irritation fired in his gut. It wasn't the fact that Ming had her head thrown back and her arms above her head that set Jason off. It was the way the guy had his hands inches from her hips and looked prepared to go where no one but Jason belonged.

Max laughed. "I know Nathan and Sebastian are ready to leave. Are you up for taking the launch in and leaving the boys to play by themselves?"

Damn right he was. "This is your party. Where you go, I go."

Eight

Rachel Lansing, bride-to-be, laughed at the photo her fiancé sent her from his bachelor party. Sitting across the limo from her, Ming wasn't the least bit amused. Her stomach had been churning for the last half an hour, ever since she'd found out that there were exotic dancers on the boat. And her anxiety hadn't been relieved when she hadn't spotted Jason amongst the half dozen men egging on the strippers. He could be standing behind Max, out of the camera's range.

She had no business feeling insecure and suspicious. It wasn't as if she had a claim to Jason beyond their oh-so-satisfying baby-making activities. Problem was, she couldn't disconnect her emotions. And heaven knew she'd been trying to. Telling herself over and over that it was just sex. Incredibly hot, passionate, mind-blowing sex, but not the act of two people in love. Just a couple of friends trying to make a baby together.

Whom was she kidding?

For the past two weeks, she'd been deliriously happy and anxiety-ridden by turn. Every time he slid inside her it was a struggle not to confide that she was falling in love with him, and her strength was fading fast. Already she was rationalizing why she and Jason should continue to be intimate long after she was pregnant.

It was only a matter of time before she confessed what she truly wanted for her future and he'd sit her down and remind her why they'd made love in the first place. Then things would get awkward and they'd start to avoid each other. No. Better to stay silent and keep Jason as her best friend rather than lose him forever.

"If you're worried about Jason, Max texted me and said he's on the upper deck with Nathan and Sebastian." Rachel gave Ming a reassuring smile.

"I'm not worried about Jason," Ming hastily assured her as she sagged in relief. She mustered a smile. "No need for me to be. We're just friends. Have been for years."

A fact Rachel knew perfectly well since the four of them had gone out numerous times since she and Max had gotten engaged. Ming had no idea why she had to keep reminding people that she and Jason were not an item.

"Jason's a great guy."

"He sure is." Ming saw where this was going and knew she had to cut Rachel off. "But he's the sort of guy who isn't ever going to fall in love and get married."

Rachel cocked her head. "Funny, that's what I thought about Max and yet he lost his favorite car to Jason over a wager that he wouldn't get married." Her blue eyes sparkled with mischief. "What's to say Jason won't change his mind, too?"

Ming smiled back, but she knew there was a big difference between the two men. Max hadn't found his father trying to kill himself because he was so despondent over the loss of his wife and daughter. And after getting the scoop about how Max and Rachel had met five years earlier, Ming suspected the reason Max had been so down on love and marriage was that he'd already lost his heart to the woman of his dreams.

"I don't know," Ming said. "He's pretty set in his ways. Besides, you weren't around when my engagement to Jason's brother ended. It made me realize that I'm happier on my own."

"Yeah, before Max, I was where you are. All I have to say is that things change." Rachel nudged her chin toward her soon-to-be-sisters-in-law. "Ask either of those two if they believed love was ever going to happen for them. I'll bet both of them felt the way you do right now."

Ming glanced toward the back of the limo, where Emma, nine months pregnant and due any second, and Missy, four months pregnant and radiant, sat side by side, laughing. They had it all. Gorgeous, devoted men. Babies on the way. Envy twisted in Ming's heart.

She sighed. "I'm really happy for all of you, but love doesn't find everyone."

"If you keep an open mind it does."

The big diamond on Rachel's hand sparkled in the low light. Ming stared at it while her fingers combed her hair into three sections. As she braided, she mused that being in love was easy when you were a week away from pairing your engagement ring with a wedding band. Not that she begrudged any of the Case women their happiness. Each one had gone through a lot before finding bliss, none more so than Rachel. But Ming just wasn't in a place where she could feel optimistic about her own chances.

She was in love with a man who refused to let his guard down and allow anyone in, much less her. Because she couldn't get over her feelings for Jason, she'd already lost one man and almost made the biggest mistake of her life. And as of late, she was concerned that having Jason father her child was going to lead to more heartache in the future.

Ming mulled Rachel's words during the second half of the forty-five-minute drive from downtown Houston to the Galveston marina where the men would be waiting. Maybe she should have gone home from the club like Rachel's sister, Hailey, instead of heading out to meet up with Jason. They'd made no plans to rendezvous tonight. She was starting to feel foolish for chasing him all the way out here.

If Jason decided to stay on the yacht with the bachelor party instead of motoring back to the dock on the launch with Max and his brothers, would she be the odd girl out when the couples reunited? Her chest tightened. Ming closed her eyes as they entered the marina parking lot.

The limo came to a stop. Ming heard the door open and the low rumble of male voices. She couldn't make her eyes open. Couldn't face the sight of the three couples embracing while she sat alone and unwanted.

"What's the matter? Did all the dancing wear you out?"

Her eyes flew open at Jason's question. His head and shoulders filled the limo's open door. Heart pounding in delight, she clasped her hands in her lap to keep from throwing herself into his arms. That was not how friends greeted each other.

"I'm not used to having that much fun." She scooted along the seat to the door, accepting Jason's hand as her foot touched the pavement. His familiar cologne mingled with the faint scent of cigars. She wanted to nuzzle her nose into his neck and breathe him in. "How about you? Did you enjoy your strippers?"

"They preferred to be called exotic dancers." He showed her his phone. "They weren't nearly as interesting as this performance."

She gasped at the picture of herself dancing. How had Jason gotten ahold of it? So much for what happens at a bachelorette party stays at a bachelorette party. She eyed the women behind Jason. Who'd ratted her out?

"It was just some guy who asked me to dance," she protested.

"Just some guy?" He kept his voice low, but there was no denying the edge in his tone. "He has his hands all over you."

She enlarged the image, telling herself she was imagining the possessive glint in Jason's eye. "No he doesn't. And if this had been taken five seconds later you would have seen me shove him away and walk off the dance floor."

"Whoa, sounds like a lover's spat to me," Rachel crowed.

Confused by the sparks snapping in Jason's blue eyes, Ming realized a semicircle of couples had formed five feet away. Six faces wore various shades of amusement as they looked on.

Jason composed his expression and turned to face the group. "Not a lover's spat."

"Just a concerned friend," Max intoned, his voice dripping with dry humor.

"Come on, we're all family here." Sebastian's gesture encompassed the whole group. "You can admit to us that you're involved."

"We're not involved." Ming found her voice.

"We're friends," Jason said. "We look out for each other."

"I disagree," Max declared, slapping Jason on the back. "I think you've finally realized that your best friend is the best thing that ever happened to you." He glanced around to see if the others agreed with him. "About time, too."

"You don't know what you're talking about." Jason was making no attempt to laugh off his friend's ribbing.

Ming flinched at Jason's resolute expression. If he'd considered moving beyond friendship, Max would be the one he'd confide in. With Jason's adamant denial, Ming had to face the fact that she was an idiot to hope that Jason might one day realize they belonged together.

"Oh!"

All eyes turned to Emma, who'd bent over, her hand pressed to her round belly.

"Are you okay?" Nathan put his arm around her waist. "Was it a contraction?"

"I don't know. I don't think so." Emma clutched his arm. "Maybe you'd better take me home."

To Ming's delight everyone's focus had shifted to Emma. What might or might not be going on between Ming and Jason was immediately forgotten. As Nathan opened the passenger door for Emma, she looked straight at Ming and winked. Restraining a grin, Ming wondered how many times Emma had used the baby in such a fashion.

"Alone at last," Jason said, drawing her attention back to him. "And the night is still young."

Ming shivered beneath his intense scrutiny. "What did you have in mind?"

"I was thinking maybe you could show me your dancing skills in private."

"Funny. I was thinking maybe you could give me a demonstration of the techniques you picked up from your strippers tonight."

"Exotic dancers," he corrected, opening the passenger door on his car so she could get in. "And I didn't pick up anything because I wasn't anywhere near their dancing."

The last of her tension melted away. "I don't believe you," she teased, keeping her relief hidden. She leaned against his chest and peered up at him from beneath her lashes. "Not so long ago you wouldn't have missed that kind of action."

"Not so long ago I didn't have all the woman I could handle waiting for me at home."

"Except I wasn't waiting for you." Lifting up on tiptoe, she pressed her lips to his and then dropped into the passenger seat.

"No, you were out on the town breaking hearts."

The door shut before her retort reached Jason's ears. Was he really annoyed with her for dancing with someone? Joy flared and died. She was reading too much into it.

"So, where are we heading?" Jason turned out of the marina parking lot and got them headed toward the bridge off the island.

"You may take me home. After all that heartbreaking, my feet are sore." She tried to smile, but her heart hurt too much. "Besides, Muffin is home alone."

"Where's Lily?"

"Supposedly she's out of town this weekend."

"Why supposedly?"

"Because I drove past Evan's house and her car was in the driveway."

"You drove past Evan's house?" Jason shifted his gaze off the road long enough for her to glimpse his alarm. "Are you sure that was a good idea?"

She bristled at his disapproving tone. "I was curious if my sister had lied to me."

"You were curious." He echoed her words doubtfully. "Not bothered that they're together?"

"No."

"Because you two were engaged not that long ago and now he's dating your sister."

"Why do you keep bringing that up?" Her escalating annoyance came through loud and clear. She'd known Jason too long not to recognize when he was picking a fight.

"I want you to be honest with yourself so this doesn't blow up between you and your sister in the future."

"You don't think I'm being honest with myself?"

"Your sister is dating the man who broke off your engagement two weeks before the wedding. I think you're trying too hard to be okay with it."

He took her hand and she was both soothed and frustrated by his touch. No matter what else was happening between them, Jason was her best friend. He knew her better than anyone. Sometimes better than she knew herself. But the warm press of his fingers reminded her that while he could act like a bossy boyfriend, she came up against his defenses every time she started to play girlfriend.

"Right now I've got my hands full with you." Ming wasn't exaggerating on that score. "Can we talk about something else? Please?"

The last thing she wanted was to argue with him when her hopes for the evening required them to be in perfect accord.

"Sure." Even though he agreed, she could tell he wasn't happy about dropping the subject. "What's on your mind?"

"I have the house to myself until late Sunday if you want to hang out."

"That sounds like an invitation to sleep over."

She made a sandwich of his hand and hers and ignored the anxious flutter in her stomach.

"Maybe it is." Flirting with Jason was fun and dangerous. It was easy to lose track of reality and venture into that tricky romantic place best avoided if she wanted their friendship to remain uncomplicated.

Or maybe she was too far gone for things to ever be the same between them again.

The part of her that wanted them to be more than just friends was growing stronger every day. It was a crazy hope, but she couldn't stop the longing any more than Jason could get past his reluctance to fall in love.

"Ming…"

She heard the wariness in his voice and held up her hand. They hadn't spent a single night together this whole week. That had been a mutual decision based on practicality. Neither of them wanted Evan to pop over late one night and find her at Jason's house. Plus, Lily had been in Houston all week and would have noticed if Ming had stayed out all night.

But she was dying to spend the night snuggled in his arms. And the craving had nothing to do with making a baby.

"Forget I said anything." Her breath leaked out in a long, slow sigh. "This past week has been fun. But you and I both know I'm past my prime fertility cycle. It makes no sense for us to keep getting together when I'm either pregnant or I'm too late in my cycle to try."

"Wait. Is that what this week has been about?" He sounded put out. "You're just using me to make a baby?"

Startled, she opened her mouth to deny his claim and realized he was trying to restore their conversation to a lighter note by teasing her. "And a few weeks from now we'll see if you've succeeded." She faked a yawn. "I guess I'm more tired than I thought."

Jason nodded and turned the topic to the bachelorette party. Ming jumped on board, glad to leave behind the tricky path they'd been treading.

By the time he turned the car into her driveway, she'd man-handled her fledgling daydreams about turning their casual sex into something more. She was prepared to say good-night and head alone to her door.

"Call me tomorrow," he told her. "I've got to go shopping for Max and Rachel's wedding present."

"You haven't done that yet?"

"I've been waiting for you to offer to do it for me."

Robbed of a dreamy night in Jason's arms and the pleasure of waking up with him in the morning, Ming let her irritation shine. "You said no about going in on a gift together, so you're on your own."

"Please come shopping with me." He put on his most appealing smile. "You know I'm hopeless when it comes to department stores."

How could she say no when she'd already agreed to help him before they'd started sleeping together. It wasn't fair to treat him differently just because she felt differently toward him.

"What time tomorrow?"

"Eleven? I want to be home to watch the Oilers at three."

"Fine," she grumbled.

With disappointment of her own weighing her down, she plodded up the stairs and let herself into her house. Muffin met her in the foyer. She danced around on her back legs, wringing a small smile from Ming's stiff lips.

"I'll take you out back in a second." She waited by the front door long enough to see Jason's headlights retreating down her driveway, then headed toward the French doors that led from her great room to the pool deck.

While the Yorkie investigated the bushes at the back of her property, Ming sat down on a lounge chair and sought the tranquility often gained by sitting beside her turquoise kidney-shaped pool. She revisited her earlier statement to Jason. It made no sense for them to rendezvous each afternoon and have the best sex ever if all they were trying to do was make a baby. Only, if she was completely honest with herself, she'd admit that a baby isn't all she wanted from Jason.

Her body ached with unfulfilled desire. Her soul longed to find the rhythm of Jason's heart beating in time with hers. From the beginning she'd been right to worry that getting intimate with her best friend was going to lead her into trouble. But temptation could be avoided for only so long when all you've ever wanted gets presented to you on a silver platter. She would just have to learn to live with the consequences.

Finding nothing of interest in the shrubbery, Muffin came back to the pool, her nails clicking on the concrete. Sympathetic to her mistress's somber mood, the terrier jumped onto Ming's lap and nuzzled her nose beneath Ming's hand.

"I am such an idiot," she told the dog, rubbing Muffin's head.

"That makes two of us."

Jason hadn't even gotten out of Ming's neighborhood before he'd realized what a huge error he'd made. In fact, he hadn't made it to the end of her block. But just because he'd figured it out didn't mean returning to Ming wasn't an even bigger mistake. So, he'd sat at a stop sign for five minutes, listening to Rascal Flatts and wondering when his life had gotten so damned complicated. Then, he'd turned the car around, used his key to get into Ming's house and found her by the pool.

"Let's go upstairs," he said. "We need to talk."

Ming pulled her hair over one shoulder and began to braid it. "We can't talk here?"

Was she being deliberately stubborn or pretending to be dense?

Without answering, he pivoted on his heel and walked toward the house. Muffin caught up as he crossed the threshold. Behind him, Ming's heels clicked on the concrete as she rushed after him.

"Jason." She sounded breathless and uncertain. She'd stopped in the middle of her kitchen and called after him as he got to the stairs. "Why did you come back?"

Since talking had only created problems between them earlier, he was determined to leave conversation for later. Taking the stairs two at a time, he reached her bedroom in record time. Unfastening his cuffs, he gazed around the room. He hadn't been up here since he'd helped her paint the walls a rich beige. The dark wood furniture, rich chestnut bedspread and touches of sage green gave the room the sophisticated, expensive look of a five-star hotel suite.

"Jason?"

He'd had enough time to unfasten his shirt buttons. Now, as she entered the room, he let the shirt drop off his shoulders and draped it over a chair. "Get undressed."

While she stared at him in confounded silence, he took Muffin from her numb fingers and deposited the dog in the hallway.

"She always sleeps with me," Ming protested as he shut the door.

"Not tonight."

"Well, I suppose she can sleep on Lily's bed. Jason, what's gotten into you?"

His pants joined his shirt on the chair. With only his boxer briefs keeping his erection contained, he set his hands on his hips.

"You and I have been best friends for a long time." Since she wasn't making any effort to slip out of that provocative halter-top and insanely short skirt, he prowled toward her. "And

I've shared with you some of the hardest things I've ever had to go through."

She made no attempt to stop him as he tugged at the thin ribbon holding up her top, but she did grab at the fabric as it began to fall away from her breasts. "If you're saying I know you better than anyone except Max, I'd agree."

Jason hooked his fingers in the top and pulled it from her fingers, exposing her small, perfect breasts. His lungs had to work hard to draw in the air he required. Damn it. They had been together all week, but he still couldn't get over how gorgeous she was, or how much he wanted to mark her as his own.

"Then it seems as if I'm doing our friendship an injustice by not telling you what's going on in my head at the moment."

Reaching around her, he slid down the zipper on her skirt and lowered it past her hips. When it hit the floor, she stepped out of it.

"And what's that?"

Jason crossed his arms over his chest and stared into her eyes. It was nearly impossible to keep his attention from wandering over her mostly naked body. Standing before him in only a black lace thong and four-inch black sandals, she was an exotic feast for the eyes.

"I didn't like seeing you dancing with another man."

The challenge in her almond-shaped eyes faded at his admission. Raw hope rushed in to replace it. "You didn't?"

Jason ground his teeth. He should have been able to contain the truth from her. That he'd admitted to such possessive feelings meant a crack had developed in the well-constructed wall around his heart. But a couple weaknesses in the structure didn't mean he had to demolish the whole thing. He needed to get over his annoyance at her harmless interaction with some random guy. Besides, wasn't he the one who'd initially encouraged her that there was someone out there for her?

To hell with that.

Taking her hand, he drew her toward the bed.

"Not one bit." It reminded him too much of how he'd lost her to his brother. "It looked like you were having fun without me."

"Did it, now?" His confession had restored her confidence. With a sexy smile, she coasted her nails from his chest to the waistband of his underwear. "I guess I was imagining that you were otherwise occupied with your exotic dancers. Did they get you all revved up? Is that why we're here right now?"

He snorted. "The only woman I have any interest in seeing out of her clothes is you."

Heaven help him—it was true. He hadn't even looked at another woman since this business of her wanting to become a mother came up. No. It had been longer than that. Since his brother had broken off their engagement.

The level of desire he felt for her had been eating at him since last weekend when she'd kissed him good-bye at the track. That had been one hell of a parting and if his knee hadn't been so banged up he never would've let her walk away.

This isn't what he'd expected when he'd proposed making love rather than using a clinic to help her conceive. He'd figured his craving for her was strictly physical. That it would wane after his curiosity was satisfied.

What he was feeling right now threatened to alter the temper of their friendship. He should slow things down or stop altogether. Yeah. That had worked great for him earlier. He'd dropped her off and then raced back before he'd gotten more than a couple blocks away.

Frustrated with himself, he didn't give her smug smile a chance to do more than bud before picking her up and dumping her unceremoniously on the bed. Without giving her a chance to recover, he removed first one then the other of her shoes. As each one hit the floor, her expression evolved from surprised to anticipatory.

It drove him crazy how much he wanted her. Every cell in his body ached with need. Nothing in his life had ever compared. Was it knowing her inside and out that made the sexual chemistry between them stronger than normal?

While he snagged her panties and slid them down her pale thighs, she lifted her arms above her head, surrendering herself to his hot gaze. The vision of her splayed across the bed, awaiting his possession, stirred a tremor in his muscles. His hands shook as he dropped his underwear to the floor.

Any thought of taking things slow vanished as she reached for him. A curse made its way past his lips as her confident strokes brought him dangerously close to release.

"Stop." His harsh command sounded desperate.

He took her wrist in a firm grip and pinned it above her head. Lowering himself into the cradle between her thighs, he paused before sliding into her. Two things were eating at him tonight: that picture of her dancing and her preoccupation with Evan and Lily's romance.

"You're mine." The words rumbled out of him like a vow. Claiming her physically hadn't rattled his safe bachelor existence, but this was a whole different story.

"Jason." She waggled her hips and arched her back, trying to entice him to join with her, but although it was close to killing him, he stayed still.

"Say it." With his hands keeping her wrists trapped over her head and his body pinning hers to the mattress, she was at his mercy.

"I can't…" Her eyes went wide with dismay. "…say that."

"Why not?" He rocked against her, giving her a taste of what she wanted.

A groan erupted past her parted lips. She watched him through half-closed eyes. "Because…"

"Say it," he insisted. "And I'll give you what you want."

Her chest rose and fell in shallow, agitated breaths. "What I want…"

He lowered his head and drew circles around her breast with his tongue. His willpower had never felt so strong before. When she'd started dating his brother, he'd been in the worst sort of hell. Deep in his soul, Jason had always believed if she'd choose anyone, she'd pick him. They were best friends. Confidants. Soul mates. And buried where neither had ventured before prom night was a flammable sexual chemistry.

Both of them had been afraid at the power of what existed between them, but he'd been the most vocal about not ruining their friendship. So vocal, in fact, she'd turned to his brother before Jason had had time to come to his senses.

"Mine." He growled the word against her breast as his mouth closed around her nipple.

She gasped at the strong pull of his mouth. "Yours." She wrapped her thighs around his hips. "All yours."

"All mine."

Satisfied, he plunged into her. Locked together, he released her wrists and kissed her hard and deep, sealing her pledge before whisking them both into unheard of pleasure.

Nine

Moving slowly, her legs wobbly from the previous night's exertions, Ming crossed her bedroom to the door, where Muffin scratched and whined. She let the Yorkie in, dipping to catch the small dog before Muffin could charge across the room and disturb the large, naked man sprawled facedown in the middle of the tangled sheets.

"Let's take you outside," she murmured into the terrier's silky coat, tearing her gaze away from Jason.

Still shaken from their passionate lovemaking the night before, she carefully navigated the stairs and headed for the back door. After cuddling against Jason's warm skin all night, the seventy-degree temperature at 7:00 a.m. made her shiver. She should have wrapped more than a silky lavender robe around her naked body.

While Muffin ran off to do her business and investigate the yard for intruders, Ming plopped down on the same lounge she'd occupied the night before and opened her mind to the thoughts she'd held at bay all night long.

What the hell had possessed Jason to demand that she admit to belonging to him? Battling goose bumps, she rubbed at her arms. The morning air brushed her overheated skin but couldn't cool the fire raging inside her. *His.* Even now the word made her muscles tremble and her insides whirl like a leaf caught in a vortex. She dropped her face into her hands and fought the urge to laugh or weep. He made her crazy. First his vow to never fall in love and never get married. Now this.

Muffin barked at something, and Ming looked up to find her dog digging beneath one of the bushes. Normally she'd stop the terrier. Today, she simply watched the destruction happen.

What was she supposed to make of Jason's territorial posturing last night? Why had he reacted so strongly to the inflammatory photo? She'd understand it if they were dating. Then he'd have the right to be angry, to be driven to put his mark on her.

Jason hadn't changed his mind about falling in love. Initially last night he hadn't even wanted to spend the night. So, what had brought him back? It was just about the great sex, right? It wasn't really fair to say he only wanted her body, but he'd shown no interest in accepting her heart.

Ming called Muffin back to the house and started a pot of coffee. She wasn't sure if Jason intended to head home right away or if he would linger. She hoped he'd stick around. She had visions of eating her famous cinnamon raisin bread French toast and drinking coffee while they devoured the Sunday paper. As the day warmed they could go for a swim in her pool. She'd always wanted to make love in the water. Or they could laze in bed. It would be incredible to devote an entire day to hanging out.

Afternoon and evening sex had been more fun and recreational than serious and committed. Ming could pretend they were just enjoying the whole friends-with-benefits experience. Sleeping wrapped in each other's arms had transported them into "relationship" territory. Not to mention the damage done to her emotional equilibrium when Jason admitted to feeling jealous.

She brought logic to bear on last night's events, and squashed the giddy delight bubbling in her heart. She'd strayed a long way from the reason she was in this mess in the first place. Becoming a mom. Time to put things with Jason in perspective. They were friends. Physical intimacy might be messing with their heads at this point, but once she was pregnant all sex would cease and their relationship would go back to being casual and supportive.

"I started coffee," she announced as she stepped into her bedroom and stopped dead at the sight of the person standing by her dresser.

Lily dropped something into Ming's jewelry box and smiled at her sister. "I borrowed your earrings. I hope that's okay."

"It's fine." From her sister, Ming's gaze went straight to the bed and found it empty. Relief shot through her, making her knees wobble. "I thought you were in Portland."

"I came back early."

Since Lily wasn't asking the questions Ming was expecting, she could only assume her sister hadn't run into Jason. "Ah, great."

Where the hell was he?

"How come Jason's car is in the driveway?" Lily asked.

Ming hovered near the doorway to the hall, hoping her sister would take the hint and come with her. "Max's bachelor party was last night. He had a little too much to drink so I drove him home and brought the car back here."

Too late she realized she could have just said he was staying in the guest room. That would at least have given him a reason to be in the house at this hour. Now he was trapped until she could get away from Lily.

Her sister wandered toward the window seat. "I put an offer in on a house."

"Really?" What was going to happen between her and Evan if she was moving away?

Lily plopped down on the cushioned seat and set a pillow in her lap, looking as if she was settling in for a long talk. "You sound surprised."

Ming shot a glance toward the short hallway, flanked by walk-in closets, that led to her bathroom. He had to be in there.

"I guess I was hoping you'd change your mind." She pulled underwear and clothes from her dresser and headed toward the bathroom. "Let me get dressed and then you can tell me all about it."

Her heart thumped vigorously as she shut the bathroom door behind her.

Jason leaned, fully clothed and completely at ease, against her vanity. "I thought you said she was spending the weekend with Evan."

"She was." Ming frowned when she realized he clearly thought she'd lied to him. "Something must have happened. She seems upset." Ming dropped her robe and stepped into her clothes, ignoring his appreciative leer. "Did she see you?"

"I was already dressed and in here when I heard you start talking." Readying himself to make a break for it.

"You were leaving?" Ming shouldn't have been surprised. Last night was over. Time to return their relationship to an easygoing, friendly place. Hadn't she been thinking the same thing? So why did her stomach feel like she'd been eating lead? "Did you intend to say goodbye or just sneak out while I was downstairs with Muffin?"

"Don't be like that."

"Why don't you tell me exactly how I'm supposed to be."

Not wanting her sister to get suspicious, Ming returned to the bedroom without waiting for Jason's answer. Her heart ached, but she refused to give in to the pain pressing on the edge of her consciousness.

Since Lily seemed entrenched in Ming's room, she sat beside her sister on the window seat. To catch Lily's attention, Ming put her hand on her knee. "Tell me about the house."

"House?"

"The one you put an offer in on."

"It's just a house."

"How many bedrooms does it have?"

"Two."

Curious about whatever was plaguing her sister, Ming was distracted by Muffin investigating her way toward the bathroom. "Nice neighborhood?"

"I think I made a huge mistake."

"Then withdraw the offer." She held her breath and waited for the terrier to discover Jason and erupt in a fit of barking.

"Not the house. The guy I've been seeing."

With an effort, Ming returned her full attention to her sister. "I thought you were just friends."

"It's gone a little further than that."

"You're sleeping together?" She asked the question even though she suspected the answer was yes.

Although the fact that her ex-fiancé was dating her sister continued to cause Ming minor discomfort, she was relieved that her strongest emotion was concern for her sister. When jealousy had been her first reaction to the realization that Lily and Evan were involved, Ming had worried that she was turning into a horrible person.

And lately, on top of all her other worries, Ming had started to wonder how Evan would feel if he found out about her and Jason. Something that might just happen if they weren't more careful.

"Yes. But it's not going anywhere."

Ming's gaze strayed to the bathroom door she hadn't completely closed. Muffin had yet to return to the bedroom. What was going on in there?

"Because you don't want it to?"

"I guess."

That tight spot near Ming's heart eased a little. "You guess? Or you know?" When her sister didn't answer, Ming asked, "Do you love him?"

"Yes." Lily stared at her hands.

Ming's throat locked up, but she couldn't blame her sister for falling for Evan. The heart rarely followed a logical path. And it must be tearing Lily apart to love the man who'd almost married her sister.

"I think you should forget about moving to Portland."

"It's not that simple."

Time to rattle her sister's cage a little. "Funny, Jason told me Evan's dating someone, but his situation is complicated, too." Ming gave a little laugh. "Maybe you two should get together and compare notes."

"I suppose we should." Lily gave her a listless smile.

Was there a way for Ming to give her sister permission to have a future with Evan? "You know, I was glad to hear that Evan had found someone and was moving on with his life."

"Really?" Despite Lily's skeptical tone, her eyes were bright with hope.

"He and I weren't mean to be. It happens."

"That's not how you felt six months ago."

"I'm not going to say that having him break off our engagement two weeks before the wedding was any fun, but I'd much rather find out then that we weren't meant to be than to get married and try to make it work only to invest years and then have it fail."

Ming's cell phone rang. She plucked it off the nightstand and answered it before Lily could respond.

"If I'm going to be stuck in your bathroom all morning, I'd love a cup of coffee and some breakfast."

"Good morning to you, too," she said, mouthing Jason's name to Lily. "How are you feeling?"

"Tired and a little aroused after checking out the lingerie drying in your shower."

"Sure, I can return your car." She rolled her eyes in Lily's direction. "Are you sober enough to drive me back here?"

"I guess I don't need to ask what excuse you gave your sister for why my car is at your house." Jason's voice was dry.

"I can follow you over there and bring you back," Lily offered.

"Hey, Lily just offered to follow me to your house so I can drop the car off."

"You're a diabolical woman, do you know that?"

"I'm sure it's no bother," Ming continued. "We're going to make breakfast first though."

"French toast with cinnamon raisin bread?"

"That's right. Your favorite." And one of the few things Ming enjoyed cooking. "Pity you aren't here this morning to have some."

"Just remember that paybacks can be painful."

"Oh, I didn't realize you needed your car to go shopping for Max and Rachel's wedding gift this morning. I'll see you in fifteen minutes." She disconnected the call. "I'm going to run Jason's car over to him and then I'll come back and we can make breakfast."

"Are you sure you don't want me to drive you over there?"

"No. I think the fresh air will do him some good."

She escorted Lily to the kitchen and settled her with a cup of green tea before she headed for the front door. Jason was already in the car when she arrived.

"Lily sounded upset this morning," Jason said. "Did I hear her say she put an offer on a house?"

"In Portland. But she seems really unsure what her next move is." She drove the car into the parking lot of a coffee shop in her neighborhood and cut the engine. "She's conflicted about going." She paused a beat. "Did you know they're sleeping together?"

Silence filled the space between her and Jason. Ming listened to the engine tick as it cooled, her thoughts whirling.

"Yes." He was keeping things from her. That wasn't like him.

"And you didn't tell me?"

"I didn't want you to get upset."

"I'm not upset." Not about Lily and Evan.

Last weekend she'd discovered what she really wanted from Jason. It wasn't a baby she would raise on her own. It was a husband who'd adore her and a bunch of kids to smother with love. She was never going to have that with him, and accepting that was tearing her apart.

"Well, you don't look happy."

"I want my sister to stay in Houston." The air inside the car became stuffy and uncomfortable. Ming shoved open the door and got out.

By the time she reached the Camaro's front bumper, Jason was there, waiting for her. "What happens if Lily and Evan decide to get married?"

Then she would be happy for them. "Evan and I were over six months ago."

"You and Evan broke up six months ago."

"Are you insinuating I'm not over him?"

"Are you?" He set his hand on his hips, preventing her from going past.

"Don't be ridiculous." She tried to sidestep him, but he shifted to keep her blocked. "Would I be sleeping with you if I was hung up on your brother?"

"If I recall, the only reason you're sleeping with me is so you can get pregnant."

She should be relieved that he believed that. It alleviated the need for complicated explanations. But what had happened between them meant so much more to her than that she couldn't stay silent.

"Perhaps you need to think a little harder about that first afternoon in your kitchen." She leaned into his body, surrendering her pride. "Did it seem as if all I was interested in was getting pregnant?"

"Ming." The guilt in his voice wrenched at her. He cupped her shoulders, the pressure comforting, reassuring.

She stared at his chest and hoped he wouldn't see the tears burning her eyes. "I knew it was going to get weird between us."

"It's not weird."

"It's weird." She circled around him and headed to the passenger side. "I should probably get back."

For a moment Jason stood where she'd left him. Ming watched him through the windshield, appreciating the solitude to collect her thoughts. It was her fault that their relationship was strained. If she'd just stuck with her plan and used a clinic to get pregnant, she wouldn't have developed a craving for a man who could never be hers. And she wouldn't feel miserable for opening herself to love.

As Jason slid behind the wheel, she composed her expression and gathered breath to tell him that they needed to go back to being friends without benefits, but he spoke first.

"Last night." He gripped the steering wheel hard and stared straight ahead. "I crossed the line."

To fill the silence that followed his confession, Jason started the Camaro, but for once the car's powerful engine didn't make him smile.

"Because of what you wanted me to say." Ming sounded irritated and unsure.

"Yes." Moments earlier, he'd considered skirting the truth, but she'd been honest about her feelings toward him.

"Then why did you?"

Making love to her had flipped a switch, lighting him up like a damned merry-go-round. He kept circling, his thoughts stuck on the same track, going nowhere. He liked that they were lovers. At the same time he relied on the stability of their friendship. So far he'd been operating under the belief that he could have it both ways. Now, his emotions were getting away from him. Logic told him lust and love were equally powerful and easily confused. But he'd begun to question his determination to never fall in love.

"Because it's how I feel."

"And that's a bad thing?"

He saw the hope in her eyes and winced. "It isn't bad. We've been close a long time. My feelings for you are strong." How did he explain himself without hurting her? "I just don't want to lead you on and I think that's what I did."

"Lead me on?" She frowned. "By making me think that you wanted to move beyond friendship into something…more?" Her fingers curled into fists. "I'm not sure who I'm more angry with right now. You or me."

If he'd known for sure that sleeping with her would complicate their friendship, would he have suggested it? Yes. Even now he wasn't ready to go back to the way things were. He had so much he longed to explore with Ming.

If he was honest with himself, he'd admit that helping her get pregnant was no longer his primary motivation for continuing their intimate relationship. He'd have to weigh a deeper connection with Ming against the risk that someday one of them would wake up and realize they were better off as friends. If emotions were uneven, their friendship might not survive.

"Do you want to stop?" He threw the car into gear and backed out of the parking spot.

"You're making me responsible for what does or doesn't happen between us? How is that fair?"

Below her even tone was a cry for help. Jason wanted to pull her close and kiss away her frown. If today they agreed to go back to the way things were, how long would he struggle against the impulse to touch her the way a lover would?

"I want you to be happy," he told her. "Whatever that takes."

"Do you?" She looked skeptical. "Last night I wanted you to stay, but you got all tense and uncomfortable." A deep breath helped get her voice back under control. When she continued, she seemed calmer. "I know it's because you have a rule against spending the night with the women you see."

"But I spent last night with you."

"And this morning you couldn't put your clothes on fast enough." She stared at him hard enough to leave marks on his face.

"So what do you want from me?"

"I'd like to know what you want. Are we just friends? Are we lovers?"

Last night he'd denied their relationship to his friends and felt resistance to her suggestion that he stay the night with her. As happy as Max and his brothers were to be in love with three terrific women, Jason could only wonder about future heartbreak when he looked at the couples. He didn't want to live with the threat of loss hanging over his head, but he couldn't deny that the thought of Ming with another man bugged him. So did her dismay that Evan had fallen in love with Lily.

"I won't deny that I think we're good together," he said. "But you know how I feel about falling in love."

"You don't want to do it."

"Can't we just keep enjoying what we have? You know I'll always be there for you. The chemistry between us is terrific. Soon you'll be busy being a mom and won't have time for me." He turned the car into her driveway and braked but didn't put the Camaro in Park. He needed to get away, to mull over what they'd talked about today. "Let's have dinner tomorrow."

"I can't. It's the Moon Festival. Lily and I are having dinner with our parents tomorrow. I'm going to tell them my decision to have a baby, and she's going to tell them she's moving." Ming sighed. "We promised to be there to support each other."

Jason didn't envy either sister. Helen Campbell was a stubborn, opinionated woman who believed she knew what was best for her daughters. At times, Ming had almost collapsed beneath the weight of her mother's hopes and dreams for her.

She hadn't talked about it, but Jason knew the breakup of her engagement had been a major blow to Ming's mother.

"What about Tuesday?" he suggested.

She put her hand on the door release, poised to flee. "It's going to be a hectic week with Max and Rachel's wedding next weekend."

Jason felt a sense of loss, but he didn't understand why. He and Ming were still friends. Nothing about that had changed.

"What's wrong?"

"It's too much to go into now."

Jason caught her arm as she pushed the door open and prevented her from leaving. "Wait."

Ming made him act in ways that weren't part of his normal behavior. Today, for example. He'd hid in her bathroom for fifteen minutes while she and her sister had occupied the bedroom. There wasn't another woman on earth he would have done that for.

Now he was poised to do something he'd avoided with every other woman he'd been involved with. "You're obviously upset. Tell me what's going on."

"I feel like an idiot." Her voice was thick with misery. "These last couple weeks with you have been fantastic and I've started thinking of us as a couple."

Her admission didn't come as a complete shock. Occasionally over the years he too had considered what they'd be like together. She knew him better than anyone. He'd shared with her things no one else knew. His father's suicide attempt. How he'd initially been reluctant to join the family business. The fact that the last words he'd spoken to his little sister before she'd died had been angry ones.

"Even knowing how you feel about love—" She stopped speaking and blinked rapidly. "Turns out I'm just like all those other women you've dated. No, I'm worse, because I knew better and let myself believe…" Her chin dropped toward her chest. "Forget it, okay?"

Was she saying she was in love with him? Her declaration hit him like a speeding truck. He froze, unable to think, unsure what to feel. Had she lost her mind? Knowing he wasn't built for lasting relationships, she'd opened herself up to heartbreak?

And where did they go from here? He couldn't ask her to continue as they'd been these past two weeks. But he'd never had such mind-blowing chemistry with anyone before, and he was a selfish bastard who wasn't going to give that up without a fight.

"Saturday night, after the wedding, we're going to head to my house and talk. We'll figure out together what to do." But he suspected the future was already written. "Okay?"

"There's nothing to figure out." She slid out of the car. "We're friends. Nothing is going to change that."

But as he watched her head toward her front door, Jason knew in the space of a few minutes, everything had changed.

Ten

Ming caught her sister wiping sweaty palms on her denim-clad thighs as she stopped the car in front of her parents' house and killed the engine. She put her hand over Lily's and squeezed in sympathy.

"We'll be okay if we stick together."

Arm in arm they headed up the front walk. No matter what their opinions were about each other's decisions, Ming knew they'd always form a unified front when it came to their mother.

Before they reached the front door, it opened and a harlequin Great Dane loped past the handsome sixty-year-old man who'd appeared in the threshold.

"Dizzy, you leave that poor puppy alone," Patrick Campbell yelled, but his words went unheeded as Dane and Ming's Yorkie raced around the large front yard.

"Dad, Muffin's fine." In fact, the terrier could run circles around the large dog and dash in for a quick nip then be gone again before Dizzy knew what hit her. "Let them run off a little energy."

After surviving rib-bruising hugs from their father, Ming and Lily captured the two dogs and brought them inside. The house smelled like heaven, and Ming suspected her mother had spent the entire weekend preparing her favorite dishes as well as the special moon cakes.

Ming sat down at her parents' dining table and wondered how the thing didn't collapse under the weight of all the food. She'd thought herself too nervous to eat, but once her plate was heaped with a sample of everything, she began eating with relish. Lily's appetite didn't match hers. She spent most of the meal staring at her plate and stabbing her fork into the food.

After dinner, they took their moon cakes outside to eat beneath the full moon while their mother told them the story of how the festival came to be.

"The Mongolians ruled China during the Yuan Dynasty," Helen Campbell would begin, her voice slipping naturally into storytelling rhythm. She was a professor at the University of Houston, teaching Chinese studies, language and literature. "The former leaders from the Sung dynasty wanted the foreigners gone, but all plans to rebel were discovered and stopped. Knowing that the Moon Festival was drawing near, the rebel leaders ordered moon cakes to be baked with messages inside, outlining the attack. On the night of the Moon Festival, the rebels successfully overthrew the government. What followed was the establishment of the Ming dynasty. Today, we eat the moon cakes to remember."

No matter how often she heard the tale, Ming never grew tired of it. As a first-generation American on her mother's side, Ming appreciated the culture that had raised her mother. Although as children both Ming and Lily had fought their mother's attempts to keep them attached to their Chinese roots, by the time Ming graduated from college, she'd become fascinated with China's history.

She'd visited China over a dozen times when Helen had returned to Shanghai, where her family still lived. Despite growing up with both English and Chinese spoken in the house, Ming had never been fluent in Mandarin. Thankfully her Chinese relatives were bilingual. She couldn't wait to introduce her own son or daughter to her Chinese family.

Stuffed to the point where it was difficult to breathe, Ming sipped jasmine tea and watched her sister lick sweet bean paste off her fingers. The sight blended with a hundred other memories of family and made her smile.

"I've decided to have a baby," she blurted out.

After her parents exchanged a look, Helen set aside her plate as if preparing to do battle.

"By yourself?"

Ming glanced toward Lily, who'd begun collecting plates. Ever since they'd been old enough to reach the sink, it was understood that their mother would cook and the girls would clean up.

"It's not the way I dreamed of it happening, but yes. By myself."

"I know how much you want children, but have you thought everything through?" Her mother's lips had thinned out of existence.

"Helen, you know she can handle anything she sets her mind to," her father said, ever supportive.

Ming leaned forward in her chair and looked from one parent to the other. "I'm not saying it's going to be a picnic, but I'm ready to be a mom."

"A single mom?" Helen persisted.

"Yes."

"You know my thoughts on this matter." Her mother's gaze grew keen. "How does Jason feel about what you're doing?"

Ming stared at the flowers that surrounded her parents' patio. "He's happy for me."

"He's a good man," her mother said, her expression as tranquil as Ming had ever seen it. "Are you hoping he'll help you?"

"I don't expect him to." Ming wondered if her mother truly

understood that she was doing this on her own. "He's busy with his own life."

Patrick smiled. "I remember how he was with your cousins. He's good with kids. I always thought he'd make a great father."

"You did?" The conversation had taken on a surreal quality for Ming. Since he never intended to get married, she'd never pictured Jason as a father. But now that her dad had mentioned it, she could see Jason relishing the role.

"What I meant about Jason…is he going to help you make the baby?" her mother interjected.

"Why would you think that?"

"You two are close. It seems logical."

Ming kept her panic off her face, but it wasn't easy. "It would mess up our friendship."

"Why? I'm assuming you're going to use a clinic."

This was all hitting a little too close to home. "That's what I figured I'd do." Until Jason came up with the crazy notion of them sleeping together. "I'd better give Lily a hand in the kitchen."

Leaving her parents to process what she'd told them, Ming sidled up to her sister.

"I shared my news." She started rinsing off dishes and stacking them in the dishwasher. "Are you going to tell them you've bought a house in Portland?"

"I changed my mind."

"About the house or Portland?"

"Both."

"Evan must be thrilled." The words slipped out before Ming realized what she was saying. In her defense, she was rattled by her father's speculation about Jason being a great dad and her mother's guess that he was going to help her get pregnant.

"Evan?" Lily tried to sound confused rather than anxious, but her voice buckled beneath the weight of her dismay. "Why would Evan care?"

The cat was out of the bag. Might as well clear the air. "Because you two are dating?"

Ming was aware that keeping a secret about her and Jason while unveiling her sister's love life was the most hypocritical thing she'd done in months.

"Don't be ridiculous."

"Evan admitted it to Jason and he told me."

"I'm sorry I didn't tell you."

"Don't you think you should have?" She didn't want to resent Lily for finding happiness.

"I honestly didn't think anything was going to happen between us."

"Happen between you when, exactly?" Ming's frustration with her own love life was bubbling to the surface. "The first time you went out? The first time he kissed you?"

"I don't want this to come between us."

"Me, either." But at the moment it was, and Ming couldn't dismiss the resentment rumbling through her.

"But I don't want to break up with him." Beneath Lily's determined expression was worry. "I can't."

Shock zipped across Ming's nerve endings. "Is it that serious?"

"He told me he loves me."

"Wow." Ming exhaled in surprise.

It had taken almost a year of dating for Evan to admit such deep feelings for her. As reality smacked her in the face, she was overcome by the urge to curl into a ball and cry her eyes out. What was wrong with her? She wasn't in love with Evan. She'd made her peace with their breakup. Why couldn't she be happy for her sister?

"Do you feel the same?"

Lily wouldn't meet her gaze. "I do."

"How long have you been going out?"

"A couple months. I know it seems fast, but I've been interested in Evan since high school. Until recently, I had no idea he saw me as anything more than your baby sister. Emphasis on the *baby*." Lily's lips curved down at the corners.

There was a five-year difference in their ages. That gap would have seemed less daunting as Lily moved into her twenties and became a successful career woman.

"I guess he's seen the real you at last."

"I want you to know, I never meant for this to happen."

"Of course you didn't."

"It's just that no one has control over who they fall in love with."

What Lily had just told Ming should have relieved her own guilt over what she and Jason were doing. Evan had moved on. He was in love. If he ever discovered what was happening between her and Jason, Evan should be completely accepting. After all, he'd fallen for her sister. All Ming was doing was getting pregnant with Jason's child. It wasn't as if they were heading down the path to blissfully-ever-after.

Struck by the disparity between the perfect happiness of every couple she knew and the failure of her own love life, Ming's heart ached. Her throat closed as misery battered her. Her longing for a man she could never have and her inability to let him go trapped her. It wasn't enough to have Jason as her best friend. She wanted to claim him as her lover and the man she'd spend the rest of her life committed to. On her current path, Ming wasn't sure how she was ever going to find her way out of her discontent, but since she wasn't the sort who moldered in self-pity, she'd better figure it out.

Unwinding in her office after a hectic day of appointments, Ming rechecked the calendar where she'd been keeping track of her fertility cycle for the past few months. According to her history, her period should have started today.

Excitement raced through her. She could be pregnant. For a second she lost the ability to breathe. Was she ready for this? Months of dreaming and hoping for this moment hadn't prepared her for the reality of the change in her life between one heartbeat and the next.

Ming stared at her stomach. Did Jason's child grow inside her? She caught herself mid-thought. This was her child. Not hers and Jason's. She had to stop fooling herself that they were going to be a family. She and Jason were best friends who wanted very different things out of life. They were not a couple. Never would be.

"Are you still here?" Terry leaned into the room and flashed his big white smile. "I thought you had a wedding rehearsal to get to."

Ming nodded. "I'm leaving in ten minutes. The church is only a couple miles away."

"Did those numbers I gave you make you feel better or worse?"

Earlier in the week Terry had opened up the practice's books so she could see all that went into the running of the business. Although part of her curriculum at dental school had involved business courses that would help her if she ever decided to open her own practice, her college days were years behind her.

"I looked them over, but until I get Jason to walk me through everything, I'm still feeling overwhelmed."

"Understandable. Let me know if you have any questions."

After Terry left, Ming grabbed her purse and headed for the door. Until five minutes ago, she'd been looking forward to this weekend. Max and Rachel were a solid couple.

Thanks to Susan Case, Max's mother, the wedding promised to be a magical event. After both Nathan and Sebastian had skipped formal ceremonies—Nathan marrying Emma on a Saint Martin beach and Sebastian opting for an impromptu Las Vegas elopement—Susan had threatened Max with bodily harm if she was denied this last chance at a traditional wedding.

Most brides would have balked at so much input from their future mother-in-law, but Rachel's only family was her sister, and Ming thought the busy employment agency owner appreciated some of the day-to-day details being handled by Max's mother.

When Ming arrived at the church, most of the wedding party was already there. She set her purse in the last pew and let her gaze travel up the aisle to where the minister was speaking to Max. As the best man, Jason stood beside him, listening intently. Ming's breath caught at the sight of him clad in a well-cut dove-gray suit, white shirt and pale green tie.

Was she pregnant? It took effort to keep her fingers from wandering to her abdomen. When she'd embarked on this journey three weeks ago, she'd expected that achieving her goal would bring her great joy and confidence. Joy was there, but it was shadowed by anxiety and doubt.

She wasn't second-guessing her decision to become a mom, but she no longer wanted to do it alone. Jason would freak out if he discovered how much she wanted them to be a real family. Husband, wife, baby. But that's not how he'd visualized his future, and she had no right to be disappointed that they wanted different things.

As if her troubled thoughts had reached out to him, Jason glanced in her direction. When their eyes met, some of her angst eased. Raising his eyebrows, he shot her a crooked grin. Years of experience gave her insight into exactly what he was thinking.

Max couldn't be talked out of this crazy event.

She pursed her lips and shook her head.

You shouldn't even try. He's found his perfect mate.

"Are you two doing that communicating-without-words thing again?"

Ming hadn't noticed Missy stop beside her. With her red hair and hazel eyes, Sebastian's wife wore chocolate brown better than anyone Ming had ever met.

"I guess we are." Ming's gaze returned to Jason.

"Have you ever thought about getting together? I know you

were engaged to his brother and all, but it seems as if you'd be perfect for each other."

"Not likely." Ming had a hard time summoning energy to repeat the tired old excuses. She was stuck in a rut where Jason was concerned, with no clue how to get out. "We're complete opposites."

"No one is more different than Sebastian and I." Missy grinned. "It can be a lot of fun."

Based on the redhead's saucy smile, Ming had little trouble imagining just how much fun the newlyweds were having. She sighed. Prior conversations with Emma, Missy and Rachel had shown her that not everyone's road to romance was straight and trouble-free, but Ming knew she wasn't even on a road with Jason. More like a faint deer trail through the woods.

"He doesn't want to fall in love."

Missy surveyed the three Case men as the minister guided them into position near the front of the church. "So make him."

Rather than lecture Missy about how hopeless it was to try changing Jason's mind about love and marriage, Ming clamped her lips together and forced a smile. What good would it do to argue with a newly married woman who was a poster child for happily ever after?

As she practiced her walk up the aisle on Nathan's arm, she had a hard time focusing on the minister's instructions. Casting surreptitious glances at Jason, standing handsome and confident beside Max, she fought against despair as she realized there would never be a day when the man she loved waited for her at the front of the church. She would never wear an elegant gown of white satin and shimmering pearls and speak the words that would bind them together forever.

"And then you separate, each going to your place." The minister signaled to the organist. "Here the music changes to signal that the bride is on her way."

While everyone watched Rachel float up the aisle, her happiness making it appear as if her feet didn't touch the ground,

Ming stared down at the floor and fought against the tightness in her throat. She was going to drive herself mad pining for an ending that could never be.

Twenty minutes later, the wedding party was dismissed. They trooped back down the aisle, two-by-two, with Nathan and Ming bringing up the rear.

"How's Emma doing?" she asked. Nathan's wife was five days past her due date.

"She's miserable." Nathan obviously shared his wife's discomfort. "Can't wait for the baby to come."

"I didn't see her. Is she here tonight?"

"No." A muscle jumped in his jaw. "I told her to stay home and rest up. Tomorrow is going to be a long day." Nathan scowled. "But if I know her, she's working on the last of her orders to get them done before the baby arrives."

Nathan's wife made some of the most unique and beautiful jewelry Ming had ever seen. Missy's wedding set was one of her designs. From what Jason had told her, Max and Rachel's wedding rings had been created by Emma as well.

"I'm worried she's not going to slow down even after the baby arrives," Nathan continued, looking both exasperated and concerned. "She needs to take better care of herself."

"Why, when she has you to take care of her?"

Nathan gave her a wry grin. "I suppose you're right. See you tomorrow."

Smiling thoughtfully at Nathan's eagerness to get home to his wife, Ming went to fetch her purse. When she straightened, she discovered Jason standing beside her. He slipped his fingers through hers and squeezed gently.

"I missed you this week."

Shivers danced along her spine at his earnest tone. "I missed you, too."

More than she cared to admit. Although they'd talked every day on the phone, their conversations had revolved around the dental practice financials and other safe topics. They hadn't discussed that Evan was in love with Lily, and Ming wasn't sure Jason even knew.

"I don't suppose I could talk you into coming home with me tonight," he murmured, drawing her after the departing couples.

Although tempted by his offer, she shook her head. "I promised Lily we'd hang out, and I have an early appointment to get my hair and makeup done tomorrow." She didn't like making up excuses, but after what she'd started to suspect earlier, the only thing she wanted to do was take the pregnancy test she'd bought on the way to the church and see if it was positive. "Tomorrow after the reception."

Jason walked her to her car and held her door while she got behind the wheel. He lingered with his hand on the door. The silence between them grew heavy with expectation. Ming's heart slowed. The crease between his brows told her that something troubled him.

She was the first to break the silence. "Evan's in love with Lily and she's decided to stay in Houston."

"How do you feel about that?"

"I'm thrilled."

"I mean about how Evan feels about her."

With a determined smile she shook her head. "I'm happy for him and Lily."

"You're really okay with it?"

"I'm going to be a mom. That's what I'm truly excited about. That's where I need to put all my energy."

"Because you know I'm here if you want to talk."

"Really, I'm fine," she said, keeping her voice bright and untroubled. She knew he was just being a good friend, but she couldn't stop herself from wishing his concern originated in the same sort of love she felt for him. "See you at the restaurant."

He stared at her for a long moment more before stepping back. "Save me a seat."

And with that, he closed her car door.

Eleven

Jason had never been so glad to be done with an evening. Sitting beside Ming while toast after toast had been made to the bride and groom, he'd never felt more alone. But it's what he wanted. A lifetime with no attachments. No worries that he'd ever become so despondent over losing a woman that he'd want to kill himself.

Logic and years of distance told him that his father had been in an extremely dark place after the death of his wife and daughter. But there was no reason to believe that Jason would ever suffer such a devastating loss. And if he did, wasn't he strong enough to keep from sinking into a hole and never coming out?

And yet, his reaction to that photo of her dancing hadn't exactly been rational. Neither had the way he'd demanded that she declare herself to be his. Oh, he'd claimed that he didn't want to lead her on. The truth was he was deathly afraid of losing her.

"I'm heading home." Ming leaned her shoulder against his.

Her breath brushed his neck with intoxicating results. "Can you walk me to my car?"

"I think I'll leave, too." The evening was winding down. Sebastian and Missy had already departed.

As soon as they cleared the front door, he took her hand. Funny how such a simple act brought him so much contentment. "Did I mention you look beautiful tonight?"

"Thank you." Only her eyes smiled at him. The rest of her features were frozen into somber lines.

They reached her car and before he could open her door, she put a hand on his arm. "This is probably not the best place for this…" She glanced around, gathered a breath and met his gaze. Despite her tension, joy glittered in her dark eyes. "I'm pregnant."

Her declaration crushed the air from his lungs. He'd been expecting it, but somehow now, knowing his child grew inside her, he was beyond thrilled.

"You're sure?"

"As sure as an early pregnancy test can be." Her fingers bit into his arm. "I took one at the restaurant." She laughed unsteadily. "How crazy is that? I couldn't even wait until I got home."

Jason wrapped his arms around her and held her against him. A baby. Their baby. He wanted to rush back into the restaurant and tell everyone. They were going to be parents. Reality penetrated his giddy mood. Except she didn't want to share the truth with anyone. She intended to raise the child on her own.

"I'm glad you couldn't wait," he told her, his words muffled against her hair. "It's wonderful news."

From chest to thigh, her long, lean body was aligned with his. How many months until holding her like this he'd feel only her rounded stomach? Or would he even get to snuggle with her, her head resting on his shoulder, her arms locked around his waist?

"Of course, this means…"

Knowing what was coming next, Jason growled. "You aren't seriously going to break up with me on the eve of Max's wedding."

"Break up with you?" She tipped her head back so he could see her smile, but she wouldn't meet his eyes. "That would require us to be dating."

But they'd sworn never to explore that path. Would they miss a chance to discover that the real reason they were such good friends was because they were meant to be together?

Are you listening to yourself? What happened to swearing you'd never fall in love?

Frustrated by conflicting desires, Jason's hold on her tightened. Her breath hitched as he lowered his head and claimed her mouth. Heat flared between them. Their tongues tangled while delicious sensations licked at his nerves. She was an endless feast for his senses. A balm for his soul. She challenged him and made him a better person. And now she was pregnant with his child. They could be happy together.

All he needed to do was let her in.

He broke off the kiss and dragged his lips across her cheek. What existed in his heart was hers alone. He could tell her and change everything.

The silence between them lengthened. Finally, Ming slid her palm down his heaving chest and stepped back.

"We're just good friends who happen to be sleeping together until one of us got pregnant," she said, her wry tone at odds with her somber eyes.

"And we promised nothing would get in the way of our friendship."

She sagged against him. "And it won't."

"Not ever."

Our baby.

Jason's words the previous night had given her goose bumps.

Almost ten hours later, Ming rubbed her arms as the sensation lingered.

My baby.

She tried to infuse the declaration with conviction, but couldn't summon the strength. Not surprising, when his claim filled her with unbridled joy. It was impossible to be practical when her heart was singing and she felt lighter than air.

Pulling into the parking lot of the salon Susan Case had selected based on their excellent reputation, Ming spent a few minutes channeling her jubilation over her baby news into happiness for Rachel and Max. It was easy to do.

The bride was glowing as she chatted with her sister, Hailey, Missy and Susan. As Ming joined the group, two stylists took charge of Rachel, escorting her to a chair near the back. Rachel had let her hair grow out from the boyish cut she'd had when Ming had first met her. For her wedding look, the stylists pinned big loops of curls all over her head and attached tiny white flowers throughout.

Unaccustomed to being the center of attention, Rachel endured being fussed over with good grace. Watching the stylists in action, Ming was certain the bride would be delighted with the results.

Because all the bridesmaids had long hair, they were styled with the front pulled away from their face and soft waves cascading down their back. When the four girls lined up so Susan could take a photo, the resulting picture was feminine and romantic.

Although the wedding wasn't until four, the photographer was expecting them to be at the church, dressed in their wedding finery by one. With a hundred or more photos to smile for and because she'd skipped breakfast after oversleeping, Ming decided she'd better grab lunch before heading to the church. She ended up being the last to arrive.

Naturally her gaze went straight to Jason. Standing halfway up the aisle, model-gorgeous in his tuxedo, he looked far more stressed than the groom. Ming flashed back to their senior prom, the evening that marked the beginning of the end for her in terms of experiencing true love.

"Don't you look handsome," she exclaimed as he drew near. Over the years, she'd had a lot of practice pretending she wasn't infatuated with him. That stood her in good stead as Jason pulled her into his arms for a friendly hug.

"You smell as edible as you look," he murmured. "Whose insane idea was it to dress you in a color that made me want to devour you?"

For her fall wedding, Rachel had chosen strapless empire waist bridesmaid dresses in muted apple green. They would all be carrying bouquets of orange, yellow and fuchsia.

Ming quivered as his sexy voice rumbled through her. If he kept staring at her with hungry eyes, she might not be able to wait until after the wedding to get him alone. A deep breath helped Ming master her wayward desires. Today was about Max and Rachel.

"Susan proposed apple green, I believe." She'd never know how she kept her tone even given the chaos of her emotions.

"Remind me to thank her later."

Ming restrained a foolish giggle and pushed him to arm's length so she could check him out in turn. "I like you in a tux. You should wear one more often."

"If I'd known how much fun it would be to have you undress me with your eyes, I would have done so sooner."

"I'm not undressing—" She stopped the flow of words as Emma waddled within earshot.

"I don't know what you're planning on taking off," the very pregnant woman said as she stepped into the pew beside them, "but I'd start with what he's wearing."

Jason smirked at Ming, but there was no time for her to respond because the photographer's assistant called for the wedding party to come to the front of the church.

With everyone in a festive mood, it was easy for Ming to

laugh and joke with the rest of Rachel's attendants as they posed for one photo after another. The photographer's strict schedule allowed little time for her to dwell on how close she'd been to her own wedding six months earlier, or whether she might be in this same position months from now if things continued to progress with Lily and Evan.

But in the half-hour lull between photos and ceremony, she had more than enough quiet to contemplate what might have been for her and to ponder the future.

She kept apart from the rest of the group, not wanting her bout of melancholy to mar the bride and groom's perfect day. Shortly before the ceremony was supposed to start, Jason approached her and squeezed her hand.

"You look pensive."

"I was just thinking about the baby."

"Me, too." His expression was grave. "I want to tell everyone I'm the father."

Ming's heart convulsed. Last night, after discovering she was pregnant, she'd longed to stand at Jason's side and tell everyone they were having a baby. Of course, doing it would bring up questions about whether or not they were together.

"Are you sure this is a good idea?"

"The only reason you wanted to keep quiet was because you didn't want to hurt Evan. But he's moved on with your sister."

"So you decided this because Evan and Lily are involved?"

"It isn't about them. It's about us. I'm going to be in the child's life on a daily basis." His expression was more determined than she'd ever seen it. "I think I should be there as his dad rather than as Uncle Jason."

He'd said *us*.

Only it wasn't about her and Jason. Not in the way she wanted. Ming's heart shuddered like a damaged window battered by strong winds. At any second it could shatter into a thousand pieces. She loved the idea that he wanted to be a father, but she couldn't ignore her yearning to have him be there for her as well.

"Come on, you two," Missy called as the wedding party began moving into position near the church's inner door. "We're on."

Jason strode to his position in line and Ming relaxed her grip on her bouquet before the delicate stems of the Gerber daisies snapped beneath the intensity of her conflicting emotions.

As maid of honor, Rachel's sister, Hailey, was already in place behind Max and his parents. The music began signaling the trio to start down the aisle. The groom looked relaxed and ready as he accompanied his parents to their places at the front of the church.

The bright flowers in Ming's hands quivered as she stood beside Nathan. He appeared on edge. His distress let Ming forget about her own troubles.

"Are you okay?" she asked.

Lines bracketed his mouth. "I tried to convince Emma to stay home. Although she wouldn't admit it, she's really having a difficult time today. I'm worried about her."

"I'm sure it's natural to be uncomfortable when you're past your due date," Ming said and saw immediately that her words had little effect on the overprotective father-to-be. "She'll let you know if anything is wrong."

"I'm concerned that she won't." He glanced behind him at the bride. "She didn't want anything to disturb your day."

Rachel put her hand on Nathan's arm, her expression sympathetic. "I appreciate both of you being here today, but if you think she needs to be at home, take her there right after the ceremony."

Nathan leaned down and grazed Rachel's cheek with his lips. "I will. Thank you."

He seemed marginally less like an overwound spring as they took their turn walking down the aisle. It might have helped that his wife beamed at him from the second row. Ming's stomach twisted in reaction to their happiness. Even for someone who wasn't newly pregnant and madly in love with a man who refused to feel the same way, it was easy to get overwhelmed by emotions at a wedding. Holding herself together became easier as she watched Rachel start down the aisle.

The bride wore a long strapless dress unadorned by beading or lace. Diamond and pearl earrings were her only jewelry. Her styling was romantic and understated, allowing the bride's beauty and her utter happiness to shine.

With her father dead and her mother out of her life since she was four, Rachel had no one to give her away. Ming's sadness lasted only until she realized this was the last time Rachel would walk alone. At the end of the ceremony, she would be Max's wife and part of his family.

Ming swallowed past the lump in her throat as the minister began talking. The rest of the ceremony passed in a blur. She was roused out of her thoughts by the sound of clapping. Max had swept Rachel into a passionate kiss. The music began once more and the happy couple headed back down the aisle, joined for life.

Because they'd been the last up the aisle, Nathan and Ming were the last to return down it. They didn't get far, however. As they drew near Emma, Ming realized something was wrong. Nathan's wife was bending forward at the waist and in obvious pain. When Nathan hastened to her side, she clutched his forearm and leaned into his strength.

"I think it might be time to get to the hospital," she said, her brown eyes appearing darker than ever in her pale face.

"How long has this been going on?" he demanded.

"Since this morning."

Nathan growled.

"I'm fine. I wanted both of us to be here for Rachel and Max. And now I'd like to go to the hospital and give birth to our son."

"Stubborn woman," Nathan muttered as he put a supporting arm around his wife and escorted her down the aisle.

"Do you want us to come with you?" Max's mother asked, following on their heels. She reached her hand back to her husband.

"No." Emma shook her head. "Stay and enjoy the party. The baby probably won't come anytime soon." But as she said it, another contraction stopped her in her tracks.

"I'm going to get the car." Handing his wife off to Ming, Nathan raced out of the church.

Ming and Emma continued their slow progress.

"Has he always been like this?" Ming asked, amused and ever so envious.

"It all started when my father decided to make marrying me part of a business deal Nathan was doing with Montgomery Oil. Since then he's got this crazy idea in his head that I need to be taken care of."

"I think it's sweet."

Emma's lips moved into a fond smile. "It's absolutely wonderful."

By the time Ming got Emma settled into Nathan's car and returned to the church, half the guests had made it through the reception line and had spilled onto the street. Since she wasn't the immediate family of the bride and groom, she stood off to one side and waited until the wedding party was free so she could tell them what had happened to Nathan and Emma.

"The contractions seemed fairly close together," Ming said in answer to Susan Case's question regarding Emma's labor. "She said she'd started having them this morning, so I don't know how far along she is."

"Hopefully Nathan will call us from the hospital and let us know," Max's father said.

Sebastian nodded. "I'm sure he will."

"In the meantime," Max said, smiling down at his glowing wife, "we have a reception to get to."

A limo awaited them at the curb to take the group to The Corinthian, a posh venue in downtown Houston's historical district. Ming had never attended an event there, but she'd heard nothing but raves from Missy and Emma. And they were right. The space took its name from the fluted Corinthian columns that flanked the long colonnade where round tables of ten had been placed for the reception. Once the lobby for the First National Bank, the hall's thirty-five-foot ceilings and tall windows now made it an elegant place to hold galas, wedding receptions and lavish birthday parties.

Atop burgundy damask table cloths, gold silverware flanked gilded chargers and white china rimmed with gold. Flickering votive candles in glass holders nestled amongst flowers in Rachel's chosen palette of gold, yellow and deep orange.

Ming had never seen anything so elegant and inviting.

"Susan really outdid herself," Missy commented as she and her husband stopped beside Ming to admire the view. "It almost makes me wish Sebastian and I hadn't run off to Las Vegas to get married." She grinned up at her handsome husband. "Of course, having to wait months to become his wife wouldn't have been worth all this."

Sebastian lifted her hand and brushed a kiss across her knuckles. The heat that passed between them in that moment made Ming blink.

She cleared her throat. "So, you don't regret eloping?"

Missy shook her head, her gaze still locked on her husband's face. "Having a man as deliberate and cautious as Sebastian jump impulsively into a life-changing event as big as marriage was the most amazing, romantic, sexy thing ever."

"He obviously knew what he wanted," Ming murmured, her gaze straying to where Jason laughed with Max's father.

Sebastian's deep voice resonated with conviction as he said, "Indeed I did."

Twelve

Keeping Ming's green-clad form in view as she chatted with their friends, Jason dialed his brother's cell. Evan hadn't mentioned skipping the wedding, and it was out of character for him to just not show. When voice mail picked up, Jason left a message. Then he called his dad, but Tony hadn't heard from Evan, either. Buzzing with concern, Jason slid the phone back into his pocket and headed for Ming.

She was standing alone, her attention on the departing Sebastian and Missy, a wistful expression on her face. Their happiness was tangible. Like a shot to his head, Jason comprehended Ming's fascination. Despite her insistence that she wasn't cut out for marriage, it's what she longed for. Evan had ended their engagement and broken her heart in the process. Her decision to become a single mom was Ming's way of coping with loneliness.

How had he not understood this before? Probably because he didn't want it to be true. He hated to think that she'd find someone new to love and he'd lose her all over again.

Over dinner, while Rachel and Max indulged the guests by kissing at every clinking of glassware, Jason pondered his dinner companion and where the future would take them after tonight. He'd been happier in the past couple of weeks than he'd been in years. It occurred to him just how much he'd missed the closeness that had marked their relationship through high school.

He wasn't ready to give up anything that he'd won. He wanted Ming as the best friend whom he shared his hopes and fears with. He wanted endless steamy nights with the sexy temptress who haunted his dreams. Most of all, he wanted the family that the birth of their baby would create.

All without losing the independence he was accustomed to.

Impossible.

He wasn't foolish enough to think Ming would happily go along with what he wanted, so it was up to Jason to figure out how much he was comfortable giving up and for her to decide what she was willing to live with.

By the time the dancing started, Jason had his proposition formed. Tonight was for romance. Tomorrow morning over breakfast he would tell her his plan and they would start hashing out a strategy.

"Hmm," she murmured as they swayed together on the dance floor. "It's been over a decade since we danced together. I'd forgotten how good you are at this."

"There are things I'm even better at." He executed a spin that left her gasping with laughter. "How soon can we get out of here?"

"It's barely nine." She tried to look shocked, but her eyes glowed at his impatience.

"It's the bride and groom's party." In the crush on the dance floor, he doubted if anyone would notice his hand venturing over her backside. "They have to stick around. We can leave anytime."

Her body quivered, but she grabbed his hand and repositioned it on her waist. "I don't think Max and Rachel would appreciate us ducking out early."

Jason glanced toward the happy newlyweds. "I don't think they'll even notice."

But in the end, they stayed until midnight and saw Max and Rachel off. The newlyweds were spending the night at a downtown hotel and flying on Monday to Gulf Shores, Alabama, where Max owned a house. The location had seemed an odd choice to Jason until he heard the story of how Max and Rachel met in the beach town five years earlier.

As the guests enjoyed one last dance, Jason slid his palm into the small of Ming's back. "Did your sister say anything about Evan's plan to miss the wedding today?"

A line appeared between Ming's finely drawn eyebrows. "No. Did you try calling him?"

"Yes. And I spoke with my dad, too. He hadn't heard from him. This just isn't like Evan."

"Let me call Lily and see if she knows what's going on." Ming dialed her sister's cell and waited for her to pick up. "Evan didn't make the wedding. Did he tell you he was planning on skipping it?" Ming met Jason's eyes and shook her head.

"Find out when she last spoke to him."

"Jason wants to know when you last heard from him. I'm going to put you on speaker, okay?"

"Last night."

It was odd for his brother to go a whole day without talking to one of them. "Is something going on with him?"

"Last night he proposed." Lily sounded miserable.

"Wow," Ming exclaimed, her excitement sounding genuine.

"I told him I couldn't marry him."

Anxiety kicked Jason in the gut. "I guess I don't need to ask how he took that."

Twice he'd seen Evan slip into the same self-destructiveness their father had once exhibited. The first time as a senior in high school when his girlfriend of three years decided to end things a week after graduation. Evan had spent the entire summer in a black funk. The second time was about a year before he and Ming had started dating. His girlfriend of two years had dumped him and married her ex-boyfriend. But Jason suspected neither of those events had upset Evan to the extent that losing Lily would.

"I don't understand," Ming said. "I thought you loved him."

"I do." Lily's voice shook. "I just can't do that to you."

Ming looked to Jason for help. "I don't blame either of you for finding each other."

While the sisters talked, Jason dialed his brother again. When he heard Evan's voice mail message, he hung up. He'd already left three messages tonight. No need to leave another.

"Do you mind if I stop by Evan's before I head home?" Jason quizzed Ming as he escorted her to where she'd left her car. "I'll feel better if I see that he's all right."

"Sure."

"Just let yourself in. I shouldn't be more than fifteen minutes behind you."

But when he got to his brother's house, he discovered why Evan hadn't made it to the wedding and hadn't called him back. His brother was lying unconscious on his living room floor while an infomercial played on the television.

An open bottle of pain pills was tipped over on the coffee table. Empty. In a flash Jason became a fifteen-year-old again, finding his father passed out in the running car, the garage filled with exhaust. With a low cry, Jason dropped to his knees beside his brother. The steady rise and fall of Evan's chest reassured Jason that his brother wasn't dead. Sweat broke out as he grabbed his brother's shoulder and shook.

"Evan. Damn it. Wake up." His throat locked up as he searched for some sign that his brother was near consciousness. Darkness closed over his vision. He was back in the shadow-filled garage, where poisonous fumes had raked his throat and filled his lungs. His chest tightened with the need to cough. His brother couldn't die. He had to wake him. With both hands on Evan's shoulders, Jason shook him hard. "Evan."

A hand shoved him in the chest, breaking through the walls of panic that had closed in on Jason.

"Geez, Jason." His brother blinked in groggy confusion. "What the hell?"

Chest tight, Jason sat on the floor and raked his fingers through his hair. Relief hadn't hit him yet. He couldn't draw a full breath. Oxygen deprivation made his head spin. He dug the heels of his palms against his eyes and felt moisture.

Grabbing the pill bottle, he shook it in his brother's face. "How many of these did you take?"

"Two. That's all I had."

And if there had been more? Would he have taken them? "Are you sure?"

Evan batted away his brother's hand. "What the hell is wrong with you?"

"You didn't make the wedding. So I came over to check on you. Then I saw you on the floor and I thought…" He couldn't finish the thought.

"I didn't make the wedding because I wasn't in the mood."

"And these?"

"I went for a bicycle ride this morning to clear my head and took a spill that messed up my back. That's why I'm lying on the floor. I seized up."

"I left three messages." Jason's hands trembled in the aftermath of the adrenaline rush. "Why didn't you call me back?"

"I turned my phone off. I didn't want to talk to anyone." Evan rolled to his side and pushed into a sitting position. "What are you doing here?"

"Lily said she turned down your proposal. I thought maybe you'd done something stupid."

But Evan wasn't listening. He sucked in a ragged breath. "She's afraid it'll hurt her sister if we get married." He blinked three times in rapid succession. "And she wouldn't listen to me when I said Ming wouldn't be as upset as Lily thinks."

Jason couldn't believe what he was hearing. Was this Evan's way of convincing himself he wasn't the bad guy in this scenario? "How do you figure? It's only been six months since your engagement ended."

Evan got to his feet, and Jason glimpsed frustration in his brother's painful movements. "I know you think I messed up, but I did us both a favor."

"How do you figure?" Jason stood as well, his earlier worry lost in a blast of righteous irritation.

"She wasn't as much in love with me as you think she was."

Jason couldn't believe his brother was trying to shift some of the blame for their breakup onto Ming. "You forget who you're talking to. I know Ming. I saw how happy she was with you."

"Yeah, well. Not as happy as she could have been."

"And whose fault was that?" He spun away from Evan and caught his reflection in the large living room windows. He looked hollow. As if the emotion of a moment before had emptied him of all energy.

"I worked hard at the relationship," he said, his voice dull.

"And Ming didn't?"

A long silence followed his question. When Jason turned around, his brother was sitting on the couch, his head in his hands.

"Ming and I were a mistake. I know that now. It's Lily I love." He lifted his head. His eyes were bleak. "I don't know how I'm supposed to live without her."

Jason winced at his brother's phrasing. His cell rang. Ming was calling.

"Is everything okay with Evan?" The concern in her soft voice was a balm to Jason's battered emotions. "It's been almost a half an hour."

He couldn't tell her what he thought was going on while

Evan could overhear. "He threw his back out in a bicycle-riding accident this morning."

"Oh, no. There should be some ice packs in his freezer."

"I'll get him all squared away and be there in a half an hour."

"Take your time. It's been a long couple of days and I'm exhausted. Wake me when you get here."

He ended the call and found himself smiling at the image of Ming asleep in his bed. This past week without her had been hell. Not seeing her. Touching her. He hadn't been able to get her out of his mind.

"Ming told me to put you on ice." Talking to her had lightened his mood. He needed to get his brother settled so he could get home. "Do you want me to bring the ice packs to you here or upstairs?"

"What the hell do I care?"

Evan's sharp retort wasn't like him. Lily's refusal had hit him hard. Fighting anxiety over his brother's dark mood, Jason bullied Evan upstairs and settled him in his bed. Observing his brother's listless state, Jason was afraid to leave him alone.

"Are you going to be okay?"

Evan glared at him. "Why aren't you gone?"

"I thought maybe I should stick around a bit longer."

"Sounds like Ming is waiting for you." Evan deliberately looked away from Jason, making him wonder if Evan suspected what Jason and Ming had been up to.

"She is."

"Then get out of here."

Jason headed for the door. "I'll be back to check on you in the morning."

"Don't bother. I'd rather be alone."

The fifteen-minute drive home offered Jason little time to process what had happened with Evan. What stood out for him was his brother's despair at losing the woman he loved.

He stepped from his garage into the kitchen, and stood in the dark, listening. The silence soothed him, guided him toward the safe place he'd created inside himself. The walled fortress that kept unsettling emotions at bay.

He glanced around the kitchen and smiled as his gaze landed on the chair where he and Ming had made love for the first time. Just one of the great moments that had happened in this room. In almost every room in the house.

He had dozens of incredible memories featuring Ming, and not one of them would be possible if he hadn't opened the doors to his heart and let himself experience raw, no-holds-barred passion.

But desire he could handle. It was the other strong feelings Ming invoked that plagued him. Being with her these past few weeks had made him as happy as he ever remembered. He couldn't stop imagining a life with her.

And this morning he'd been ready to make his dreams reality.

But all that had changed tonight when he'd mistaken what was going on with Evan and relived the terror of the night he'd found his father in the garage. The fear had been real. His pledge to never fall in love—the decision that had stopped making sense these last few weeks—became rational once more.

He couldn't bear to lose Ming. If they tried being a couple and it didn't work out, the damage done to their friendship might never heal. Could he take that risk?

No.

Jason marched up the stairs, confident that he was making the right decision for both of them. He'd expected to find her in his bed, but the soft light spilling from the room next door drew him to the doorway. In what had been his former den, Ming occupied the rocking chair by the window, a stuffed panda clutched against her chest, her gaze on the crib. Encased in serenity, she'd never looked more beautiful.

"Where's all your stuff?" she asked, her voice barely above a whisper.

"It's in the garage."

Gone was the memorabilia of his racing days. In its place stood a crib, changing table and rocker. The walls had been painted a soft yellow. The bedding draped across the crib had pastel jungle animals parading between palm trees and swinging from vines.

She left the chair and walked toward him past the pictures that had graced her childhood bedroom. He'd gotten them from her parents. Her father was sentimental about things like that.

"Who helped you do this?"

"No one." His arms went around her slim form, pulling her against his thudding heart. He rested his chin on her head. "Except for the paint and new carpet. I hired those out."

"You picked all this out by yourself?"

Jason had never shopped for a Christmas or birthday present without her help, and Ming was obviously having a hard time wrapping her head around what he'd accomplished in such a short time.

"Do you like it?" he prompted, surprised by how much he wanted her approval.

"It's perfect."

Nestled in Jason's arms, Ming wouldn't have believed it was possible to fall any deeper in love with him, but at that moment she did. The room had been crafted with loving care by a guy who was as comfortable in a department store as a cat in a kennel of yapping dogs.

He was an amazing man and he would be a terrific father. She was lucky to have such a good friend.

Jason's arms tightened. "I'm glad you like the room. It turned out better than I expected."

"I love you." The courage to say those words had been building in her ever since Jason told her he wanted to go public about his part in her pregnancy. She'd always been truthful with Jason. She'd be a fool and a coward to hide something so important from him.

He tensed.

She gestured at the room. "Seeing this, I thought…" Well, that wasn't true. She'd been reacting emotionally to Jason's decision to be an active father and to his decorating this room to surprise her. "I want to be more than your best friend. I want to be a family with you and our baby."

Fear that he'd react badly didn't halt her confession. As her love for him strengthened with each day that passed, she knew she was going to bare her soul at some point. It might as well be sooner so they could talk it through. "I know that's not what you want to hear," she continued. "But I can't keep pretending I'm okay with just being your best friend."

When his mouth flattened into a grim line, Ming pulled free of his embrace. Without his warmth, she was immediately chilled. She rubbed her arms, but the cold she felt came from deep inside.

"Evan knew how you felt, didn't he?" Jason made it sound like an accusation. "Tonight. He told me you weren't as in love with him as I thought."

"Why did he tell you that?"

"I assumed because he was justifying falling for Lily."

"I swear I never gave him any reason to suspect how I felt about you. I couldn't even admit it to myself until I saw you crash. You've always been so determined not to fall in love or get married." Ming's eyes burned as she spoke. "I knew you'd never let yourself feel anything more for me than friendship, so I bottled everything up and almost married your brother because I was completely convinced you and I could never be."

He was silent a long time. "I haven't told you what happened with Evan tonight."

"Is he okay?"

"When I got to his house I found him on the floor with an empty bottle of painkillers beside him. I thought he was so upset over Lily refusing to marry him that he tried to kill himself."

Ming's heart squeezed in sympathy. The wound he'd suffered when he'd found his father in the garage with the car running had cut deeper than anyone knew. The damage had been permanent. Something Jason would never be free from.

"Did he?" She'd been with Evan for three years and had never seen any sign of depression, but Jason's concern was so keen, she was ready to believe her ex-fiancé had done something to harm himself.

"No. He'd only taken a couple." A muscle jumped in Jason's jaw. He stared at the wall behind her, his gaze on a distant place. "I've never seen him like this. He's devastated that Lily turned him down."

"They're not us."

"What does that mean?" Annoyance edged his voice, warning her that he wasn't in the mood to listen.

She refused to be deterred. "Just because they might not be able to make it work doesn't mean we can't."

"Maybe. But I don't want to take the risk." He gripped her hands and held on tight.

"Have you considered what will happen if we go down that road and it doesn't work out between us? You could come to hate me. I don't want to lose my best friend."

Ming had thought about it, but she had no easy answer. "I don't want to lose you, either, but I'm struggling to think of you as just my best friend. What I feel for you is so much deeper and stronger than that."

And here's where things got tricky. She could love Jason to the best of her ability, but he was convinced that loving someone meant opening up to overwhelming loss, and she couldn't force him to accept something different. But she could make him face what he feared most.

"I love you," she said, her voice brimming with conviction. "I need you to love me in return. I know you do. I feel it every time you touch me." She paused to let her words sink in. "And because we love each other, whether you want to admit it or not, our friendship is altered. We're no longer just best friends. We're a whole lot more."

Through her whole speech he regarded her with an unflinching stare. Now he spoke. "So, what are you saying?"

"I'm saying what you're trying to preserve by not moving our relationship forward no longer exists."

A muscle jumped in his jaw as he stared at her. Silence surrounded them.

"Is this an ultimatum?"

Was it? When she started, she hadn't meant it to be.

"No. It's a statement of intent. Our friendship as it once was is over. I love you and I want us to be a family."

"And if I don't accept that things have to change?"

She made no attempt to hide her sadness. "Then we both lose."

Half an hour after her conversation with Jason, Ming plopped onto her window seat and stared at the dark backyard. She didn't bother changing into a nightgown and sliding between the sheets. What was the point when there was no way she was going to be able to sleep? Her conversation with Jason played over and over in her mind.

Could she have handled it better? Probably not. Jason was never going to relish hearing the truth. He liked their relationship exactly the way it was. Casual. Comfortable. Constant. No doubt he'd resent her for shaking things up.

Dawn found her perched on a stool at the breakfast bar, her gaze on the pool in her backyard. She cradled a cup of coffee in her hands.

"You're up early." Lily entered the kitchen and made a beeline for the cupboard where she kept the ingredients for her healthy breakfast shake. "Couldn't sleep?"

"You're an idiot." Ming knew it wasn't fair to take her frustration out on her sister, but Lily was throwing away love.

Her sister leaned back against the countertop. "Good morning to you, too."

"I'm sorry." Ming shook her head. Her heart hurt. "I'm sitting here thinking how lucky you are that Evan wants to marry you. And it just makes me so mad that you turned him down."

"Are you sure that's what you're mad about?"

Ming blinked and focused her gaze on Lily. "Of course."

"The whole time you were with Evan I was miserable."

Seeing where her sister was going, Ming laughed. "And you think I'm unhappy because Evan loves you?"

"Are you?"

"Not even a little."

"Then why are you so upset?"

With shaky hands, Ming set her cup down and rubbed her face. "I'm pregnant."

After all the arguments she'd had with her sister, the last thing Ming expected was for Lily to rush over and hug her. Ming's throat closed.

"Aren't you going to scold me for doing the wrong thing?" Ming asked.

"I'm sorry I've been so unsupportive. It wasn't fair of me to impose my opinions on you. I'm really happy for you." Lily sounded sincere. "Why didn't you didn't tell me you'd gone to the clinic?"

"Because I didn't go."

"Then how…?" Lily's eyes widened. "Jason?"

"Yes." Ming couldn't believe how much it relieved her to share the truth.

"Have you thought about what this is going to do to Evan?" It was natural that this would be Lily's reaction. She loved Evan and wanted to protect him.

"I was more worried about it before I knew he'd moved on with you." Ming crossed her arms. "But now you've turned down his proposal, and neither Jason nor I want to keep his involvement a secret."

"Why did you have to pick Jason?" Lily shook her head.

Ming refrained from asking Lily why Evan had picked her. "When I decided to have a baby, I wasn't keen on having a stranger's child. Jason understood, and because he's my best friend, he agreed to help."

"So you slept with him."

Ming's cheeks grew warm. "Yes."

"Does that mean you two are a couple?"

"No. As much as I want more, I understood that us being together was a temporary thing. Once I got pregnant, we'd stop."

"But now you're in love with him." Not a question, a statement. "Does he know?"

"I told him last night."

Lily squeezed Ming's hands. "How did he react?"

"Exactly how I'd expected him to." Ming put on her bravest smile. "He has his reasons for never falling in love."

"What are you talking about? He loves you."

"I know, but he won't admit to anything stronger than friendship."

"A friend he wants to sleep with." Lily's smile was wry.

"We have some pretty fabulous chemistry." The chuckle that vibrated in Ming's chest was bittersweet. "But he won't let it become anything more."

"Oh, Ming."

"It's not as if I didn't know how he feels." Ming slid off her stool and looped her arm through Lily's. She tugged her sister toward the stairs. "It just makes it that much more important for you to accept Evan's proposal." Closing her ears to her sister's protests, Ming packed Lily an overnight bag and herded her into the garage. "One of us deserves to be madly in love."

Fifteen minutes later, they pulled up in front of Evan's house. The longing on Lily's face told Ming she'd been right to meddle. She scooped up her sister's overnight bag and breezed up the front walk, Lily trailing slowly behind.

"Are you sure about this?" Lily questioned as they waited for Evan to answer the door.

"Positive. What a horrible sister I would be to stand in the way of your happiness."

Evan opened his door and leaned on it. He looked gray beneath his tan. "Ming? What are you doing here?"

"My sister tells me she turned down your marriage proposal."

His gaze shot beyond Ming to where Lily lingered at the bottom of his steps, but he said nothing.

Not being able to fix what was wrong in her own love life didn't mean she couldn't make sure Lily got her happily-ever-after. "She claims she turned you down because she thinks I would be hurt, but I'm moving on with my life and I don't want to be her excuse for not marrying you." Ming fixed her ex-fiancé with a steely gaze. "Do you promise you'll love her forever?"

"Of course." Evan was indignant.

Fighting to keep her composure intact, Ming headed down the steps to hug her sister. Confident they were out of Evan's hearing, she whispered, "Don't you dare come home until you've got an engagement ring on your finger."

Lily glanced at Evan. "Are you going to take your own advice and go talk to Jason?"

Ming shook her head. "Too much has happened over the last few days. We both need some time to adjust."

"He'll come around. You'll see."

But Ming didn't see. She merely nodded to pacify her sister. "I hope you're right."

Finding Evan passed out last night had reaffirmed to Jason how much better off he was alone. After such a powerful incident, Ming was convinced he'd never change his mind.

"Hey, Dad." It was late Sunday morning when Jason opened his front door and found his father standing there. "What's up?"

"Felt like having lunch with you."

From his father's serious expression, Jason wondered what he was in for, but he grabbed his keys and locked the house. "Where to?"

"Where else?"

They drove to his dad's favorite restaurant, where the pretty brunette hostess greeted Tony by name and flirted with him the whole way to the table.

"She's young enough to be your daughter," Jason commented, eyeing his father over the menu.

Tony chuckled. "She's young enough to be my granddaughter. And there's nothing going on. I love my wife."

When Tony had first announced that he was marrying Claire, Jason had a hard time believing his father had let himself fall in love again. But he'd reasoned that fifteen years of grieving was more than enough for anyone, and there was no question that Claire made his father happy. But his father's optimistic attitude toward love didn't stop Jason from wondering what would happen if Claire left.

Would his father collapse beneath the weight of sadness again? There was no way to know, and Jason hoped he never had to find out. "So, what's on your mind, Dad?"

"I spoke with Evan earlier today. Sounds like he and Lily are engaged."

"Since when?"

"Since this morning. Apparently Ming dropped her sister off and told her not to come home until she was engaged." Tony grinned. "I always loved that girl."

"Good for Evan. He was pretty beat up about Lily last night."

"He said you weren't doing too great, either."

Jason grimaced. "I found Evan on his living room floor, an empty bottle of pain pills next to him and I assumed…"

"That he'd tried to kill himself the way I had when you were fifteen." Tony looked older than his sixty-two years. The vibrancy had gone out of his eyes and the muscles in his face were slack. "That was the single darkest moment of my life, and I'm sorry you had to be the one to experience it with me."

"If I hadn't you'd be dead." They'd never really talked about what had happened. As a teenager Jason had been too shocked by almost losing a second parent to demand answers. And since Evan had been away at college, the secret had remained between Jason and his father while questions ate away Jason's sense of security.

"Looking back, I can't believe I allowed myself to sink so low, but I wasn't aware that I needed help. All I could see was a black pit with steep sides that I couldn't climb out of. Every day the hole seemed deeper. The company was months away from layoffs. I was taking my professional worries out on your mother, and that was eating me up. Then the car accident snatched her and Marie away from us. I was supposed to have driven them to the dress rehearsal for Marie's recital that night, but I was delayed at the office." Tony closed his eyes for a few seconds before resuming. "Those files could have waited until morning. If I had put my family first, they might still be alive. And in the end, all my work came to nothing. The job we'd bid went elsewhere and the company was on the verge of going under. I was to the point where I couldn't live with my failure as a husband, father or businessman."

So, this was the burden his father had carried all these years. Guilt had driven him to try to take his life because he'd perceived himself a failure?

And just like that, Jason's doctrine citing the dangers of falling in love lost all support.

"I thought you were so desperately in love with Mom that you couldn't bear to live without her anymore."

"Her death was devastating, but it wasn't why I started drinking or why I reached the point where I didn't want to go on. It was the guilt." His father regarded Jason in dismay. "Is that why you and Ming never dated? Were you afraid you'd lose her one day?"

"We didn't date because we're friends."

"But you love her."

"Of course I love her." And he did. "She's my—"

His father interrupted to finish. "Best friend." He shook his head in disgust. "Evan had another bit of news for me." Tony leaned his forearms on the table and pinned Jason with hard eyes. "Something Lily told him about Ming."

Now Jason knew why his father had shown up at his house. "She's pregnant."

"And?"

"The baby's mine."

So was Ming. His. Just as he'd told her the night of Max's bachelor party. He'd claimed her and then pushed her away because of a stupid pledge he'd made at fifteen. Had he really expected her to remain his best friend just because that's how it had always been for them?

And now that he knew the truth behind his father's depression, Jason could admit that he wanted the same things she did. Marriage. Children. The love of a lifetime.

But after he pushed her away last night, would she still want those things with him?

Jason's chair scraped the floor as he got to his feet. He threw enough money on the table to cover their tab and gestured for his father to get up. "We have to go."

"Go where?" Tony followed his son out the door without receiving an answer. "Go where?" he repeated, sliding behind the wheel of his BMW.

"I have an errand to run. Then I'm going to go see Ming. It's way past time I tell her how I really feel."

Ming swam beneath the pool's surface, stroking hard to reach the side before her breath gave out. After leaving Evan's house hours earlier, she'd been keyed up. After cleaning her refrigerator and vacuuming the whole upstairs, she'd decided to burn off her excess energy, hoping the cool water would calm both her body and her mind.

The exercise did its job. By the time she'd completed her twentieth lap, her thoughts had stopped racing. Muffin awaited her at the edge of the pool. As soon as Ming surfaced, the Yorkie raced forward and touched her nose to Ming's. The show of affection made her smile.

"What would I do without you?" she asked the small dog and received a lick in response.

"I've been asking myself the same question since you left last night."

A shadow fell across her. Ming looked up, her stomach flipping at the determined glint in Jason's blue eyes. Relief raced through her. The way their conversation had ended the previous night, she'd worried their friendship was irrevocably damaged.

"Luckily you aren't ever going to find that out." She accepted Jason's hand and let him pull her out of the water.

He wrapped her in a towel and pulled her against him. Dropping his lips to hers, he kissed her slow and deep. Ming tossed aside all the heartache of the past twelve hours and surrendered to the powerful emotions Jason aroused.

"I was wrong to dump all that stuff about Evan on you last night," he told her.

"I'm your friend. You know I'm always there for you."

"I know I take that for granted."

He took her by the hand and led her inside. To Ming's delight he pulled her toward the stairs. This wasn't what she'd expected from him after she confessed her feelings. She figured he'd distance himself from her as he'd done with women in the past.

But when they arrived in her bedroom, he didn't take her in his arms or rip the covers off the mattress and sweep her onto the soft sheets.

Instead, he kissed her on the forehead. "Grab a shower. I have an errand to run and could use your help."

An errand? Disappointment sat like a bowling ball in her stomach. "What sort of an errand?"

"I never got Max and Rachel a wedding present."

"Oh, Jason." She rolled her eyes at him.

"I'm hopeless without you," he reminded her, nudging her in the direction of the bathroom. "You know that."

"Does it have to be today?"

"They're leaving for Alabama tomorrow morning. I want them to have it before then." He scooped up the Yorkshire terrier and the dog's stuffed squirrel toy. "Muffin and I will be waiting for you downstairs."

"Fine."

Half an hour later Ming descended her stairs and found Jason entertaining Muffin with a game of fetch. She'd put on a red sundress with thin straps and loved the way Jason's eyes lit up in appreciation.

She collected the Yorkie's leash and her purse and headed out the front door. When she spotted the car in front of her house, she hesitated. "Why are you driving the 'Cuda?"

"I told you, I never got Max and Rachel a wedding present."

Understanding dawned. "You're giving him back the car?"

"The bet we made seems pretty stupid in light of recent events."

"What recent events?"

He offered her his most enigmatic smile. "Follow me and you'll find out."

When they arrived at Max and Rachel's house, Jason didn't even have a chance to get out of the car before the front door opened. To his amusement, Max looked annoyed.

"Why are you driving the 'Cuda?" he demanded as Jason slowly got to his feet. "Do you have any idea what the car's worth?"

"I don't, since you never told me what you paid for it." Jason took Ming's hand as she reached his side and pulled her close.

"Look, I'm sorry that I didn't get you anything for your wedding. Ming was supposed to help me pick something, but she backed out at the last minute."

"Jason." She bumped her hip against him in warning. "You are perfectly capable of shopping on your own."

"No, he's not," Max put in.

"No, I'm not. So, here." Jason held out the keys.

"You're giving me back the 'Cuda?" Max's thunderstruck expression was priceless.

"I realize now that I had an unfair advantage when we made the bet. You were already in love with Rachel, just too stubborn to realize it."

Max took the keys and nodded. "Being stubborn when it comes to love means you lose out on all sorts of things."

Jason felt the barb hit home. He had missed a lot with Ming. If he hadn't been so determined never to be hurt, she might have married his brother, and Jason could have ended up with a lifetime of pain.

Rachel had come out to join them. She snuggled against her husband's side and looked fondly at the bright yellow car. "What's going on?"

"Jason's giving me back the 'Cuda," Max explained with a wry grin. "Can I interest you in a ride?"

To Jason's surprise, the blonde's cheeks turned pink. Unwilling to delve too deeply into whatever subtext had just passed between husband and wife, he reached for the passenger seat and pulled out a box wrapped in white-and-silver paper and adorned with a silver bow.

"And because the car is a really lousy wedding present," he continued, handing the gift to Rachel, "I got this for you."

Rachel grinned. "I think the car is a lovely present, but thank you for this."

Jason shut the 'Cuda's door and gave the car one last pat. "Take good care of her," he told Max.

"I intend to." Max leaned down and planted a firm kiss on his wife's lips.

"I meant the car," Jason retorted, amused.

"Her, too."

After spending another ten minutes with the newlyweds, Ming and Jason returned to her car.

"What was that about?" she asked, standing beside the driver's door. "You didn't need me to help deliver the car. You could have had Max come pick it up."

"It was symbolic." He could feel her tension growing and decided he'd better tell her what was on his mind before she worked herself into a lather. "I won the car because I bet against love. It sits in my garage, a testament to my stubbornness and stupidity. So I decided to give it back to Max. Apparently in addition to its financial value it has some sentimental value to him, as well."

Her lips curved. "I'm happy to hear you admit that you were idiotic and pigheaded, but what caused your enlightenment?"

He leaned against the car and drew her into his arms.

"My dad swung by my house earlier and we had a long talk about what happened after my mother and sister died."

She sighed and relaxed against him. "You've talked with him about it before, haven't you?"

"We talked about his depression, but I never understood what was at the root of him trying to take his life."

"I thought it was because he was so much in love with your mom that he couldn't live without her."

"That's what I believed. Turns out I didn't know the whole story."

"There's more?"

"Today I found out why he was so depressed after my mother and sister died. Apparently he stayed at work when he was supposed to drive them the night they died. He thinks if he'd chosen his family over the business they might still be alive. It was eating him up."

"You mean he felt guilty?"

Jason nodded. "Guilty because he'd failed her. Not devastated by loss. All these years I was wrong to think love only led to pain." He watched Ming's expression to gauge her reaction to his tale. "When my dad fell in love with Claire, I thought he was nothing more than an optimistic fool." Jason winced. He'd spoken up against his father marrying her and a rift had formed between them. "Then Max fell in love with Rachel. Until he met her, he'd had a block of ice where his heart should be."

"But Rachel's great."

Jason nodded. "And she's perfect for Max, but when he fell head over heels for her, I was even more convinced that love made everyone else crazy and that I was the only sane one."

It scared her how firmly he clung to his convictions. "And now your brother has gone mad for Lily."

"That he has." He gave her a sheepish smile. "Max and his brothers. My dad. Evan. They're all so damned happy."

"You're happy."

"When I'm with you." He set his forehead against hers. "I've been a stubborn idiot. All this time I've been lying to myself about what I wanted. I thought if you and I made love, I could keep things the way they were between us and manage to have the best of both worlds."

"Only I had to go and fall in love with you."

"No. You had to go and tell me you wanted us to be together as a family." At last he was free to share with her what lay in his heart. "Did you know when you chose me to help you get pregnant that a baby would bind us together forever?"

"It crossed my mind, but that isn't why I decided on you." She frowned defensively. "And I'd like to point out that you agreed to help me. You also had to realize that any child I gave birth to would be part of us."

"From the instant you said you wanted me to be your baby's father, all I could think about was how much I wanted you." He took her hand and kissed her palm, felt her tension ease.

"After prom night I ran from the way I felt about you. It went against everything I believed. I've been running for the last fifteen years."

"And what is it you want?"

"You. More than anything. Marry me. I want to spend the rest of my life showing you how much I love you." He produced a diamond ring and held it before her eyes.

Heart pounding, she stared at the fiery gem as he took her left hand and slid the ring onto her finger. It fit perfectly.

"Yes. Yes. Of course, yes."

Before she finished her fervent acceptance, he kissed her. As his lips moved with passionate demand against hers, she melted beneath the rush of desire. He took his time demonstrating how much he loved her until his breath was rough and ragged. At last he lifted his head and stared into her eyes. Her stark joy stopped his heart.

Grinning, he hugged her hard. "And just in case you're worried about everyone's reaction, I cleared this with your sister and parents and my brother. The consensus seems to be that it's about time we take things from friends…"

"To forever." She laughed, a glorious sound of joy. "How lucky can a girl be?" she murmured. "I get to marry my best friend and the man I adore."

Jason cupped her face and kissed her gently. "What could be better than that?"

Ming lifted onto her tiptoes and wrapped her arms around his neck. "Not one single thing."

Epilogue

One year later

Bright afternoon sunshine glinted off the brand new paint on the galaxy blue Mustang parked in the driveway. Ming adjusted the big red bow attached to the roof and waved goodbye to the Stover brothers, who'd dropped the repaired race car off moments before. With her anniversary present for Jason looking absolutely perfect, she glanced toward the colonial's front door. The delivery had not been particularly quiet and she was surprised her husband of one year hadn't come out to see what the commotion was about.

She headed inside and paused in the foyer. From the family room came the sounds of revving engines so she followed the sound. Jason sat on the couch in front of the sixty-inch TV, absorbed in a NASCAR race. Muffin slept on the back of the couch near his shoulder.

"Jason?"

Muffin's head came up and her tail wagged, but Jason didn't

react at all. She circled the couch and discovered why he hadn't heard the delivery. He was fast asleep. So were their twin three-month-old sons, Jake and Connor, one on either side of him, snuggled into the crooks of his arms.

Ming grinned at the picture of her snoozing men and hoped this nap meant Jason would have lots of energy later tonight because she had plans for him that required his full strength. But right now she was impatient to show him his gift.

"Jason." She knelt between his knees and set her hands on his thighs. Muffin stretched and jumped down to lick Connor's cheek. "Wake up and see what I got you for our anniversary." When her words didn't rouse him, she slid her palms up his thigh. She was more than halfway toward her goal when his lips twitched upward at the corners.

"Keep going."

"Later."

He sighed, but didn't open his eyes. "That's what you always say." But despite his complaint, his smile had blossomed into a full-blown grin.

"And I always come through." She stood and slapped his knee. "Now come see your present."

She scooped up Jake and waited until Jason draped Connor over his shoulder and got to his feet before she headed back through the house. Muffin raced ahead of them to the foyer. Tingling with anticipation, Ming pulled open the front door and stepped aside so Jason could look out. The shock on his face when he spotted the car was priceless.

"You had the Mustang repaired?" He wrapped his free arm around her waist and pulled her tight against him.

"I did." She smiled up at him and his lips dropped onto hers for a passion-drenched kiss that curled her toes. When he let her breath again, she caught his hand and dragged him down the steps. "I think you should start racing again."

He hadn't been anywhere near the track since he'd crashed the Mustang over a year ago. Between getting married, her taking over the dental practice and the birth of their twins, they'd been plenty busy.

"Are you sure that's what you want?" Jason ran his hand along the front fender with the same appreciation he'd lavished on her thigh the previous night. "It'll take me away some weekends."

"I never wanted you to stop doing what you love."

"What I love is being your husband and a father to Jake and Connor."

"And I love that, too." She nudged her body against his. "But racing is your passion, and Max is bored to death without you to compete against."

He coasted his palm over her hip and cupped her butt, drawing her up on her toes for a slow, thorough kiss. The babies began to fuss long before Ming was done savoring her husband's fabulous technique and they broke apart with matching regretful sighs.

"More of that to come later," she assured him, soothing Jake.

While they were distracted, a car had pulled up behind the Mustang. Max and Rachel got out. "Get a room you two," Max called good-naturedly, picking up the excited terrier.

"That's the plan," Ming retorted, handing off her son to Rachel.

"Great to see you guys." Jason switched Connor to his other arm so he could give Max a man hug. "Are you staying for dinner?"

"They're staying," Ming said. "We're leaving. They're going to babysit while we celebrate our anniversary." Since the twins were born, uninterrupted time together was pretty much non-existent, and Ming was determined that she and Jason should make a memorable start to their second year of marriage.

Jason eyed Max. "Are you sure you're up for this?"

"I think I could use a little parenting practice."

"I'm pregnant," Rachel announced, beaming.

While Jason congratulated Max, and Rachel cooed over

Jake, Ming marveled at her good fortune. She'd married her best friend and they had two healthy baby boys. Her practice was thriving. Lily and Evan were getting married in the spring. Everything that had been going wrong a little over a year ago was now sorted out. It wasn't perfect, but it was wonderful.

Jason looked over and caught her watching him. The blaze that kindled in his eyes lit an answering inferno deep inside her. For twenty-five years he'd been her best friend and that had been wonderful, but for the rest of her life he was going to be her husband and that was perfect.

* * * * *

MILLS & BOON®
By Request

RELIVE THE ROMANCE WITH THE BEST OF THE BEST

0917/05

Join Britain's BIGGEST Romance Book Club

- **EXCLUSIVE** offers every month

- **FREE** delivery direct to your door

- **NEVER MISS** a title

- **EARN** Bonus Book points

Call Customer Services

0844 844 1358*

or visit

millsandboon.co.uk/subscriptions

* This call will cost you 7 pence per minute plus your phone company's price per minute access charge.

BKCB3